John Hamilton Davies

The Life of Richard Baxter of Kidderminster

Preacher and Prisoner

John Hamilton Davies

The Life of Richard Baxter of Kidderminster
Preacher and Prisoner

ISBN/EAN: 9783744760515

Printed in Europe, USA, Canada, Australia, Japan

Cover: Foto ©Raphael Reischuk / pixelio.de

More available books at **www.hansebooks.com**

RICHARD BAXTER.

[illegible] of the Trustees from the original painting in Dr. Williams' Library, Red Cross Street

THE LIFE

OF

RICHARD BAXTER,

OF KIDDERMINSTER,

Preacher and Prisoner.

BY

JOHN HAMILTON DAVIES, B.A.,

RECTOR OF ST. NICHOLAS', WORCESTER;

Fellow of the Royal Historical Society, etc.

"*I would almost as soon doubt the Gospel verity as Baxter's veracity.*"

SAMUEL TAYLOR COLERIDGE.

London:

W. KENT AND CO., PATERNOSTER ROW.

1887.

THIS BOOK IS INSCRIBED

TO THE

RIGHT REV. HENRY PHILPOTT, D.D.,

BISHOP OF WORCESTER.

CONTENTS.

THE LIFE OF RICHARD BAXTER.

CHAPTER I.

INTRODUCTORY.

DURING the latter part of the sixteenth century, the Reformation produced great changes among all classes of the English people. Some of them thought these changes had not gone far enough; especially those persons who had associated with the pastors in Wittenberg, Frankfort, and Geneva, and who were not content that any of the symbols of the Latin ritual should be retained in the Anglican Church. They asserted that their Protestantism was the public acknowledgment of their personal responsibility, and their declaration against hypocrisy and priestly domination, their demand for freedom of conscience, and for religious independence. They wished everything to be removed from the temples of the Lord which bore any trace of what they held to be the old superstition, and which could remind the people of "the Babylonian woe" from which they had been delivered. Forgetting that Christianity can never be entirely free from the influence of the creations of genius, they held the beauties of ancient sacred art of little account; and some of them regarded roods and screens, and the storied windows which shed the light of day in variegated loveliness of colour on wall and floor, as the memorials of an idolatry which they had renounced. The contest with Rome had ceased, but the Church in England was disturbed.

Even the strong hand of Elizabeth had failed to hush the discords of them who clamoured for the simpler service which obtained in Geneva, and for the abolition in religious worship of that which they deemed to debase reason and to lower the dignity of man. To the end of her reign the ultra-reforming element became the stronger in proportion to her attempts to repress it.

Among the infinite follies of men, few, perhaps, are more injurious than religious contentions. If there are various views of truth, there must necessarily be in the Church divergencies of thought; and it is impossible to conceive of any corporate form of religionists in which perfect unity obtains. No reasonable men can really believe that all revealed truth, and the practical goodness it produces, are confined within the arbitrarily assigned limits of their own circle; for the test of Christianity is charity. It has often been the error of despotical government to insist, if not on unity of creed and worship, on uniformity at least of their expression; and the attempt—frequently cruel in its procedure, and sometimes unsuccessful—to restrict large communities to one form of religious observance, has produced some of the most grievous of the evils which have afflicted the Christian nations.

James I. ascended the throne with the determination to enforce among his subjects implicit obedience to his will, both in Church and in State. To his innate love of arbitrary power were added the obstinacy of a perverse mind and the vanity which is fed by adulation. Without the advantage of a wise tuition, he never had the good fortune to see truth at first hand, to acquire self-control, and to learn the better method of managing men. He was educated among persons, with one signal exception, of the narrowest views, and of little knowledge of affairs, who held one part of their creed with little heed of the other; adding to natural asperity the bitterness of theological rancour. At the Hampton-Court conference, James acted on the principles in which he had been trained, and which always more or less governed him.

He said to the assembled divines, "I will have one doctrine, one discipline, one religion in substance and ceremony: never speak more to that point, how far you are bound to obey. No bishop, no king. I will make them conform, and that quickly too, or they shall hear of it. If they are of an obstinate and turbulent spirit, I will have them enforced to conform." The king's conduct at that conference confirmed the resolution of several of the younger members of the House of Commons to demand from their sovereign civil and religious freedom.

On the accession of Charles I. two opposing currents moved English thought. On the one hand, the Hampton-Court conference had revived in some of the Anglican clergy more or less sympathy with the ceremonial of the Latin Church, and had produced an increasing aversion to the particularist doctrines of the French and Swiss Reformers; which they regarded as limiting the extent of the Divine mercy, and as denying to a great degree the free-agency and responsibility of man. Some of them desired to subordinate the Church to the State, and thus to make the king supreme in both; so that he should not only bear the august title, "Defender of the Faith," which the most despotic of the Tudors had received from the Pope; but that he should be acknowledged to have both the Divine right to rule, and to determine for his subjects the standard of truth and belief.

On the other hand, in both Houses of Parliament, and especially in that daily increasing body of merchants and traders, the representatives of our upper middle classes, there was not only a growing discontent with the despotism of the king and with the assumption of secular power by the prelates, but many of them held those principles which the foreign reformers had introduced into this country,—that man is responsible for his faith to God only, and that Revelation in Holy Scripture, made to and preserved by the Church, and not patristic authority alone, nor the decrees of councils, nor tradition, are to define faith and to direct Christian life.

These primary truths all the reformed communities held, and in greater or less degree still retain, and with many differences of Church-order and administration. It may reasonably be questioned why such dissensions should then have existed amongst them, since they believed so much in common; and that the sects, as they had power and opportunity, should have harassed and afflicted one another. But, until a recent period, Christians generally knew little or nothing of the healthful doctrine of toleration. They did not understand that revealed truth may be regarded from different points of view, and that one class of religionists may see more clearly and with wider range than another. If the knowledge of these facts had obtained at an earlier period of ecclesiastical life, what conflicts and sufferings might have been avoided, and what shame to Christianity might have been prevented, during years of dissension and persecution! But the history of the Church has often illustrated the statement of Cyprian, that men prove unfaithful for faith, and irreligious for religion.

The legal and mercantile classes, the country gentlemen of lesser estate, and their sons at the universities and inns of court, generally maintained that men had a natural right to judge for themselves in matters of religion, and that they must make their final appeal to the Bible alone as the Word of God, the ground of faith and hope; and which—as, long afterwards, Goethe said—became to them more beautiful the more they studied it. In fact, the Bible was the one book of the English people. It was read by the peer, the country-gentleman, the merchant, the yeoman, the mechanic; so that Grotius said of England, "Theology rules there." All classes diligently studied the Scriptures, which governed their thoughts, guided their conduct, and enriched their language.

Ames, who was supposed to have presumed to answer the "Ecclesiastical Polity" of Hooker, explained the points of difference between his party and the Anglican clergy. He said, "The state of the dispute is this: we, as it becometh

Christians, stand on the sufficiency of Christ's institution for all kinds of worship. THE WORD, say we, and nothing but the Word in matters of religious worship. The prelates rise up on the other side, and will needs have us allow and use certain human ceremonies in our Christian worship. Christ we know, and all that cometh from Him we are ready to embrace; but these human ceremonies we know not, nor can have anything to do with them."

Between these opposing religionists compromise appeared to be impossible. Political difference, embittered by theological disagreement, prevailed in many portions of the community; envenomed the books they read and the sermons they heard; disturbed the discussions of councils and the decorum of the legislature; corrupted the manners of men, kindled anger in their families; and at length produced the greatest of all the calamities which can afflict a state—the long-continued civil war. The conflict cast down the Throne, silenced the Church, revived in England some of the ferocity of mediæval warfare, and caused thousands to mourn over the intemperance of the human mind and the madness of religious animosity.

CHAPTER II.

1615—1633.

ON the twelfth day of November, 1615, Richard Baxter was born at Eaton Constantine, a village in Shropshire, between the Severn and the Wrekin Hill. His father was a country gentleman, who had lessened his estate by gambling. Abandoning that vice before the birth of his son, he was compelled to husband what remained of it with scrupulous care. He listened to the inner voice which never deceives, and he resolved on other ways and better deeds. But the counsellors of his soul were few. In the Autobiography of his son, a precious memorial of his age, and one of "the ablest text-books of Church history," written when his strifes and sufferings were nearly at an end, he has described to some extent the manner of clergymen who in his childhood ministered in some of the villages of Shropshire. In their churches the prayers were duly said on Sundays, but in some of them there was little preaching, or, if any, of an absolutely negative kind; resembling the sermons Bahrdt was accustomed to hear in Berlin, in the early days of Frederick the Great, when it was thought by the court-chaplains enough to discourse on friendship, frugality, the right use of time, and kindred subjects, but with only the slightest allusion to any specifically Christian truths. In the township nearest to Eaton Constantine there had been four curates in less than seven years, two of whom were suspected of immorality; and in Baxter's own village there was a resident clergyman who never preached, holding two livings twenty miles from each other, and so failing in sight that he was obliged to say the public prayers from memory, and to employ a labourer to read the appointed lessons. In some of the adjacent towns and villages there were other incompetent clergymen, whose lives were of evil repute, blind leaders of the blind; among them, however, as lights in the darkness, were faithful parish-priests, thoroughly doing their duty. Such men were held in little favour by the inhabitants of some of the rural districts, many of whom delighted in fairs and revels, danced round the maypoles and played at cricket on Sundays, baited bulls, loved prize-fights, ravaged orchards and fields, and drank ale with ribald songs in the Church's hours of prayer.

Richard Baxter's narrative of his own confirmation attests the prevailing ecclesiastical negligence of the villages. He says:—"When I was a schoolboy, about fifteen years of age, the bishop coming into the country, many went to him to be confirmed; we that were boys each went out to see the bishop among the rest, not knowing anything of the meaning of the business. When we came thither, we met about thirty or forty in all, of our own stature and temper, that had come to be *bishopped*, as it was then called. The bishop examined us, not at all in one article of faith, but in a churchyard; in haste we were set in a rank, and he passed hastily over us, laying his hands on our heads, and saying a few words, which neither I nor any that I spoke with understood, so hastily were they uttered, and a very short prayer recited, and there was an end. But whether we were Christians or infidels, or knew so much as that there was a God, the bishop little knew nor inquired. And yet he was esteemed one of the best bishops in England. And though the canons require that the curate or minister send a certificate that the children have learned the catechism, there was no such thing done, but we ran of our own accord to see the bishop only, and almost all the rest of the country had not this much; this was the old careless practice of this excellent duty of confirmation."

Episcopal supervision at that time was often inefficient. The account of the incumbent's routine of work, which the bishop now demands of each of his beneficed clergy, once a year, and in which the facts of the public clerical life are officially communicated, was either ill-made, or not made at all, in the earlier part of the seventeenth century. The extent of the diocese, the badness of the roads, the general difficulties of travelling, excepting in the days of summer, and the lack of the means necessary for communicating and receiving intelligence, necessarily led to occasional neglect on the bishop's part, and to remissness among some of the rural clergy. The orderly visitation of his parishes, which in our days the prelate makes with the regularity of the seasons; the periodical confirmation of the young; his sermons at the opening of new or of restored Churches; his constant association with the clergy; his animating influence on every charitable organisation; and his counselling or directing improvements in education, and other religious works in his diocese, were few and feeble in comparison with those of our own period of presumed ecclesiastical reformation.

Richard Baxter's early education was conducted under bad auspices. The curates of the village were successively his instructors, and of them he retained no good impressions. He long had reason to remember one of them, who had been clerk to a lawyer, but by dissipation he lost his employment, and entered into holy orders "for a morsel of bread." Baxter once heard him preach; but he was drunk at the time, and his ecclesiastical and tutorial duties came to an end. Then for two years he was placed with a clergyman of character and ability, whose theological library consisted of a Greek Testament, Augustine's "De Civitate Dei," and Bishop Andrewes' "Sermons." From him, he says, he received no useful instruction, but tedious iterations on the evils of the times, the grandeur of the Church, and the malignity of Puritanism. Afterwards he studied with Mr. Owen, the master of Wroxeter School, with whom he read the classics; and on his recommendation he was placed with

Mr. Wickstead, chaplain to the Council at Ludlow, who was allowed to have one pupil. He taught him very little, but gave him a large number of books, which he read with delight.

The lack of such instruction as he would have received at a university was a lifelong loss to Baxter. His sagacity led him to perceive his disadvantage, and he determined to live the laborious days of the student, with almost incredible industry, acquiring, in however desultory a manner, large stores of knowledge, partly from the works of the Fathers, but chiefly from the scholastic writers. Narrating in his Autobiography his early difficulties, he says that in his sixteenth year one of his father's poor neighbours lent him "Resolution," a book written by Parsons the Jesuit, and which had been edited by Bunny, rector of Bolton Percy. This book, which is the first part of Parsons' larger work, "The Christian Directory," was intended to produce serious thoughts in the younger members of the Roman Catholic Church, and in this respect it had had great success in England and abroad. Many persons in both communions confessed their indebtedness to it; and it was the first of the series of books treating upon practical religion, which are still held in estimation. He read also "The Bruised Reed," the well-known work of Dr. Richard Sibbes, one of the most able divines of the Anglican Church, in the earlier part of the seventeenth century—a book once of great and well-deserved reputation, replete with biblical theology, expressed in ingenious antithetical language, with much epigrammatic wit, which has not yet lost its charm for the reader, and with many admirable expositions of the method by which man's spiritual misery may be removed by the gracious and effective goodness of God, and of the wisdom and advantage of holy living. With these and with other invigorating Anglican and Puritan books, the young student nurtured his mind. He is the more to be commended that he acquired knowledge in adverse circumstances; and there is a manifest propriety in the answer he gave to Anthony à Wood, the author of "Athenæ Oxonienses," who inquired where he had been educated,—"As to myself, my faults are no disgrace to any university, for I was of none. I have little but what I read out of books, and inconsiderable helps of country tutors. Weakness and pain helped me to study how to die; that set me on studying how to live; beginning with necessities, I proceeded by degrees, and now am going to see that for which I have lived and studied."

Some of the theological works which Baxter read in his younger years were casuistical and mystic. The latter had their type in "The Imitation of Christ," a book often ascribed to Thomas à Kempis, but also attributed to Gerson, and which, translated into many languages, and having passed through more than eighteen hundred editions, has been read wherever Christianity obtains. It may be questioned whether religious reading can wisely be restricted to that class of writing or that school of thought, for the mind may become habituated to self-inspection, until all that is objective in truth may be disregarded; and thus the Christian law may be in effect disobeyed, which demands not merely devotional feeling, but active service from each one who professes to make the life of the Saviour the example of his own. The illustrious instances of Pascal, Quesnel, and Madame Guyon could not give permanence to that which existed only in the contemplation of "pure love," apart from the practical application of principles, and a regulated course of duty; for the history of the Church gives prominence to the fact that religion is strong in proportion to its activity. From frequent self-inquiry, even in his early days, Baxter was harassed by doubts of his salvation. He sought for direct evidence of the work of the Holy Spirit upon his heart, and he was grieved to discover the difficulty of demonstration in a matter at once so profound and awful. In looking back long afterwards upon this period of his life, when the truth which had ripened on his lips ruled his mind, Baxter wrote: "I was once wont to meditate most on my own heart, and to dwell all at home. I was still poring over either my sins or wants, or examining my sincerity. But now, though I am greatly convinced of the need of heart-acquaintance and employment, I see more the need of higher work, and that I should look oftener on God, and Christ, and heaven, than upon my own heart. At home I can find distempers to trouble me, and some evidences of my peace; but it is above that I must find matter of delight, and joy, and love, and peace itself. I would, therefore, have one thought at home, on myself and sins; and many thoughts above, on the amiable and beatifying objects."

Through all his life Baxter suffered, more or less, from nervous irritation, accompanying his chronic state of ill-health. When a boy he was attacked by small pox, a disease frequently mentioned in the biographies of the seventeenth century, in terms such as now might be used in writing of the terrible ravages of cholera or diphtheria. Want of due regard to the danger of exposure to atmospheric changes, during the process of his recovery from that dreadful disease, no doubt produced the pulmonary disorders which remained throughout his life. He often and dolefully relates his afflictions, and the means adopted for their removal. In reflecting how modern diagnosis and treatment have improved upon the former attempts at this conjectural art, which, as the witty philosopher wrote, "sometimes assists nature, and sometimes destroys her," it may be questioned whether the diseases or the drugs were the worse to be endured. To the inquiries his friends made as to the state of his health, Baxter might often have replied in the words, had he known them, of one of the able women whose charming letters grace the literature of France—"I have recovered from the disorder, but not from the medicines." His life, even to old age, afflicted by varying forms of disease, was a continuous struggle with death. He was harassed by a constant cough. He was in peril of consumption. He had frequent bleedings from the nose; on one occasion for three days without cessation. He had distressing chronic dyspepsia, "with incredible flatulency." He was tortured by lancinating pains in the head. He had that miserable state of body, well understood by physicians of the nineteenth century, in which a scratch upon the skin, or the extraction of a tooth, is followed by hæmorrhage difficult to be checked. His fingers, sometimes denuded of the ill-nourished and attenuated cuticle, became so raw that he could scarcely hold his pen. He was repeatedly threatened by dropsy. He was afflicted by renal pains. He suffered from periodical depression, when clouds darkened the eye of his mind, and doubt whispered at the ear of his heart. But even with these evils his life was not altogether unhappy; he had many cheerful hours, joyous gleams between the storms. He resorted to the physicians, and there were few of the more eminent of them who had not made practical speculations upon him; some of them differing from others, both as to the cause of his diseases, and as to the treatment appropriate to them, and occasionally with that acrimonious assertion of individual wisdom and superiority, which since their day Hogarth vividly depicted. Their drugs, few and poor as they were, seem to have been improvements upon those which were generally prescribed in the days of Henry VIII., Edward VI., and in the earlier part of Elizabeth's reign, when the most disgusting compounds were employed by men who, ignorant of causes, and able to judge empirically by effects only, in their attempts and failures to remove pain, and to smooth the path to the grave, must have been weary of guessing. There is a remarkable record in "Baxter's Autobiography," which may illustrate the medical treatment at the time. He says: "I was restored from illness, by the mercy of God, and the help of Dr. Bates, and the moss of a dead man's skull, which I had from Dr. Michlethewait." His state of health may have induced him sometimes to meditate upon the history of the woman healed by the Saviour, who "had suffered many things of many physicians." He had endured the experiments of more than thirty of them, in that twilight time of science, who occasionally agreeing, but perhaps oftener contradicting one another, but unable to discover the cause of his diseases, had copiously given, as the dramatist said, drugs of which they knew little to a body of which they knew less. But even in the weakness and discomfort produced by diseases so often returning, Baxter had days of tranquil happiness, when with prodigious industry he wrote one or other of his many books on doctrinal, controversial, and practical theology, which remain as memorials of his great labour, his delight in disputation, his wide-ranging charity, and his admirable devotedness to sacred truth.

CHAPTER III.

1633—1638.

BAXTER continued his studies of scholastic theology until he was eighteen years old. Charles I. had lately been crowned, and the young student was recommended to seek employment at the Court, where his circumstances would give him reasonable hope of advancement. His tutor, Mr. Wickstead, with the consent of Baxter's parents, introduced him to Sir Henry Newport, the master of the revels, who took him to Whitehall. The palace was as a new world to the youth accustomed to the simple manners and early hours of rural life, and to the temperate regularity of his father's house; and it seemed to him to have an atmosphere in which religion could not exist. The Sunday especially was passed there in laxity and dissipation. He says: "I had quickly enough of the Court when I saw a stage-play instead of a sermon on the Lord's Days in the afternoon, and saw what course was there in fashion." It was customary for the royal family, no doubt by the wish of the Queen, to be entertained in the evening of the day by a comedy,—a practice which not only changed the character of the Sunday, but which many persons at the time believed to have had a demoralising effect upon all classes of English society. In the period preceding the Reformation there was an increasing relaxation in that strict observance of the Lord's Day which had obtained at an earlier time. The well-known Italian ecclesiastical jurist, Pelliccia, the author of the "Polity of the Christian Church," may be referred to as a sufficient authority for the fact. He says: "It is evident how widely the discipline observed by Christians in the first ages of the Church, in this matter of Sunday observance, differed from that of our own day—their joy was assuredly not what we call pleasure, but was the effect of their religion itself, since they spent the day, not in banqueting and comic amusements, as is customary among us in Italy, but in reading of the Scriptures, the singing of psalms, assembling for worship, etc. Such was the religious observance even down to the fourteenth century, since which period, even down to our times, Christians have been falling away in no slight degree from ancient strictness."

Baxter had been taught from his childhood to believe that the manner of observing the Lord's Day is the best evidence of the state of religion in a nation; and that although the observance had been changed by the Church from the seventh to the first day of the week, the moral obligation of dedicating it to religious work and meditation still remains. So that, while the school of Churchmen, whose exponent was Archbishop Laud, insisted that it should be held merely as a holiday, Baxter's education led him to believe then, what indeed he afterwards maintained, that the apostles, in arranging the times and modes of Church service, appointed the first day of the week "for holy worship, especially in Church assemblies; and that this act of theirs was done by the guidance or inspiration of the Holy Ghost, which was given them." He ever held that the spirit of the Ten Commandments was to direct all the religious life, and that in the observance of the Lord's Day the examples of the Apostles and early Fathers should determine Christian conduct. He has given an illustration of the effect of the "Book of Sports," originally ordered to be published by James I., and which Laud afterwards, with disastrous folly, endeavoured to compel the clergy to enforce upon their parishioners. Baxter says: "I cannot forget that in my youth, in those late times, when we lost some of our conformable godly teachers for not publicly reading the

'Book of Sports' and dancing on the Lord's Day, one of my father's own tenants was the town piper, hired by the year, for many years together, and the place of the dancing assembly was not a hundred yards from our door. We could not, on the Lord's Day, either read a chapter, or pray, or sing a psalm, or catechise or instruct a servant, but with the noise of the pipe and tabor, and the shoutings in the streets continually in our ears. Even among a tractable people we were the common scorn of all the rabble in the streets, and called Puritans, precisians, and hypocrites, because we rather chose to read the Scriptures than to do as they did, though there was no savour of Nonconformity in our family. And when the people by the book were allowed to play and dance out of public service time, they could so hardly break off their sports, that many a time the reader was fain to stay till the piper and player would give over. Sometimes the morris-dancers would come into church in all their linen, and scarves, and antic dresses, with morris-bells jingling at their legs; and as soon as Common Prayer was read, did haste and presently to their play again."

To Baxter the practice of the Court was so distasteful that, after remaining at Whitehall for a month, he withdrew from his duties there. Tidings of his mother's ill health determined him to return to his home. He set out upon his journey to Shropshire, in the long-remembered, terrible winter of 1633. Leaving London a little before Christmas, he was overtaken by frightful storms, and the snow was so heavy and continuous that flocks were overwhelmed and cottages destroyed by it. In all the west-midland districts of the country "Winter reigned tremendous o'er the conquered year." Travelling then was always more or less dangerous, when the roads were deep in snow or mire, and the lowlands flooded far and wide. Men journeyed on horseback, happy if they escaped successive dangers, for the public ways were hardly to be distinguished from the ploughed fields at their sides; the bridges were often insecure; and marauders were many and bold, wandering beggars expelled from parishes where they could prove no right of settlement, and disbanded or disgraced soldiers making their way to their homes. On this journey Baxter narrowly escaped death. In the frozen road running between banks, meeting a heavily-laden waggon, he thought to avoid it by urging his horse up the steep side of the highway; his girths broke, and he was thrown before the wheel of the waggon. Suddenly the horses stopped as if by a marvellous instinct, and he was dragged away from destruction.

The incident is recorded here, because he regarded it as warning him of the many hazards attending human life, and of the Providence which often by simple means averts impending harm. From that hour the needle of his heart pointed towards heaven. What thoughts crowded upon his soul in that day of deliverance from untimely death!—The life of man, what a shadow it is; a semblance of being, how unreal among all existing things! What instability of condition, gone in a moment; in the current of it all things moving, nothing staying; his days a passing shadow, his departure as the awakening from a dream! Yet is the end the crown or the ruin of all? When he has gone, how small a gap remains, how quickly filled by another, who in his turn falls and passes! This world is an inn, and not a home, all soon to be quitted; nothing continues, and man hurries on, learning many truths, meeting many difficulties, happy if only at length he may reach the Stay of life—the Centre of the everlasting rest and peace. Baxter determined on an amended course. He perceived what before he had but dimly or partly apprehended; he, hitherto without definite resolve or aim, now first began to understand his relation to the Father of spirits. He had been merciful, and He would be helpful to him, who needed strength and guidance. How had he lived uselessly so long in the world; how now had his life been spared in extremity of danger! Would not He Who had been so compassionate direct his way, teach him how he might work for what was best and highest, and shape his end? From that hour of danger and of deliverance, he resolved on giving himself to holy meditation and service. He would defend the truth. He would arouse men from their indifference, shame them from their sensuality, convince them of their danger, and rescue them from destruction. His thoughts should be much in heaven, his sympathies with the good, the suffering, and the self-denying; and his unwearying labour for the Church which Christ had founded on earth, and which He royally governed in His glory. He would be as they were of whom he had read, the heroes who had fought their fight and finished their course. He would labour like Augustine, devote himself like Francis of Assisi and Xavier, and others of the sacramental host of God's elect, and, like repenting Loyola, he would do all to the glory of the Lord. He deemed he had received a Divine impulse in his soul. Heaven called him, and he could not disobey the voice which spoke to his spirit. His heart was thrilled by hope that he might be accepted as a servant of Him Whose mercy had saved him from death. Then began that life of prayer and devotedness, of toil and suffering, which for more than fifty eventful years was given to the service of the Saviour, and in which, as he said with all the emphasis of fact, in the strange variety of his afflictions, in the uncertainty sometimes of being able to live through a day of pain and weariness:

> "He preached as one who ne'er should preach again,
> And as a dying man to dying men."

With such thoughts, and with so firm a resolution, he reached his father's house. He found that much had been changed during the short period of his absence from it. Its peace and calm content were disturbed by the sudden illness of his mother; but she lovingly welcomed home her son, and he told her the thoughts which burned within him, and of his resolution to devote himself entirely to the service of God. After the terrible winter, and when spring was renewing the verdure and loveliness of the world, he had the grief of one who mourneth for his mother. In his Autobiography he says but little of her; and of his father he does not make frequent mention, except that, among other notices of him, this is conspicuous,—that in the following year he married a daughter of Sir Thomas Hunks, who long outlived him, attaining her ninety-sixth year. She had the happiness of seeing the days when the religious discords were at an end, when toleration prevailed, and the persecutions ceased, which in the seventeenth century had injured and disgraced the English government.

His reflections on the loss of his mother gave strength to his resolution to devote himself to the service of the Saviour. He had lately escaped death; he was sorrowing for her whom he loved with all the strong affection of his tender and sensitive nature; and from the general feebleness of his health, he feared he himself might not long survive. The morning of his life was already clouded, and he hardly expected he should live to see its noon. But his lofty mind looked far and wide, and saw on all sides the sins, miseries, and needs of men, and the means which the amazing goodness of God had provided for at once pardoning and mitigating them. In the purity and simplicity of his heart, as if forecasting his high destiny, he determined not to be beguiled and ensnared by the deceits and evils of the earthly life, and he resolved he would not live in vain. He would have the grand and recompensing future ever in view, he would pass his time in proclaiming and defending truth; that, when summoned to depart, he might leave the world without regret, as one quits his inn where he has sojourned for a time; and as with words like those of the Roman philosopher, upon which he had often admiringly pondered, he might bless the day when, freed from the rude and disordered human society, he might enter upon that august council and assembly where friendship is renewed, where the life is immortal, and the employment beneficent and sublime. He knew that the Saviour came to the world and died, not merely that men might be pardoned for unrighteous deeds wilfully done, but that they might be freed from the condition of sinful thought and affection, and that the dignity and high offices of their nature might be restored; that under His teaching all of life might be a time of education for heaven, and that for these purposes God was daily calling them by His Spirit to His eternal glory, bidding them to look to that mark, and to strive to attain it.

Baxter resolved not to urge upon others that of which he was himself ignorant; but, returning from his mother's grave, he determined to keep that pure and happy future life before his mind. He thought of it continually. He looked upon his frail state of earthly being as the soldier looks upon the tent in which he is to pass days and nights not without alarm and attack, until warfare shall end in peace. He would inure himself to the fact of his dissolution. He would anticipate its hour by mortifying that which most of all might make the world dear to him; for he daily thought he was not doomed to long exile and imprisonment in his frail body; but he would not live in gloom and dread, but in the happy activities of a consecrated and hopeful life, employing it both in labour for the Church, and in submission to his lot; for he had already learned that resignation is wisdom, and that to be patient is to be divine.

Baxter's father had carefully trained him to the faith of the English Church. Within its walls from his childhood he had been accustomed to pray. Mr. Garbet, his tutor, had taught him its distinctive truths, and had directed him to careful study of the works of Burgess, Downham, and other polemical writers. He carefully read "The Ecclesiastical Polity" of Richard Hooker, which had already attained to great repute; the Pope, Clement VIII., had deemed it worthy of his commendation, and its ability was acknowledged even by men who held little else in common. A careful examination of Baxter's controversial works will give evidence that he had learned much from Hooker's book, and the reader of those works is often reminded of that great divine's method of meeting the arguments of opponents. There can be little doubt that, as the writings of John Howe had afterwards much influence in suggesting the arguments of Bishop Butler and of Paley, so Hooker was one of the chief educators of Baxter both in his dogmatical and polemical treatises. If Baxter had not Hooker's wide range of learning in ecclesiastical archæology, and in the history of doctrine, he certainly was but little inferior to the great Churchman in the capacity of accumulating substantial evidence from every quarter to strengthen his conclusions, nor in effective eloquence to maintain and enforce them.

As yet Baxter had had but occasional contact with Nonconformists, and those of them he had seen were men of inconsiderable attainment and of small power. Of their literature at this time he seems to have known comparatively nothing; so that he was not biassed by their prejudices, nor hindered by any imaginary scruples from attaching himself to the Anglican Church. He had not then, he confessed, read the Homilies, nor even carefully studied the Church's Articles of Religion, nor wasted his strength and vexed his spirit by attempting to improve upon the phraseology of the Prayer-Book. He says of himself: "My teachers and books made me think, in general, that the Conformists had the better cause; so that I kept out all particular scruples by that opinion." He wisely accepted them all without practical dissension, and he was contented to use those forms in which, for more than forty generations, penitent and faithful men had offered at the gates of heaven the incense of praise and thanksgiving. He was a true Protestant, adapted to the age in which he lived; of moderation, and yet of progress; and, as has been said of Herder, a man of ancient and modern times, as he was able to bring forth things old and new from his treasure, and to blend them wisely; yielding where he ought to yield, but clinging at the risk of his life to what he ought to hold. How much is there in the great Prussian, John Godfrey Herder, which may remind men of the integrity and heroism of Baxter's later years!

Baxter was, then, happily uninfected by the disease of disputation, of entering upon the wearying contention of words, and of wishing to substitute new phrases in the Prayer-Book for those which a wise antiquity had adopted, not without Divine illumination; which long-continued use had made familiar and dear to all hours of devotion, and which the Church had consecrated in the observance of fast and of festival for more than a thousand years. He was in fact at that time a sober-minded and persistent English Churchman. At no period of his life had he the least sympathy with the principles which are understood to distinguish modern Dissent; and it is not uncharitable to infer, that his works give evidence that they would have been entirely without his approval. The Nonconformists in our days bear the name of their predecessors, but they occupy other grounds of secession, and they seek other ends than theirs. In that age men differed for the most part from the Church of England rather on forms of worship than on matters of doctrine; but it is simply fair to them to state, that while, in some instances, conscience may have led them to object, the unwise Government of the time compelled them to offer resistance to demands which were tyrannical, to exactions which were unjust, and to authority which had become intolerable.

It is said there is a time when a man, who is to do a considerable work in the world, is conscious that the germ of his calling is growing within him. Old thoughts pass away, everything becomes new; he feels the passionate impulses which nothing can check. Restrained no more, he resolves to act, and his whole life takes a new course. In the early dedication of himself to the service of the Church, Richard Baxter had the purest and highest aims. Selfishness had no place in his heart. He, who in the bitterness of angry controversies continuing for many years, and in the varied sufferings of his life, could fervently say at its close that "he would as willingly be a martyr for charity as for truth," began his course with the noble purpose of inducing men to see and to acknowledge the diffusive goodness of God; especially in the spiritual means He has graciously directed to be used, for their recovery from the multiform results of their disobedience to eternal laws. He had thoroughly learned of St. Paul to give himself wholly to the meditation of sacred Truth, "that his profiting might appear to all; taking heed to himself and to his teaching, and continuing in them, that he might both save himself and them that heard him;" and thus that he might have some share in the Church's Divine work.

With such resolutions, in 1638, when in his twenty-third year, Baxter sought ordination at the hands of the venerable Dr. Thornborough, Bishop of Worcester, at that time ninety years old, vigorous in the kindly winter of his age; and in the stately cathedral which overlooks the Severn, he was admitted by him to the ministry of the English Church. Mr. Foley, the ancestor of the well-known family of that name, had recently built and endowed a school-house at Dudley, and he offered Baxter the post of head master to it, which the young candidate was glad to accept, and which was acknowledged by the Bishop as giving a sufficient title to ordination. Baxter willingly undertook to perform the duties of the office, which would allow him time for continuing his studies, and many opportunities of preaching in the town and in the neighbouring villages, without his having also the constant responsibility of a parish. He entered upon his work there, not without some scruples which recent association with Nonconformists had suggested to him. With the frivolous objections of some of the agitating religionists of the time, often disputing simply for the sake of differing, he not only had no sympathy, but he decried and resisted their habit of dissension, and of unseemly bickering. He had early learned from Bishop Davenant the charitable opinion, that "he who believes the things contained in the Apostles' Creed, and endeavours to live a life agreeable to the precepts of Christ, ought not to be expunged from the roll of Christians, nor be driven from communion with the other members of any Church whatsoever."

With the irritable differences and weak scrupulousness of some of the Nonconformists of his day Baxter could have no agreement. His studies had already led him to the conclusion, that there is a contention for religion which is in itself right, and that there is a contention for religion which is a sin; and that charity should govern all things which pertain to the components, opinions, and duties of the Christian society. That the Church should be in conflict with every power which is extraneous to it, is in accordance with its essential state, and with its historical consistency; but that it should have contention and discord within, indicates weakness and confusion. Its spiritual life and strength can be maintained only when the Church has peace in itself. The age of the bitterest animosities of Christian communities has always been the age of religious deadness.

Intemperate angers among Churchmen are ever injurious to Christianity. The evils which negligence and deadening custom have produced are not to be removed by what has been happily termed the rough touch of an ungentle hand; nor can such reformation be undertaken by them whose element is contention, who love the fire of controversy, and who are ingenious in finding matters of dispute. With such men Baxter had neither kinship of thought nor desire of association. Even then he mourned over the animosities among Protestants, the mutual censures of those who held the same truths, and who differed chiefly in matters which were trivial. He knew that discord increases as religion is enfeebled; and that a Church divided against itself is weakened within, and incapable of successful action without. Even at the commencement of his course, he was not unfamiliar with the truth afterwards uttered by Tillotson, that charity is above rubrics, and that they who are seeking the same heaven should not fall out by the way.

CHAPTER IV.

1638—1640.

BAXTER'S first sermon was preached in the church at Dudley, and in that town he remained for a year. The place was not congenial to him. He began his work there with the enthusiasm and energy of one who knew the dignity but not the difficulty of his office. He thought as, we may infer from Luther's reproof of his too sanguine expectation, Melanchthon thought, that his success would be immediate and signal, and that the fortresses of iniquity would yield to his summons. But, habituated transgression is not readily to be abandoned merely at the words of an enthusiast. Men do not quickly step out of the track of lifelong habits. The strongholds of their sins are to be gained rather by the sap and mine of a protracted and fiercely-resisted siege than by impetuous assault; and mild expostulation will often gain it, where energetic argument or vehement declamation has failed.

At the request of Mr. Madstard, the vicar of Bridgnorth, to become his curate, Baxter removed to that town. He speaks of him as "a grave and severe divine, very honest and conscientious, an excellent preacher, but somewhat affected with want of maintenance, but more with a dead-hearted, unprofitable people." Many of the inhabitants were very poor and ignorant; few of them could read. Their homes were little superior to the Highland hovels at the beginning of our century. Their weekly wages were at a very low rate. A farm-servant would not receive more than fourpence a day. Thirty years later, on the estate of Philip Henry, his Diary informs us he paid his "labourers seven groats for seven days' work"; a bricklayer only at the rate of fourpence a yard for building a barn wall; and the joiner who worked in his house received "tenpence a day, and meat and drink." After thirteen years of service in his family, his cook had for her wages only thirty-six shillings a year; yet Philip Henry was a benevolent gentleman, a considerable landholder, and a generous master. In London, and in the home-counties, the rate of payment was necessarily more, but in agricultural districts, especially in those distant from the metropolis, the wages of the poor did not average fivepence a day. In summer the scale of wages would be higher than in winter, but in the dreary months from November to March, when from rain and frost the farm-lands gave little employment to the poor, their poverty was great, and their sufferings extreme. Their clothing was scanty, their food was unwholesome, their diseases were many, and their lives were shortened by hardships. A large proportion of their children died in their infancy, or grew up crippled and weakened by insufficient and irregular nourishment. Baxter had but little success among people so ignorant and poor, gaining their scanty subsistence chiefly from agriculture, and knowing nothing of manufactures, or the healthful rivalries of trade. He says: "There I continued in my liberty of preaching the Gospel at Bridgnorth about a year and three-quarters; which I took to be a great mercy in those troublesome times."

There can be no doubt that laxity of conduct existed then among some of the country clergy. The activities of the Reformation-period had been followed by a reaction of indifference and indolence. Where episcopal visitation was occasional or intermittent, disorder was sure to obtain among the inferior incumbents. The public services were sometimes conducted in a cold, perfunctory manner, and the kindling influence of the earnest preacher was frequently wanting. Generally the churches were opened for Divine worship only on Sunday; and the day itself, beneficently appointed by heavenly wisdom for rest from toil and for spiritual thoughts and duties, was often regarded as the week's holiday for sports, revelling, and jollity. The refining and elevating influences of its wise and cheerful observance, which have been so evident in Great Britain in our own time, had little effect then. On that day the farmers guarded croft and field from the attacks of bands of plunderers from the towns. The apprentices went out to shoot at the butts, or met for football or cricket on the green or village common. If a bull were to be baited, or cocks were to be matched against each other by the sons of the squires, or a long-standing quarrel to be settled by a fight at single-stick or boxing, or the publican's last brewage of ale to be tasted by the artisans from city or town, or hares to be coursed through the lanes and fields,—Sunday would be the occasion selected for them all. It happened often that the curate, and the few parishioners who assembled with him in the church, were disturbed in lesson and litany by the cry of men urging the hounds, or by the roar of the ale-drinking multitude at the success of a favourite pugilist, or by the shouts of the youths who kicked the ball triumphantly. Some parts of society were almost in a state of moral dissolution. Intrigues were many, often leading to bloodshed. Chicanery and knavery abounded. Vices corrupted young and old. Where any of the clergy were negligent of their public and pastoral duty, careless of the mode of life which became them who were dedicated to the awful service of religion, their parishioners too quickly followed the evil examples. In some parishes the spirit of goodness was all but quenched, and mechanical services were an evil and a shame in the hours of prayer. Where the shepherd is faithless and unwatchful, the flock strays to its ruin. Nothing has a more deteriorating effect upon a community than the lack of personal religion in its spiritual teacher and guide; especially when this is manifested by irreverence or indifference in the conduct of the Divine service, by the wilful neglect of private visitation and counsel, and by the evident want of restraint of appetites and passions in social and family life. Notwithstanding his arbitrary temper, his narrowness of view, and his superstition, there was every reason why the spirit of Archbishop Laud was stirred within him when he learned, both by his personal observation and by the reports of his agents, of the disorders which obtained in the lives and duties of some of his clergy; and though his ministration may have been on the whole unwise, and his methods severe and even cruel, no one can deny that, in that age, in some districts of the country, there was need of the sagacious watchfulness of the master-mind, the promptness of a just decision, and the determination to effect a quick and thorough reform of neglects and abuses which disgraced the Church, and injured the State. Something of that which popular tradition has affirmed of the evil courses of monks and friars, may be alleged with truth of certain of Baxter's contemporaries who ministered in holy things. The irregularity and inefficiency of the clergy might be justly estimated by the increase and vigour of the Nonconformists; although it would be historically incorrect to term the Puritans of the seventeenth century dissenters. As, in our own day, it is observed that dissent often languishes and diminishes where the clergyman is able and active in the discharge of his duty, so, in the period immediately preceding the civil war, the incompetence and disorder of some of the parochial ministers might be known by the growth and activity of their opponents. In our own time, there is demonstration of the fact that the renewed life and energy of English Churchmen have greatly checked the increase of Nonconformist communities; and the sterling good sense of our countrymen instinctively perceives that an ordered and well-managed system works more readily and productively than others which lack firm coherence, and which, however zealously maintained for a time, are readily disintegrated at the will or caprice of their components.

Some of the parochial clergy, curates of absentee-vicars

for the most part, whom Baxter knew in his youth, were men who in their manner of living happily have no successors among ourselves. If they had been students at either university, they had quitted collegiate residence and literature at the same time. The stipends of many of the country priests were very small. Their books were few, and their means were scanty for increasing professional knowledge. Their homes wanted the conveniences and comforts which now every clergyman's dwelling contains. There was little in their associations to animate and elevate them. Seldom invited to the tables of nobles and country gentlemen, some of the rural curates dined with yeomen, visited the alehouses, and tippled with traders and rustics at markets. These, however, may have been but a small minority. Numbers of the stricter class of the parochial clergy had been silenced by the bishops for their suspected Puritan tendencies, as for their directly refusing to use the sign of the cross in the baptism of infants, and the ring in the celebration of the marriage-service. When Laud became Archbishop of Canterbury, he found that seven-eighths of the English people were attached to Puritanism ; he determined to overthrow it, and to use against it for that purpose all the powers of the High Commission Court, which was in fact the English form of the Roman Inquisition in Protestant hands. He resolved to put an end to that which was popularly known as "Gospel-preaching," and to suspend and deprive all incumbents who refused to yield to his demand. He suppressed the lectures which had been founded in towns, and which merchants and tradesmen supported in days when books were few, nurture for the mind scarce and costly, and when as yet newspapers and serials were not. He even went so far as to refuse country gentlemen the right of keeping chaplains in their houses, which had been hitherto undisputed; thus needlessly making that large and important class his enemies, and thereby hastening the end. Laud became more and more tyrannical as he became more conscious of the extent of his power, and of the endurance of the clergy. He was the Strafford of the Church, in which he resolved to establish a thorough despotism. He would allow the Genevan Bibles to be no longer imported and purchased by Englishmen. The editions of this translation, which were in great favour with the people, were such as could be carried in the pocket, and which the merchant could take easily with him on his journeys; with some explanatory notes in the margins, which gave great offence at Canterbury. Laud believed that the English observance of the Lord's Day fostered Puritanism, and greatly impeded the sacerdotal reaction, upon the success of which all his heart was set; and he determined not only to republish the Book of Sports, which explained what games could be played on the sacred Day, but also to compel every clergyman to read from his pulpit the king's declaration in favour of Sunday-amusements. Englishmen were indignant at the dictation, presumptuous folly, and "the exorbitant power of the Archbishop of Canterbury"; and the clergy, ever the advocates of freedom, resisted his imperious demand. Many hundreds of them were at once deprived of their livings; in Norfolk alone thirty were driven from home and means of sustenance. No one, who reads of these and of other of Laud's greater tyrannies, can wonder that the road on which he went his way led to the scaffold. Tradition relates that one clergyman in London, Dr. Dawson, after saying the Ten Commandments, obeyed his domineering Archbishop by reading the king's declaration for destroying the sanctity of the Lord's Day, but that he immediately added: "You have heard read, good people, both the commandment of God and the commandment of man. Obey which you please."

In 1640, both Houses of Convocation formed new regulations for the clergy, which contained that which was generally known as the *et cætera* oath, in which each ordained person was directed to affirm: "I will never give my consent to alter the government of this Church by archbishops, bishops, deans, archdeacons, *et cætera*, as it stands now established, and ought to stand." The refusal to take the oath was punishable by suspension and deprivation. The whole country was in a ferment of discontent and animosity. The ill-advised attempt of Charles I. to impose the English Prayer-Book upon the Scotch added to the general disquietude and confusion; and led them not only to the formation of the Solemn League and Covenant against popery and prelacy, but to cross the English border with a formidable army. Charles came to a compromise with them at Newcastle; but the effervescence in England continued unabated. Men's minds were agitated by discontent with the present state, and by apprehension of dangerous changes, suspicions of the intentions of the government, and fearful of being compelled to absolute subjection to the monarch's despotical authority. Petitions were sent in large numbers to the Long Parliament against some of the clergy, with complaints of their irreverent service and of their unseemly habits. Strafford and Laud, the two chief advisers of the policy of the king, were hated by that assembly, many of whom were resolved to resist at all hazards the innovations attempted in Church and State; and the religious members of the Lower House, with no sympathy with the crude theories of others, who in their hearts longed for the establishment of a democratical form of government, were determined to oppose to the uttermost the attempted changes in the English Church, the High Commission Court, and Star Chamber, and the ejection from their benefices of eminent clergymen for their refusal to read the king's declaration of the Book of Sports. Never, in all the varied history of the Church, were the bishops so unpopular as in that year. Their extreme harshness to some clergymen of unblemished life, whom they had driven from their cures, and the measures which, by the direction of Archbishop Laud, they had adopted towards men who had been sentenced, for unimportant differences with their prelates in religious opinion, to long imprisonment or to perpetual exile, had roused a spirit of resistance in the Long Parliament, which neither the king nor his two chief counsellors Laud and

Strafford could have foreseen, and which ultimately brought both the monarch and his ministers to destruction. There can be little doubt, from the mass of historical evidence now collected, that Laud was one of the chief factors in producing the grievous troubles which overthrew the throne, silenced the voice of the Church, and brought unnumbered calamities upon English homes. The spirit of opposition to royal and ecclesiastical tyranny grew stronger and bolder. The Parliament passed an Act to abolish the Star Chamber, and to restrict the bishops to the possession of spiritual authority only; and they formed a committee to receive and to investigate the complaints, which came to them from several counties, of the immorality, idleness, and general incompetency of certain clergymen.

While Baxter was at Bridgnorth, the parishioners of Kidderminster threatened to petition Parliament against their vicar, of whom they complained that he was often in the alehouses, was sometimes seen to be drunk, and was generally ignorant and feeble in his office; and that the curate who assisted him had all the failings of the elder clergyman, and, in addition to other malpractices, made money by trafficking in unlawful marriages. The behaviour of the two ministers was a general scandal; but all good principle and right feeling had not died out in the town. Grieved and wounded as is the public conscience whenever the teachers of religion are men of vice and shame, the natural kindness and forbearance of the English people make them always unwilling to expose to the eyes of strangers the ill-doings of nefarious clergymen, and to proceed to extremities against them. An English parish will always endure much from its erring shepherd before it determines to publicly restrain and punish his evil behaviour. The Vicar of Kidderminster, well aware of this social generosity, resolved to make such compromise with the townspeople as should shield him from further exposure, and from ultimate punishment, and which should be effectual in silencing the damaging complaints against him. He agreed to dismiss the obnoxious curate; and he offered to give up his pulpit to any lecturer whom the parishioners might select, to whom he promised to do the part of an assistant in the duties of the church and parish, to allow him full liberty of preaching, and to assign him a stipend of sixty pounds a year. A committee of parishioners was formed, who accepted the terms proposed by the Vicar, and on the ninth day of March, 1640, they invited Baxter to be their lecturer. In the following spring he was legally instituted to the office.

Baxter was glad to be appointed to such a post of duty. Kidderminster at first had no attraction to him. Many of the inhabitants were ignorant, ill-mannered, and dissolute, addicted more or less to the practice of drunkenness, so prevalent and so destructive in their century. The town was as a field overgrown with thistles and thorns, which by judicious care would amply repay the cost and pains of cultivation. The church was large, and well suited to him. Some of the better class of townspeople received him kindly, and promised to co-operate with him in his endeavours to effect a religious reformation in the parish. In referring to this important incident in his life, he says: "Thus I was brought by the gracious providence of God to that place which had the chiefest of my labours, and yielded me the greatest fruits of comfort; and I noted the mercy of God in this, that I never went to any place in my life which I had before desired or thought of, much less sought, till the sudden invitation did surprise me." With happy recollections of this town in which his happiest days were passed, and where his preaching had wonderful success, he wrote in his "Poetical Fragments":—

"Where I did make my best and longest stay,
And bore the heat and burden of the day,
Mercies grew thicker there than summer flowers,
They over-numberèd my days and hours.
There was my dearest flock and special charge,
Our hearts with mutual love Thou didst enlarge:
'Twas there Thy mercy did my labours bless
With the most great and wonderful success."

Baxter was appointed to the lectureship at Kidderminster in 1640, and he entered upon his duties not only in the spirit of the resolution made on his escape from sudden death in his winter-journey from London, but with the chastened mind of a man whose increasing weaknesses caused him to live in the certainty of having only a very short time in which to serve the Church, and to win men to the knowledge, preparation, and hope of the better life. His purpose was not to teach them a selfish religion, so that they should congratulate themselves they were safe and happy, whatever might betide the rest of mankind; nor that they should be actuated merely by the fear of escaping condemnation at last, as though they were to aim at nothing higher than personal security in the future audit of the world; nor that they should presumptuously attempt to form a contract with Heaven, that present advantage and happiness should accrue to them just as they either abstained from the grosser, open depravity of the age, or shunned secret vices, or with some show of self-denial followed a prescribed routine of private or public prayer. He who had so long watched for truth, with constant study of the revealed, everlasting Word, and of the writings of the Fathers and Confessors, who had loved, lived, and taught it, saw that religion affected all human relations, and that the Church—the enduring evidence to the facts of historical Christianity—was to be no other than the place of welcome, of healing, and of rest, for a diseased, unquiet, and disordered world. For Baxter believed that which, long afterwards, the German philosopher, Johann Gottlieb Fichte, taught, that "Religion is not mere devotional dreaming; it is not a business which can be followed on certain days, or at certain hours, independent of other business; but it is the inner spirit which penetrates all our thoughts and actions, and immerses them in itself." Baxter would refer all holy influences to Christ; and therefore he taught his flock that it is the glory of the blessed Saviour that they who are conscious of their wants should find satisfaction in Him, able to live only as He empowers them; so that they should ever regard Him as the Lord of life, in Whom they might trust at all times, at once their solace and delight. He urged them to imitate the example of their Redeemer, to love purity, to confide in His ever-present and all-containing goodness; to believe therefore in the world-wide range of His redemptive purpose; and that humanity itself should not only be recovered from guilt and loss, but also should be supremely happy in possessing the glorious qualities of a nature restored to likeness and to union with God, Who is both light and love; and that in His all-comprehending compassion, the regulations of His government are to restrain or to lessen the evils of life, to promote amendment, to encourage faithful service, and to guide struggling virtue to a safe and happy end. With all the ardour of his soul, with the tender entreaty of his kindly heart,—his face, pale and worn by frequent suffering, kindling as with celestial fire,—he exhorted them to look beyond the outline of the present state, and to the serene and compensating future, rejoicing in hope of the glory of God; by the anticipations of faith seeing how He Who is ever happy diffuses joy among all the brotherhood of the just made perfect, receiving their praise, and returning them His blessing. He would have them ever to remember that only a short time would intervene between the hoping soul and the happiness which awaits it, so that they might well endure with patience the discipline of life. Thus he taught them a religion neither darkened by fears, nor blended with fables, nor degraded by cunning deceits.

Baxter's chief object seems to have been to urge his parishioners to form that habit of communion with God, that humble confession of the soul to Him Who knows its wants and woes, and which the devout men of all Christian churches hold to be essential to a life of religion. He writes: "To walk with God is a word so high, that I should have feared the guilt of arrogance in using it, if I had not found it in the Holy Scriptures. It is a word that importeth so high and holy a frame of soul, and expresseth such high and holy actions, that the naming of it striketh my heart with reverence, as if I had heard the voice to Moses, 'Put off thy shoes from off thy feet, for the place whereon thou standest is holy ground.' Methinks he that shall say to us, 'Come see a man that walks with God,' doth call me to see one that is an angel or glorified soul. It is a far more reverend object in my eye than ten thousand lords or princes, considered only in their fleshly glory. It is a wiser action for people to run and crowd together to see a man that walks with God than to see the pompous train of princes, their entertainments, or their triumph. O happy man that walks with God, though neglected and contemned by all about him! What blessed sights doth he daily see! What ravishing tidings, what pleasant melody doth he daily hear! What delectable food doth he daily taste! He seeth, by faith, the God, the glory, which the blessed spirits see at hand by nearest intuition. He seeth that in a glass darkly, which they behold with open face. He seeth the glorious majesty of his Creator, the Eternal King, the Cause of causes, the Composer, Upholder, Preserver, and Governor of all worlds. He beholdeth the wonderful methods of His Providence; and what he cannot reach to see, he admireth, and waiteth for the time when that also shall be open to his view. He seeth by faith the world of spirits, the hosts that attend the throne of God; their perfect righteousness, their full devotedness to God, their ardent love, their flaming zeal, their ready and cheerful obedience, their dignity and shining glory, in which the lowest of them exceeds that which the disciples saw on Moses and Elias, when they appeared in the holy mount, and talked with Christ. He hears by faith the heavenly concert, the high and harmonious songs of praise, the joyful triumphs of crowned saints, the sweet commemoration of the things that were done and suffered on earth, with the praises of Him that redeemed them by His blood, and made them kings and priests unto God. Herein he hath a sweet foretaste of the everlasting pleasures which, though it be but a little, as Jonathan's honey on the end of his rod, or as the clusters of grapes which were brought from Canaan into the wilderness; yet they are more excellent than all the delights of sinners."

The public services at Baxter's parish church differed in some respects from those which obtain among ourselves. The rubrics then, as now, regulated the order of public prayer, but no rubrics existed to prescribe the mode and length of the preaching. The wisdom of brevity was little understood by our forefathers, whether Anglican or Puritan. Even Calamy admits, that such services as theirs few clergymen could have gone through without inexpressible weariness both to themselves and their auditors. His description of those, on occasions of public fast-days, to which John Howe accustomed his congregation in the parish church at Torrington, may give some idea of the painful labour of the minister, and of the wonderful patience of his congregation. He says: "I shall not easily forget the account he once gave me in private conversation of the great pains he took, without any help or assistance, on the public fasts, which in those days returned pretty frequently, and were generally kept with very great solemnity. He told me it was upon these occasions his common way to begin about nine in the morning, with a prayer for about a quarter of an hour, in which he begged a blessing on the work of the day; and afterwards read or expounded a chapter or a psalm, in which he spent about three-quarters; then prayed for about an hour, preached for another hour, and prayed for about half an hour. After this, he retired and took some little refreshment for about a quarter of an hour or more (the people singing all the while), and then came again into the pulpit and prayed for another hour, and gave them another sermon of about an hour's length; and so concluded the service of the day, at about four o'clock in the evening, with about half an hour or more in prayer. But he had a strong head, a warm heart, and a good bodily constitution: and the more he spent himself in his Master's service, the more was he beloved by the inhabitants of his parish."

Soon after his appointment to the parish of Kidderminster,

Baxter determined to attempt an improvement in the service of sacred song in his church. To him, as to John Milton, music was a minister of grace to the soul. He loved the stately airs of the older time, many of which probably were brought from Germany to England by them who in perilous days had found shelter at Frankfort and Wittenberg from the severities of the English government—such tunes as are now sometimes heard in rural churches in the lands of the Oder and the Rhine; and some of which survive in our own country, where there is now in fashion a lighter musical expression of the deep feelings of the heart, when offering public praise and thanksgiving to the Eternal Majesty. In his later years he writes: "For myself I confess that harmony and melody are the pleasure and elevation of my soul. I have made a psalm of praise in the holy assembly the chief delightful exercise of my religion and my life, and have helped to bear down all the objections I have heard against church music, and against the 149th and 150th Psalms. It was not the least comfort that I had in the converse of my late dear wife, that our first in the morning and last at night was a psalm of praise, till the hearing of others interrupted it. Let those that savour not melody leave others to their different appetites, and be content to be so far strangers to their delights." Sacred music and poetry were his enjoyment throughout his busy, troubled life. His friend Sylvester writes of Baxter, in his later days of suffering, that "when his sleep was intermitted, or removed in the night, he then sang much; and on the Lord's Days he thought the service very defective without some considerable time were spent in singing; nay, he believingly expected that his angelical convoy would conduct him through all the intermediate regions to his appointed mansion in his heavenly Father's house, with most melodious hallelujahs, or with something equally delightful."

Such was the manner of him who transformed the sacred service in Kidderminster church, and kindled religious life and fervour among his parishioners; teaching them to sing those tunes by which both miners in the Hartz mountains and English artisans long preserved religious truth, when much around them was dark and dreary. In our own day, the improvement effected in sacred melody is not the least of those changes in ecclesiastical procedure which all good men must commend. For, so far as relates to the Christian world, one of the chief requirements of religion is, that everything which hath breath should praise the Lord.

CHAPTER V.

1640—1642.

THE most interesting page of Baxter's history is that which records his work at Kidderminster. His service there is an example to all clergymen of what may be accomplished by devout and earnest labour in the noblest employment. He early learned the truths which the Church in her warfare bears upon her golden shield—that prayer is life, and life is prayer; that prayer is work, and work is prayer. He had dedicated himself to the service of the Saviour, and he relied absolutely upon the ready help of the gracious Lord for success in the duties he had undertaken. He firmly held the reasonable doctrine of the grace of God,—that which in his system might be termed belief in the prevenient acts of His mercy. He had been educated to the opinion of some of the ancient philosophers, that religion and not reason is the specific difference of man, and that it is as impossible for any human society to be without it "as for a bird to be without wings;" but that, to be effectual, it must be essentially a religion of Divine impression on the one part, and of submission, trust, and hope on the other. He held also, as the very heart of his creed, that He, Whose last words to His Church were the command to go out to teach the world, was near to strengthen and to direct all who faithfully obeyed Him. So Baxter laboured to persuade his flock to live the better life; but he knew that the only way to it—if men were to be gained—was by the conviction of conscience, and that they could be gained only as they saw the real importance and necessity of that which they were urged to do. When one is compelled in his own judgment to admit the reasonableness of the Divine claim, and of the submission of the once resisting soul to its rightful Lord, much is done towards the full reception of truth; and the clergyman's animating hope of success depends on the fact that conscience may be thus convinced. Thus he was above all things solicitous for the result of his work, and the more so from the necessary uncertainty of attaining it: whether the higher life will be secured to the glorious service and bliss of goodness, or whether it will be utterly lost to them. But the very anxiety consoled him when tempted to doubt his own sincerity; for if he had no honest purpose to restore the lost, there would be no cause for that anxiety. Each day of his labour convinced him more and more that everything depended upon gaining the consciences of his flock, and then that what was admitted to be right in their enlightened judgment might become their law and rule of life and of conduct. On this success his heart was set; if he might only rescue some of them from the madness and deformity of wicked and useless living, raise them to see and to rejoice that they were the fallen children of the ever-merciful, eternal Father and Saviour, and win them to love and obey Him. How would he often remember the words of the gracious Lord that, in such circumstances of service, and of uncertainty of attainment, "men ought always to pray,"—how would his chamber at Kidderminster witness his cries to the Spirit of mercy, of power, and of truth, to help him in his duty; that He Who is the Life and the Light of men would scatter the darkness from the minds of his flock, and would make the wilderness a fruitful field! It is said of the greater masters of Italian art, that they never ventured to place sketch or colour on wall or canvas until they had first kneeled down to implore the help and guidance of the Holy Spirit; so that their "pencils embodied the language of prayer," and their works of beauty are the perpetual admiration and joy of the civilised world. So Richard Baxter, greatest of all English preachers, if success is to be estimated by the results of his work, presumed not to study the oracles of God, nor to prepare those sermons whose breathing thoughts and burning words gave life and faith to the souls of his cure, without the often-uttered supplication that the Lord of the Church would enlighten the darkness of his mind, raise him to higher views of truth, inspire his thoughts, and give him strength to work, while gathering in the precious fruits o the land given him to till,—that He Whom he loved might accept the labour which had first received His blessing, and thus that all might be well at eventide.

In his home Baxter mourned over his sinfulness of nature and feebleness of service, prayed for the help which never fails, and lived with the hope which makes not ashamed. There he learned those sublime truths which, when spoken in his melodious words, with the animated gesture and the flashing eye, moved, convinced, melted his congregation to tears, or determined them to immediate amendment, or filled them with peace and joy in believing. How they hung upon his lips! how the accents of that perfect voice gained the ear of the heart! how he strengthened the believer in his grasp of truth, compelled the reckless to reflection, the indifferent to attention, the guilty to confession, the mocker to pray. Benches, aisles, galleries, and every spot on which men could stand, were occupied by them who wept at his entreaties, or trembled at his denunciations, or who, at his eloquent pleading, opened their hearts to his appeals; the nailers and weavers, who could get no admission at the crowded entrances, climbing up the waterspouts, lying on the leads, to hear through the opened windows how readily the Heavenly Father receives and pardons the sinner who asks for mercy,—how freely and truly the Redeemer loved them all,—how the gracious Spirit of His goodness had long waited for the hour of their repentance and amendment of life, and how happy would be the glorious Easter-time of the world, when, in the consummation of His compassions, God should restore humanity, and "with a smile repair" all that had been ravaged and wasted by the revolt of man. Can it be wondered that the poor labourers, for whose souls hitherto no one had duly cared, should delight to hear him speak of the possibility of a better and happier life in this world, and of that other state to which the present is but the vestibule?

Towards the end of his life, in referring to his work at Kidderminster, Baxter writes: "In the place where God most blessed my labours, at Kidderminster in Worcestershire, my first and greatest success was upon the youth; and, which was a marvellous way of Divine mercy, when God had touched the hearts of young men and girls with love of goodness and delightful obedience to the truth, the parents, and grandfathers, who had grown old in an ignorant, worldly state, did many of them fall into a liking and love of piety, induced by the love of their children, whom they perceived by it to be made much wiser, and better, and more dutiful to them. God, by His unexpected, disposing providence, having now for twenty years placed me in and near London, where, in a variety of places and conditions (sometimes under restraint by men, and sometimes at more liberty), I have preached, but as to strangers, in other men's families, as I could, and not to any special flock of mine, I have been less capable of judging of my success; but by much experience I have been made more sensible of the necessity of warning and instructing youth than I was before. The sad reports of fame have taught it to me; the sad complaints of mournful parents have taught it me; the sad observation of the wilful impenitence of some of my acquaintance tells it me; the many scores, if not hundreds, of bills that have been publicly put up to me to pray for wicked and obstinate children, have told it me; and by the grace of God, the penitent confessions, lamentations, and restitutions of many converts, have more particularly acquainted me with their case, which moved me, on my Thursday's lecture, awhile to design, the first of every month, to speak to youth and those that educate them."

It may not be easy to account altogether for the remarkable success of Baxter as a preacher then and afterwards. His sermons were unlike anything which his congregation had heard before. He spoke with remarkable ardour; and a public assembly is generally sympathetic. Tears generate tears, as fire produces fire. Everything he uttered was the result of careful study. He observed to the utmost the golden rules laid down by Quintilian and by other great teachers of rhetoric, observed by the ablest speakers down to the present time, and commended by the experience of all who have spent laborious days in fitting themselves for public discourse, that everything depends upon careful preparation. In that age, differing in many things from our own, when multifarious duties occupy so much of the time of all oral instructors and debaters,—without the incessant harassment of public meetings, of attendance upon committees, and of the daily weariness of diffuse correspondence, Baxter had ample leisure for the constant study of the Scriptures, and for careful forethought and arrangement as to what was best, both in matter and in manner, for the religious education of his flock. He had that love for books which is said to be one of the greatest gifts of Heaven to man. With a full use of them, he had ample time to arrange the logical connection of his thoughts, to choose the words most suitable for giving them effect, whether to teach the ignorant, to arouse the indifferent, or to increase the growth in knowledge of the communicants. The vigour and simplicity of his style are conspicuous in his nervous language, which gave force to admonition and appeal; but he was by no means a skilful rhetorician. He had no regard for harmonious expressions, redundant epithets, gracefully rounded periods; by the artful use of which expedients men of lesser attainment often gain a lucrative popularity. He could never be classed with them whom Lord Bacon condemns for employing themselves "more in hunting after words than matter; more after the choiceness of the phrase, and the round and clean composition of the sentence, and the sweet falling of the clauses, and the varying and illustration with tropes and figures, than after the weight of matter, worth of subject, soundness of argument, life of invention, or depth of judgment." He had no fear of men's censures, and he cared nothing for their applause. He wrote and spoke that he might convince and win assent; as a faithful ambassador, whose brief expressions have point and elegance enough if they convey the wishes of his king. He stooped to none of those arts by which declaimers often succeed,—by weeping at pre-arranged times, and by using tender tones, to attract attention and to win admiration for the favourite speaker; nor did he employ an unrestrained imagination, the offensive faculty ever obtruding beyond its proper sphere, as Bishop Butler wrote of it, to charm or to beguile the susceptible hearers; but he spoke with voice, and eye, and hand, as one who knew he had hearts to gain, lives to reform, men to save, and the Holy Saviour to honour above all. He spoke in glowing words of what his honest mind knew to be the truth, and to which all his life was obedient. With what power of language! with what directness of purpose! with what gentleness of spirit, and in what terms of compassion!—if only he might be faithful to his trust, successful in his service, and mindful that he worked always under the great Taskmaster's eye.

Failure to such a man, acting on such principles, and using such methods, was simply impossible under that spiritual government to which all are subject; whose unvarying law is, that the wealth of labour accrues to patient industry; that no self-denial or wearisome toil is forgotten, or is ever unfruitful in the ministrations of religion; and that, as in nature, with all its forces of growth, and its wonderful arrangement for universal sustenance and preservation, so in the higher world of the spiritual life, all that is sympathetic is coherent, and like begets like, by the unvarying law of reproduction and renewal. Baxter's eminent personal religion; his animated countenance, and the remarkable light of his lustrous and speaking eye, demonstrating sincerity; his almost incredible industry and energy.

his consummate ability as a theologian of an unbiassed mind, as a careful and close reasoner, and, above all, as a preacher whose force and success were remarkable; his gentle bearing and his daily actions of benevolence, made him for half a century one of the greatest powers in the kingdom, charitable to a large degree, and thrifty only in the employment of time. Nothing is more striking than the sagacity of his conduct both as a clergyman and as a citizen, in all he did both in church and at home. Like other great leaders of men, he considered nothing to be trifling, or unworthy of careful consideration, if it would help him in convincing the judgment and securing the assent of them whom he sought to benefit. He had respect to their prejudices, he bore with their narrowness of thought, he abstained from opposing their harmless predilections, so that he might lead his flock to the Saviour. His behaviour in the town was singularly prudent. His liberality and courtesy were unfailing. He interested himself in the affairs of his parishioners; he loved their children; he gave all he could part with to the poor; he sedulously cared for the infirm; he offered medicine to the sick; he distributed many useful books, and in one year it is said he expended £100 in purchasing Bibles for poor families. Without curiosity, he listened to their tales of sorrow, and without a thought of recompense he counselled them in their various perplexities and troubles. He carried the sacred truth from the church to the home, going with orderly diligence from house to house. He sought out individuals of whose doubts or temptations or difficulties of belief he had accurate knowledge. By his example of devotedness, kindness, and energy, he induced them to help one another in acquiring Christian truth, and in fulfilling Christian duty. He applied in each day to his sacred work more time than that which the merchant or the lawyer gives to his calling; and, by a judicious management of his hours, while he left no part of his parish unseen by his watchful eye, he was able to write the earlier of those numerous volumes, which remain as memorials of the amazing application and industry of a man whose strength was made perfect in weakness; for his body was one of the feeblest and most suffering in which a human spirit has ever dwelt. Tortured by pain, disturbed in his rest, irritated by nervous debility, afflicted by varying forms of disease, he lived in constant expectation of death. But he gave full proof of the thoroughness of his service. He revived the religious life of the town, and he turned the waste land into a fruitful field.

For two years he laboured with increasing encouragement. At first the intemperate and disorderly of the townspeople opposed and maligned him. They were angry that their vices were condemned and decried, and that so many of the parishioners were reformed in their habits and conduct. They misrepresented his sermons, they accused him of giving horrible ideas of the severity and vindictiveness of the government of God. They gathered mobs, who roared fiercely around his door, and threatened him with personal violence and public dishonour. But his earnest diligence, the sincerity, kindness, and impartiality of his procedure, soon silenced the angry spirit of hatred and animosity, and he lived down the slanders of the vicious and the malignant.

The outbreak of the war between Charles I. and the Parliament compelled Baxter to leave Kidderminster. He hated democracy, and he looked always with suspicion and dislike upon the Independents, who were then becoming numerous and powerful. He thought both sides were wrong in hastily resorting to violence. He condemned some of the adherents of the Parliament; although he seems to have considered that there was some just cause for remonstrance and resistance from the popular party; especially Sir Henry Vane and Lord Brooke, for their imprudence in demanding too much from the Court, and for the rashness with which they took up arms. But from the commencement of the discords until they terminated in war, Baxter doubted—as since his day M. Guizot and others have doubted—the sincerity and truth of the king. At the beginning of the war, Charles manifested the distinctive fault of all his house—an unreadiness to forgive, and an incapability of making a compact with the honest intention of keeping it. If his advisers gave him from first to last injurious counsels, his habitual insincerity was one of the causes of his ruin. Charles always seemed to take the second step before he had determined on the first—the stigma which Frederick the Great applied to the Austrian Emperor—or he would not have summoned the northern army, nor moved against the free action of the House of Commons, nor endeavoured to seize the five members of it, nor indeed resorted to other rash and dangerous measures, which embittered the differences between himself and the Parliament, and made accommodation not only difficult but impossible. But his inherited obstinacy of belief in his Divine right to rule, his love of despotic authority, with the constant stimulus of the counsel of the queen, that "he should be a king as the king of France was," and the reckless words of the noblemen on whose advice he relied, led him to the final step of taking up arms to compel the submission of those who resisted his prerogative. He assembled his troops, formed a regular army at Nottingham, and prepared for the vigorous prosecution of war. The Parliament on their side collected their forces, and they gave the command of them to the Earl of Essex. The noblemen and country-gentlemen were mostly on the side of the king, with their tenants and a large number of the agricultural population, who were more dependent upon the wealthy families, and more closely associated with their interests, in those days than they are in our own time. The merchants, the greater number of the yeomen, and persons engaged in trade, were almost entirely in favour of the Parliament; and with them the question was mainly that of religion. Many of them were hostile to the bishops, who were then generally believed by the people to be opposed to the extension of liberty, and to freedom of conscience. Indeed, episcopacy was the matter mainly in dispute from first to last. These classes bitterly hated Archbishop Laud, who was thought to have been all along the adviser of some of the extreme measures to which the king had resorted, and who himself was regarded as a persecutor of some of their clergymen who advocated political liberty, and who had sympathy with the principles of Puritanism.

The severities of the bishops' courts; their silence in protesting against the king's levying taxes upon his own authority alone; their general sympathy with him in his manner of government; their unwillingness to condemn the Book of Sports; and their refusal to assent to the popular request for a larger number and better kind of preachers, made the middle classes of the people more furious against the prelates than against the king. But it was evident that the cause of Charles I. was also the cause of the bishops; that if he were successful, episcopacy would be supreme; and that if the chances of war were against the king, the Anglican Church would be endangered by his defeat. Baxter writes: "Before 1640, in the place where I first lived and the country round about, the people were of two sorts. The generality seemed to mind nothing seriously, but the body and the world. They went to church, and could answer the parson in responses, and thence to dinner, and then to play. They never prayed in their families; but some of them going to bed would say over the Creed and the Lord's Prayer, and some of them the Hail Mary. They read not the Scriptures, nor any good book or catechism: few of them indeed could read, or had a Bible. They were of two ranks: the greater part were good husbands, as they called them, and minded nothing but their business or interest in the world; the rest were drunkards. Most were swearers, though they were not all equally gross. The other class were such as had their conscience awakened to some regard for God and their everlasting state; and, according to the various measures of their understandings, did speak and live as serious in the Christian faith, and would inquire what was their duty, what was sin, and how to please God, and to make sure of salvation. This being the fundamental division, some of those who were called Puritans and hypocrites, for not being hypocrites but serious in the religion they professed, would sometimes get together, and meet after sermons on the Lord's Days, to repeat the sermon and sing a psalm and pray. For this and for going from their own parish-churches, they were first envied by the readers and day-teachers, whom they sometimes went from, and next prosecuted by apparitors, officials, archdeacons, commissaries, chancellors, and other episcopal instruments. When these conformable Puritans were thus prosecuted, it bred in them hard thoughts of bishops and their courts, as enemies to serious piety, and persecutors of that which they should promote. Suffering induced this opinion and aversion; and the ungodly rabble rejoiced at their troubles, and applauded the bishops for it, and were everywhere ready to set the apparitors on those, or to ask them, 'Are you holier and wiser than the bishops?' When the persons of bishops, chancellors, officials, apparitors, etc., were come under such repute, it is easy to believe what would be said against their office. And the more the bishops thought to cure this by punishment, the more they increased the opinion that they were persecuting enemies of godliness. The civil contentions arising, those called Puritans were mostly against that side to which they saw the bishops and their neighbours enemies. Yet they desired, wherever I was, to have lived peaceably at home; but the drunkards and the rabble that formerly hated them, when they saw the war beginning, grew enraged; for if a man did but pray and sing a psalm in his house, they would say, 'Down with the Roundheads!' (a word then new made for them), and put them in fear of sudden violence. Afterwards they brought the king's soldiers to plunder them of their goods, which fain made them run into holes to hide their persons; and when their goods were gone, and their lives in continual danger, they were forced to fly for food and shelter. To go amongst those that hated them they durst not, when they could not dwell among such at home. And thus thousands ran into the parliamentary garrisons, and having nothing there to live upon, became soldiers."

On both sides were many devout persons, who had that dislike of extreme opinions which has been ever since characteristic of the reflecting, unprejudiced Englishman; who held that wisdom is in moderation, and that nothing is ever gained by advocating revolutionary principles, by vehemence of denunciation, and by violence of conduct. Some of them questioned the lawfulness of resisting the sovereign. A deep religiousness of nature induced others to submit to arbitrary government, rather than to sanction discord and insurrection; and some of them distrusted equally the profligate nobles, who recruited for the king, and the furious levellers, who used religious pretexts and phrases to advance their own interests, and to accumulate money for themselves out of the angers, confusions, and ravages of a civil war.

Such prudent and temperate men were silenced and overborne by furious partisans hastening to conflict. Their silence was wilfully misunderstood; their reasons were ridiculed; or their withdrawment from participation in choosing a side, and taking an active part in violent measures, rendered them objects of suspicion, and involved them in danger of injury from both contending hosts indiscriminately. Baxter writes of these circumstances: "For my own part, I freely confess I was not judicious enough in politics and law to decide this controversy. Being astounded at the Irish massacres, and persuaded fully both of the Parliament's good endeavours for reformation and of their real danger, my judgment of the main cause much swayed my judgment in the matter of the wars; and the arguments *a fine, et a naturâ, et necessitate*, which common wits are capable of discerning, did not too far incline my judgment in the cause of the war, before I well understood the arguments from our particular laws. The consideration of the quality of the persons also, that sided for each cause, did greatly work with me, and more than it should have done. I verily thought, that if that which a judge in court saith is law must go for law to the subject as to the decision of that cause, though the king send his broad seal against it, then that which the Parliament saith is law, is law to the subject about the dangers of the commonwealth, whatever it be in itself. I make no doubt that both parties were to blame, as it commonly falleth out in most wars and contentions; and I will not be he that will justify either of them. I doubt not but the headiness and rashness of the younger, inexperienced sort of religious people made many Parliament men and ministers overgo themselves to keep pace with those Hotspurs. No doubt but much indiscretion appeared, and worse than indiscretion, in the tumultuous petitioners; and much sin was committed in the dishonouring the king, and in the uncivil language against the bishops and liturgy of the Church. But these things came chiefly from the sectarian, separating spirit, which blew the coals among foolish apprentices. And as the sectaries increased, so the insolence increased. One or two in the House, and five or six ministers that came from Holland, and a few relicts of the Brownists (Independents) that were scattered in the city, did drive on others, and sowed the seeds which afterwards spread all over the land. But I then thought, whoever was faulty, the people's liberties and safeties should not be forfeited. I thought that all the subjects were not guilty of all the faults of king or Parliament, when they defended them; yea, that if both their causes had been bad as against each other, yet that the subjects should adhere to that party which most secured the welfare of the nation, and might defend the land under their conduct without owning all their cause. And herein I was then so zealous, that I thought it a great sin for men who were able to defend their country to be neuter; and I have been tempted since to think I was a more competent judge upon the place, when all things were before our eyes, than I am in the review of those days and actions so many years after, when distance disadvantageth the apprehension."

On the side of the king were some noblemen and gentlemen of vicious life, who could endure no rebuke of their profligacy, and whose hatred of strictly religious persons was intense. They had a large following of men of tastes and habits like their own, who had loose opinions in religion, and worse practices in morals; and by them the Puritan and Parliamentary adherents were regarded as precisians and hypocrites. In their barracks and around their camp-fires they imitated their alleged nasal tones in their long preaching. They mimicked them both in the phrases and in the gestures of their extemporaneous prayers. They ridiculed their scrupulousness of conduct, laughed at their short hair and plain clothes, plundered their homesteads, and abused their wives and daughters, as opportunities occurred, during the various incidents of battle and siege in the civil war.

But Charles I. had also men of great virtue and patriotism among his adherents, who willingly parted with money and plate, mortgaged their land to supply the royal exchequer, and with loyalty and devotion abandoned their homes and followed his fortunes, acting, as they deemed, on the highest principles of religion; and some of them, with their means exhausted, and their credit gone, when disaster and defeat had ruined the royal cause, went into a long and miserable exile; leaving their native land to the terror and wretchedness of that military despotism which invariably succeeds violent revolution. Such men as Lord Falkland would have given dignity and glory to any principle which conscience led them to adopt and maintain. With clear views of the philosophy of political causes and effects, and with comprehensive knowledge of the better methods of government, acquired not only by their own experience, but by accurate acquaintance with the history of the ancient commonwealths; they mourned over evils they could not prevent, foresaw the calamities which would certainly result from the conflict between the king and his subjects, and they tried various means of procuring peace. By nature, education, and reflection, such men were opposed to democratic principles. They abhorred popular violence. They were taught by their religious feelings and views to defend the person and to uphold the authority of the sovereign at all hazards. They regarded him as the vicegerent of God. They would proceed with him only by petition and remonstrance; for they looked upon armed rebellion as one of the deadly sins, to which the people may be urged by their giving heed to the fanaticism and denunciations of demagogues. They held that the art of government was understood only by the few who had made it their study, and that nations are to be ruled, not in the market-place and in the camp, but in the Cabinet; that the general mass of men, as they are naturally ignorant of the first principles of political economy, liable to be swayed by the invective, and deceived by the fallacies of agitating declaimers, are quite incapable of determining public affairs; that calm deliberations and safe conclusions are not to be had among the harangues and recriminations of a clamorous assembly; and that practical wisdom is not to be found in the factions and heats of the multitude. As such men, from their position and wealth, could not be neutral, they necessarily adhered to the side of the king.

Among the members of the House of Commons, on the other hand, were some of the ablest of them who, during the many ages of its long-continued existence, have had seats in that popular assembly. In the opinion of many of them, resistance to the king was merely giving practical effect to their unheeded demand for relief from unlawful exactions, and for religious liberty. Opposition to him, in their view, was opposition to Archbishop Laud, and to his inquisitorial and oppressive ecclesiastical courts. The demand for constitutional government—especially, that taxation should not depend upon the will and needs of the sovereign, but upon the free consent of the representatives of the nation assembled in Parliament—was supported by the insistence for freedom of opinion in religion. The claim for liberty of conscience was the logical and inevitable sequence of the Reformation. If men are taught to believe that they are not to rely upon the decisions and decrees of a central and irresponsible authority, they will conclusively form their own opinions of sacred truth. It may be that generally they are no more able to judge what is best for their individual interests in religion, than in the important matters of law and of medicine; but that they need in all of these to be guided by wisdom and knowledge superior to their own. Whether that supposition be true or false, it is certain that there is no medium between absolute submission to ecclesiastical authority and decision, and the right of judging for one's self in the awful matters of religious belief, duty, and responsibility.

Such was the opinion of the leading members in the Lower House who resisted the king. The spirit of the time was quickened. They, who had themselves carefully studied the causes and effects of the reformation produced in the Anglican Church by severing its connection with the papal chair; whose fathers had warred with the Spaniard, had gained hard-won victories against Alva and Spinola, and had sunk fleets and stormed fortresses in the glorious days of Elizabeth's conquests on the seaboard of the Mediterranean and of the New World, were not to be intimidated by royal manifestoes from Whitehall and Oxford, nor to be restrained by threats of punishment and by attempts at personal violence, from endeavouring to secure freedom both in Church and in State. Men who have conquered tyranny abroad are not likely to submit to it at home. The extreme imprudence of the king; his determination to admit no question of his right to absolute authority; the passionate entertainment of the remonstrances of the House of Commons; the attempt to imprison the more obnoxious members of it; and the arrogance of some persons in his family and court, all tended to enlarge the field of contention, and to destroy the last hope of conciliation and of peace. The wound became every day deeper and more painful, until it was past healing.

Their ardent zeal for religion, and their love of liberty, were the motives of the conduct of the more eminent members of the Lower House; but there were others in that Chamber who were not influenced by such honourable principles. Dissatisfied with their own position, and discontented that they were poorer in resources and lower in station than the members of the Court, they allied themselves to the popular party, and were clamorous for thorough changes in Church and State, with the hope of gaining some lasting advantage from the general confusion and overthrow. Such adventurers abound in all days of violent political movement. We have seen again and again in our own time verbose advocates of popular rights, who announced themselves as universal reformers, and were zealous in denouncing real or imaginary grievances; deluding the credulous masses by promising advantages which could never be attained, by artfully fomenting discords, and by inciting their adherents to insist upon changes which would, if completed, dissolve all the bonds which hold human society together; and when the Government of the day, glad to be rid of offensive exponents, placed them in lucrative offices, the declaimers and their grievances became suddenly silent and unheeded, and the much-enduring public ear was no longer vexed by the outcries of the reformers, who were sincere in nothing but in seeking their own advancement. In the various phases of modern European political life, the historical philosopher sometimes discovers the scoundrel in the guise of the patriot; and observes that the more zealously he decries some presumed existing injustice, the more determinately he is aiming at that which shall permanently repay his efforts to attain it. No doubt Cromwell, Milton, Marvell, and others knew that there were many such interested partisans among them who overthrew the Church, and who discrowned and destroyed their king.

CHAPTER VI.

1642—1646.

AFTER he had been two years at Kidderminster, Baxter found, in the autumn of 1642, that he could remain longer there only at the risk of losing his life. The whole county had declared itself for the king. The town was entirely under the influence of the Royalist families living in its neighbourhood, whose money circulated among the traders; and it became the head-quarters of all Charles's adherents in a wide extent of country. One of the magistrates had publicly denounced Baxter as a traitor. Recruiting officers were stationed in the parish. Every townsman who was suspected of siding with the popular party was liable to be plundered and beaten. The Parliament had passed a resolution that all images and crucifixes should be removed from the churches. Baxter was thought to sympathise with this decree, and a furious mob, urged to violence by the vehemence of some of the king's officers, assembled before his door, shrieking horrible invectives against him, and threatening him with death. He saw that it would not be prudent for him to remain where his parochial services could not be continued, and he withdrew to Gloucester. In a short time, at the request of some of his parishioners, he returned to Kidderminster; but as he found the town and its neighbourhood held by a division of the royal army, and as he was suspected of disaffection, and threatened with violence, he withdrew from it, and found shelter in Warwickshire. In the meantime, the king and the

Parliament actively prepared for war. Depôts were formed, arms imported, cannon cast, and thousands of men were drilled in various districts of the country. Manufactures were suspended, excepting those of weapons and military accoutrements; trade was disturbed, and the whole land was agitated and distressed by the rage of contending hosts, and by their forced requisitions for provision and forage. After desultory skirmishes, the two armies approached each other, and fought their first battle at Edgehill. Baxter gives a vivid account of it. He says: "Upon the Lord's Day, October 23rd, 1642, I preached at Alcester for my reverend friend, Mr. Samuel Clark. As I was preaching, the people heard the cannon play, and perceived that the armies were engaged. When the sermon was done in the afternoon, the report was more audible, which made us all long to hear of the success. About sun-setting many troops fled through the town, and told us that all was lost on the Parliament's side, and that the carriages were taken and the waggons plundered before they came away. The townsmen sent a messenger to Stratford-on-Avon to know the truth. About four o'clock in the morning he returned, and told us that Prince Rupert wholly routed the left wing of the Earl of Essex's army; but while his men were plundering the waggons, the main body and the right wing routed the rest of the king's army; took his standard, but lost it again; killed General the Earl of Lindsay, and took his son prisoner; that few persons of quality on the side of the Parliament were lost, and no nobleman but Lord St. John, eldest son to the Earl of Bolingbroke; that the loss of the left wing happened through the treachery of Sir Frederick Fortescue, major to Lord Fielding's regiment of horse, who turned to the king when he should have charged; and that the victory was obtained mainly by Colonel Hollis's regiment of London redcoats, and the Earl of Essex's own regiment and lifeguard, where Sir Philip Stapleton, Sir Arthur Haselrigge, and Colonel Urrey did much. Next morning, being desirous to see the field, I went to Edgehill, and found the Earl of Essex, with the remaining part of his army, keeping the ground, and the king's army facing them upon the hill, about a mile off. There were about a thousand dead bodies in the field between them; and many, I suppose, were buried before. Neither of the armies moving towards the other, the king's army presently drew off towards Banbury, and then to Oxford. The Earl of Essex's went back to provide for the wounded, and refresh themselves at Warwick Castle, belonging to Lord Brooke. For myself, I knew not what course to take. To live at home I was uneasy; but especially now, when soldiers on one side or other would be frequently among us, and we must still be at the mercy of every furious beast that would make a prey of us. I had neither money nor friends; I knew not who would receive me in any place of safety, nor had I anything to satisfy them for my diet and entertainment. Hereupon I was persuaded by one that was with me to go to Coventry, where an old acquaintance, Mr. Simon King, was minister; so thither I went, with a purpose to stay there till one side or other had got the victory, and the war was ended; for so wise in matters of war was I, and all the country beside, that we commonly supposed that a very few days or weeks, by one other battle, would end the wars. Here I stayed at Mr. King's a month; but the war was then as far from being likely to end as before. While I was thinking what course to take in this necessity, the committee and governor of the city desired me to stay with them, and lodge in the governor's house, and preach to the soldiers. The offer suited well with my necessities; but I resolved that I would not be chaplain to a regiment, nor take a commission; yet, if the mere preaching a sermon once or twice a week to the garrison would satisfy them, I would accept of the office till I could go home again. Here, accordingly, I lived in the governor's house, followed my studies as quietly as in a time of peace for about a year, preaching once a week to the soldiers, and once on the Lord's Day to the people; taking nothing from either but my diet."

Baxter went for a short time into Shropshire, and then came back to pass another year in his chaplaincy at Coventry. The whole country was in confusion and distress. Much land lay untilled. Farm-houses were often plundered, sometimes deserted and burned. Wounded soldiers, disabled from further service, begged on all the highways. Deserters from both armies ill-treated travellers, searched waggons, forced themselves upon wives and families whose husbands were absent at the war, lived at free quarters upon the helpless, robbed the hen-roosts, and, sometimes taken in the act, were recognised by former comrades and speedily hanged. Many of the churches were shut. Few clergymen were to be found to say prayers, and only scanty congregations assembled, except in those country districts which were happily left in peace by the opposing armies. Many persons took refuge in the metropolis and in the larger towns. Large numbers of the labourers were compelled to join one or other of the contending forces, and their wives remained at home, as happened mostly in the wars in France, the Netherlands, and Germany, to reap the wheat, and to work generally on field and farm for their daily bread.

The conflict was waged by the king at first with some advantage, but time and means were on the side of the Parliament; and the successive engagements showed every day more clearly the limit of the royal resources, the difficulty of recruiting them, and the probable issue of the war. In his Autobiography Baxter gives many details of the king's alternate victories and defeats, and of his own share in some of the great events of the time. He says, "Naseby being not far from Coventry, where I was, and the noise of the victory being loud in our ears, and I having two or three who had been my intimate friends in Cromwell's army, whom I had not seen for above two years, I was desirous of seeing whether they were dead or alive; so to Naseby field I went, two days after the fight, and thence by the army's quarters before Leicester, to seek my acquaintance. When I found them, I stayed with them a night; and understood from them the state of the army much better than ever I had done before. We that lived quietly in Coventry kept to our old principles, and thought all others had done so too. Except a very few inconsiderable persons, we were unfeignedly for king and Parliament; we believed that the war was only to save the Parliament and kingdom from papists and delinquents, and to remove the dividers; that the king might again return to his Parliament, and that no changes might be made in religion but by the laws which had his free consent. We took the true happiness of king and people, Church and State, to be our end, and so we understood the covenant, engaging both against papists and schismatics; and when the Court News-Book told the world of the swarms of Anabaptists in our armies, we thought it had been a mere lie, because it was not so with us, nor in any of the garrisons or county forces about us. But when I came to the army, among Cromwell's soldiers I found a new face of things which I never dreamed of; I heard the plotting heads very hot upon that which intimated their intention to subvert both Church and State. Independency and Anabaptistery were more prevalent; Antinomianism and Arminianism were equally distributed; and Thomas Moor's followers (a weaver of Wisbitch and Lynn, of excellent parts) had made some shifts to join these two extremes together. Abundance of the common troopers and many of the officers I found to be honest, sober, orthodox men; others were tractable, ready to hear the truth, and of upright intentions. But a few proud, self-conceited, hot-headed sectaries had got into the highest places, and were Cromwell's chief favourites; and by their very heat and activity bore down the rest, or carried them along with them. These were the soul of the army, though much fewer in number than the rest, their strength being in the General's, in Whalley's, and in Rich's regiments of horse, and among the new-placed officers in many of the rest. I perceived they took the king for a tyrant and an enemy, and really intended absolutely to master him or to ruin him.

They thought if they might fight against him, they might also kill or conquer him; and if they might conquer, they were never more to trust him further than he was in their power. They thought it folly to irritate him either by war or contradiction in Parliament, if so be they must needs take him for their king, and trust him with their lives when they had thus displeased him. 'What were the lords of England,' said they, 'but William the Conqueror's colonels; or the barons, but his majors; or the knights, but his captains!' They plainly showed that they thought God's providence would cast the trust of religion and the kingdom upon them as conquerors; they made nothing of all the most wise and godly in the armies and garrisons that were not of their way. *Per fas aut nefas*, by law or without it, they were resolved to take down not only bishops, and liturgy, and ceremonies, but all who did withstand them. They were far from thinking of a moderate episcopacy, or of any healing method between the Episcopalians and the Presbyterians; they most honoured the Separatists, Anabaptists, and Antinomians; but Cromwell and his council took upon them to join themselves to no party, but to be for the liberty of all. Two sorts, I perceived, they did so commonly and bitterly speak against, to make them odious to the soldiers, and to all the land; and these were the Scots, and with them all the Presbyterians, but especially the ministers, whom they called priests and priestbyters, dryvines and the dissembly-men, and such like. The committees of the several counties, and all the soldiers that were under them, that were not of their mind and way, were the other objects of their displeasure. Some orthodox captains of the army partly acquainted me with all this, and I heard much of it from the mouths of the leading sectaries themselves. This struck me to the very heart, and made me fear that England was lost by those that it had taken for its chief friends. Upon this I began to blame other ministers and myself. When the Earl of Essex went out first, each regiment had an able preacher; but at Edgehill fight almost all of them went home; and as the sectaries increased, they were the more averse to go into the army. And if it had brought reproach upon themselves from the malicious, who called them *Military Levites*, the good which they had done would have wiped off that blot much better than the contrary course would have done. I reprehended myself also, who had before rejected an invitation from Cromwell, when he lay at Cambridge with that famous troop with which he began his army. His officers purposed to make their troop a gathered Church, and they all subscribed an invitation to me to be their pastor, and sent it to me to Coventry. I sent them a denial, reproving their attempt, and told them wherein my judgment was against the lawfulness and convenience of their way, and so I heard no more from them; but afterwards meeting Cromwell at Leicester, he expostulated with me for denying them. These very men that then invited me to be their pastor were the men that afterwards headed much of the army, and some of them were the forwardest in all our changes; which made me wish that I had gone among them, however it had been interpreted; for then all the fire was in one spark. When I had informed myself to my sorrow of the state of the army, Captain Evanson (one of my orthodox informers) desired me yet to come to their regiment, which was the most religious, most valiant, and most successful of all the army. I was unwilling to leave my studies, and friends, and quietness, at Coventry, to go into an army so contrary to my judgment; but I thought the public good commanded me, and so I gave him some encouragement. Whereupon he told his colonel (Whalley), who also was orthodox in religion, but engaged by kindred and interest to Cromwell, who invited me to be the chaplain to his regiment. I told him I would take but a day's time to deliberate, and would send him an answer, or else come to him. As soon as I came home to Coventry I called together an assembly of ministers, Dr. Bryan, Dr. Grew, and many others. I told them the sad news of the corruption of the army, and that I thought all we had valued was likely to be endangered by them; seeing the army having first conquered at York, and now at Naseby, and having left the king no visible army but Goring's, the fate of the whole kingdom was likely to follow the disposition and interest of the conquerors. We had sworn to be true to the king and his heirs in the oath of allegiance. All our soldiers here think that the Parliament is faithful to the king, and have no other purpose themselves. If the king and Parliament, Church and State be ruined by these men, and we look on and do nothing to hinder it, how are we true to our allegiance, and to the covenant which bindeth us to defend the king, and to be against schism, as well as against popery and profaneness? For my part, said I, I know that my body is so weak that it is likely to hazard my life to be among them; but yet, if your judgment take it to be my duty, I will venture my life. The ministers did unanimously give their judgment for my going. Hereupon I went straight to the committee, and told them that I had an invitation to the army, and desired their consent to go. They consulted a while, and then left it wholly to the governor. It fell out that Colonel Barker, the governor, was just then to be turned out as a Member of Parliament, by the self-denying vote, and one of his companions, Colonel Willoughby, was to be colonel and governor in his place. Hereupon Colonel Barker was content, in his discontent, that I should go out with him, that he might be missed the more; and so he gave me his consent. I then sent word to Colonel Whalley that to-morrow, God willing, I would come to him. As soon as this was done, the elected governor was much displeased; and the soldiers were so much offended with the committee for consenting to my going, that the committee all met again in the night, and sent for me and told me I must not go. I told them that by their consent I had promised, and I must go. They told me that the soldiers were ready to mutiny against them, and they could not satisfy them, and therefore I must stay. In a word, they were so angry with me that I was fain to tell them all the truth of my motives and design, what a case I perceived the army to be in, and that I was resolved to do my best against it. I knew not till afterwards that Colonel William Purefoy, a Parliament man, and one of the chief of them, was a confidant of Cromwell's; and as soon as I had spoken what I did of the army, magisterially he answereth me, 'Let me hear no more of that; if Nol Cromwell should hear any soldier but speak such a word, he would cleave his crown. You do them wrong. It is not so.' So I parted with them that had been my very great friends, in some displeasure. The soldiers, however, threatened to stop the gates, and keep me in; but being honest, understanding men, I quickly satisfied the leaders of them—and some of them accompanied me on my way. As soon as I came to the army, Oliver Cromwell coolly bade me welcome, and never spoke to me more while I was there; nor once, all that time, vouchsafed me an opportunity to come to the headquarters, where the councils and meetings of the officers were; so that most of my design was thereby frustrated. His secretary gave out that there was a reformer come to the army to undeceive them, and to save Church and State, with some such other jeers; by which I perceived that all I had said the night before to the committee had come to Cromwell before me, I believe by Colonel Purefoy's means; but Colonel Whalley welcomed me, and was the worse thought of for it by the rest of the cabal.

"Here I set myself from day to day to find out the corruptions of the soldiers, and to discourse and dispute them out of their mistakes, both religious and political. My life among them was a daily contending against seducers, and gently arguing with the more respectable; but another kind of warfare I had than theirs. I found that one-half almost of the religious party among them were such as were either orthodox or but very slightly touched with heterodoxy; and almost another half were honest men, that stepped further into the contending way than they could well get out of again, but who, with competent help, might be recovered. There were a few fiery, self-conceited men among them who kindled the rest, and made all the noise and bustle, and carried about the army as they pleased; for the greatest part of the common soldiers, especially of the foot, were ignorant men, of little religion; abundance of them were such as had been taken prisoners, or turned out of garrisons under the king, and had been soldiers in his army. These would do anything to please their officers, and were ready instruments for the seducers, especially in their great work, which was to cry down the covenant, to vilify all parish ministers, but especially the Scots and Presbyterians; for the most of the soldiers that I spoke with never took the covenant, because it tied them to defend the king's person, and to extirpate heresy and schism. When I perceived that it was a few, then, who bore the bell, and did the hurt among them, I acquainted myself with those men, and would be oft disputing with them, in the hearing of the rest. I found that they were men who had been in London, hatched up among the old Separatists, and had made it all the matter of their study and religion to rail against ministers, parish churches, and Presbyterians; whereas many of those honest soldiers who were tainted, but with some doubts about liberty of conscience and independency, were men who would discourse of the points of sanctification and Christian experience very seriously. I so far prevailed in opening the folly of these revilers and self-conceited men, as that some of them became the laughing-stock of the soldiers before I left them; and, when they preached—for great preachers they were—their weakness exposed them to contempt. A great part of the mischief was done among the soldiers by pamphlets, which were abundantly dispersed, such as Overton, Martin Mar-Priest, and more of his; and some of J. Silburne's, who was one of the preaching-officers; and divers against the king, and against the ministry, and for liberty of conscience, etc. The soldiers being usually dispersed in quarters, they had such books to read, when they had none to contradict them. But there was a yet more dangerous party than these among the soldiers, who took the direct Jesuitical way.

They first most vehemently declaimed against the doctrine of election, and for the power of free-will, and all other points which are controverted between the Jesuits and Dominicans, the Arminians and Calvinists. They then as fiercely cried down our present translations of the Scriptures, and debased their authority, though they did not deny them to be Divine. They cried down all our ministry, Episcopal, Presbyterian, and Independent, and all our churches. They vilified almost all our ordinary worship; they allowed of no argument from Scripture, but what was brought in its express words; they were vehement against both king and all government, except popular; and against magistrates meddling in matters of religion. All their disputing was with as much fierceness as if they had been ready to draw their swords upon those against whom they disputed. They trusted more to policy, scorn, and power than to argument. They would bitterly scorn me among their hearers, to prejudice them before they entered into dispute. They avoided me as much as possible; but when we did come to it they drowned all reason in fierceness, and vehemency, and multitude of words. They greatly strove for places of command; and when any place was due by order to another that was not of their mind, they would be sure to work him out, and be ready to mutiny if they had not their will. I thought they were principled by the Jesuits, and acted all for their interest, and in their way. But the secret spring was out of sight. These were the same men that afterwards were called Levellers, who rose up against Cromwell and were surprised at Burford, having then deceived and drawn to them many more. Thompson, the general of the Levellers, who was slain then, was no greater a man than one of the corporals of Bethel's troop; the cornet and others being much worse than he."

From this "taste of his employment in the army," the narrative which Baxter has given to posterity in his Autobiography, much is to be inferred as to the political and military condition of the country. Legal authority was cast down, and all the time was out of joint; society was disorganised, and almost every man was out of his proper place in it. The love of disputation was the curse of the age. In all parts of England there was the unhealthy effervescence of misunderstanding, and the confusion engendered by strife. Rightful power sat no longer in the seat of justice. The base and malignant, whom the storm had brought to the surface, swarmed in every part of life. The devout and learned were here and there clamoured down in the tumult of fanatical disputation. Many good men withdrew from association with bitter sectaries, who argued with vehemence on subjects they did not comprehend. Tolerated liberty of opinion was understood by none of them who cried out for freedom. Good men on both sides were blind to the evil of persecuting those who differed from them. Many of them looked only upon one side of truth.

In the parliamentary army were devout persons who studied the Word of God with enlightened conscience. Endeavouring to diffuse the spirit of religion among the soldiery, they mourned that the disease of the time was to be remedied by the sword. Such men were but few in comparison with the numbers of them who were political levellers, hating the restraints of law, and the unequal distribution of property; hypocrites, who prayed by the hour, descanted with gleeful energy on the slaughter of the priests of Baal, and on the havoc countenanced by Hebrew prophets and kings in cleansing the shrines of sin and abomination. They held one part of Scripture to the wilful suppression of another, and while declaiming upon the fact, which cannot be disputed, that oppression makes wise men mad, they were unwilling to believe in the duty of submission to any other form of government than to that which they might themselves resolve upon, either by majority of votes or by tumultuous show of hands. While keen to resent infringement of their personal freedom, they did not hesitate to harass the quiet in the land, who would not join in their religious fervours and political excesses; and their violence made the condition of the rectors and vicars in the country places, who desired to be allowed to live and labour in peace, one of the most afflictive that has ever fallen to the lot of them who have suffered undeservedly. Reason could speak no intelligible word in the roar of heated sectaries, quarrelling in camp and market over the revelations of infinite mercy, and the promises of Divine goodness and truth; for when men have reached a certain point of religious fanaticism, they become unreasonable and ungovernable. Learning painfully acquired; the wisdom which comes of profound thought and wide research; the eloquent tongue, which argues from wise principles to just conclusions; the sagacity which foresees evil, and which provides security from hazard and refuge from danger, were unavailing before the flood of violence which swept through the country. The intemperance of the human mind was extreme, and moderation had ceased to be a factor in the life of the English brotherhood. If the land is unhappy which has a child for its ruler, woeful is the state where the ancient landmarks are torn up by the hand of fury, and dreadful the condition of a people when ignorance is armed with power!

Baxter writes:—"As soon as I came to the army, it marched speedily down into the west, because the king had no army left there but the lord Goring's, and it would not suffer the fugitives of Naseby fight to come thither to strengthen them. We came quickly down to Somerton, when Goring was at Langport; which lying upon the river, Massey was sent to keep him in on the further side, while Fairfax attended him on this side with his army. One day they faced each other and did nothing; the next day they came to their ground again. Betwixt the two armies was a narrow lane, which went between some meadows in a bottom, and a small brook crossed the lane with a narrow bridge. Goring planted two or three small pieces at the head of the lane to keep the passage, and there placed his best horse; so that none could come to them but over that narrow bridge, and up that steep lane upon the mouth of those pieces. After many hours' facing each other,

—Fairfax's great ordnance affrighting more than hurting Goring's men—and some musqueteers being sent to drive them from under the hedges, at last Cromwell bid Whalley send three of his troops to charge the enemy, and he sent three of the General's own regiment to second them—all being of Cromwell's own regiment. Whalley sent Major Bethel, Captain Evanson, and Captain Grove to charge; Major Desborough, with another troop or two, came after, as they could go but one or two abreast over the bridge. By the time Bethel and Evanson, with their troops, were got up to the top of the lane, they met with a select party of Goring's best horse, and charged them at sword's point, whilst you could count three or four hundred, and then put them to retreat. In the flight they pursued them too far to the main body, for the dust was so great, being in the very hottest time of summer, that they who were in it could scarce see each other; but I, who stood over them upon the brow of the hill, saw all. When they saw themselves upon the face of Goring's army, they fled back in haste, and by the time they came to the lane again, Captain Grove's troop was ready to relieve them, and Desborough behind them. They then rallied again, and the five or six troops together marched towards all Goring's army; but before they came to the front, I could discern the rear begin to run, and so beginning in the rear, they all fled before they endured any charge; nor was there a blow struck that day but by Bethel's and Evanson's troops on that side, and a few musqueteers in the hedges. Goring's army fled to Bridgewater, and very few of them were either killed or taken in the flight or the pursuit. I happened to be next to Major Harrison as soon as the flight began, and heard him with a loud voice break forth into the praise of God with fluent expressions, as if he had been in a rapture.

"Goring immediately fled with his army further westward to Exeter, but Fairfax stayed to besiege Bridgewater, and after two days it was taken by storm, in which Colonel Hammond's service was much magnified. Mr. Peters, having come to the army from London but a day before, went presently back with the news of Goring's rout, when a hundred pounds' reward was voted to himself for bringing the news, and to Major Bethel for his service; but no reward was given to Captain Evanson, because he was no sectary. Bethel alone had all the glory and applause from Cromwell and from that party. From Bridgewater the army went back towards Bristol, where Prince Rupert was taking Nunny Castle and Bath in the way. At Bristol they continued the siege about a month. After the first three days I fell sick of a fever, the plague being round about my quarters. As soon as I felt my disease I rode six or seven miles back into the country, and the next morning, with much ado, I got to Bath. Here Dr. Venner was my careful physician; and when I was near death, far from all my acquaintance, it pleased God to restore me, and on the fourteenth day the fever ended in a crisis. But it left me so emaciated and weak, that it was long ere I recovered the little strength I had before. I came back to Bristol siege, three or four days before the city was taken. The foot, which were to storm the works, would not go on unless the horse, who had no service to do, went with them. So Whalley's regiment was fain to go on to encourage the foot, and to stand to be shot at before the ordnance, while the foot stormed the forts. Here Major Bethel, who in the last fight had his thumb shot, had a shot in his thigh, of which he died, and was much lamented. The outworks being taken, Prince Rupert yielded up the city upon terms that he might march away with his soldiers, leaving their ordnance and arms.

"After this, the army marched to Sherborne Castle, the Earl of Bristol's house; which, after a fortnight's siege, they took by storm, and that on a side which one would think could never have been that way taken. While they were there, the countrymen called Clubmen rose near Shaftesbury, and got upon the top of a hill. A party was sent out against them up the hill, and routed them, though some of the valiantest men were slain in the front.

"When Sherborne Castle was taken, part of the army went back, and took in a small garrison by Salisbury, called Langford House, and so marched to Winchester Castle, and took that after a week's siege, or little more. From thence Cromwell went with a good party to besiege Basing House, the Marquis of Winchester's, which had frustrated great sieges heretofore. Here Colonel Hammond was taken prisoner into the house, afterwards the house was taken by storm, and he saved the Marquis and others, and much riches were taken by the soldiers.

"In the meantime the rest of the army marched down again towards the lord Goring, and Cromwell came after them. When we followed lord Goring westward, we found that, above all other armies of the king, his soldiers were most hated by the people, for their incredible profaneness, and their unmerciful plundering, many of them being foreigners. A sober gentleman, whom I quartered with at South Pederton, in Somersetshire, averred to me that, when with him, a company of them pricked their fingers, and let the blood run into the cup, and drank a health to the devil in it; and no place could I come into, but their horrid impiety and outrages made them odious. The army marched down by Hunnington to Exeter, where I continued near three weeks among them at the siege, and then Whalley's regiment, with the General's, Fleetwood's, and others, being sent back, I returned with them, and left the siege, which continued till the city was taken. The army following Goring into Cornwall, there forced him to lay down arms, his men going away beyond sea, or elsewhere, without their arms; and at last Pendennis Castle and all the garrisons there were taken.

"In the meantime Whalley was to command the return of the party of horse, to keep in the garrison of Oxford till the army could come to besiege it; and so in the extreme winter he quartered about six weeks in Buckinghamshire, and then was sent to lay siege to Banbury Castle, where Sir William Compton was governor, who had wearied out one long siege before. There I was with them above two months, till the castle was taken; and then he was sent to lay siege to Worcester, with the help of the Northampton and Warwick and Newport Pagnell soldiers, who had assisted him at Banbury. At Worcester he lay in siege eleven weeks, and at the same time, the army being come up from the west, lay in siege at Oxford.

"By this time Colonel Whalley, though Cromwell's kinsman and commander of the trusted regiment, grew odious among the sectarian commanders at the headquarters. For my sake he was called a Presbyterian, though neither he nor I were of that judgment in several points; Major Salloway not omitting to use his industry in the matter to that end. When he had brought the city to a necessity of present yielding, two or three days before it yielded, Colonel Rainsborough was sent from Oxford, which had yielded, with some regiments of foot, to command in chief; part that he might be governor there, and not Whalley, when the city was surrendered. So, when it was yielded, Rainsborough was governor, to head and gratify the sectaries, and settle the city and county in their way; but the committee of the county were for Whalley and lived in distaste with Rainsborough, and the sectaries prospered there no further than Worcester city itself,—a place which deserved such a judgment; but all the country was free from their infection.

"When we were quartered at Agmondesham, in Buckinghamshire, some sectaries of Chesham had set up a public meeting for conference, to propagate their opinions through all the county; and this in the church, by the encouragement of an ignorant sectarian lecturer, one Bramble, whom they had got in, while Dr. Cook the pastor, and Mr. Richardson his curate, durst not contradict them. When this public talking day came, Bethel's troopers, with other sectarian soldiers, must be there to confirm the Chesham men, and make men believe the army was for them. I thought it my duty to be there also, and took divers sober officers with me, to let them see that more of the army were against them than for them. I took the reading pew, and Pitchford's cornet and troopers took the gallery. And there I found a crowded congregation of poor, well-meaning people, who came in the simplicity of their hearts to be deceived. Then did the leader of the Chesham men begin, and afterwards Pitchford's soldiers set in, and I alone disputed against them from morning until almost night; for I knew their trick, that if I had but gone out first, they would have prated what boasting words they listed when I was gone, and made the people believe they had baffled me, or got the best; therefore I stayed it out till they first rose and went away. The abundance of nonsense which they uttered that day may partly be seen in Mr. Edwards's 'Gangrœna;' for I had wrote a letter of it to a friend in London, so that and another were put into Mr. Edwards's book, without my name. But some of the sober people of Agmondesham gave me abundance of thanks for that day's work, which they said would never be there forgotten. I heard also that the sectaries were so discouraged that they never met there any more. I am sure I had much thanks from Dr. Cook and Mr. Richardson, who being obnoxious to their displeasure for being for the king, durst not open their mouths themselves. After the conference I talked with the lecturer, Mr. Bramble, and found him little wiser than the rest.

"The chief impediments to the success of my endeavours I found were only two—the discountenance of Cromwell and the chief officers of his mind, which kept me a stranger from their meetings and councils; and my incapacity of speaking to many, as soldiers' quarters are scattered far from one another, and I could be but in one place at once. So that one troop at a time ordinarily, and some few more extraordinarily, was all that I could speak to. The most of the service I did beyond Whalley's regiment was, by the help of Captain Lawrence, with some of the General's regiment, and sometimes I had converse with Major Harrison and a few others; but I found that if the army had had only ministers enough, who would have done such little as I did, all their plot might have been broken, and king, Parliament, and religion might have been preserved. I, therefore, sent abroad to get some more ministers among them, but I could get none. Saltmarsh and Dell were the two great preachers at the headquarters, but honest and judicious Mr. Edward Bowles kept still with the General. At last I got Mr. Cook, of Foxhull, to come to assist me, and the soberer part of the officers and soldiers of Whalley's regiment were willing to remunerate him out of their own pay. A month or two he stayed and assisted me, but was quickly weary, and left them again. He was a very worthy, humble, laborious man, unwearied in preaching, but weary when he had not opportunity to preach, and weary of the spirits he had to deal with.

"All this while, though I came not near Cromwell, his designs were visible, and I saw him continually acting his part. The Lord-General suffered him to govern and do all, and to choose almost all the officers of the army, so that by degrees he had headed the greatest part of the army with Anabaptists, Antinomians, Seekers, or Separatists, at best. All these he led together by the point of liberty of conscience, which was the common interest in which they did unite. Yet all the sober party were carried on by his profession, that he only promoted the universal interest of the godly, without any distinction or partiality at all; but still, when a place fell void, it was twenty to one a sectary had it, and if a godly man, or of any other mind or temper, had a mind to leave the army, he would secretly or openly further it. Yet did he not openly profess what opinion he was of himself; but the most that he said for any was for Anabaptism and Antinomianism, which he usually seemed to own. He would not dispute with me at all; but he would in very good discourse very fluently pour out himself in the extolling of free grace.

"All the two years that I was in the army, even my old bosom friend, who had lived in my house and been dearest to me, James Berry, then captain, after colonel and major-general, then lord of the Upper House, who had formerly invited me to Cromwell's old troop, did never once invite me to the army at first, nor invite me to his quarters after, nor ever once came to visit me, or even saw me, save twice or thrice that we met accidentally. So potent is the interest of ourselves, and our opinions with us, against all other bonds whatever. He that forsaketh himself in forsaking his own opinions, may well be expected to forsake his friend who adhereth to the way which he forsaketh. When Cromwell made him his favourite, and his extraordinary valour was crowned with extraordinary success, and when he had been awhile most conversant with those who, in religion, thought the old Puritan ministers were dull, conceited men, and that new light had declared I knew not what to be a higher attainment, his mind, his aim, his talk, and all were altered accordingly. And as ministers of the old way were lower, and sectaries much higher, in his esteem than formerly; so he was much higher in his own esteem when he thought he had attained much higher than he was before, when he sat with his fellows in the common form.

"After this he was president of the agitators, a major-general and lord, a principal person in the changes, and the chief executioner in pulling down Richard Cromwell; and then one of the governing council of state. As he was the chief in pulling down, so he was one of the first that fell; for Sir Arthur Haselrigge taking Portsmouth, his regiment of horse, sent to block it up, went most of them to Sir Arthur. And when the army was melted to nothing, and the king ready to come in, the council of state imprisoned him, because he would not promise to live peaceably; and afterwards he (being one of the four whom General Monk had the worst thoughts of) was closely confined in Scarborough Castle; but being released, he became a gardener, and lived in a safer state than in all his greatness.

"When Worcester siege was over, having seen with joy Kidderminster and my friends there once again, the country being now cleared, my old flock expected that I should return to them, and settle in peace among them. I accordingly went to Coventry, and called the ministers again together who voted me into the army. I told them that the forsaking of the army by the old ministry, and the neglect of supplying their places by others, had undone us; that I had laboured amongst them with as much success as could be expected in the narrow sphere of my capacity, but that was little to all the army; that the active sectaries were the smallest part of the army among the common soldiers, but that Cromwell had lately put so many of them into superior command, and their industry was so much greater than others, they were likely to have their will; that whatever obedience they pretended, I doubted not but they would pull down all that stood in their way in State and Church, both king, Parliament, and ministers, and set up themselves. I told them that for the little that I had done I had ventured my life, and weakened my body (weak before), but that the day which I expected was yet to come; and that the greatest service with the greatest hazard was yet before—whereupon they all voted me to go and leave Kidderminster yet longer, which accordingly I did.

"From Worcester I went to London to Sir Theodore Mayern about my health; he sent me to Tunbridge Wells, and after some stay there to my benefit, I went back to London, and so to my quarters in Worcestershire, where the regiment was. My quarters fell out to be at Sir Thomas Rous's, at Rous-Lench, where I had never been before. The Lady Rous was a godly, grave, understanding woman, and entertained me not as a soldier, but as a friend. From thence I went into Leicestershire, Staffordshire, and at last into Derbyshire. One advantage of this moving life was that I had opportunity to preach in many counties and parishes; and whatever came of it afterward I know not, but at the time they commonly seemed to be much affected.

"I came to Major Swallow's quarters, at Sir John Cook's house, at Melbourn, on the edge of Derbyshire, beyond Ashby-de-la-Zouch, in a cold and snowy season; and the cold, together with other things coincident, set my nose on bleeding. When I had bled about a quart or two, I opened four veins, but that did no good. I used divers other remedies for several days to little purpose; at last I gave myself a purge, which stopped it. This so much weakened me, and altered my complexion, that my acquaintances who came to visit me scarcely knew me. Coming after so long weakness, and frequent loss of blood before, it made the physicians conclude me *deplorate*, supposing I could never escape a dropsy.

"Thus God unavoidably prevented all the effect of my purposes in my last and chiefest opposition of the army, and took me off the very time when my attempt should have begun. My purpose was to have done my best, first, to take off that regiment I was with, and then, with Captain Lawrence, to have tried upon the General's, in which two were Cromwell's chief confidants, and then to have joined with others of the same mind; for the other regiments were much less corrupted. But the determination of God against it was most observable; for the very time that I was bleeding, the council of war sat at Nottingham, where, as I have credibly heard, they first began to open their purpose and act their part; and, presently after, they entered into their engagement at Triploe Heath. As I perceived it was the will of God to permit them to go on, I afterwards found that this great affliction was a mercy to myself; for they were so strong and active, that I had been likely to have had small success in the attempt, and to have lost my life among them in their fury. And thus I was finally separated from the army.

"When I had stayed at Melbourn in my chamber three weeks, being among strangers, and not knowing how to get home, I went to Mr. Nowell's house, at Kirby-Mallory, in Leicestershire, where, with great kindness, I was entertained three weeks. By that time the tidings of my weakness came to the Lady Rous, in Worcestershire, who sent her servant to seek me out; and when he returned, and told her I was afar off, and he could not find me, she sent him again to find me, and bring me thither, if I were able to travel. So, in great weakness, thither I made shift to get, where I was entertained with the greatest care and tenderness, while I continued the use of means for my recovery; and when I had been there a quarter of a year, I returned to Kidderminster."

Baxter had not been able to accomplish much during his service in the army. The evils of the camp were many: some of them he had lessened or removed, but he could not repress the spirit of dissension. When the soldiers were not fighting, they were disputing on religious doctrines, on questions of Church-order and discipline, or as to the best form of civil government; and when they discussed, it was often with vehemence, which soon became anger, and sometimes with a heat which produced violence. Ever agitating around fresh centres of thought, the parliamentarian army had more creeds than regiments, more preachers than captains, more definitions of doctrine than the scholastic expositors had propounded, more sermons and exhortations than the works of the Fathers contain. Baxter delighted in theological discussion. Questions of casuistry were dear to his soul. He loved division and subdivision in expounding sacred truth. Logical distinctions, and the minute definition of the essential and the accidental, attracted, employed, and amused him. But he found that Cromwell's gunners and bandoleer-men had no fear of his powers of debate, felt no force in his philosophical disquisitions, disputed his expositions of Scripture, and argued with him as his equals on the abstractions of predestination, necessity, and freedom of the will. While admiring the purity of his character, the unfailing kindness of his life among them, his energy in his work as a clergyman in his attention to the sick and the wounded, and his wide and practical knowledge of the Holy Scriptures, in which few theologians have ever surpassed him; many of them were neither convinced by his arguments nor silenced by his eloquence. The sturdy obstinacy of the English seceder was often more than the chaplain could overcome, and he found it well to withdraw from association with men who were neither awed by his learning nor won by his reasoning.

CHAPTER VII.

1646—1647.

NOTHING is more characteristic of Baxter's remarkable industry, and of his habitual care in using fragments of time, than that in the period he passed in the army of the Parliament, although frequently engaged in discussions with officers or private soldiers, on their favourite topics in policy or theology, he was able to write two of his chief books. The first was called "The Aphorisms of Justification;" a small work, which was the first of his doctrinal treatises, and written, as he said, "in his immature youth, and the crudity of his new conceptions." His intention in writing it,—holding the middle way between High Calvinism and the Arminian theory,—was to explain the Pauline doctrines of faith, justification, and good works. He says: "It was overmuch valued by some, and overmuch blamed by others; both contrary to my own esteem of it. It cost me more than any of the books I have written; not only by men's offence, but especially by putting me on long and tedious writings. But it was a great help to my understanding, for the animadverters were of several minds, and what one approved another confuted, being further from each other than any of them were from me."

Many divines assailed the opinions which Baxter had published in his book. Criticism was beneficial to him, as it is generally to writers who have not had much experience of the public temper, and of the diversities of sentiment and of taste which obtain among persons of intellect and of culture;

and it compelled him to the conclusion, that the deeper knowledge and the sounder views of theology are to be gained not from the books of men, but, as is more consonant with reason, from the Word of God. So he admitted it, as: "Being in sickness cast far from home, where I had no book but my Bible, I set to study the truth from thence, and so by the blessing of God discovered more in one week than I had done before in seventeen years' reading, hearing, and wrangling." Attacked on all sides, he consoled himself—as he afterwards wrote to his friend and companion in the army, Commissary-general Whalley—by reflecting that "the diversity of opinion in these days should not diminish our estimation of Christianity, nor make us suspect that all is doubtful, because so much is doubted of. . . . He that wonders to see wise men differ, doth but wonder that they are yet imperfect, and know but in part . . . such wonderers know not what man is, and are too great strangers to themselves."

This book, which was the first he published, was also the cause of many of the controversies in which his life was passed; it was the fountain from which they flowed in ever-increasing stream. But polemical discussion was his delight. He was never more at home than in arguing with opponents and guiding the course of debate. He who is prone to contend will always find them who are ready to gratify his taste for controversy, and who are more eager to dispute about that of which they are ignorant, than to make practical use of the knowledge they have. There are those who like to live in stormy latitudes, and who find real happiness in the strife of tongues.

Whatever part he took in religious discussion and in literature, Baxter was eminent. Few men have thought more deeply than he, or have written more copiously upon the noblest subjects in which the mind of man can be engaged. In controversy, when not overborne by clamour, he was seldom at a disadvantage. As a writer on practical theology he has never been surpassed. In various circumstances, with the best opportunities, he had studied the many sides of human nature. He was thoroughly versed in the philosophy of religion, and he knew, as few have ever known, the sacred Scriptures, which reveal all that man really is, and which declare something of that which he will become, when Christ shall have restored the spiritual life of humanity.

"The Saint's Everlasting Rest," the first work which Baxter wrote, was published after "The Aphorisms." He says: "Almost all the book itself was written when I had no book but the Bible and a Concordance; and I found that the transcript of the heart hath the greatest force on the hearts of others. While I was in health, I had not the least thought of writing books, or of serving God in any more public way than preaching; but when I was weakened with great bleeding, and left solitary in my chamber at Sir John Cook's, in Derbyshire, without any acquaintance but my servant about me, and was sentenced to death by the physicians, I began to contemplate more seriously on the everlasting rest, which I apprehended myself to be just on the border of. That my thoughts might not too much scatter in my meditation, I began to write something on that subject, intending but the quantity of a sermon or two; but being continued long in weakness, when I had no books and no better employment, I followed it on till it was enlarged to the bulk in which it is published. The first three weeks I spent on it was at Mr. Nowell's house, at Kirkby Mallory, in Leicestershire; and a quarter of a year more, at the seasons which so great weakness would allow, I bestowed on it at Sir Thomas Rous's, in Worcestershire, and I finished it shortly after at Kidderminster." He divided the book into four parts. Three of them were addressed to all who had received his ministrations. The last part he calls, "a testimony of his love to his native soil, and to his many godly and faithful friends there living."

The book had what in those days must have been a quick and large sale. In little more than twelve years, nine editions of it had been sold, and when the great fire of

London took place, the work must have been in the hands of many thousands of Englishmen, both at home and in America. A curious circumstance is connected with the last editions published during the author's lifetime. In the earlier he had included the names of Pym, John Hampden, and Lord Brooke among those whom he hoped to see and to associate with in heaven; but after the death of Cromwell these names were omitted from the book. Yet Hampden and the author had been firm friends, and Baxter speaks of him as "the most eminent for prudence, and piety, and peaceable counsels; having the most universal praise of any gentleman that I remember of that age." Baxter excuses himself for the omission:—"The need which I experienced of taking away from before such men as Dr. Jane anything which they might stumble at, made me blot out the names of Lord Brooke, Pym, and Hampden in all the impressions of the book that were made since 1659: yet this did not satisfy. But I must tell the reader that I did it not as changing my judgment of the persons, well-known to the world."

But the fact may well be recorded here, in evidence of the intolerant censorship of the press, which the bishops were commanded to maintain under the government of Charles II., when public liberty was at its lowest point.

"The Saint's Everlasting Rest" was designed by the author to be "a directory for getting and keeping the heart in heaven, by heavenly meditation." The second part of it shows the superstition which still governed the world, and from which Baxter and his ablest contemporaries were not altogether free. He inserts narratives of ghosts and witches, and of contracts made by madmen with the devil. The new learning and the light of the Reformation had not as yet dispelled the ignorance and darkness from the human mind. The clouds of the deep night of darker ages hung heavily in some portions of the sky, and it was not yet full day. Unhappy women suspected, or at least accused, by their acquaintances, were still tried,—even by a judge as eminent as Sir Matthew Hale,—convicted, and burned for supposed powers and practices of necromancy and bewitchment; and base wretches, living in city lanes, lurked in the foul corners of the law-courts, who were ready, at the bribe of jealousy or malice, to swear that they had suffered personal indignities and injuries from the spells of feeble old neighbours, whom they affirmed they had seen keeping Sabbath with Satan, or feeding on the bodies of murdered infants, consorting with hideous spectres, or dancing with fiends. We may wonder, not that the ignorant were deluded, but that barristers could be contented to prosecute diseased or bewildered women, and that grave judges could listen to the evidence against them, and for imaginary crimes condemn them, without pity or remonstrance, to horrible sufferings. But psychology was then among the dreams or speculations of the future. Medicine was not as yet matured into a science. The numerous morbid influences of the atmosphere upon the brain were unknown, and little of the structure of the nervous system had been discovered. Materialism held sway. Men lived in dread of the forces of nature, which we now know to be ministers of good to the world; and cruelty rioted where superstition reigned.

"The Saint's Everlasting Rest," notwithstanding these occasional or accidental blots in it, is one of the most useful and delightful books of that literature in which England is intrinsically and peculiarly rich. It has a charm for old and young. The statesman and divine, the economist and lawyer, the trader and the artisan, in their days of languor and of age have read its pages with comfort and gladness; thankful, amid the sufferings and the exhaustions of decaying nature, to be consoled by anticipations of that blissful life, in which the merciful Saviour gives welcome to them who escape from the pollutions and wrecks of time, in the home of perpetual goodness, of happy service, and of perfect peace. So that the sufferer who reads it learns contentment with his lot, endures with greater resignation the discipline to which submission is inevitable, and is able to acquiesce cheerfully in the dispositions of the government which is at once Divine and paternal.

Such subjects of meditation, the holiest upon which man can employ his reason, were familiar to Baxter; for, having hardly rest for a day from pain of body, and from apprehension of mind in a continual expectation of death, he lived on the border of that world whither his devout thoughts tended, and on which his best affections were set.

In his work as a clergyman, distressed by the view of the atrocities and sufferings of the conflict around him; maligned and harassed by them who either suspected his motives, or charged him with publishing heretical opinions, he often soothed himself by the hope of rest and peace in that world where the law of existence is goodness, the eternal city of God. To him it was sweet to think of that immortal state, in which happiness and obedience are one; where the purest and best associations of human life are restored; where all are happy because all are good; where every service of duty is a transacted thanksgiving, and where war is learned no more. Baxter was assured that such a future state is one of constant activity in the highest employment of the spiritual nature, that no one should regret suffering and dying, if he might attain that fulness of joy, and that enough has been revealed to allure men thither. He would keep the image of that future bliss ever before his mind. The thought of it would inspire his meditations, and would strengthen him in his ministry; the expectation of it would make him patient in affliction, and resigned to be daily educated in that course which would best enable him to triumph over the weakness of his frail humanity.

Of all Baxter's books, "The Saint's Everlasting Rest" has been the most useful. It is still read in every land in which the English language is spoken. "There reigns in it," as Archbishop Trench writes, "a robust and masculine eloquence, nor does it want from time to time rare and unsought felicity of language, which once heard can scarcely be forgotten." Baxter's description of a Christian's thoughts in prospect of his departure expressed his own anticipations of the rest he hoped to attain: "As Moses, before he died, went up into mount Nebo, to take a survey of the land of Canaan, so he ascended the mount of contemplation, and by faith surveyed his heavenly rest. He looked on the delectable mansions, and said, 'Glorious things are deservedly spoken of thee, thou city of God.' He heard, as it were, the melody of the heavenly choir, and said, 'Happy the people that are in such a case; yea, happy is that people whose God is the Lord.' He looked upon the glorious inhabitants, and exclaimed, 'Happy art thou, O Israel! Who is like unto thee, O people saved by the Lord!' He looked on the Lord Himself, Who is their glory, and was ready with the rest to fall down and worship Him that liveth for ever and ever. He looked on the glorified Saviour, and was ready to say 'Amen' to that new song, 'Blessing, and honour, and glory, and power be unto Him that sitteth upon the throne, and unto the Lamb.' He looked back upon the wilderness of this world, and blessed the believing, patient, despised saints; he pitied the ignorant, obstinate, miserable world. For himself, when thus employed, he said with Peter, 'It is good to be here;' or with Asaph, 'It is good for me to draw near to God.' Like Daniel in his captivity, he daily opened his window, looking towards the Jerusalem that is above, though far out of sight. Like Paul's affections towards his brethren, though absent in the flesh from the glorified saints, he was yet with them in spirit, joying and beholding their heavenly order."

Many who have read "The Saint's Everlasting Rest," in the fading light of life, nourished and comforted by it, have been able to sympathise with Baxter when he writes: "As the lark sings sweetly while she soars on high, but is suddenly silenced when she falls to earth; so is the frame of the soul most delightful and Divine while it keepeth God in view by meditation. But, alas! we make there too short a stay, and lay by our music." The book is concluded by a prayer, which is a transcription of Baxter's heart, declaring his devout humility and earnest goodness:—"O Thou, the merciful Father of spirits, the attractive of love, and ocean of delight! draw up these drossy hearts unto Thyself, and keep them there till they are spiritualised and refined! Second Thy servant's weak endeavours, and persuade those that read these lines to the practice of this delightful, heavenly work. O suffer not the soul of Thy most unworthy servant to be a stranger to those joys which he describes to others; but keep me, while I remain on earth, in daily breathing after Thee, and in a believing affectionate walking with Thee. And when Thou comest, let me be found so doing; not serving my flesh, nor asleep with my lamp unfurnished, but waiting and longing for my Lord's return. Let those who shall read these pages not merely read the fruit of my studies, but the breathing of my active hope and love; that if my heart were open to their view, they might read Thy love most deeply engraven with a beam from the face of the Son of God; and not find vanity, or lust, or pride within, where the words of life appear without; that so these lines may not witness against me; but proceeding from the heart of the writer, may be effectual through Thy grace upon the heart of the reader, and so be the savour of life to both!"

Baxter withdrew from his chaplaincy in the camp, the scene of incessant agitation and faction. The violence of the contending parties disgusted and grieved him; for he was in heart no sectarian, and in all his stormy disputations he never forgot that where goodness exists, charity is supreme. Regret at his failing to appease the religious discords in the parliamentarian army, and to restore its loyalty, brought on a return of some of his severer illnesses. He resolved to go back to the parish where his ministry was thankfully remembered, and where he was revered. In his Autobiography he says of this period: "I have related how after bleeding a gallon of blood by the nose, that I was left weak at Sir Thomas Rous's house, at Rous-Leach, where I was taken up with daily medicines to prevent a dropsy; and being conscious that my time had not been improved to the service of God as I desired it had been, I put up many an earnest prayer, that God would restore me and use me more successfully in His work. Blessed be that mercy which heard my groans in the day of my distress; which brought my deliverance when men and means failed, and gave me opportunity to celebrate His praise. Whilst I continued there, weak and unable to preach, the people of Kidderminster had again renewed their articles against their old vicar and his curate. Upon trial of the cause, the committee sequestered the place, but put no one into it; and placed the profits in the hands of divers of the inhabitants, to pay a preacher till it were disposed of. These persons sent to me, and desired me to take it, in case I was again enabled to preach; which I flatly refused, and told them I would take only the lecture, which, by the vicar's own consent and bond, I held before. Hereupon they sought others to accept the place, but could not meet with any one to their minds; they therefore chose Mr. Richard Serjeant to officiate, reserving the vicarage for someone that was fitter.

"When I was able, after about five months' confinement, to go abroad, I went to Kidderminster, where I found only Mr. Serjeant in possession; and the people again vehemently urged me to take the vicarage. This I declined; but got the magistrates and burgesses together into the town-hall, and told them, that though I had been offered many hundred pounds per annum elsewhere, I was willing to continue with them in my old lecturer's place, which I had before the wars, expecting they would make the maintenance an hundred pounds a year and a house; and if they would promise to submit to that doctrine of Christ which as His minister I should deliver them, I would not leave them. That this maintenance should neither come out of their own purses, nor any more of it out of the tithes, save the sixty pounds which the vicar had before bound himself to pay, I undertook to procure an augmentation for Milton (a chapel in the parish) of forty pounds per annum. This I afterwards did; and so the sixty pounds and that forty pounds were to be my part, and the rest I should have nothing to do with.

"The covenant was drawn up between us in articles, and subscribed; in which I disclaimed the vicarage and pastoral charge of the parish, and only undertook the lecture. Thus the sequestration continued in the hands of the townsmen, as aforesaid, who gathered the tithes, and paid me (not a hundred pounds as they promised) but eighty pounds per annum, or ninety pounds at most, which was all I had at Kidderminster. The rest they gave to Mr. Serjeant, and about forty pounds per annum to the old vicar; six pounds per annum to the king and lord for rents, and a few other charges.

"Besides this ignorant vicar, there was a chapel in the parish, where was an old curate as ignorant as he, that had long lived upon ten pounds a year and the fees for celebrating unlawful marriages. He was also a drunkard, and a railer, and the scorn of the country. I knew not how to keep him from reading, though I judged it a sin to tolerate him in any sacred office. I got an augmentation for the place and an honest preacher to instruct them, and let this scandalous fellow keep his former stipend of ten pounds for nothing; yet could never keep him from forcing himself upon the people to read, nor from celebrating unlawful marriages, till a little before death did call him to his account. I have examined him about the familiar points of religion, and he could not say half so much to me as I have heard a child say. These two in this parish were not all; in one of the next parishes, called 'The Rock,' there were two chapels, where the poor ignorant curate of one got his living by cutting faggots, and the other by making ropes. Their abilities being answerable to their studies and employments."

Thus Baxter resumed his work at Kidderminster, under circumstances which can be justified only by the irregularity resulting from the disorder which then prevailed. He had no renewal of his licence from the bishop of the diocese to re-enter on his work as a lecturer in the parish, and he had not ceased to be an Anglican clergyman. On entering upon the duties, he had, if any title at all, only that which the commissioners of the Parliament could sanction, founded upon his election to the office by some of the townsmen. He had taken no step to obtain the preferment; he had no part in the ejection of the incompetent vicar, nor did he possess himself of the proceeds of the parochial income. He had the singular misfortune to enter upon the office, with a compact as to the payment of his stipend, which depended for its fulfilment only upon the goodwill of the contributors; and which, as still often happens, when one relies for his maintenance upon voluntary contributions to it, was soon broken on the one side, and could not be enforced on the other. In such cases the unhappy dependent frequently finds, as Baxter found, that they who promise to give what they can soon learn to give what they please; and that few men in any calling are more to be pitied, than they, who for sacred service efficiently done, have to rely for their daily bread upon either the pleasure or the caprice of others. They, who are so slavishly bound, often receive the means of living, only so long as they can satisfy or can amuse their supporters.

When Baxter was resuming his office at Kidderminster, the course of the war began to turn against the king. The parliamentary army, new modelled by Cromwell, and guided by his consummate military skill, was superior to all which Charles could oppose to him. The noblemen who sided with the king had exhausted their means. No more money could be raised either by the mortgage of estates or by the sale of plate and of pictures. The Cavaliers had lost so much and so often; and the Ironsides and other picked troops in Cromwell's army, at Naseby, Marston Moor, and on other well-fought fields, had so swept all before them; and so many royal strongholds, one after another, had either yielded or been stormed, that the king's affairs were all but desperate.

The capture of Charles's camp, and especially of his private cabinet, which contained the letters of the queen, gave such clear evidence of his insincerity in negotiating, and of his determination to re-establish arbitrary government should success attend him, that the leaders of the parliamentary forces abandoned all hope of coming to an equitable arrangement with him, which should assure civil and religious liberty, and secure peace. Both the House of Commons and the army, however much they might differ in other matters, were agreed in the resolution to have a settlement of the national affairs on no other terms than these.

Baxter had no belief in the honest intentions of some of the leading men in Parliament; he suspected that they might insist upon the public recognition of a sectarian form of religion, to the exclusion or to the injury of the Church; and he sagaciously suspected that the ambition of some of the generals might lead to the establishment of a military oligarchy, in which public freedom would be in peril. His testimony is very valuable, not merely because he was an eyewitness of some of the chief transactions of the time, but that he observed with clearness, and wrote with truth.

In his Autobiography he says:—" I must now look back to the course and affairs of the king; who, after the siege of Oxford, having no army left, and knowing that the Scots had more loyalty and stability in their principles than the sectaries, resolved to cast himself upon them, and so escaped to their army in the north. The Scots were very much troubled at this honour that was cast upon them, for they knew not what to do with the king. To send him back to the English Parliament seemed unfaithfulness, when he had cast himself upon them; to keep him, they knew would divide the kingdoms, and draw a war upon themselves from England, which they were now unable to sustain. They kept him, therefore, awhile among them with honourable entertainment, till the Parliament sent for him, and they saw that the sectaries and the army were glad of it, as an occasion to make them odious, and to invade their land. Thus the terror of the conquering army made them deliver him to the Parliament's commissioners upon two conditions: 1. That they should promise to preserve his person in safety and honour, according to the duty which they owed him by their allegiance; 2. That they should presently pay the Scots army one-half of what was due to them for their services, which had long been unpaid.

"Hereupon, the king delivered to the Parliament, they appointed Colonel Richard Greaves, Major-General Richard Brown, with others, to be his attendants, and desired him to abide awhile at Holmby House, in Northamptonshire. While he was here, the army were hatching their conspiracy; and on the sudden, one Cornet Joyce with a party of soldiers fetched away the king, notwithstanding the Parliament's orders for his security. This was done as if it had been against Cromwell's will, and without any order or consent of theirs; but so far was Joyce from losing his head for such a treason, that it proved the means of his preferment; and so far were Cromwell and his soldiers from returning the king in safety, that they detained him among them, and kept him with them, till they came to Hampton Court, and there they lodged him under the guard of Colonel Whalley, the army quartering all about him. While he was there, the mutable hypocrites pretended an extraordinary care of the king's honour, liberty, safety, and conscience. They blamed the austerity of Parliament, who had denied him the attendance of his own chaplains, and of his friends in whom he took great pleasure. They gave liberty to his friends and to his chaplains to come to him, and pretended that they would save him from the incivilities of the Parliament and the Presbyterians.

"Whether this was while they tried what terms they could make with him for themselves, or while they acted any other part, it is certain that the king's old adherents began to extol the army. At last, on the sudden, the judgment of the army changed, and they began to cry for justice against the king; and with vile hypocrisy to publish their repentance, and cry God's mercy for their kindness to the king; and confess that they were under a temptation: but in all this, Cromwell and Ireton, and the rest of the council of war, appeared not. The instruments of all this work must be the common soldiers. Two of the most violent sectaries in each regiment are chosen by them, by the name of agitators, to represent the rest in these great affairs. All these together made a council, of which Colonel James Berry was the president, that they might be used, ruled, and dissolved at pleasure. No man that knew them will doubt that this was done by Cromwell's and Ireton's direction. This council of agitators take not only the Parliament's work upon themselves, but much more; they draw up a paper called 'The Agreement of the People,' as the model or form of 'a new commonwealth.' When Cromwell had awhile permitted them thus to play themselves, partly to please them, and confirm them to him, and chiefly to use them in his demolishing work; at last he seemed to be so much for order and government, as to blame them for their disorder, presumption, and headiness, as if they had done it without his consent. This emboldened the Parliament, not to censure them as rebels, but to rebuke them, and prohibit them, and claim their own superiority; and while the Parliament and the agitators were contending, a letter was secretly sent to Colonel Whalley, to intimate that the agitators had a design suddenly to surprise and murder the king. Some thought this was sent by a real friend, but most thought it was contrived by Cromwell to frighten the king out of the land, or into some desperate course which might give them advantage against him. Colonel Whalley showed the letter to the king, which put him into much fear of such ill-governed hands; so that he secretly got horses, and slipped away towards the sea with two of his confidants only. On coming to the sea, near Southampton, they were disappointed of the vessel which they expected to transport them, and so were fain to pass over into the Isle of Wight, and His Majesty was committed to the trust of Colonel Robert Hammond, who was governor of a castle there. For a day or two all were amazed to think what had become of the king; and then a letter from the king to the House acquainted them that he was fain to flee thither from the cruelty of the agitators, who, as he was informed, thought to murder him; and urging them to treat about ending all these troubles. But here Cromwell had the king in a pinfold, and was more secure of him than before.

"When at the Isle of Wight, the Parliament sent him some propositions, to be consented to in order to his restoration. The king granted many of them; and some he granted not. The Scottish commissioners thought the conditions more dishonourable to the king than was consistent with their covenant and duty, and protested against them; for which the Parliament blamed them as hinderers of the desired peace. The chief thing which the king stuck at was the utter abolishing of episcopacy, and the alienating of the bishops' and the dean and chapter lands. Hereupon, with the commissioners, certain divines were sent down to satisfy the king, viz., Mr. Stephen Marshall, Mr. Richard Vines, Dr. Lazarus Seaman, etc.; who were met by many of the king's divines, Archbishop Ussher, Dr. Hammond, Dr. Sheldon, etc. The debates here being in writing were published, and each party thought they had the better. The parliamentary divines came off with great honour.

"They seem to me, however, not to have taken the course which should have settled these distracted Churches. Instead of disputing against all episcopacy, they should have changed diocesan prelacy into such an episcopacy as the conscience of the king might have admitted, and as was agreeable to that which the Church had in the two or three first ages. I confess Mr. Vines wrote to me, as their excuse in this and other matters of the assembly, that the Parliament tied them up from treating or disputing of anything at all but what they appointed or proposed to them; but I think plain dealing with such leaders had been best, and to have told them, This is our judgment, and, in the matters of God and His Church, we will serve you according to our judgment, or not at all.

"Archbishop Ussher there took the right course, who offered the king his *reduction* of episcopacy to the form of presbytery. He told me himself that formerly the king had refused it, but at the Isle of Wight he accepted it; and as he would not when *others* would, so *others* would not when *he* would. So also, when Charles II. came in, we tendered Ussher's scheme of union to him; but then he would not. Thus the true, moderate, healing terms are always rejected by those that stand on the higher ground, though accepted by them that are lower, and cannot have what they will; from whence it is easy to perceive whether prosperity or adversity, the highest or the lowest, be ordinarily the greater hinderer of the Church's unity and peace. I know that if the divines and Parliament had agreed for a moderate episcopacy with the king, some Presbyterians of Scotland would have been against it, and many Independents of England; and the army would have made it the matter of odious accusations and clamours; but all this ought not to have deterred foreseeing, judicious men from those healing counsels which must close our wounds whenever they are closed.

"The king, sending his final answers, the Parliament had a long debate upon them, whether to acquiesce in them as a sufficient ground for peace. Many members spake for resting in them, and, among others, Mr. Prynne went over all the king's concessions in a speech of divers hours long with marvellous memory, and showed the satisfactoriness of them all; so that the House voted that the king's concessions were a sufficient ground for a personal treaty with him, and suddenly gave a concluding answer, and sent for him up. But at such a crisis it was time for the army to bestir themselves. Without any more ado, Cromwell and his confidants sent Colonel Pride with a party of soldiers to the House, and set a guard upon the door; one part of the House who were for them they let in; another part they turned away, and told them that they must not come there; and the third part they imprisoned. To so much rebellion, perfidiousness, perjury, and impudence can error, selfishness, and pride of great successes transport men of the highest pretensions to religion.

"For the true understanding of all this, it must be remembered that, though in the beginning of the Parliament there was scarce a noted, gross sectary known but Lord Brooke in the House of Peers, and young Sir Harry Vane in the House of Commons, yet by degrees the number increased in the Lower House. Major Salloway and some few others, Sir Henry Vane had made his own adherents; many more were carried part of the way to Independency and liberty of religions; and many that minded not any side in religion, did think that it was not policy ever to trust a conquered king, and therefore were wholly for a parliamentary government. Of these, some would have lords and commons, or a mixture of aristocracy and democracy; others would have commons and democracy alone; and some thought that they ought to judge the king for all the blood that had been shed. Thus, when the two parts of the House were ejected and imprisoned, the third part, composed of the Vanists, the Independents, and other sects, with the democratical party, was left by Cromwell to do his business under the name of the Parliament of England; which, by the people in scorn, was commonly called the Rump of the Parliament. The secluded and imprisoned members published a writing, called their 'Vindication;' and some of them would afterwards have thrust into the House, but the guard of soldiers kept them out, and the Rump were called the *honest men*. And these are the men that henceforward we have to do with in the progress of our history as called The Parliament.

"As the Lords were disaffected to these proceedings, so were the Rump and soldiers to the Lords; so that they passed a vote, supposing that the army would stand by them, to establish the government without a king and a House of Lords; and thus the Lords were dissolved, and these

Commons sat and did all alone. Being deluded by Cromwell, and verily thinking that he would be for democracy, which they called a commonwealth, they gratified him in his designs, and themselves in their disloyal distrust and fears. They accordingly called a high court of justice to be erected, and sent for the king from the Isle of Wight. Colonel Hammond delivered him, and to Westminster Hall he came, and refusing to own the court and their power to try him, Cook, as attorney, having pleaded against him, Bradshaw, as president and judge, recited the charge, and condemned him. Before his own gate at Whitehall they erected a scaffold, and in the presence of a full assembly of people beheaded him. In all this appeared the severity of God, the mutability and uncertainty of worldly things, the fruits of a sinful nation's provocations, the infamous effects of error, pride, and selfishness prepared by Satan, to be charged hereafter upon reformation and godliness, to the unspeakable injury of the Christian name and Protestant cause, the rejoicing and advantage of the papists, the hardening of thousands against the means of their own salvation, and the confusion of the actors when their day should come.

"The Lord-General Fairfax all this while stood by, and with high resentment saw his lieutenant do all this by tumultuous soldiers, tricked and overpowered by him; neither being sufficiently on his guard to defeat the intrigues of such an actor, nor having resolution enough to lay down the glory of all his conquests and forsake him. At the king's death he was in wonderful perplexities, and when Mr. Calamy and some ministers were sent for to resolve him, and would have further persuaded him to rescue the king, his troubles so confounded him, that his servants durst let no man speak to him: and Cromwell kept him, as it was said, in praying and consulting till the stroke was given, and it was too late to make resistance. But not long after, when war was determined against Scotland, he laid down his commission, and never had to do with the army more; and Cromwell became General in his stead.

"If you ask, What did the ministers all this while? I answer, they preached and prayed against disloyalty; they drew up a writing to the Lord-General, declaring their abhorrence of all violence against the person of the king, and urging him and his army to take heed of such an unlawful act. They presented it to the General when they saw the king in danger; but pride prevailed against their counsels."

From the beginning to the end of the civil troubles Baxter was a Royalist at heart. He had a wise conservatism of character, which prevented him from being blind to the faults of the king, and from being deceived by the specious excuses of some of the parliamentary leaders for their violent usurpation of authority in the country, for their readily yielding to the clamour of unprincipled sectarians, and for their cruel treatment of Charles I. Baxter at that time had a strong dislike of Cromwell, of whose public course he had seen much. He charged him with dissimulation and perfidy, and with artfully contriving the condemnation and execution of the king. That unwise reprisal he always held to be the crime which spoiled the success and disgraced the cause of the popular party. Many of them who had dislike of Archbishop Laud, and of the Star Chamber, and of King Charles's arbitrary attempts to raise taxes upon his own authority alone, and, indeed, of the general principles of his government, regarded his execution not only as a fatal mistake, but as a public wickedness and shame. In the "Diaries" of Philip Henry—for the recent publication of which his descendant, Mr. Matthew Henry Lee, vicar of Hanmer, deserves the thanks of historical students—there is a record that he and other religious men, who could not take part with the king, condemned and deplored his execution. He writes: "At the later end of the year, 1648, I had leave given me to goe to London to see my Father, and during my stay there at that time at Whitehal it was that I saw the Beheading of King Charles the First; He went by our door on Foot each day that he was carry'd by water to Westminster, but hee took Barge at Garden Stayres where wee liv'd, and once he spake to my Father and sayd, 'Art thou alive yet!' On the day of his execution, which was Tuesday, Jan. 30, I stood amongst the crowd in the street before Whitehal gate, where the scaffold was erected, and I saw what was done, but was not so near as to hear anything. The Blow I saw given, and can truly say it with a sad heart; at the instant whereof, I remember well, there was such a Grone by the thousands then present, as I never heard before and desire I may never hear again. There was according to Order one Troop immediately marching from-wards charing-cross to Westminster, and another from-wards Westminster to charing-cross, purposely to masker the people, and to disperse and scatter them, so that I had much adoe amongst the rest to escape home without hurt."

CHAPTER VIII.

1647—1648.

IN the Autobiography which he bequeathed to his country, rich in historical memorials, bearing on every page evidence of its truth, and which Coleridge declares to be one of the most remarkable pieces of writing that has come down to us, Baxter gives a description of the ambitions, effervescence, and animosities of some of the religionists in the period which Milton called, "the æra of sects and schisms." Baxter observed carefully, knew thoroughly, and wrote faithfully an account of the religious parties who abounded in that eventful time. These seceders were produced by the reaction following the civil and ecclesiastical repression, which existed in the reigns of Elizabeth and of James I. The fountains of the great deep were broken up, and universal disorder ensued upon the sudden removal of restraint. Among some of the sects the differences were more verbal than real; but disputes upon trifles have often produced hatred and hostility. Baxter attributed the rapid increase of sects, and their mutual enmity and rancour, to the intrigues and contrivances of the Jesuits: for at that time the Society of Jesus was one of the most potent and active forces in the life of the world.

With the hope of putting an end to the spiritual supremacy of the English Church, and of placing all sects on an equality in public regard, the Parliament ordered a body of divines to meet in London for the purpose of defining Christian doctrine. Some members who were

Presbyterians no doubt hoped that their own sect would carry all before it, and would give prominence to their form of religion, which Charles II. used to say was "unfit for a gentleman." Milton probably had reasons of his own for his dislike of it, the causes of which are not clear to us; but his well-known line may suffice to show his prejudice against it: "New Presbyter is but Old Priest writ large."

They were termed the "Westminster Assembly." Baxter was not appointed one of them; but as a contemporary, and having personal friendship with some of the constituents, his opinion of the body may be regarded as just. In his Autobiography he writes: "This synod was not a Convocation, according to the diocesan way of government; nor was it called by the votes of the ministers, according to the Presbyterian way; for the Parliament, not intending to call an assembly which should pretend to a divine right to make obligatory laws or canons, but an ecclesiastical council to be advisers to itself, thought it best knew who were fitted to give advice, and therefore chose them all itself. Two were to be chosen from each county, though some counties had but one, that it might be impartial and give each party liberty to speak. Over and above this number, it chose many of the most learned episcopal divines; as, Archbishop Ussher, Dr. Holdsworth, Dr. Hammond, Dr. Wincop, Bishops Westfield and Prideaux, and many more; but they would not come, because the king declared himself against it. Dr. Featley, and a few more of that party, however, came; but, at last, he was charged with sending intelligence to the king, for which he was imprisoned.

"The divines there congregated were men of eminent learning, godliness, ministerial abilities, and fidelity; and being not worthy to be one of them myself, I may the more freely speak the truth, even in the face of malice and envy; that, as far as I am able to judge by the information of all history of that kind, and by any other evidences left us, the Christian world, since the days of the Apostles, had never a synod of more excellent divines than this and the synod of Dort. Yet highly as I honour the men, I am not of their mind in every part of the government which they would have set up. Some words in their catechism I wish had been more clear; and, above all, I wish that the Parliament and their more skilful hand had done more than was done to heal our breaches, and had hit upon the right way, either to unite with the Episcopalians and Independents, or at least had pitched on the terms that are fit for universal concord, and left all to come in upon these terms that would."

Lord Clarendon had only an imperfect knowledge of the components of the Assembly, and in his "History of the Rebellion" he writes of them as one might be expected to write whose king had been publicly put to death, and whose Church had been given over to the spoiler. He says: "Of the whole number of that assembly, there were not above twenty who were not declared and avowed enemies to the doctrine or discipline of the Church of England; some of them infamous in their lives and conversations, and most of them of very mean parts in learning, if not of scandalous ignorance; and of no other reputation than of malice to the Church of England. So that that convention hath not since produced anything that might not then reasonably have been expected from it."

The account Milton has given of the Assembly, in his "Fragment of a History of England," will show how another contemporary regarded it. Clarendon and he are the best representatives of the two prominent and contradictory opinions of the time. The former wrote as a Cavalier whose heart and fortune had been given to his unhappy king: the latter as a Republican who hated domination in religion and oppression in civil government, whether under a monarchy or a democracy. Milton says of the divines: "They taught compulsion without convincement, which, long before, they complained of as executed unchristianly against themselves—setting up a spiritual tyranny by a secular power, to the advancing of their own authority above the magistrate, whom they would have made their executioner to punish Church delinquencies. And well did their disciples manifest themselves to be no better principled than their teachers; trusted with committeeships, and other gainful offices, upon their commendations for zealous and (as they hesitated not to term them) godly men, but executing their places like children of the devil, unfaithfully, unjustly, unmercifully, and where not corruptly, stupidly. So that between them, the teachers, and these, the disciples, there hath not been a more ignominious and mortal wound to faith, to piety, to the work of the Reformation, nor more cause of blaspheming given to the enemies of God and truth, since the first preaching of the Reformation."

The Assembly in its deliberations discussed economical and polemical questions, on which they were not thoroughly agreed. Unity of decision was difficult among its members, who represented numerous parties. The Assembly ultimately separated with many important matters not distinctly concluded, and, to some extent, the purpose failed for which the Parliament called it together. Among men, some of whom were of singular eminence both as scholars, divines, and lawyers, and whose names are still of renown in the history of our national literature, it is remarkable that no practical decision was arrived at, which might have formed the ground for a religious peace. It might have been justly expected that men so able as Selden and Whitelocke the eminent jurists, Lightfoot and Arrowsmith the illustrious Rabbinical and Biblical scholars, with generals of so much repute as Manchester and Essex, all of them members of that Assembly, would have effected that good result.

Baxter well knew the sentiments and characters of the chief components of the Assembly. He deplored the religious dissensions, he grieved that the household of his Lord should be divided. He had no sympathy with the bitter sectarians who clamoured for the destruction of the Anglican

Church, in which he had been ordained, and in one of whose parishes he had laboured with success. He desired to maintain a liberal and tolerant episcopate; but the majority of the Assembly were Presbyterians, holding firmly Calvin's theological doctrines and his principles of Church government. Many of the chief men in the House of Commons, and some of the generals in the army, belonged to this party, and for them Baxter had more regard than for any of the others who dissented from the English Church.

In his Autobiography are many interesting memorials of the Assembly, and reflections upon their proceedings. He says: "The Episcopal party seemed to have reason on their side in this, that in the primitive Church there were apostles, evangelists, and others, who were general unfixed officers, not tied to any particular charge, but who had some superiority over fixed bishops or pastors. And as to fixed bishops of particular churches, that were superior in degree to presbyters, though I have nothing at all in Scripture for them, yet I saw that the reception of them was so very early and so very general, I thought it most improbable that it was contrary to the mind of the Apostles.

"As for the Presbyterians, I found that the office of preaching presbyters was allowed by all who deserved the name of Christians; that the office did participate, subserviently to Christ, in the prophetical or teaching, the priestly or worshipping, and the governing power; and that Scripture, antiquity, and the nature of Church government clearly show that all presbyters were church-governors, as well as church-teachers. I saw also in Scripture, antiquity, and reason, that the association of pastors and churches for agreement, and their synods in cases of necessity, are a plain duty, and that their ordinary stated synods are usually very convenient. I disliked their orders of lay-elders, who had no ordination, or power to preach, or to administer sacraments; for though I grant that lay-elders, or the chief of the people, were often employed to express the people's consent and preserve their liberties, yet these were no church-officers at all, nor had any charge of private oversight of the flocks. I disliked also the course of some of the more rigid of them, grasping at a kind of secular power. They reproach the ministerial power, as if it were not worth a straw, unless the magistrate's sword enforce it. What then did the primitive Church for three hundred years? Till magistrates keep the sword themselves, and learn to deny it to every angry clergyman who would do his own work by it, and leave them to their own weapons, the Word and spiritual keys, and, *valeant quantum valere possunt*, the Church will never have unity and peace. I disliked also some of them that were not tender enough to dissenting brethren, but too much against liberty, as others were too much for it, and thought by votes and numbers to do that which love and reason would have done."

Baxter was opposed to the Independents. Philip Henry also objected to their principles and conduct, "that they unchurch the nation, that they pluck up the hedge of parish-order, and that they throw the ministry common, and allow persons to preach who are unordained." Baxter says: "In the Independent way I disliked many things. They made too light of ordination. They also had their office of lay-membership. They were commonly stricter about the qualification of Church members than Scripture, reason, or the practice of the universal Church would allow; not taking a man's bare profession as credible, and as sufficient evidence of his title to Church communion, unless either by a holy life, or the particular narration of the passages of the work of grace, he satisfied the pastors and all the Church that he was truly holy; whereas every man's profession is the valid evidence of the thing professed in his heart. If once you go beyond the evidence of a serious, sober confession, as a credible and sufficient sign of a title to church-membership, you will never know where to rest. The Church's opinion will be both rule and judge, and men will be let in or kept out according to the various latitude of opinion or charity in the several officers or churches, so that he will be passable in one Church who is intolerable in another.

"I disliked also the lamentable tendency of this their way to divisions and subdivisions, and the nourishing of heretics and sects. But above all I disliked that most of them made the people, by majority of votes, to be church-governors, and so they governed their governors and themselves. They also too much exploded synods, refusing them as stated, and admitting them but upon some extraordinary occasions. I disliked also their over-rigidness against the admission of Christians of other Churches to their communions. And their making a minister to be no minister to any but his own flock, and to act to others but as a private man; with divers other such irregularities and dividing opinions.

"Among all these parties I found that some were naturally of mild, calm, and gentle dispositions, and some of sour, froward, passionate, peevish, or furious natures. Some were young, raw, and inexperienced; and these were like young fruit, sour and harsh, addicted to pride of their own opinions, to self-conceitedness, turbulences, censoriousness, and temerity, and to engage themselves for a cause and party before they understood the matter, judging of sermons and persons by their fervency more than by the soundness of the matter and the cause. Some I found on the other side to be ancient and experienced Christians, that had tried the spirits, and seen what was of God, and what of man, and noted the events of both in the world.

"But I found not all these alike in all the disagreeing parties, though some of both sorts were in every party. The Diocesan party consisted of some grave, learned, godly bishops, and some sober, godly people of their mind; and withal of almost all the carnal politicians, temporizers, profane, and haters of godliness in the land, and all the rabble of the ignorant, ungodly vulgar.

"The Presbyterians consisted of grave, orthodox, godly ministers, together with the hopefulest of the students and young ministers, and the soberest, godly, ancient Christians, who were equally averse to persecution and to schism; and of those young ones who were educated and misled by these, —as also of the soberest sort of the well-meaning vulgar, who liked a godly life, though they had no great knowledge of it. This party was most desirous of peace.

"The Independent party had many very godly ministers and people, but with them many young, injudicious persons, inclined much to novelties and separations, abounding more in zeal than knowledge; usually doing more for subdivisions than the few sober persons among them could do for unity and peace; too much mistaking the terms of church-communion.

"The Anabaptist party consisted of some (but fewer) sober, peaceable persons, and orthodox in other points, but withal of abundance of young, transported zealots, and a medley of opinionists, who all hasted directly to enthusiasm and subdivisions, and by the temptation of prosperity and success in arms, and the policy of some commanders, were led into rebellions and hot endeavours against the ministry, and other scandalous crimes, and brought forth the horrid sects of Ranters, Seekers, and Quakers in the land. I thought it my duty to labour to bring them all to a concordant practice of so much as they were agreed in; to set all that together which was true and good among them all, and to reject the rest; and especially to labour to revive Christian charity, which faction and disputes had lamentably extinguished."

A remarkable fact in Baxter's career, and to which he frequently refers, was his antipathy to the Quakers, who appeared first at the time of the civil wars. It may be regarded as one of the strange repetitions of the facts of history, that the same diversities of sentiment reappear at certain periods in the course of human society; for this sect appears to be a revival of a secession from the uniformity of the general Christian commonwealth in the time of the primitive Church. In our days the Quakers, or Friends as they are more courteously termed, are among the most religious, peaceable, and orderly of English citizens. They are singularly prudent, industrious, and often very successful in commerce; devoted to works of benevolence, supporting useful institutions, zealous for education, and for the moral and material improvement of their fellow-citizens; opposed to the wasteful iniquity of war; contributors to societies whose object is to diffuse a knowledge of revealed truth; and some of them with facile pen and eloquent tongue have done much to advance the nobler interests of mankind. Either their principles and social conduct must have entirely changed from those of the early days of their party, or they were then misunderstood and misrepresented.

Baxter often complains of their behaviour to himself. In his bitterness of feeling, he says: "The Quakers were but the Ranters turned from horrid profaneness and blasphemy to a life of extreme austerity on the other side. Their doctrines were mostly the same with the Ranters; they made the light which every man hath within him to be his sufficient rule; and, consequently, the Scripture and ministry were set light by. They spake much for the dwelling and working of the Spirit in us, but little of justification and the pardon of sin, and our reconciliation with God through Jesus Christ. They pretend their dependence on the Spirit's conduct, against set times of prayer, against sacraments, and against their due esteem of Scripture and ministry. They will not have the Scripture called the Word of God; their principal zeal lieth in their railing against the ministers as hirelings, deceivers, false prophets, etc.; and in refusing to swear before a magistrate, or to put off their hats to any, or to say *you* instead of *thou* or *thee*, which are their words to all. At first they did use to fall into tremblings, and sometimes vomiting in their meetings, and pretended to be violently acted on by the Spirit; but now that is ceased. They only meet, and he that pretendeth to be moved by the Spirit speaketh; and sometimes they say nothing, but sit an hour or more in silence, and then depart. One while divers of them went naked through several chief towns and cities of the land, as a prophetical act; some of them have famished, and drowned themselves in melancholy; and others have undertaken, by the power of the Spirit, to raise the dead. Their chief leader, James Nayler, acted the part of Christ at Bristol, according to much of the history of the Gospel, and was long laid in Bridewell for it, and his tongue bored as a blasphemer by the Parliament Act. Many Franciscan friars, and other papists, have been proved to be distinguished speakers in their assemblies, and to be among them; and it is like are the very soul of all these horrible delusions. But of late one William Penn is become their leader, and would reform the sect and set up a kind of ministry among them."

So one of the kindest hearts of the seventeenth century, in an age beclouded by theological differences, judged of the originators of a sect now distinguished among us by the virtues and charities which humanize society. That such a sentence as that Baxter mentions was inflicted upon Nayler is probable, and that he bore it with the strength and patience of a man who is willing to endure all things for that which he holds to be truth; for the spirit of the time was horribly cruel. Both Royalists and Parliamentarians harassed one another to the death. The sentences upon criminals then pronounced by the judges, and as indeed they have sometimes been since, were frequently atrocious; and even to a recent period successive British governments were not ashamed to garnish their walls and gateways, like the Ashantees, with the reeking heads of their enemies. On the great roads then, and for ages afterwards, on the numerous gibbets hung the decaying bodies of political opponents of Stuarts and Georges; and, many times in a year, an obscene and half-drunken rabble sang ribald songs, and shouted horrible blasphemies round Tower Hill, as the heads of noblemen and gentlemen fell by the axe of the executioner, and who died there for having risen in rebellion against intolerable tyranny and wrong.

Baxter's quarrel with the Quakers seems to have been bitter

and long-continued. He says: "The Quakers in their shops, when I go along London streets, say, 'Alas! poor man, thou art yet in darkness.' They have often come into the congregation when I had liberty to preach Christ's Gospel, and cried out against me as a deceiver of the people. They have followed me home, crying out in the streets, 'The day of the Lord is coming, when thou shalt perish as a deceiver.' They have stood in the market-place, and under my window, year after year, crying out to the people, 'Take heed of your priests, they deceive your souls'; and if they saw any one wear a lace or a neat clothing, they cried out to me, 'These are the fruit of thy ministry.' If they spake to me with the greatest ignorance or nonsense, it was with as much fury and rage as if a bloody heart had appeared in their faces; so that though I never hurt, nor occasioned the hurt of, any one of them that I know of, their tremulent countenances told me what they would have done had I been in their power. This was from 1656 to 1659.

"The Quakers say we are idle drones that labour not. The worst I wish you is, that you had my ease instead of your labour. I have reason to take myself for the least of saints, and yet I fear not to tell the accuser that I take the labour of most tradesmen in the town to be a pleasure to the body, in comparison with mine; though, for the ends and pleasure of my mind, I would not change it with the greatest prince. Their labour preserveth health, and mine consumeth it; they work in ease, and I in continual pain; they have hours and days of recreation, I have scarce time to eat and drink. Nobody molesteth them for their labour, but the more I do, the more hatred and trouble I draw upon me. If a Quaker ask me what all this labour is, let him come and see, or do as I do, and he shall know!"

Baxter's numerous animadversions on the chief Nonconformists who cast in their lot with the Parliament, evince his complete loyalty,—which never wavered even in the days of his persecution and sufferings,—his indignation at the treatment the king received at the hands of his conquerors, and his disgust at the lack of principle in the conduct of some of the violent sectaries, who disturbed and confused all departments of the state, and contributed nothing towards a peaceful settlement. He seems always to have distrusted and disliked Cromwell, as ambitious and perfidious. After the discovery of many of Cromwell's private letters, posterity without doubt has considerably modified this opinion of the Protector's conduct and character. The natures of the two men were so entirely dissimilar, their habits of thought, their affections, and pursuits were so contrary to each other, that it would have been impossible for sympathy and unity to have existed between them. There may have been some private misunderstanding or personal offence, which disposed Baxter to regard Cromwell with so much disfavour. In the early days of the conflict, that great general had invited him to be his army-chaplain; but there was no kinship of spirit between them, for Baxter says: "As soon as I came to the army, Cromwell coolly bade me welcome, and never spake one word more to me while I was there." Long afterwards, he says of his conduct towards the Protector: "I did, seasonably and moderately, by preaching and printing, condemn his usurpation, and the deceit which was the means to bring it to pass. I did in open conference declare Cromwell and his adherents to be guilty of treason and rebellion, aggravated by perfidiousness and hypocrisy. But yet I did not think it my duty to rave against him in the pulpit, or to do this so unseasonably and imprudently as might irritate him to mischief. And the rather because, as he kept up his approbation of a godly life in general, and of all that was good, except that which the interest of his sinful cause engaged him to be against; so I perceived it was his design to do good in the main, and to promote the gospel and the interests of godliness more than any had done before him; except in those particulars which were against his own interest. The principal means that henceforward he trusted to for his establishment, was doing good, that the people might love him, or at least be willing to have his government for that good, who were against it as it was usurpation. I made no question but when the rightful governor should be restored, the people who had adhered to him, being so extremely irritated, would cast out multitudes of the ministers, and undo the good which the usurper had done, because he did it, and would bring abundance of calamity upon the land. Some men thought it a very hard question, whether they should rather wish the continuance of a usurper who did good, or the restitution of a rightful governor whose followers would do hurt. For my part I thought my duty was clear, to disown the usurper's sin, what good soever he should do, and to perform all my engagements to a rightful governor, leaving the issue of all to God; but yet to commend the good which a usurper doth, and to do every lawful thing which might provoke him to do more, and to approve of no evil which is done by any, whether a usurper or a lawful governor.

"At this time Lord Broghill and the Earl of Warwick brought me to preach before Cromwell, the Protector; which was the only time that I ever preached to him, save once long before, when he was an inferior man, amongst other auditors. I knew not which way better to provoke him to his duty than by preaching on 1 Corinthians i. 10, against the divisions and distractions of the Church, and showing how mischievous a thing it was for politicians to maintain such divisions for their own ends, that they might fish in troubled waters and keep the Church by its divisions in a state of weakness, lest it should be able to offend them; and showing the necessity and means of union. My plainness, I heard, was displeasing to him and his courtiers; but they put it up. A little while after, Cromwell sent to speak with me, and when I came, in the presence of only three of his chief men, he began a long and tedious speech to me of God's providence in the change of the government, and how God had owned it, and what great things had been done at home and abroad, in the peace with Spain and Holland, etc. When he had wearied us all with speaking thus slowly about an hour, I told him it was too great condescension to acquaint me so fully with all these matters which were above me; but I told him that we took our ancient monarchy to be a blessing and not an evil to the land; and humbly craved his patience that I might ask him how England had ever forfeited that blessing, and unto whom that forfeiture was made? I was fain to speak of the form of government only, for it had lately been made treason, by law, to speak for the person of the king.

"Upon that question he was awakened into some passion, and then told me it was no forfeiture, but God had changed it as pleased Him; and then he let fly at the Parliament, which thwarted him; and especially by name at four or five of those members who were my chief acquaintances, whom I presumed to defend against his passion; and thus four or five hours were spent.

"A few days after, he sent for me again, to hear my judgment about liberty of conscience, which he pretended to be most zealous for, before almost all his privy-council; where, after another slow tedious speech of his, I told him a little of my judgment. And when two of his company had spun out a great deal more of the time in such-like tedious but more ignorant speeches, some four or five hours being spent, I told him, that if he would be at the labour to read it, I could tell him more of my mind in writing in two sheets, than in that way of speaking in many days; and that I had a paper on the subject by me, written for a friend, which, if he would peruse, and allow for the change of the person, he would know my sense. He received the paper afterwards, but I scarcely believe that he ever read it; for I saw that what he learned must be from himself; being more disposed to speak many hours, than to hear one; and little heeding what another said, when he had spoken himself."

CHAPTER IX.

1646—1658.

IF it is to be estimated by its usefulness, the most important part of Baxter's public life was that which he passed in the fourteen years of the second period of his work at Kidderminster. The civil war had ended in the complete defeat of the king, his capture, trial, and execution. When the conflict terminated, some of the causes of dissension and agitation ceased. Men learned then, that which indeed before and since has often occurred in the experiences of a nation, that violent resistance to authority which has been long established, especially if it proceed to the extremity of war, loosens all the relations of life; extends much farther than its promoters had originally designed; produces unforeseen changes, sometimes beneficial, sometimes disastrous; and ultimately replaces one class of evils by another, no less injurious to the state than the first had been. If changes can be effected on principles of reason and of justice, they oftentimes enlarge and strengthen, and materially improve the commonwealth; increase the possession and enjoyment of public liberty; introduce a better method of government, with more legal equality of the citizens; and make the condition of the people happier than before.

But when that resistance becomes necessary, in consequence of an arbitrary and oppressive administration, and civil war follows, a long time elapses before order reigns, and security and confidence are re-established. Such a country resembles a town which has been subject to extensive conflagration, or a district which has been devastated by a flood. The fire has been extinguished, and the raging waters have subsided; but what wide-ranging ruin have they left behind them! how long a time must pass before streets can be formed, and churches and market-halls be rebuilt, and before the fields can be cleansed, ploughed, and sown with grain! So Baxter found that the war had left terrible ravage in his parish. Many fathers and sons had fallen in battle; the industry of the town had become sluggish, and the religion of many had grown faint and cold. The mutual hate and passion of them who were lately contending for rival interests had left social irritations. If the wounds had healed, the scars remained.

On his return to the parish, he did not conceal his sympathy for the cause of the king, but he could not with prudence show any opposition to the military despotism which the Protector had found it necessary to establish; and he was allowed to continue his ministrations in the town without threat or molestation from the government. The young prince, afterwards known as Charles II., had landed in Scotland, in hope that the Presbyterians of that country, who fretted under the republican rule, might be willing to rise in arms and to help him to recover his father's throne; but he found himself with little freedom of action, although nominally at the head of a considerable army. He was surrounded by men of rigid faith and of strict morals, whose form of sacred service he detested. He had no tolerance for ardent religionists, who spoke to him with phrases taken from Psalmists and Prophets; who reminded him in their admonitions of the curses pronounced upon the kings of Canaan, if he failed to root out heresy, to maintain the Genevan form of Church-government, and to make that the chief object of his reign; who urged him to repent, to abstain from vices very dear to him, and to conduct himself with the gravity and decorum becoming the anointed of the Lord. The young prince, educated among the frivolities and immorality of Paris, living hitherto in the unrestrained enjoyment of sensual pleasures, accustomed to luxury and ease, turned with disgust from voluble preachers, who lectured him by the hour, who keenly watched his manner of life, the companions of his table, the amusements of his leisure, and above all his observance of the Day of Rest, and reproved him for the oaths which were profuse in his conversation, for the lays of sunny France which he delighted to sing, and for the unrestrained gaiety of his conduct.

Charles may have been glad when tidings reached him that Cromwell, resolved to carry the war into Scotland, had already crossed the Tweed, and had reached the neighbourhood of Edinburgh with but trifling opposition. His many counsellors and monitors urged upon the prince that the issues of the war were uncertain; the Northern troops, the best Scotland ever had, were thirty thousand strong, in good discipline, and under the command of the sagacious and experienced Leslie; the English general had indeed been uniformly successful, and had defeated the armies of his father; but the country was wasted, provisions were destroyed, and the enemy could be fed only from the sea, while the Scotch were fighting in their own country, with the advantage of local knowledge, and with all their resources at hand. The soldiers were brave and well equipped; and if long exhortations, terrible denunciations, and frequent prayers could quicken energy, maintain enthusiasm, and give hope of victory, the chances of his success were neither few nor small. But in the battle of Dunbar, on the 3rd of September, 1650, the Scottish army was completely defeated.

On the first day of 1651, Charles was crowned at Scone. At this coronation he took oath, "in the presence of Almighty God, to fully establish the Presbyterian government of religious affairs in Scotland, which he would never change, nor alter anything in confession of faith and catechisms as approved by the General Assembly of the Kirk." He also signed a declaration, in which he admitted that his father was guilty of marrying into an idolatrous family, and of all the blood which had been shed in the civil war; and the young king acknowledged his own sins, his detestation and abhorrence of popery, superstition, idolatry, and prelacy; and that he would not tolerate them in any part of his dominions. He was obliged to be often present at the long prayers and longer sermons of his spiritual advisers. Bishop Burnet says: "I remember in one fast day, there were six sermons preached without intermission. He was not allowed to walk abroad on Sundays; and if at any time there had been any gaiety at court, as dancing or playing at cards, he was severely reproved for it; which contributed not a little to beget in him an aversion to all strictness in religion."

Wearied by the endless exhortations and reproofs of the preachers, Charles took the desperate resolution of marching into England, in hope that the many royalists there would enable him to make good his claim to his father's throne. But the quick decision of the general, and the rapid march of the victorious army of the Parliament, daily enlarged by reinforcements in its pursuit of the royal forces, again destroyed the young king's hope; and in the hotly-contested battle of Worcester, on September 3rd, 1651, Cromwell once more overthrew and dispersed his troops. Baxter gives interesting details of these events: "When the soldiers were going against the King and the Scots, I wrote letters to some of them to tell them of their sin; and desired them at least to begin to know themselves. Some of them were startled at these letters, and thought me an uncharitable censurer, who would say that they could kill the godly, even when they were on the march to do it; for how bad soever they spake of the cavaliers (and not without too much desert as to their morals), they confessed that abundance of the Scots were godly men. Afterwards, however, those that I wrote to better understood me. At the same time, the Commonwealth, which so much abhorred persecution, and were for liberty of conscience, made an order that all ministers should keep certain days of humiliation, to fast and pray for their success in Scotland; and that we should keep days of thanksgiving for their victories; and this upon pain of sequestration! So that we all expected to be turned out: but they did not execute upon any, save one, in our parts. For myself, instead of praying and preaching for them, when any of the committee or soldiers were my hearers, I laboured to help them to understand what a crime it was to force men to give God thanks for all their bloodshed, and to make God's ministers and ordinances vile and serviceable to such crimes, by forcing men to run to God on such errands of blood and ruin; and what it is to be such hypocrites to persecute and cast out those that preach the Gospel, while they pretend the advancement of the Gospel, and the liberty of tender consciences, and leave neither tenderness nor honesty in the world.

"My own hearers were all satisfied with my doctrine, but the committeemen looked sour, yet let me alone. The soldiers said I was so like Love, that I would not be right till I was shorter by the head. Yet none of them ever meddled with me, farther than by the tongue; nor was I ever by any of them in those times forbidden or hindered to preach one sermon, except only one assize-sermon which the high-sheriff had desired me to preach, and afterwards sent me word to forbear, as from the committee; which told Mr. Moor, the Independent preacher at the College, Worcester, that they desired me to forbear, and not to preach before the judges, because I preached against the state. But afterwards they excused it, as done merely in kindness to me, to keep me from running myself into danger and trouble.

"The greater part of the [royal] army passed close by Kidderminster, and the rest through it. Colonel Graves sent two or three messages to me, as from the king, to come to him; and after, when he was at Worcester, some others were sent; but I was at that time under so great an affliction of sore eyes, that I was scarcely able to see the light, and unfit to stir out of doors. Being not much doubtful of the issue which followed, I thought if I had been able it would have been no service at all to the king, it being so little, on such a sudden, that I could add to his assistance.

"When the king had stayed a few days at Worcester, Cromwell came with his army to the east side of the city, and after that made a bridge of boats over the Severn, to hinder them from foraging on the other side; but because so great an army could not long endure to be pent up, the king resolved to charge Cromwell's men. At first the Scottish foot charged very gallantly, some chief persons among the horse, the Marquis of Hamilton, late Earl of Limerick, being slain; but at last the hope of security so near their backs encouraged the king's army to retreat into the city, and Cromwell's soldiers followed them so close at the heels, that Major Swallow, of Whalley's regiment, first, and others after him, entered Sidbury Gate with them; and so the whole army fled through the city quite away, many being trodden down and slain in the streets; so that the king was fain to fly with them northward. The Lord Wilmot, the Earl of Lauderdale, and many others of his lords and commanders, fled with him. Kidderminster being but eleven miles from Worcester, the flying army passed some of them through the town, and some by it. I had nearly gone to bed when the noise of the flying horses acquainted us with the overthrow; and a piece of one of Cromwell's troops, that guarded Bewdly Bridge, having tidings of it, came into our streets, and stood in the open market-place, before my door, to surprise those that passed by. So, when many hundreds of the flying army came together, and the thirty troopers cried 'Stand!' and fired at them, they either hastened away or cried quarter, not knowing in the dark what number it was that charged them. Thus as many were taken there as so few men could lay hold on; and, till midnight, the bullets flying towards my door and windows, and the sorrowful fugitives hastening by for their lives, did tell me the calamitousness of war.

"The king, parted at last from most of his lords, went to Boscobel, by the White Ladies, where he was hid in an oak, in a manner sufficiently declared to the world; and thence to Mosely, and so with Mrs. Lane away as a traveller, and escaped all the searchers' hands, till he came safe beyond sea, as is published at large by divers."

These great events were not without effect on the second ministry of Baxter at Kidderminster. His Autobiography, with evidence of truth in every line of the narrative, gives a clear view of the labours, difficulties, and successes in that town, with which his great name is associated, and where his memory is still fragrant. There was the chief work of his life. There he completely performed the vow of his youth, after deliverance from untimely death. There, in the round of labour, in church and parish, conscientiously and fully done, he found time to write sixty of his books. There, worn with sickness, patient in frequent adversities, busy in many controversies, abounding in words and deeds of kindness,—praying, toiling, warning,—he served his Lord. Ignorance yielded to his persuasion, and laboured to learn. Brutal vice at his entreaty tried to walk in the path of virtue. The avaricious, understanding the joy and advantages of charity, opened his hand, and gave to the widow and the poor. The little children, whose well-being no one hitherto had regarded, compelled to work with tender hands where their rugged fathers wrought in iron and coal, found in the pallid clergyman a teacher and friend. He gathered them together for instruction, bought books for them out of his own scanty stipend, and urged them who had leisure to help him teach the little ones to read and to pray. He carefully visited the infirm and the diseased, many of whom suffered from ague, one of the common scourges of the poor man's family at that time, or from the more destructive fever, produced by neglect of public health in the habitual filth of streets and gutters; and he would often go to their huts, smoky, damp, and dark, where their chambers, according to the fashion of the age, were securely closed against every breath of healthful air. The sick murmured their expressions of thankfulness and gladness when he entered their dwellings, and willingly took the medicines he profusely bestowed; listened to his words of instruction and comfort; and the eye of the dying was enlightened by hope, when Baxter spoke to him of the Love which saves, and of the Mercy which prepares a home for the blessed who die in the Lord. While he lamented that "there was scarcely any such thing as Church Government or discipline known in the land, that in all his life he had never lived in the parish where one person was publicly admonished or brought to public penitence, but that the ancient discipline of the Church was unknown," in his own parish he maintained a careful vigilance of morals and conduct; and he was able to effect great reforms by his own purity of life, and by his industrious devotedness to duty, which secured him forbearance from enemies and the confidence and affection of his friends. His example gained them whom his words never reached. His influence was not only that of a clergyman, whose goodness and eloquence all men admitted, but also that of a social reformer, who was indifferent to nothing which could give happiness to the community among whom he lived.

Baxter's work at Kidderminster points him out as the very model of a conscientious, faithful clergyman; successful not so much from his moving appeals, and his affectionate entreaties, as from his complete devotion to his office, his unceasing industry in it, and his absolute reliance upon prayer, which he knew—as the Talmud expresses it—is the good man's only weapon. In what manner holy influences affect the mind, except through well-known appointed means, has not yet been declared. The affinities of the spiritual world, its laws of communication, and of the exquisite sympathy which obtains between its higher agents and the weaknesses and necessities of the lowly and penitent among mankind, have yet to be fully revealed. Little as has been discovered of the forces of the material world, some simple and effective modes of transmitting thought have been brought into hourly practical use; and there may be other methods of such communication which will be gradually made known in the progress of humanity; when to the aggregate of men, Christianity, Revelation, and Church are no more empty sounds, but beneficent realities. It may reasonably be conjectured that this world, which has been the scene of great events, and on which perhaps some of the higher facts of spiritual government are to be both manifested and explained, for the instruction and advantage of other parts of the creation of God, may never be without the effective sympathy of the mightier holy powers who may be appointed to watch over mankind; to receive the expressions of their desire for the gifts of Divine compassion; to defend them from the malignant attempts of all that is hostile to goodness; and to maintain the life of the soul often threatened and often in danger. The office of prayer may be the very means which attracts to the lower, struggling nature the beneficent higher influences, and which moves the sympathies of those sublime beings who are not encumbered by the mortal "vesture of decay," but whose instinct is kindness, and whose endowment is that of capacity to give instant succour to the humble and devout.

Baxter had apprehended some of these possibilities, ever mindful of the principle contained in the well-known maxim, "Act and pray; pray and act; expect all of God": convinced that prayer may be a part of the established order of the universe. The words of Revealed Truth taught the duty and philosophy of prayer, and experience convinced him of its direct advantage. The excessive weakness of his constitution made it his unceasing resort. Gratitude made it his delight. They who knew him best, both at Kidderminster and in the stormy times which followed his labours there, have related, that "when he prayed, his soul took wing for heaven, and wrapt up the souls of others with him."

The influence of Baxter's preaching affected not only the town where he lived, but the county. The blessed Saviour's life, death, and resurrection were the chief topics on which he meditated at home, and which he proclaimed to his parishioners in church. With unerring wisdom he saw at the beginning of his ministry that the Creed, the Lord's Prayer, and the Ten Commandments—"the things to be believed, to be desired, and to be done"—contain in wonderful concentration Divine revelation and the whole duty of man. He lived the faith he taught; and that which was enforced upon others was fully observed by himself. He had that absolute dependence upon God, which is the essence of religion; for he knew that all progress in spiritual life results from conscious communion with Him, and that the highest attainment of our nature is to advance in His wisdom and knowledge. As fresh air destroys the germs of disease, so in the purer atmosphere of that communion low desires perish in the soul.

The truths he believed, Baxter impressed upon his parishioners with all the earnestness of one whose own heart had proved their reality and power. No one was too poor to have his care, none too ignorant to be without repeated efforts at his instruction, none too fearful to be without the comforting words of holy promises, none too hard of heart to weary out the patient labour of gaining him to the life of goodness: for the great preacher's one desire was that his talent might be well employed. Who could resist the entreaties of a pleader so devout, gentle, and earnest? Who could remain insensible to the charm of those appeals, uttered by a voice of remarkable sweetness and compass, whose variety of articulation Baxter had carefully studied, and in the management of which he was a consummate master; as others have been, whose words commanded the applause of senates and guided the councils of kings? Some of them, who were his friends in his Worcestershire parish, and afterwards in London, have left such portraiture of him as words can give; and which renders it easy to see in his tall and attenuated form, not without dignity, in the lineaments of the pale countenance upon which a gentle smile seemed always to rest, and in the wonderful brightness of his large and benignant eye, one made to improve and to lead mankind. He wasted no hour which could add to his knowledge, and increase his capability of attracting and winning the hearts of men. He perfectly anticipated the opinion of some of the ablest ecclesiastics of our own day, that the efficiency of the Church does not depend on multiplying churches and clergymen, but in the energetic spirit in which parishes are worked, sermons preached, and homes visited. He lived with the greatest temperance, that he might have the more to give to the needy and the diseased, to buy useful books for the education of children and for distribution among the poor; for his life as a clergyman was passed in holy meditation, in untiring labour, and in diffusive charity. Dr. Bates, who knew him better than most of them who delighted to call him friend, relates of Baxter that which may account in some measure for his remarkable success in the parish of Kidderminster, where he always acted upon the conviction that preaching is a real power. He says: "In his sermons there was a rare union of arguments and motives to convince the mind and gain the heart; all the fountains of reason and persuasion were open to his discerning eye. There was no resisting the force of his discourses, without denying reason and Divine revelation. He had a marvellous felicity and copiousness in speaking. He that was solicitous for the salvation of others was not negligent of his own; but his first care was to prepare himself for heaven. In him the virtues of the contemplative and active life were eminently united. His time was spent in communion with God, and in charity to men; he lived above the sensible world, and in solitude and silence conversed with God. His life was a practical sermon, a drawing example; there was an air of humility and sanctity in his mortified countenance; his deportment was becoming a stranger upon earth and a citizen of heaven. In him there was a rare union of sublime knowledge with the lowest opinion of himself. He wrote to one, who sent him a letter full of expressions of honour and esteem, 'You admire one you do not know; knowledge will cure your error. The more we know God, the more we see reason to admire Him; but our knowledge of man discovers his imperfections, and lessens our esteem.' He desired some clergymen, his chosen friends, to meet at his house, and to pray with him for his direction in a matter of moment; before the duty was begun, he said, 'I have desired your assistance at this time, because I believe God will sooner hear your prayers than mine.' He imitated Augustine both in his penitential confessions and retractions. In conjunction with humility, he had great candour for others. He was severe to himself, but candid in excusing the faults of others; whereas the busy inquirer and censurer of the faults of others is usually the easy neglecter of his own. I never knew any person less indulgent to himself, and more indifferent to his temporal interest. The offer of a bishopric was no temptation to him; for his exalted soul despised the pleasures and profits which others so earnestly desire; he valued not an empty title upon his tomb. Love to the souls of men was the peculiar character of his spirit. In this he imitated and honoured our Saviour, who prayed, died, and lives for the salvation of souls. All his natural and supernatural endowments were subservient to this blessed end. It was Baxter's meat and drink, the life and joy of his life, to do good to souls. His industry was almost incredible in his studies. He had a sensitive nature, as desirous of ease as others; yet such was the continual application of himself to his great work, as if the labour of one day had supplied strength for another, and the willingness of the spirit had supported the weakness of the flesh."

It cannot be questioned that such a clergyman was a living force in his parish, which made itself felt in every home of it. Men admired if they did not altogether understand him. The rude nailers and weavers, attracted by his energy, the eloquence both of face and of tongue, wept as he told them of their sins, felt their disease, and learned the remedy. The poor cottagers, hitherto beasts of burden or slaves of toil, so oppressed and destitute, with dreary prospects and hopeless minds, found that for the first time in their lives they had a constant friend to sympathise with them in their sorrows, and in some degree to lessen their terrible poverty. They delighted to hear him; they opened their hearts to him as to a brother; they obeyed his injunctions; they abandoned their vices. Hope smiled upon their wretchedness; and among the privations and afflictions in the lives of the English labourers at that time, the filth and misery of their dwellings, the insufficiency and unhealthiness of their food, their patience in want, their uncomplaining endurance of a hard and unchangeable state, their great kindness to each other,—qualities which, in our own day, make the conduct of the British poor the admiration of economists and philosophers,—in circumstances of penury and woe they learned the healthful truths of their Saviour's compassion; bore the indigence and wretchedness of their earthly life, in hope of gaining the bliss of heaven,—that imperishable personal existence for which our nature craves.

Such a clergyman was in every sense a reformer of his age; animated by the assurance that, when the glorious light shall end all controversies, the effects of devout and industrious labour in the Church will be permanent as goodness, and various as its pleasures. In the first part of his Autobiography, Baxter relates some of the events of his ministry, and of the causes of his success in his parish. The readers will be well repaid by a perusal of his dispassionate review of the work he had accomplished, made, without passion or prejudice, in the languors of an existence which was continued from year to year by little less than a miracle. He says: "I shall next record to the praise of my Redeemer the comfortable employment and success which He vouchsafed me during my abode at Kidderminster, under all my weaknesses. Before the wars, I preached twice each Lord's Day; but after the war, but once, and once every Thursday, besides occasional sermons. Every Thursday evening, my neighbours who were most desirous, and had opportunity, met at my house, and there one of them repeated the sermon; afterwards, they proposed whatever doubts any of them had about the sermon, or any other case of conscience; and I resolved their doubts. Last of all, I caused sometimes one and sometimes another of them to pray, to exercise them, and sometimes I prayed with them myself; which, beside singing a psalm, was all they did. Once a week also, some of the younger sort, who were not fit to pray in so great an assembly, met among a few more privately, where they spent three hours in prayer together. Every Saturday night, they met at some of their houses to repeat the sermon of the former Lord's Day, and to pray and prepare themselves for the following day. Once in a few weeks, we had a day of humiliation, on one occasion or other. Every religious woman that was safely delivered, instead of the old feastings and gossipings, if she was able, did keep a day of thanksgiving with some of her neighbours, with them praising God, singing psalms, and soberly feasting together. Two days every week, my assistant and myself took fourteen families between us for private catechising and conference; he going through the parish, and the town coming to me. I first heard them recite the words of the catechism, and then examined them about the sense; and lastly urged them with all possible engaging reason and vehemency to answerable affection and practice. I spent about an hour with each family, and admitted no others to be present; lest bashfulness should make it burdensome, or any should talk of the weaknesses of others.

"Besides all this, I was forced, five or six years, by the people's necessity to practise physic. A common pleurisy happening one year, and no physician being near, I was forced to advise them to save their lives; and I could not afterwards avoid the importunity of the town and country round about. Because I never once took a penny of any one, I was crowded with patients; so that almost twenty would be at my door at once; and though God, by more success than I expected, so long encouraged me, yet, at last, I could endure it no longer; partly because it hindered my other studies, and partly because the very fear of miscuring and doing any one harm did make it an intolerable burden to me. So that, after some years' practice, I procured a godly, diligent physician to come and live in the town, and bound myself by promise to practise no more, unless in consultation with him, in case of any seeming necessity; and so with that answer I turned them all off, and never meddled with it again.

"But all these my labours (except my private conference with the families), even preaching and preparing for it, were but my recreation, and, as it were, the work of my spare hours; for my writings were my chief daily labour; which yet went the more slowly on, that I never one hour had an amanuensis to dictate to, and especially because my weakness took up so much of my time. All the pains that my infirmity ever brought upon me were never half so grievous an affliction as the unavoidable loss of time which they occasioned. I could not bear, through the weakness of my stomach, to rise before seven o'clock in the morning, and afterwards not till much later; and some infirmities I laboured under made it above an hour before I could be dressed. An hour I must of necessity have to walk before dinner, and another before supper; and after supper I could seldom study. All of which, besides times of family duties, and prayer, and eating, etc., left me but little time to study, which hath been the greatest external personal affliction of all my life.

"Every first Wednesday in the month was our monthly meeting for parish discipline; and every first Thursday of the month was the ministers' meeting for discipline and disputation. In those disputations it fell to my lot to be almost constant moderator; and for every such day, I usually prepared a written determination; all which I mention as my mercies and delights, and not as my burdens. Every Thursday besides, I had the company of divers godly ministers at my house after the lecture, with whom I spent that afternoon in the truest recreation, till my neighbours came to meet for their exercise of repetition and prayer.

"For ever blessed be the God of my mercies, who brought me from the grave, and gave me after wars and sickness fourteen years' liberty in such sweet employment! How strange that in times of usurpation, I had all this mercy and happy freedom; when under our rightful King and Governor, I, and many hundreds more, are silenced and laid by as broken vessels. I have mentioned my secret and acceptable employment; let me, to the praise of my gracious Lord, acquaint you with some of my success—for it is the sacrifice of thanksgiving which I owe to my most gracious God.

"My public preaching met with an attentive, diligent auditory. Having broke over the brunt of the opposition of the rabble before the wars, I found them afterwards tractable and unprejudiced. The congregation was usually full, so that we were fain to build five galleries after my coming thither; the church being very capacious, and the most commodious and convenient that ever I was in. Our private meetings also were full. On the Lord's Days there was no disorder to be seen in the streets; but you might hear a hundred families singing psalms and repeating sermons as you passed through them. In a word, when I came thither first, there was about one family in a street that worshipped God; and when I came away, there were some streets where there was not one poor family in the side that did not so; and that did not, by professing serious godliness, give us hopes of their sincerity. And in those families which were the worst, being inns and alehouses, usually some persons in each house did seem to be religious.

"Though our administration of the Lord's Supper was so

ordered as displeased many, and the far greater part kept away, we had six hundred that were communicants; of whom there were not twelve that I had not good hopes of as to their sincerity; those few who consented to our communion, and yet lived scandalously, were excommunicated afterwards. I hope there were also many who had the fear of God that came not to our communion in the sacrament, some of them being kept off by husbands, by parents, by masters, and some dissuaded by men that differed from us. When I set upon personal conference with each family, and catechising them, there were very few families in all the town that refused to come; and those few were beggars at the town's ends, who were so ignorant that they were ashamed it should be manifest. God was pleased also to give me abundant encouragement in the lectures I preached about in other places, as at Worcester, Cleobury, etc., but especially at Dudley and Shiffnal. At the former of which, being the first place that I ever preached in, the poor nailers, and other labourers, would not only crowd the church as full as ever I saw any in London, but also hang upon the windows and the leads without.

"Having related my comfortable success in this place, I shall next tell you by what and how many advantages this was effected, under that grace which worketh by means, though with a free diversity. One advantage was, that I came to a people who never had any awakening ministry before, but a few formal cold sermons from the curate; for if they had been hardened under a powerful ministry, and been sermon-proof, I should have expected less. I was then also in the vigour of my spirits, and had naturally a familiar moving voice (which is a great matter with the common hearers), and doing all in bodily weakness as a dying man, my soul was the more easily brought to seriousness, and to preach as a dying man to dying men. For drowsy formality and customariness doth but stupefy the hearers and rock them asleep. It must be serious preaching which will make men serious in hearing and obeying it. Another advantage was, that most of the bitter enemies of godliness in the town, who rose in tumults against me before, in their hatred of Puritans, had gone out into the wars, into the king's armies, and were quickly killed, and few of them ever returned again. Another advantage which I found was the acceptation of my person among the people. Though to win estimation and love to ourselves only be an end that none but proud men and hypocrites intend, yet it is certain that the gratefulness of the person doth ingratiate the message, and greatly prepareth the people to receive the truth. Another advantage which I had was the zeal and diligence of the godly people of the place. They thirsted after the salvation of their neighbours, and were in private my assistants; and, being dispersed through the town, were ready in almost all companies to repress seducing words, and to justify godliness, convince, reprove, and exhort men according to their needs; as also to teach them how to pray, and to help them to sanctify the Lord's Day. For those people who had none in their families who could pray, or repeat the sermons, went to their next neighbour's house who could do it, and joined with them; so that some of the houses of the ablest men in each street were filled with them that could do nothing, or little, in their own. Their holy, humble, blameless lives were also a great advantage to me. Our unity and concord were a great advantage to us, and our freedom from those sects and heresies with which many other places were infected. We had no private church, and though we had private meetings, we had not pastor against pastor, or church against church, or sect against sect, or Christian against Christian.

"Our private meetings were a marvellous help to the propagation of godliness, for thereby truths that slipped away were recalled, and the seriousness of people's minds renewed, and good desires cherished. Their knowledge also was much increased by them, and the younger sort learned to pray by frequently hearing others. I had also the opportunity of knowing their case; for, if any were touched and awakened in public, I should frequently see them drop into our private meetings. Idle meetings and loss of time were greatly prevented; and so far were we from being by this in danger of schism or divisions, that it was the principal means to prevent them; for here I was usually present with them, answering their doubts, silencing objections, and moderating them in all.

"Another advantage was the great honesty and diligence of my assistants, and the presence and countenance of honest justices of peace, who ordinarily were godly men, and always such as would be thought so, and were ready to use their authority to suppress sin and promote goodness. Another help to my success was the small relief which my low estate enabled me to afford the poor; though the place was reckoned at near two hundred pounds per annum, there came but ninety pounds, and sometimes only eighty pounds, to me. Beside which, some years I had sixty or eighty pounds a year of the booksellers for my books; which little dispersed among them much reconciled them to the doctrine that I taught. I took the aptest of their children from the school, and sent divers of them to the universities; where, for eight pounds a year, or ten at most, by the help of my friends I maintained them. Some of these are honest, able ministers, now cast out with their brethren; but two or three, having no other way to live, turned great conformists, and are preachers now. In giving the little that I had, I did not inquire whether they were good or bad, if they asked relief; for the bad had souls and bodies that needed charity most. And this truth I will speak to the encouragement of the charitable, that what little money I have now by me, I got it all, I scarce know how, at that time when I gave most; and since I have had less opportunity of giving, I have had less increase.

"Another furtherance of my work was the books which I wrote, and gave away among them. Of some small books I gave each family one, which came to about eight hundred; and of the bigger I gave fewer; and every family that was poor, and had not a Bible, I gave a Bible. I had found myself the benefit of reading to be so great, that I could not but think that it would be profitable to others. It was a great advantage to me that my neighbours were of such a trade as allowed them time enough to read or talk of holy things. For the town liveth upon the weaving of Kidderminster stuffs; and, as they stand in their looms, the men can set a book before them, or edify one another; whereas ploughmen and many others are so wearied, or continually employed either in the labours or the cares of their callings, that it is a great impediment to their salvation. Freeholders and tradesmen are the strength of religion and civility in the land; and gentlemen, and beggars, and servile tenants are the strength of iniquity. Though among these sorts there are some that are good and just, as among the other there are many bad. And their constant converse and traffic with London doth much promote civility and piety among tradesmen.

"I found also my *single life* afforded me much advantage; for I could the easier take my people for my children, and think all that I had too little for them, in that I had no children of my own to tempt me to another way of using it. Being discharged from most of family cares, and keeping but one servant, I had the greater vacancy and liberty for the labours of my calling. God made use of my practice of physic among them also as a very great advantage to my ministry; for they that cared not for their souls did love their lives and care for their bodies; and by this they were made almost as observant as a tenant is of his landlord. Sometimes I could see before me in the church a very considerable part of the congregation, whose lives God had made me a means to save, or to recover their health; and doing it for nothing so obliged them that they would readily hear me. It was a great advantage to me, that there were at last few that were bad, but some of their own relations were converted; many children did God work upon, at fourteen, fifteen, or sixteen years of age; and this did marvellously reconcile the minds of the parents and elder sort to godliness. They that would not hear me would hear their own children. They that before could have talked against godliness would not hear it spoken against when it was their children's case. Many who would not be brought to it themselves were proud that they had understanding, religious children; and we had some old persons of eighty years of age, who I hope are in heaven, and the conversion of their own children was the chief means to overcome their prejudice, and old customs, and conceits.

"Another great help to my success at last was the formerly described work of personal conference with every family apart, with catechising and instructing them. That which was spoken to them personally, and which put them sometimes upon answers, awakened their attention, and was easier applied than public preaching, and seemed to do much more upon them. The exercise of Church-discipline was no small furtherance of the people's good; for I found plainly that without it I could not have kept the religious sort from separation and division. Another advantage which I found to my success was by ordering my doctrine to them in a suitableness to the main end, and yet so as might suit their dispositions and diseases. The things which I opened to them, and with greatest importunity laboured to imprint upon their minds, were the great fundamental principles of Christianity contained in their baptismal covenant, even a right knowledge and belief of, and submission and love to, God the Father, the Son, and the Holy Ghost, love to all men, and concord with the Church and with one another. I did so inculcate the knowledge of God, our Creator, Redeemer, and Sanctifier, love and obedience to God, unity with the Church catholic, and love to men, and the hope of life eternal, that these were the matter of their daily cogitations and discourses, and indeed of their religion. Yet did I usually put something in my sermon which was above their own discovery, and which they had not known before; and this I did that they might be kept humble, and still perceive their ignorance, and be willing to keep in a learning state. For when preachers tell their people of no more than they know, and do not show that they excel them in knowledge, and scarcely overtop them in abilities, the people will be tempted to turn preachers themselves, and think that they have learned all that the ministers can teach them, and are as wise as they. The bare authority of the clergy will not serve the turn without overtopping ministerial abilities. I gave the opening of the true and profitable method of the Creed, or doctrine of faith; the Lord's Prayer, or matter of our desires; and the Ten Commandments, or the law of practice.

"Another thing that helped me was not meddling with tithes or worldly business; whereby I had my whole time, except what sickness deprived me of, for my duty, and my mind more free from entanglements than else it would have been; and also I escaped the offending of the people, and contending by any law-suits with them. Three or four of my neighbours managed all those kinds of businesses, of whom I never took account; and if any one refused to pay his tithes, if he was poor, I ordered them to forgive it him. In my own family I had the help of my father and step-mother, and the benefit of a godly, understanding, faithful servant, an ancient woman, near sixty years old, who eased me of all care, and laid out all my money for housekeeping: so that I never had one hour's trouble about it, nor ever took one day's account of her for fourteen years together, as being certain of her fidelity, providence, and skill.

"Finally, it much furthered my success that I stayed still in this one place, near two years before the wars, and above fourteen years after; for he that removeth oft from place to place may sow good seed in many places, but is not likely to see much fruit in any, unless some other skilful hand shall follow him to water it. It was a great advantage to me to have almost all the religious people of the place of my own instructing and informing; and that they were not formed into erroneous and factious principles before; and that I stayed to see them grow up to some confirmedness and maturity. So much of the way and helps of those successes, which I mention because many have inquired after them, as willing with their own flocks to take that course which other men have by experience found to be effectual."

CHAPTER X.

1646—1658.

AT Kidderminster Baxter found, during his ministry there, that, as Milton says: "Then was the time in special, to write and speak what might help to the further discussing of matters in agitation. The temple of Janus, with his controversial faces, might not insignificantly be regarded as set open. All the winds of doctrine were let loose to play upon the earth; but Truth was prepared to grapple with falsehood, and sustained no injury in a free and open encounter." In his parish Baxter mostly confined himself to the study and enforcement of practical religion. Books nourished him, and they were his consoling friends, as Le Maistre found them to be; and he loved, with John Milton, "to contemplate the bright countenance of Truth in the quiet and still air of delightful studies."

He had devoted his whole existence to the work of doing good. It was the chosen employment of his life to gain men to repentance and faith, to amendment of conduct, and to the service of the Saviour. It was his delight so to study the Scripture as to find passages of it capable of simple explanation, and of appeal, which would fasten readily upon the hearer's mind, and would occupy his daily thoughts, until he was entirely possessed by the fact of the immediate necessity and wisdom of guiding himself by it. Of all the large number of admirable preachers, who for hundreds of years have influenced the religious life of the English people, Baxter unquestionably has the pre-eminence.

No one has so convincingly reasoned in the pulpit as he, so powerfully urged, or so effectively taught, and moved the conscience to right decision; and in his success, that which has recently been stated is found to be eminently true, that nothing can withstand the force of the man who, upon the most awful of all subjects, is absolutely sure of what he says, and is resolved that others shall be so too; and that in our own day, as in his, "the preacher is the master of the situation." In this respect his great knowledge of the Word of God gave him signal advantage.

In our own time the clergyman addresses a congregation who admit more or less the chief truths of Christianity, and many of whom would think it little less than profanity to express doubt as to the reasonableness and validity of any one of them; but Baxter for the most part had to teach labouring people, very ignorant and pitiably poor, who heard Christian words without having been led to understand the truths contained in them. Their lives were vicious, and their hearts were sad. The mass of literature now published, and of which most of the houses of the working men have some portion, then had no existence. Readers were few, and books still fewer. Everything at that time, contributory to popular instruction and improvement, depended upon the life and efficiency of the public teaching in the Church. Baxter thoroughly understood there is no power like eloquence. He had copious knowledge, vivid and restrained imagination, the ability of strikingly expressing thought, and a voice which he had carefully trained to variety of modulation; but he was singularly free from the methods to which in modern times declaimers have often resorted to gain popular assent. He descended to no familiar jocularity. He was not happy in seeing his congregation alternately the disciples of Democritus and Heraclitus, weeping on one occasion and laughing on another. He sought not to ingratiate himself with the weak and frivolous by using tender tones and emphatic whispers, nor were his discourses replete with epithets in which the manner overbore the matter of the argument. He was too honest in heart, and too earnest in purpose, to trifle with the great duties committed to him; but all his effort was to give men such knowledge of themselves as would induce them, in obedience to the precepts of their Redeemer, to seek freedom from evil of mind, from wilful estrangement to goodness, and to learn the method of attaining future happiness.

Two of his books, written during the period of his ministry at Kidderminster, the "Treatise on Conversion," and "A Call to the Unconverted," contained the substance of sermons which he had preached in the church; for the latter is addressed "to all unsanctified persons who shall read the book, especially his hearers in the parish of Kidderminster." These volumes may give some idea of the substance of his preaching, but without the charm of the personal presence and the stirring voice of the speaker. He says that the "Treatise on Conversion," dedicated to the inhabitants of the borough and foreign of Kidderminster, "was the substance of some plain sermons on conversion, which Mr. Baldwin, who lived in my house, and learned the short-hand character in which I wrote my pulpit-notes, had transcribed. Though I had no leisure, for this or other writings, to take much care of the style, or to add any ornaments or citations of authors, I thought it might better pass as it was than not at all; and that if the author missed the applause of the learned, the book might yet be profitable to the ignorant, as it proved, through the great mercy of God." A few sentences from his address to his parishioners will represent the benevolence and fervour of the preacher: "As it was the unfeigned love of your souls, that hath hitherto moved me much to print what I have done, that you might have the help of those truths which God hath acquainted me with, when I am dead and gone, so it is the same affection that hath persuaded me to send you this familiar discourse. It is the same that you heard preached; and the reasons that moved me to preach it do move me now to publish it, that if any of you have forgot it, it may be brought to your remembrance; or if it worked upon you in the hearing, yet in the deliberate perusal it may work. I bless the Lord that there are so many among you that know by experience the nature of conversion, which is the cause of my abundant affection towards you above any other people that I know. But I see that there is no place or people upon earth that will answer our desires, or free us from those trials that constantly attend our earthly state. I have showed you the certain misery of an unconverted condition; I have earnestly besought and begged of you to turn; and if I had tears at command, I should have mixed all these exhortations with my tears; and if I had but time and strength (as I have not), should have made bold to have come once more among you, and sit with you in your houses, and entreated you on behalf of your souls, even twenty times for one that I have entreated you.

"The commonness and the greatness of men's necessity commanded me to do anything that I could for their relief, and to bring forth some water to cast upon this fire, though I had not at hand a silver vessel to carry it in, nor thought it the most fit. The plainest words are the most profitable oratory in the weightiest matters. Fineness is for ornament, and delicacy for delight; but they answer not necessity, though sometimes they may modestly attend what answers it. Yea, it is hard for the necessitous hearer or reader to observe the matter of ornament and delicacy, and not to be carried from the matter of necessity; and to hear or read a neat, concise, sententious discourse, and not to be hurt by it; for it usually hindereth the due operation of the matter, keeps it from the heart, stops it in the fancy, and makes it seem as light as the style. We use not to stand upon compliment when we run to quench a common fire, nor to call men out of it by an eloquent speech. If we see a man fall into the fire or water, we stand not upon mannerliness in plucking him out, but lay hands upon him as we can without delay."

Towards the end of 1657, Baxter published his "Call to

the Unconverted," one of the most successful of all his books, and to which thousands of religious persons have owed their first serious repentant thoughts. His friend Archbishop Ussher had suggested both this and the former work, and never was advice more seasonable and profitable. Baxter alludes to the fact: "In the short acquaintance I had with that reverend, learned servant of Christ, Bishop Ussher, he was oft, from first to last, importuning me to write a Directory for the several ranks of professed Christians, which might distinctly give each one their portion; beginning with the unconverted, and then proceeding to the babes in Christ, and then to the strong; and mixing some special helps against the several sins they are addicted to. By the suddenness of his motion at our first congress, I perceived it was in his mind before; and I told him both that it was abundantly done by many already, and that his unacquaintedness with my weakness might make him think me fitter for it than I was. But this did not satisfy him; he still made it his request. I confess I was not moved by his reasons, nor did I apprehend any great need of doing any more than is done in that way, nor that I was likely to do more. And, therefore, I parted with him without the least purpose to answer his desire. But since his death, his words often came into my mind; and the great reverence which I bore to him did the more incline me to think with some complacency of his motion. Having of late years intended to write 'A Family Directory,' I began to think how congruously the fore-mentioned work should lead the way, and the several conditions of men's souls be spoken of, before we come to the several relations."

It may be justly questioned if any other modern book has had so happy an effect as this has had in stirring and enlightening the minds of those persons whose occupations and means allowed them but scanty time for reading, and who had to rely for religious instruction and admonition, either on the unassisted perusal of the Bible, or on the public teaching provided by the Church. "The immortal mind craves objects that endure," and the instincts of his humbler contemporaries assured them that this volume would be of lasting advantage to themselves and to posterity. None of the popular works, which are intended to awaken the sluggish mind to a consideration of the reasonableness, advantage, and importance of religion, can be placed in comparison with Richard Baxter's "Call to the Unconverted." Many writers have attempted to imitate it, as painters of the ruder hand have ventured to imitate Titian, Raffaelle, Rembrandt, and our own Reynolds and Turner; but the educated and experienced eye discovers at once where the master's touch is wanting, and where only the copyist excels. The sale of this book was immediately large, and editions followed one another in rapid succession. Baxter had the joy of beholding a quickly-grown and abundant harvest of his toil. Men wept over it, and thanked God they possessed it, not only in every district of Britain, but throughout Europe, and among nations whose untutored minds had learned only what natural observation and reflection might teach them of the Creator and Governor of all things. Baxter in his Autobiography remarks of this volume: "God blessed it with unexpected success, beyond all I have written, except the 'Saint's Rest.' In a little more than a year there were about twenty thousand of them printed by my own consent, and about ten thousand since, besides many thousands by stolen impression, which poor men stole for lucre' sake. Through God's mercy I have had information of almost whole households converted by this small book, which I set so light by; and as if all this in England, Scotland, and Ireland were not mercy enough to me, God, since I was silenced, hath sent it over as His message to many beyond the seas. For when Mr. Elliot had printed all the Bible in the Indians' language, he next translated this my 'Call to the Unconverted,' as he wrote to us here; and though it has been thought prudent to begin with the 'Practice of Piety,' because of the envy and distaste of the times against me, he had finished it before the advice came to him. Yet God would make some further use of it, for Mr. Stoop, the pastor of the French Church in London, being driven hence by the displeasure of superiors, was pleased to translate it into elegant French, and print it in a very curious letter; and I hope it will not be unprofitable there, nor in Germany, where it is printed in Dutch."

Many who have carefully read the "Call to the Unconverted," observing how in it the unwilling mind is approached on all sides, and how many methods of obtaining his end have been adopted, lest the author might fail in one or more of them, will call to mind the opinion expressed by Dr. Isaac Barrow, Professor of Mathematics in the University of Cambridge, and tutor of Sir Isaac Newton—that Baxter's practical writings were never mended, and his controversial ones seldom refuted.

Baxter well understood that if men were to be gained to the life of practical religion, it could be only as they were convinced of its essential truth, and of its importance to themselves; and that it were not enough to enrol them, so many times every year, among the number of the communicants, unless they lived under the hallowing influence of the Christian faith; and that they would not obtain the ultimate advantages of it, unless each one was in spiritual union with his Saviour. It was of the highest moment, therefore, to give his parishioners instruction in the great principles of Christianity, especially in reference to the central truth that Christ is the Life and Light of men, from Whom every spiritual benefit is received. Knowledge must precede action, and with St. Augustine he would urge that the Lord must be loved to be known. Let them first love the Saviour, and all else of right principle and of holy living would necessarily follow. That the Redeemer should intervene in this world in the higher matters of man's spiritual life, is not evident at first sight; and yet this is the truth of which, most of all, the conscience must be convinced, and by which the repentant and amended life is to be guided.

Baxter demanded that each one should examine the doctrine of Christ upon its own evidence. He held, with his contemporary John Locke, that no one is made better merely by having rules laid down for his conduct; but he maintained, that a practically religious life can proceed only from union between the several constituents of the Church and their Lord, their Head and King; and that this unity does not consist merely in their possessing exact and large knowledge of His truth, and a form of faith in harmony with it, but in having within themselves as a vital force that spiritual influence which produces all the fruits and acts of goodness. Religion is not in word but in deed, not merely in functional observance, but in willing submission to the government of Christ, in resignation to His guidance, and in constant dependence upon His merciful mediation. So he taught his flock, that revealed truth carries convictive evidence to the conscience, just because, when willingly received, each one becomes capable of judging of it, and of seeing the loss and unreasonableness of a self-indulgent and useless life. So he argued with them, that the lamentable state of the world generally is that men who, in their conscience, know Divine revelation to be true, and of the utmost importance to them, refuse even to think of it; take no care to avoid that which foreseeing goodness has forbidden to be done; but are contented to live all their time without inquiring if their state is safe; and allow day after day to pass by, as though all things were well, and as if the grand realities and responsibilities of human existence were but the imaginations of a dream. He taught them that he who is not religious is necessarily miserable; because his mind is the place of conflict, in which the better principle is always overcome, and the inclination and unrestrained passions of his nature successfully resist the power of his conscience. So that his unhappiness consists in the fact that, while the voice of his soul tells him what is right to be done, he has no moral strength to enable him to do it; and that happiness can be secured to him only when the light of conscience and the inclination of the mind are in agreement.

Baxter understood the fact of the threefold life of man: since defined as that which is outward, which the world sees; as that which is social, which his family observe; and as that which is inner and spiritual, known only to the Searcher of hearts. The true happiness of man in his mortal state is, when he sees the right way and walks in it; knows that his Lord should be loved and served, and therefore loves and serves Him; knows that His Spirit is the only safe guide, and follows His guidance; knows that conscience should rule, and obeys it. Baxter's Church ministry was really a constantly forcible appeal to conscience. The plainest language is generally the most direct, and this he used. Advice is always best taken when the evident motive of it is kindness, and affection and tenderness marked all he said. Success is generally the result of prudent and honest endeavour: sincerity illumined all his public conduct. Industrious use of power in wise hands has generally a happy productiveness; so he laboured incessantly, that he might win their hearts and reform their lives. "To live, and act, and serve the future hour," he made it the chief aim of his ministry at Kidderminster to awaken the moral sense among his flock, and thus to gain the verdict of their conscience; so that they might know their happiness would be assured, when there was an agreement between their knowledge of what was right to be done and their inclination in doing it. He urged upon them those awful facts of the religious life, that when a man prays he attracts to himself the regard, the sympathy, and the help of the beneficent powers of goodness; but that when he closes the ear of his heart to the secret voice which speaks to him of the better way, and prompts him to walk in it, then does the Holy Influence withdraw from him, grieved and quenched; and the benignant agencies of the spiritual world, who "come to succour us that succour want," as if pained that the unhappy one refuses to co-operate with them in their endeavour to rescue him from ruin, leave him with regret. As when a virtuous family mourn over a brother, whom suffering will not compel, and whom affection cannot induce, to abandon a vicious habit which is impoverishing and destroying him.

Baxter often thought of the first time of the Church after the Ascension of its Lord, when thousands were gained in a day by the appeals of the Apostles, the electric word passing from heart to heart, melting away ancient prejudice, overcoming stubborn resistance to conviction and submission, and producing new views of truth and of duty to the enlightened mind. To him all that Pentecostal triumph of his Lord was vividly present. He saw the impassioned penitent, a waverer no more, speaking in the name of Him he had lately betrayed; declaring His dignity and glory, and as His ambassador commanding men to repent of their individual and national sin, and to yield to their King and Saviour. He thought often of the gathering thousands, who came to hear, and went to their homes to repent and to believe; of the awful gifts at the great festival, when the Twelve assembled the converts to pray for the blessing promised by their Saviour; of the alarm and agitation among the priests; of the young and vigorous life of the Church going forth in obedience to the word of the Lord, to teach all nations of His goodness and redemptive mercy.

How emulous was Baxter of that great success! how would he gladly gain his thousands, as Apostles and martyrs had gained theirs! how he daily prayed that he might be permitted to sweep away the shrines of the heart's idolatry, and to induce men to believe in, and serve, and delight in their Saviour! How he wept in his chamber at home, when he reflected that so many souls had been committed to his cure, and of a few only could he hope that they had yielded their hearts to Him Who loved them, and had given Himself for them. One by one they passed before the eye of his mind; some he would especially remember, whom he had visited in sickness, but who had no newness of life; others whom he had counselled in trouble, and had helped by timely gifts, but whose hearts offered no tribute of thankfulness to the Giver of all good. In his days of suffering the thoughts of such as these would add pain to his affliction. In the long nights of winter, when his rest was dispelled by the anguish which his occult disease produced in his attenuated body, he would pray for the older persons in his parish, who had hitherto made no signs of religion, whose autumn-days were becoming shorter and darker, and their sere and yellow leaf fluttering to its fall. On other occasions, when sleep, "Dear mother of fresh thoughts and joyous health," refused him her gifts, he would think tenderly of the children, towards whom his heart yearned; planning how he might apply some part of his stipend to buy them books, or that he might write that which would usefully help them through dangers and difficulties.

Baxter had "an infinite capacity for taking trouble," which has been said to be another name for genius itself. He knew that truth which, long afterwards, Goethe expressed, that man is properly the only object that interests man. All his soul was intent upon his work; and toil and reproach and shame were not worthy of consideration, if he might but be found faithful, and his labour accepted.

Few men have better understood the awful responsibility of the clergyman's office,—that in his appeals to the human conscience he is always under the eye of God, to Whom the motive, the aim, and the progress of the work are perfectly known; and the fact that he serves Christ animates him, when conscious of failure from personal infirmity, Who discerns every condition of the labour. It is enough if He approve. The condemnation of men cannot affect the judgment of God. In His Church there is no waste of strength and toil, no forgetfulness of the good intention. Even the wish to be more successful in duty is accepted. Nothing is lost by them who work in the wilderness: the very fragments are gathered up for good uses. Joy is set before him who, in that service, bears his burden, and despises the shame. The everlasting remembrance is the gift of Divine love to him who has done what he could. It is simply equitable that the clergyman should have respect to the recompense of reward, and that he is to work in hope of eternal life.

What can fatally discourage him who, in faith in the living Saviour, strong in the spirit of prayer, in no darkness of seclusion or mystery of office, has no other object of his existence but to convince men of the wasteful folly of the life which is not devoted to God, and thus to recover them to the nobler purposes of it? He who can speak to another, in his weariness or distress, a strengthening or comforting word, simple in itself as the cup of cold water given by the Arab in his tent to the thirsty traveller, has a special reward, by the provision of the Divine government, that good ever produces good. The martyr dies, but the truth is propagated. The enemies rage, and threaten its destruction; but time reaps them, and the Church endures. The minister of that Church, with such ability as has been given him, toiling in his allotted field, that God in all things may be glorified through Jesus Christ, must necessarily accept in resignation the painful conditions of his service; comforted when successful, trustful when troubled, praying when he fears—"Through love, through hope, and faith's transcendent dower,"—until darkness fall, and it is night.

The clergyman who is so faithful to his trust as thoroughly to ascertain the kind and degree of spiritual life among his parishioners—and which can be learned only by frequent contact and association with them, and by that confidential intercommunication which his office permits and secures—knows that the best things when corrupted become the worst, and that there is an external and an internal Christianity; and his utmost skill and care are necessary to give such wise and timely counsel, that reliance may not be placed upon the one to the certain loss of the benefits resulting from the other. As the first condition of the Christian life, there must be a living union between each component of the Church and the Lord. The tendency of human nature is to rely upon that which is external, and which sets religion upon an easy condition. Few things are more readily done than those which are simply perfunctory; and there are few which are more directly injurious to the healthful growth of the spiritual life, if reliance for acceptance with God be placed upon these only. The temptation is to exaggerate the importance of one part of Christian duty, to the lessening or abandonment of the other. Many things are necessary in spiritual education, which are only temporary or subsidiary; just as a scaffold, which is of great use while a house is being built, would be a disfigurement and an injury if it were retained when the structure had been completed. So the difficulty for the clergyman is, to bring his parishioners to understand the difference between that in religion which is non-essential, and that which is necessary to its very existence, maintenance, and acceptance; between those duties which have merely a relation to Church-order, and those which pertain to the very continuance of the Christian life itself. The imminent danger is, that some of them should be contented with only mechanically following the appointed course of public observance, delighting to be where prayer is accustomed to be said, and where the memorials of Gethsemane and of Calvary are celebrated with joyful thanksgiving; but who are practically ignorant of the fact, that under holy influences the heart is to become the real temple of sacred service, that the Christian is to be the priest of his own spiritual sacrifice and dedication. That which the Church is, in its entirety of praise, confession, and eucharist, each component is to become in the temple of the consecrated soul. There each Christian must find his present heaven, where he exercises a just authority over himself, and where obedience to the Saviour is the only true freedom.

All the practical works of Baxter declare, that one chief object of his ministrations was to be successful in persuading his parishioners to yield themselves to God. He regarded the state of mankind as that of rebellion, and that recovery would follow upon submission, and thus pardon would be secured. His early education in the doctrines of the English Church, his diligent reading of the better writers in scholastic divinity, his long and careful study of Richard Hooker's "Ecclesiastical Polity," kept him closely to what may be termed constitutional doctrines both in Church and in State. A sincere Royalist, he had learned by bitter experience how oppressive is the tyranny which democracy can establish. An able theologian, he had turned with disgust from the endless disputes and the grievous animosities of contending religionists, who had removed the ancient landmarks of doctrinal definition, and had found no rest i wrangling in endless subdivisions over their own confused and contradictory propositions. But there is always consonance in truth; and that which the earlier Fathers had learned from the Apostles, and which Augustine, the Hilaries, Prosper, our own Anselm and Bradwardine, and other renowned teachers of Christian doctrines maintained, Baxter believed. He well knew that listeners require reason and sense; and he therefore gave his parishioners only new views of those doctrines which have for their authority all the argument which antiquity can give, what the best men everywhere and always have held, and which are derived from Revelation itself.

Thus he taught that repentance is no expiation, but that the violation of the law of life made a Mediator necessary to procure man's restoration to God; an intervention founded on sacrifice, and such as in its essential dignity should bear relation to the enormity of the transgression to be forgiven. The truth revealed to Apostles, maintained to the death by martyrs of the Eastern and Western Churches, and explained by saintly Fathers, is: that heaven and earth were united in Christ, the gracious Mediator and Intercessor, for the sake of Whose holy life, and as the consequence of His death, the gates of mercy are opened for mankind; and every prayer is offered, and all happiness is derived through Him alone, the exalted Prince and Saviour, from Whose royal hand are granted repentance and forgiveness,—the King of life, the Light of hope for the world. All the ministry of Baxter was successful, because he taught the ancient creed with such devotedness and energy as his parishioners had not known before: but it was always the truth in its close relation to the duty and responsibility of each one of them; that they should live as consecrated to their Lord, and under the constant guidance of His Holy Spirit, daily improving themselves in His service; acting worthily of Him who had received them into His kingdom, and with reliance on the happy fact in their spiritual life, that their former transgressions were pardoned, and that they might work happily all their days under their Saviour's provident and unfailing care. With such truths he nourished faith, restored life to his Church, and reformed the town.

CHAPTER XI.

1646—1659.

DURING the period of his ministry at Kidderminster, Baxter wrote one of the most useful of his practical works, "Gildas Salvianus, The Reformed Pastor." Gildas and Salvianus were two writers of the fifth and sixth centuries. The former, surnamed "the Wise," a Welsh monk, is the oldest British historian (A.D. 511); the latter was a Presbyter of Marseilles (A.D. 426), author of "De Gubernatione Dei," etc. Baxter says of them: "I pretend not to the sapience of Gildas, nor to the sanctity of Salvian, as to the degree; but by their names I offer an excuse for plain dealing. If it was used in a much greater measure by men so wise and holy as these, why should it in a lower measure be disallowed in another? At least from hence I have this encouragement, that the plain dealing of Gildas and Salvian being so much approved by us now they are dead, how much soever they might be despised or hated while they were living by them whom they did reprove, at the worst I may expect some such success in times to come." The book was one of the sermons, of prodigious length, customary during the years of the Commonwealth, written for a day of humiliation which the clergy of the county had agreed to keep at Worcester, at the beginning of December, 1655. At that time in England there were no Sunday-schools for the children of the poor. The idea of employing some part of the Lord's Day for the instruction of the labourers' children seems to have been originated by

Cardinal Borromeo, in Italy, in the sixteenth century; but his was a single effort of benevolence. In England such schools had no place. Provision had indeed been made for catechising the young, before or after evening prayer; but in some parishes either it had been discontinued, or it was done in a negligent and almost useless manner. Baxter saw the importance of this part of the clergyman's duty, and he resolved to attempt its restoration. He had formerly urged upon his parishioners the advantage of religious teaching at home, and to effect this he wrote catechisms of much utility. He says: "If parents would but do their parts in reading good books to their households, it might be a great supply where the ministry is defective; and no ministry will serve sufficiently without men's own endeavours for themselves and families." In 1656, he published "The Agreement of Divers Ministers, in the county of Worcester and some adjacent parts, for catechising or personally instructing all in their several Parishes that will consent thereunto," and he secured the signatures of several of them who consented to his proposal. Of his own practice in catechising he says: "Of all the works that ever I attempted this yielded me most comfort. All men thought that the people, especially the ancienter sort, would never have submitted to this course, and so that it would have come to nothing; but God gave me a tractable, willing people, and also gave me interest in them; and when I had begun, and my people had given a good example to other parishes, and especially the ministers so unanimously concurring, that none gainsayed, it prevailed with the parishes about. I set two days a week apart for this employment; my faithful, unwearied assistant and myself took fourteen families every week; those in the town came to us to our houses; those in the parish my assistant went to, to their houses; besides what a curate did at a chapelry. First they recited the catechism to us, a family only being present at a time, and no stranger admitted; after that, I first helped them to understand it, and next inquired modestly into the state of their souls; and lastly endeavoured to set all home to the convincing, awakening, and resolving of their hearts according to their several conditions; bestowing about an hour and the labour of a sermon with every family, I found it so effectual, with the blessing of God, that few went away without seeming humiliation, conviction, and purposes and promise for a holy life. Except half-a-dozen or thereabouts of the most ignorant and senseless, all the families in the town came to me; and though, the first time, they came with fear and backwardness, after that they longed for their turn to come again. So that I hope God did good to many by it; and yet this was not all the comfort I had in it."

Baxter found that no part of the pastoral work is more directly useful than this, by which spiritual instruction is given in the homes of the people, "And pure religion, breathing household laws." To the clergyman who has tact and kindness every door in his parish is open. So that the visit to them is well-timed, there are few among those who are called working-men who are not pleased by it; and where opportunity is so happily given, wisdom suggests that it should be promptly and methodically used for admonition or encouragement, and for promoting the work he is especially commissioned to do. His life should be in every sense the book of the ignorant.

"The Reformed Pastor" is singularly useful to all who have consecrated themselves to the service of the Church; which, whatever difficulties may attend it, is of all human work the most consoling in the review, as it is the most satisfactory in the result. Baxter never forgot that the clergyman's office is to bring men to the Saviour, the Fountain of Life, that they may be educated for the everlasting existence, by being gradually freed from the present power of sin. This he is commanded and taught to do, with such promise of sublime recompense in turning men to righteousness, that in his hereafter state he shall be as lustrous and useful as a star; and that in the work of mercy, he is actually associated with those nobler agents of the Divine government, whose employment would seem to consist in guarding the Church in its earthly struggle and service. The clergyman is to preach the word of life, and to live it; assured that it declares the method which God has appointed to recover the lost, to build up the Christian society, and to honour the Redeemer. He is to proclaim the Truth, whose seed is in itself, with the power of endless reproduction.

Nothing more directly commends religion than excellence of character in them who teach it, and the evidence of their devotedness to their duty. Earnestness makes its own way. Determination to gain one's end is often the guarantee to success. Example is one of the most forcible teachers. To the generality of men theological doctrines may be abstruse, and difficult of ready comprehension. Decrees of councils may seem merely as the authorised publication of opinions, which long since have lost their influence upon the thought and conduct of the world. The disputes of rival schools in polemics or philosophy have little interest for them, whose lives are passed in the various employments by which the means of living are procured. But all men can understand and approve the excellence of industrious attention to duty, of patient labour, and unselfish charity. The clergyman, who is faithful to his office, is a living exponent of the truth which he is appointed to enforce and to defend. His life is an argument for his doctrine. With sincere mind he is ever to promote Christianity in his parish, and to keep his thoughts directed to that end; assured that his intentions will be accepted, although the visible result of his labour may be small; for its thoroughness cannot always be estimated by the success which seemed to attend it. Andrew Marvell might have studied the career of Baxter at Kidderminster, when he wrote his celebrated tractate in defence of John Howe, and in contrasting his sober application to duty with the contentions and controversies of some other theologians. He says: "Of all vocations to which men addict themselves, or are dedicated, I have always esteemed that of the ministry to be the most noble and happy employment; as being more peculiarly directed to those great ends, the advancement of God's glory and the promoting of man's salvation. It hath seemed to me as if they who have chosen, and are set apart for that work, did, by the continual opportunity of conversing with their Maker, enjoy a state like that of Paradise; and in this superior, that they are not also as Adam, put in 'to dress and keep a garden'; but are, or ought to be, exempt from the necessity of all worldly avocations. Yet upon nearer consideration, they likewise appear to partake of the common infelicities of human condition. For although they do not, as others, eat their bread in the sweat of their brows (which some divines account to be, though in the pulpit, undecent), yet the study of their brain is more than equivalent; and even the theological ground is so far under the curse that no field runs out more in thorns and thistles, or requires more pains to disencumber it. Such I understand to be those peevish questions which have overgrown Christianity; wherewith men's minds are only rent and entangled, but from whence they can no more hope for any wholesome nourishment, than 'to gather grapes from thorns, or figs from thistles.' And (if I may so far pursue the allegory) this curse upon divinity, as that upon the earth, seems also to have proceeded from taking that forbidden fruit of 'the tree of knowledge of good and evil.' For, in general, many divines, out of a vain affectation of learning, have been tempted into inquiries too curious, after those things which the wisdom of God hath left impervious to human understanding further than they are revealed. And hence, instead of those allowed and obvious truths of faith, repentance, and the new creature (yet these too have their proper weeds which pester them), there have sprung up endless disputes concerning the unsearchable things of God; and which are agitated by men, for the most part, with such virulence and intricacy, as manifest the subtlety and malice of the serpent that hath seduced them. But, more particularly, that very knowledge of good and of evil, the disquisition of the causes from whence, and in what manner, they are derived, hath been so grateful to the controversial *female* appetité, that even the divines have taken of it 'as fruit to be desired to make them wise,' and given to their people, and they have both eaten, at the peril of God's displeasure and of their own happiness."

Baxter had so much of the prerogative of genius, that in the tranquillity of his mind, and in habitual communion with God, he knew well the extent of his powers—"the length of his line," as it is called by the philosopher Locke. He had "Thoughts that do often lie too deep for tears"; and he had long been assured there were many depths in the mighty ocean of truth which it were vain to attempt to fathom. It were better to make full use of that which has been revealed of the nature and government of God, than to waste time by vainly speculating on things which can never be known and determined. It were wiser to employ opportunity to the utmost. Time changes all things; nothing long continues. They, who might well have been admonished or entreated yesterday to repent and amend, are hurried away to-day as by an invisible flood. Their hours of labour have ended. The time of rescue is past. Then, if he, to whose faithful care they were committed, has been neglectful of his duty; if the blind has led the blind; if he, whose office it is to show the way of salvation, has not been able to find it for himself, and has been incapable of leading men into it,—how hard his lot! how unavailing his lamentation, that the day is at an end which he has ill employed, that they are gone from his care, with all their sins upon their heads, whom he might have guided to blissful life! and that he can no more teach the ignorant, remove doubt, encourage trembling goodness; but that eternity has suddenly intervened between him and his neglected duty, and that which he might have timely heeded and wisely tended is irrecoverably gone.

Such reflections were frequent in Baxter's mind, and they led him to form a practical method for his own conduct in his parish, and with so much success that he gave the details of it to others. His whole conduct was influenced by his belief, that the Sermon on the Mount is really the Magna Charta of the kingdom of God; and that the Church is the salt of the earth, to give healthful freshness to humanity. In "The Reformed Pastor" he describes in seven chapters the duties of the clergyman, and the manner in which they should be done. In all he maintains continuity of work to be of the utmost importance. He regarded the church as the place in which it should begin, but the home as that in which it should be carried on. In his church men were appealed to in masses, but in their own houses he had the advantage of reasoning with them individually. Thus he gradually learned their spiritual condition and mental capacities, and was enabled to educate each as his character and condition required. Religion is to be determined, not by impulses of goodness, but by habitual conduct; not so much by right actions as by the motives which produced them. It is necessary that the whole nature should be brought under transforming influences. This result can be attained only by the patient labour of the clergyman, and by a willing and assiduous attention from his flock; but in this field, more than in any other, the industrious hand reaps largely; and he, who relies on the merciful help of God, is satisfied with the fruits of his toil.

Baxter maintains, that a clergyman's work "consists in the prudent, effectual management of searching men's hearts, and setting home the saving truths; and that he must, therefore, seek out the people, and not expect they will necessarily come to him; in all things to shepherd the church; and that the parish should be no greater than the pastor can personally oversee, so that he may take heed to all the flock." His address is first to the clergy themselves, that they are not to be strangers to the religion they proclaim; that they live not in those sins which they preach against in others; that they be not spiritually or mentally unfit for the great employment they have undertaken: for how can such work be done "by raw, unqualified men"? What skill does every part of the work require, and of how much moment is every part! It is not, he asserts, a mere taste of study that will make a sound divine; but study, prayer, "conference," and practice are to be industriously used to ensure success; above all, that there be no disproportion between the clergyman's preaching and living. "Many will study hard to preach exactly, and study little or none at all to live exactly. All the week long is little enough to speak two hours; and yet one hour seems too much to study how to live all the week. What differences between their pulpit speeches and their familiar discourse! We must study as hard how to live well as how to preach well. In studying, your thoughts should be, What shall I say that is most likely effectually to convince them, and convert them, and tend to salvation? If saving of souls be your end, you will certainly intend it as well out of the pulpit as in it. Oh that this were your daily study, how to use your wealth, your friends, and all you have for God, as well as your tongues!" He dwells much upon the necessity for the personal religion of the clergyman—that there can be no sadder case than for a man, who made it his very trade and calling to proclaim salvation, to be himself shut out. That many eyes are upon him, and if he fall, "all the world will ring of it;" for a great man, a teacher of others, cannot commit a small sin; "all your preaching will be but dreaming and trifling hypocrisy, till the work be thoroughly done upon yourselves"—no one can care for the salvation of another who neglects his own. "All that a preacher does is a kind of preaching"; "men will give you leave to preach against their sins as much as you will, and talk as much goodness in the pulpit, so you will but let them alone afterwards, and be friendly and merry with them when you have done, and talk as they do, and live as they live." "Every flock should have its own pastor (one or more), and every pastor his own flock:

every company in a regiment must know its own captain. There must be so many souls assigned to each pastor as he is able to take heed of. Will God require of any bishop to take the charge of a whole county, or of so many thousands of souls, as he is not able to oversee? If there is to be discipline, it is unavoidably excluded where it is made to be his work who (from the extent of his diocese) is naturally incapable of performing it: the pastoral work must be done by the pastor himself. He may not delegate to a man that is no pastor to baptize or administer the Lord's Supper. I must profess, for my own part, I am so far from their boldness that dare venture on the sole government of a county, that I would not for all England have undertaken to have been one of the two that should do all the pastoral work that God enjoineth to that one parish where I live, had I not this to satisfy my conscience, that through the Church's necessities more cannot be had, and, therefore, I must rather do what I can than leave all undone, because I cannot do all. Oh, happy Church of Christ, were the labourers but able and faithful, and proportioned in number to the number of souls!"

Baxter urges, that the motive of the clergyman's work is "the pleasing and glorifying God. A man that is not heartily devoted to God, and attached to His service and honour, will never set heartily about the pastoral work. No man is fit to be a minister of Christ that is not of a public spirit as to the Church, and delighteth not in its beauty, and longeth not for its felicity; as the good of the commonwealth must be the end of the magistrate, so must the felicity of the Church be the end of the pastors of it. The subject-matter of the ministerial work is that which concerns the pleasing of God and the salvation of the people." He says: "Having shown them the right end, our next work is to acquaint them with the right means of attaining it. We have the great mystery of redemption to disclose; the person, natures, incarnation, perfection, life, miracles, suffering, death, burial, resurrection, ascension, glorification, dominion, and intercession of the blessed Son of God; as also the terror of His promises, the conditions imposed upon us, the duties which He hath commanded us. How much of our corruptions and sinful inclinations to root out! We have the depth of God's bottomless love and mercy, the depth of the mystery of His designs and works of creation, redemption, providence, justification, adoption, sanctification. We must teach them as much as we can of the word and works of God. Oh, what two volumes are these for a minister to speak upon! How great, how excellent, how wonderful, how mysterious! The Church is Christ's school, we are His ushers; the Bible is His grammar: this is what we must daily teach them. But each member of our charge must be taken heed of. Paul taught them publicly, and from house to house. It is our duty to take care of every individual person in our flock. Look after every member of the flock, even though it were the meanest servant-man or maid. Have you not so much maintenance yourself as might serve yourself and another? If you have but a hundred pounds a year, it is your duty to live upon part of it, and allow the rest to a competent assistant, rather than that the flock you are over should be neglected. If you say this is hard measure, your wife and children cannot so live, I answer, do not many families in your parish live upon less? This poverty is not so bad and dangerous a business as it is pretended to be. You must not leave off the work of personal oversight, nor refuse to deal particularly with any, because you cannot do it with all. The work of conversion is the great thing we must first drive at, and labour with all our might to effect; then to build up those that are already truly converted. Our work is all reducible to three particulars—confirmation, progress, preservation and restoration; for the world is better able to read the nature of religion in a man's life than in the Bible. Another part of our work is to guide our people, and be as their mouth in the public prayers of the Church, and in the public praises of God; also to bless them in the name of the Lord. The sacerdotal part of the work is not the least. A great part of God's services in the Church assemblies was wont in all ages of the Church, till of late, to consist in public praises and eucharistical acts in Holy Communion, and the Lord's Day was still kept as a day of thanksgiving. I am as apprehensive of the necessity of preaching as some others; but yet, methinks, the solemn praises of God should take up more of the Lord's Day than in most places they do."

Baxter insists on the immense importance that the clergyman should have especial care and oversight of *each member of his flock*. This he often repeats: "A minister is not only for public preaching, but to be a known counsellor for their souls, as the lawyer for their estates, and the physician for their bodies; so that each man that is in doubts and straits should bring his case to him and desire resolution. But the minister should not be troubled with every small matter. We must press them publicly to come to us for advice in such cases of great concernment to their souls. One word of seasonable and prudent advice given by the minister to persons in necessity hath done that good that many sermons would not have done. Persuade them that the master of the family will every Lord's Day at night cause all his family to repeat the catechism to him, and give him some account of what they have learned in public that day. Get masters of families to their duties, and they will spare you a great deal of labour with the rest, and further much the success of your labours." He impresses on the clergy the importance of careful and continual visitation of the sick, "helping them to prepare either for a fruitful life or a happy death. It requires extraordinary care when time is almost gone, and they must be now or never reconciled to God, and possessed of His grace. Oh, how doth it concern them to redeem those hours, and lay hold upon eternal life! And when we see we are likely to have but a few days or hours more to speak to them, what man that is not an infidel, or a block, would not be with them, and do all that he can for their salvation in that short space!

Stay not till strength and understanding be gone, and the time so short that you scarcely know what you do, but go to them as soon as you hear that they are sick, whether they send for you or not. When the time is so short, three things must chiefly be insisted on. 1. The end: the certainty and greatness of the glory of the saints in the presence of God, so that their hearts may be set upon it. 2. The sufficiency of redemption by Jesus Christ, and the fulness of the Spirit, which we may and must be partakers of. This is the principal way to the end, and the nearer end itself. 3. The necessity and nature of faith, repentance, and resolutions for new obedience, as there shall be opportunity. If they should recover, be sure to mind them to their promises."

Much stress is laid by him upon Church discipline: "I confess much prudence is to be exercised in such proceedings, lest we do more hurt than good. To be against discipline is to be against the ministry; to be against the ministry is to be *tantum non*, to be absolutely against the Church; and to be against the Church is near to being absolutely against Christ. In the ministry it is not serving God but ourselves, if we do it not for God but for ourselves. They that make a trade of it for a livelihood will find that they have chosen a bad trade, though a good employment. Self-denial is of absolute necessity in every Christian, but of a double necessity in a minister. We are seeking to uphold the world, to save it from the curse of God, to perfect the creation, to attain the ends of Christ's redemption, to save ourselves and others from condemnation, to overcome the devil and demolish his kingdom, and set up the kingdom of Christ, and attain and help others to the kingdom of glory. Are these works to be done with a careless mind and a slack hand? No man was ever a loser by God. If we can but teach Christ to our people, we teach them all. Get them well to heaven, and they will have knowledge enough. All our teaching must be as plain and evident as we can make it. Painted, obscure sermons (like the painted glass in the windows that keep out the light) are too often the mark of painted hypocrites. If you would not teach men, what do you do in the pulpit? If you would, why do you not speak so as to be understood? Our whole work must be carried on in pious, believing dependence upon Christ—must be managed with great humility, as beseemeth them that believe the presence of God. I hate that preaching which tendeth to make the hearers laugh, or to move their mind with tickling levity, and affect them as stage-players use to do, instead of affecting them with a holy reverence of the name of God,—and all our work must be done spiritually, as by men possessed of the Holy Ghost. Our whole work must be carried on in a tender love to our people; we must let them see that nothing pleaseth us but what profiteth them. As Augustine says, *Dilige et dic quicquid voles.* Our business is to humble ourselves before the Lord for our former negligence, especially of catechising and personally instructing those committed to our charge. In all my life I never lived in a parish where one person was publicly admonished, or brought to public penance, or excommunicated. The ancient discipline of the Church was unknown, and indeed it was impossible, when one man that lived at a distance from them, and knew not one of many hundreds of the flock, did take upon him the sole jurisdiction, and executed it not by himself, but by a lay chancellor, excluding the pastors of the several congregations, who were but to join with the churchwardens and the apparitors in presenting men and bringing them into their courts. Yet, through the mercy of God, it was not all the prelates of the Church that thus miscarried; we have yet surviving our Ussher, our Hall, our Morton—learned, godly, and peaceable men; whose names are as dear to us as any man's alive. Oh that it had been the will of God that all had been such! Then had we not been like to have seen those days of blood that we have seen; nor those great mutations in Church and State. But so far were these good men from being able to do the good that they would, that they were maligned for their piety and soundness in the faith; and many a time have I heard them despised as well as others, and scorned as Puritans for all they were prelates.

"We have as sad divisions among us in England as most nations under heaven have known. The most that keeps us at odds is but about the right form and order of Church government. Is the distance so great that Presbyterian, Episcopal, and Independent might not be well agreed? Were they but heartily willing and forward for peace, they might—I know they might. Did we but agree among ourselves, our words would have some authority with the people. The most common cause of our divisions and unpeaceableness is men's high estimation of their own opinions. So it is with the Anabaptists, they must now in the end of the world have a new church for Christ. Never since the creation can it be proved that God had anywhere a Church on earth where infants were excluded from being members, if there were any among them. Yet this disturbing vice doth work by setting a higher rate of necessity upon some truths than the Church of Christ hath ever done."

Baxter returns, and often returns, to press the importance of industry and efficiency in ministerial work. He says: "In the study of our sermons we are too negligent. We must study how to convince and get within men, and how to bring each truth to the quick, and not leave all this to our extemporary promptitude. Experience will teach you that men are not made learned or wise without hard study and unwearied labours. How few ministers preach with all their might! There is nothing more unsuitable to such a business than to be slight and dull. What! speak coldly for God and for men's salvation!

"Ruling is as essential a part of the pastor's office as preaching. I confess I think that the magistrates should be the hedge of the Church, and defend the minister, and improve his power to the utmost to procure an universal obedience to Christ's laws, and restrain men from the apparent license of them. I am against the two extremes of universal license and persecuting tyranny. Too much interposition of the sword with our discipline would do more harm than good. It would but corrupt it by the mixture, and make it a human thing. If the magistrate do but give us protection and liberty, especially if he will but restrain deceivers from preaching against the unquestionable truths of the Gospel, and give public countenance and encouragement to those master-truths, I shall not fear, by the grace of God, but a prudent, sober, unanimous ministry will ere long shame the swarm of vanities that we think so threatening.

"Those ministers that have the larger maintenance must be larger in doing good; often, if they have an assistant, it is but some young man to ease them about baptisms or burials, and not one that will faithfully and diligently watch over the flock, and afford them that personal instruction which is so necessary. Oh, what a charge have we undertaken! And shall we be unfaithful? Have we the stewardship of God's own family, and shall we neglect it? Have we the conduct of those saints that must live for ever with God in glory, and shall we neglect them? See that the work of saving grace be thoroughly wrought in your own souls. It is a fearful thing to be an unsanctified preacher. When you pen your sermons, little do you think you are drawing up indictments against your own souls. O miserable life, that a man should study and preach against himself, and spend all his days in a course of self-condemnation! Oh, what an aggravated misery, to famish with the bread of life in our hands, while we offer it to others, and urge it on them! It is the danger and calamity of the Church, to have so many men become preachers before they are Christians; to be sanctified by dedication to the altar as God's priests, before they are sanctified by hearty dedication to Christ as His disciples. Oh that all our students in the university would well consider this!"

Often Baxter urges upon the clergy the necessity for

their own personal religion. "Watch over your own hearts. Be much in secret prayer and meditation. There you fetch the heavenly fire that must kindle your sacrifices. You cannot neglect your duty to your own hurt alone; many will be losers by it as well as you. Whatever you do, let the people see you are in good earnest. You cannot break men's hearts by jesting with them, or telling them a smooth tale, or patching up a gaudy oration. Men will not cast away their dearest pleasures upon a drowsy request. A great matter lies in the very pronunciation and tone of speech. The best matter will scarcely move them, if it be not movingly delivered. See that there be no affectation, but speak as familiarly to our people as we would do if we were talking to any of them personally. Satan will not be charmed out of his profession. We must lay siege to the souls of sinners who are his garrisons. In preaching there is intended a communion of souls, and a communication from ours unto theirs. I have observed that God seldom blesseth any man's work so much as his whose heart is set upon success. If God set us to wash negroes, and cure those that will not be cured, we shall not lose our labour, though we perform not the cure.

"Condescend to men of low estate, be not strange to the poor of your flock. They are apt to take your strangeness for contempt. A kind and winning carriage is a cheap way of advantage to do men good. Go to the poor, and see what they want, and show at once your compassion to soul and body. Buy them a catechism, and some small books that are likely to do them good. Stretch your purse to the utmost, and do all the good you can. Think not of being rich; seek not great things for yourselves or posterity. If you believe that God is your safest purse-bearer, and that to expend in His service is the greatest usury, and the most thriving trade, show them that you believe it. You lose no great advantage for heaven by becoming poor. The self-sufficient are the most deficient."

Baxter pressed the clergy "to maintain unity; if only

Vincentius's test might serve, *quod ubique, quod semper, quod ab omnibus creditum est, hoc est etenim verè proprièque Catholicum.* Many corruptions may be in a Church, and yet it may be a great sin to separate from it. There is a strange inclination in proud men to make the Church of Christ much narrower than it is, as if they were loath to have too much company in heaven. The most godly people in your congregation will find it worth their labour to learn the very words of a catechism; and if you would safely edify and establish them, be diligent in this work. If physicians should only read a public lecture of physic, their patients would not be much the better for them; nor would a lawyer secure your estate by reading a lecture of law. The charge of a pastor requires personal dealing as well as any of these. Let us show the world this by our practice, for most men are grown regardless of bare words. Lest we should seem to favour auricular confession, we have too commonly neglected all personal instruction. There is much more to be done, if taking heed to the flock is another business than careless, lazy ministers do consider. I will instance my own case. We are together two ministers, and a third at a chapel, willing to bestow every hour of our time in Christ's work. We are engaged to set apart two days every week from morning to night for private catechising and instruction. Unless we will omit this personal instruction, we must needs run thus unprepared into the pulpit. When we have set two whole days apart for the work, it will be as much as we shall be able to do, to go over the parish but once a year, there being in it about eight hundred families; and what is worse than that, we shall be forced to cut it short, having above fifteen families to visit in a week. How small a matter is it to speak to a man only once a year! Many ministers in England have ten times, if not more, the number of parishioners that I have; so that if they should undertake the work that we have done, they can go over the parish but once in ten years. Thus, while we are hoping for opportunities to speak to them, we hear of one dying after another, and to the grief of our souls are forced to go with them to their graves before we could ever speak a word to them personally to prepare them for their change. Moreover, they will do good to many ministers that are apt to be idle, and mis-spend their time in businesses, journeys, or recreations. People used to say, Such a minister can sit in an alehouse, or tavern, or spend his time at bowls, or other sport, or vain discourse; why may we not do so as well as he? If you will but faithfully perform the business of catechising and personal instruction, you will do more for the true Reformation that is so desirable. In public, by length and speaking alone, we lose their attention, but privately we can easily cause them to attend, and engage them by promises before we leave them, which in public we cannot do. Oh! then, for a clear conscience that can say, I live not for myself, but to Christ; I spared no pains, I hid not my talent, I concealed not men's misery, nor the way of their recovery. Oh! happy Church, if the physicians were but healed themselves. We may take time for necessary recreation for all this. An hour or half an hour's walk before meat is as much recreation as is of necessity for the health of most of the weaker sort of students. Though I have a body that hath languished under great weakness many years, and my diseases have been such as require as much exercise as almost any in the world, I have found exercise the principal means of my preservation till now. What have we our time and strength for, but to lay both out for God? What is a candle made for but to burn? What comfort will it be at death that you lengthened your life by shortening your work? He that works much, lives much. I profess I wonder at those ministers that can hunt, shoot, bowl, or use the like recreations two or three hours, yea, whole days together; that can sit an hour together in vain discourses, and spend whole days in complimental visits, and journeys to such ends. Good Lord! what do these men think on? It is the chief misery of the Church that so many are made ministers before they are Christians. We shall be judged according to our works. Bishop Ussher, in his sermon before King James at Wanstead, said, 'Your Majesty's care can never sufficiently be commended, in taking order that the chief heads of the catechism should in the ordinary ministry be diligently propounded and explained unto the people throughout the land; the laying of the foundation skilfully is the matter of the greatest importance in the whole building, for let us preach never so many sermons to the people, our labour is but lost, as long as the foundation is unlaid, and the first principles untaught, upon which all other doctrine must be builded.' The preaching truth is the most successful way of confuting error. If you cannot go from house to house, call the people to come to you, and learn of you at your own house, or the Church-house, so that you will but give them that personal instruction which their conditions do require. For my own part, I am not able to go from house to house; there being not one house of many among the poor people, where I can stand half an hour in the midst of summer without taking cold, to the apparent hazard of my life."

In urging the great importance of instructing the young and the untaught in the first principles of religion, Baxter says: "I believe that Christ Himself is the author of the ancient creed, expressly in St. Matthew xxviii. 19; and I fully believe that before the New Testament was written, the Apostles taught their catechumens and persons admitted to baptism the sum of the gospel or Christian religion in a few distinct articles. It is certain they could not deliver all the history or doctrine of Christ to every convert; for the essentials of the subjective Christianity are the image and effects of the essentials of objective Christianity or faith."

These quotations, from one of the most useful of Baxter's writings, show the principles which guided him in his work at Kidderminster, and the cause of his great success there. Few books more really useful than this could be in the hands of English clergymen, many of whom do not know how great is its treasury of devout and practical wisdom; often neglected with other works of the literature by which our country is enriched, and which lie unheeded in libraries —as, in the gold-fields of the south and west, the settler sows his land and reaps his harvest, sometimes wholly unaware of the precious metal which is hidden beneath it.

CHAPTER XII.

1648—1658.

DURING the fourteen years of Baxter's ministry at Kidderminster, in which his chief public work was done, various and important changes occurred in the political and social condition of England. Agitation was general and long-continued. The waves were high, though the severity of the storm had passed away. When revolutions have ceased, men do not easily return to their former ways and habits of life. The old landmarks are not readily traced in fields which have been devastated by a flood. After disruption, a community which has been so disordered is long liable to confusion and unrest, before it returns to the pursuits and enjoyments of peace. The tempest which purifies the atmosphere, disperses malarious vapours, and perhaps prevents the visitation of pestilence, often leaves behind it wreck and destruction: as though a law obtained in the world, that that which is itself good must ever have an accompaniment of evil. In a civil revolution, such as that of 1648, produced either by the tyranny of reckless government on the one hand, or by the ambitions and plots of demagogues on the other, the whole social and religious order of a country is dissolved, and liberty, so long previously withheld, is violently abused. At that time many of the English dissidents had little regard for the belief and practice of antiquity, either as to Christian doctrine or as to ecclesiastical constitution. Every day produced a new opinion, or increased the adherents of the sects. The Seekers especially, as their name indicates, were ever looking out for fresh illuminations. Others were waiting to be inspired. Fanatics declared that they had met angels in the streets, or had wrestled at midnight with filthy demons, the enemies of the soul; and some of them, maddened and naked, ran through the streets, denouncing their spiritual enemies with horrible imprecations. Some of them vociferated that the clergy were useless drones, every way injurious to religion. Others, in a vague manner imitating Hobbes of Malmesbury, held that the magistrates should determine religious opinion and the mode of public worship. Unclothed prophets foretold terrible judgments on prelate and priest, and infuriated women "broke trenchers before Parliament, as a sign and testimony." The clamouring religionists, hating each other, pretended in some instances to Divine enlightenment; and few of them would admit that there might be truth or justice in the argument of an opponent. It is impossible to avoid the conclusion, that sometimes the suspicions of indifferent spectators of these theological disputes were not altogether groundless—that with an ostensibly religious fervour, there was often the commingling of hypocrisy.

Baxter well knew some of them who took part in these controversies, and who endeavoured to affect the parliamentary and military leaders with their opinions. During the time of his service in the army he had opportunities of hearing their declarations, and of judging of their characters and motives. He had rebuked their mutual malignity and their theological rancour. These were the men whom Cromwell endeavoured to gain to his party. His successful conduct of the war, and his great sagacity and tact, had raised him to supreme power. How was he to weld these discordant elements together, and to make them at once submissive and peaceful? Disturbing forces surrounded him. Every day produced a new plot against him. Conspiracies were formed, and if discovered and unmercifully punished, they were renewed; until no small part of the work of government was watchfulness against its own overthrow. How was the victorious general to govern men who proclaimed themselves to be the saints into whose hands the judgment of the world was committed? How was he to restrain the furious turbulence of fanatics, who avowed that they had visions of angels, revealing to them that which the greatest Apostle declared to be unutterable? How was he to silence the clamour of disordered prophets, who ran unclothed from street to street, foretelling coming disasters, especially that a volcano of Divine wrath was about to burst upon London, and which would destroy all them who were not in the kingdom of the holy? If Cromwell did not believe in the possibility of that union of all good men who agreed in holding the chief Christian doctrines, and which Baxter ever desired to effect, in order to put a perpetual end to religious discords; his policy was to give full liberty to all, excepting to hostile Royalists, but to allow superiority to none of them.

In the difficulties of composing such strifes, his sagacity led him to select the ablest men for his advisers, whose names would be of authority even in days of anarchy, and whose judgments would be uninfluenced by clamour and outrage. It is impossible not to admire the wisdom of the Protector in selecting John Milton for his secretary, and John Howe for his chaplain, two of the most eminent of the illustrious men whose thoughts have given strength to the mind of England, and who may be regarded justly as representatives of the culture and genius of that age, one of the most distinguished in all the history of our literature. The correspondence between Baxter and Howe, on the propriety of his taking so important an office in the court of a ruler, who, in the opinion of some of his contemporaries, by bye-paths and trackless ways had met his crown, is not the least interesting of all that enormous mass of letters which are among the existing Baxter-manuscripts, and some of which are as large as a modern pamphlet.

Always desirous of effecting such a comprehension of orthodox religionists, on the basis of the Creed, the Lord's Prayer, and the Ten Commandments, Baxter says, in one of his letters to John Howe, referring to the Protector's wish for such unity: "The welfare of the Church, and the peace of the nations, lies much on the public reputation of good magistrates, which therefore we should not diminish but promote. The Lord Protector is noted as a man of a catholic spirit, desirous of the unity and peace of all the servants of Christ. We desire nothing in the world (at home) so much as the exercise and success of such a disposition; but more is to be done for union and peace. Would he, 1st, but take some healing principles into his own consideration; 2nd, when he is satisfied in them, expose them to one or two leading men of each party (Episcopalian, Presbyterian, Congregational, Erastian, Anabaptist), and privately feel them, and get them to a consent; 3rd, and then let them be printed, to see how they will relish (with the reasons annexed); 4th, and then let a free-chosen assembly be called to agree upon them,—he would exceedingly oblige and endear all nations to him; and I am confident, as I live, that by God's blessing he may happily accomplish so much of this work, if he be willing, as shall settle us in much peace, and prevent and heal abundance of our dissensions. I pray you to persuade men not to despise those they call Royalists and Episcopalians, either because they are now under them, or because of contrariety of worldly interests; for these things signify less than carnal hearts imagine—and who knows what a day (and a righteous God) may bring forth?"

But in the heat and passion which remained after the great conflict—for the ashes of the conflagration were still glowing—Cromwell assumed supreme power. The work before him had stupendous difficulties. He endeavoured to obtain the assistance of men able to give him judicious counsel, and of experience and knowledge of affairs; but he found it easier to command regiments and brigades, and to direct those movements in the field of battle which he saw to be necessary to gain victory, than to attract the affections, influence the opinions, and secure the allegiance of men, who had cast down the throne, silenced the Church, and, intoxicated by their successes, dreamed of having no restraints in the license of universal liberty. He could neither acquire their esteem, nor protect himself from the arrows which wound all unseen, their malicious calumnies and bitter revilings. To restore religious peace was impossible; but for every interest it was necessary that, until public order could be re-established, the administration should be strong. The history of the time demonstrates that, if arbitrary government is galling, there is no tyranny worse than that of an unrestrained liberty. Without control each man is his own tyrant, but true freedom is enjoyed in that state only which is ruled and moderated by law.

These and other difficulties Cromwell had to encounter, after he had taken the government of England into his own hands. If he had at first good intentions, if he were desirous of consolidating upon a permanent basis the new form of public liberty which the Parliament had gained by its victory over the king, he found that he was compelled to swerve from his purpose. The oppositions to him were so various and so numerous; the intrigues were so frequent of them who were disappointed at the turn affairs had taken, contrary to their desires and expectations; the personal dislike and jealousy of the Protector, on the part of his defeated antagonists, and of some of them who had been his comrades in battles and sieges, were so bitter and constant; and the force at his command was composed of men with so many varieties of religious opinion,—that if government were to be maintained at all, it could be secured only by the establishment of a vigilant military despotism. He had been fully convinced that a great nation cannot be governed by vociferous declaimers in a heated chamber; and that nothing is more hazardous to the well-being of the state, than that the mass of the people, who are entirely ignorant of the principles of legislation, should interfere in the course of policy adopted by them to whom the administration of affairs is entrusted.

Baxter thoroughly understood the character of Cromwell. He was an eyewitness of some of the prominent occurrences of the time; and the account which he gives in his Autobiography of the transactions, and of the chief figure in them, has a peculiar interest. He says:—

"Cromwell having thus far seemed to be a servant to the Parliament, and to work for his masters, the Commonwealth, did next begin to show whom he served, and take that impediment also out of the way. To this end, he first did by them as he did by the Presbyterians, make them odious by hard speeches against them throughout his army; as if they intended to perpetuate themselves, and would not be accountable for the money of the Commonwealth. He also treated privately with many of them, to appoint a time when they would dissolve themselves, so that another free Parliament might be chosen. But they perceived the danger, and were rather for filling up their number by new elections, which he was utterly against.

"His greatest advantage to strengthen himself against them by the sectaries was their owning the public ministry and its maintenance; for though Vane and his party set themselves to make the ministers odious, and to take them down by reproachful titles, still the greater part of the House did carry it for a sober ministry and for a competent maintenance. When the Quakers and others openly reproached the ministry, and the soldiers favoured them, I drew up a petition for the ministry; got many thousand hands to it in Worcestershire, and Mr. Thomas Foley and Colonel John Bridges presented it. The House gave it a kind and promising answer, which increased the sectaries' displeasure against the House. When a certain Quaker wrote a reviling censure of this petition, I wrote a defence of it, and caused one of them to be given to each parliament-man at the door; but, within one day after this, they were dissolved. For Cromwell, impatient of any more delay, suddenly took Harrison and some soldiers with him, as if God had impelled him; and, as in a rapture, went into the House and reproved the members for their faults. Pointing to Vane, he called him a juggler; and to Henry Martin, called him a whoremaster,—and having two such to instance in, took it for granted that they were all unfit to continue in the government of the Commonwealth, and out he turned them. No sort of people expressed any great offence that they were cast out; though almost all, save the sectaries and the army, did take him to be a traitor who did it.

"The young Commonwealth being already headless, you might think that nothing was left to stand between Cromwell and the crown. For a governor there must be, and who should be thought fitter? But yet there was another pageant to be played, which had a double end: first, to make the necessity of his government undeniable; and, secondly, to put his own soldiers, at last, out of love with democracy; or, at least, to make those hateful who adhered to it. A Parliament must be called, but the ungodly people are not to be entrusted with the choice; therefore the soldiers, as more religious, must be the choosers; and two out of a county are chosen by the officers, upon the advice of their sectarian friends in the country. This was called, in contempt, the Little Parliament. Harrison became the head of the sectaries, and Cromwell now began to design the heading of a soberer party, who were for learning and a ministry, but yet to be the equal protector of all. Hereupon, in the little sectarian Parliament, it was put to the vote, whether all the parish ministers in England should at once be put down; and it was accidentally carried in the negative by two voices. It was taken for granted, that the tithes and universities would at the next opportunity be voted down; and so Cromwell must be their saviour, or they must perish; when he had purposely cast them into the pit, that they might be beholden to him to pull them out. But his game was so grossly played, that it made him the more loathed by men of understanding and sincerity. So Sir Charles Wolsley and some others took their time, and put it to the vote, whether the House, as incapable of serving the Commonwealth, should go and deliver up their power to Cromwell, from whom they had received it; which was carried in the affirmative. So away they went, and solemnly resigned their power to him; and now who but Cromwell and his army?

"The intelligent sort by this time did fully see that Cromwell's design was, by causing and permitting destruction to hang over us, to necessitate the nation, whether it would or not, to take him for its governor, that he might be its Protector. Being resolved that we should be saved by him or perish, he made more use of the wild-headed sectaries than barely to fight for him. They now served him as much by their heresies, their enmity to learning and the ministry, and their pernicious demands, which tended to confusion, as they had done before by their valour in the field. He could now conjure up at pleasure some terrible apparition of agitators, levellers, or such like, who, as they affrighted the king from Hampton Court, affrighted the people to fly to him for refuge; that the hand that wounded them might heal them. Now he exclaimed against the giddiness of these unruly men, and earnestly pleaded for order and government, and must needs become the patron of the ministry; yet so as to secure all others their liberty."

A government, beset during its whole course by so many dangers as that of Cromwell, was compelled to adopt every method of defence. As in a siege it is necessary that the mine should be met by the counter-mine, so, to detect the schemes and plots of his enemies, the Protector resorted to the use of secret means of obtaining information. He had agents at the chief European courts, and in every portion of English society he had persons in his employment, who reported to him all that could be obtained by association with them who were in a greater or less degree disaffected to him. By these means, some of which perhaps all administrations occasionally find it expedient to adopt, he had early and trustworthy intelligence of much that was said, proposed, and designed for his overthrow. He had more to fear from plots than from the perils of personal violence; although it has been alleged, that for some years he thought it necessary for his safety to wear some kind of defensive armour, and to carry weapons in his pockets. But they who were his most dangerous antagonists, and especially so as they were the more difficult of detection, were the Jesuit emissaries; who were so clever in their methods of disguise, that they were able to pass through his guards, to escape the vigilance of his spies, and to find places of concealment and of refuge in every county of the kingdom. Cromwell had also to encounter the unceasing hatred and animosity of certain members of the Anglican clergy, who corresponded with kinsmen or friends at the courts of Louis and of Charles, and who had signs of communication with each other, and means of imparting information, which, seldom detected, baffled the observation of the officers of the government.

Among the agents whom Cromwell made use of to discover the plots, and to counterwork the intrigues of his adversaries, some of the Puritan ministers no doubt were the most efficient. Several of these men, who had distinguished themselves at the universities both of England and of Holland, were thoroughly competent to manage difficult affairs with skill and discretion, and especially to conduct secret negotiations with consummate prudence and dexterity. They were quite equal to their opponents in making political investigations with wariness and success; and sometimes they were able to obtain knowledge of intended movements on the part of the exiles, earlier than their adversaries at home; from the fact that the Protestants at the Hague, in Utrecht, Breda, and even in Paris, sympathised with the brethren of their faith in England, and were able to keep them completely furnished with the latest intelligence of all that transpired among the exiled Royalists in France and in the Netherlands. Even so eminent a man as John Howe, the Protector's chaplain, and certainly one of the ablest of the divines of the seventeenth century, was often compelled to engage in such negotiations. Calamy says: "Whilst Howe continued in Cromwell's family, he was often put upon secret services; but they were always honourable, and such as, according to the best of his judgment, might be to the benefit either of the public, or of particular persons. And when he was once engaged, he used all the diligence and secrecy and despatch as he was able. Once, particularly, I have been informed, he was sent by Oliver in haste upon a certain mission to Oxford, to a meeting of ministers there; and he made such despatch, that though he rode by St. Giles's church at twelve o'clock, he arrived at Oxford by a quarter after five."

In his administration two things were necessary for Cromwell—to be able to maintain a strong government, and to keep it in his own hands. If man is ever satisfied by attainment, he had reached the object of his ambition. He had won a brilliant renown, but he was not so biassed by fanaticism, nor blinded by success, as not to be assured that when the nation had recovered calmness, and had time for reflection, and when the exhausted strength of the large Royalist party had to some extent been restored, his position would be hazardous, if not held by a power it would be vain to resist and impossible to overthrow. The necessities of tyranny urged him to courses which his better judgment could not have approved. He strengthened himself to the utmost by concentrating the military force, and by surrounding himself by the wisest counsellors. His sagacity in appointing Matthew Hale to be one of his judges, and John Milton one of his secretaries, confirms the observation of Bishop Burnet: "In nothing was his good understanding better discovered than in seeking out able and worthy men for all employments." The longer he held power, the sweeter it became to him. He could not renounce his ambition, nor could he silence detracting tongues, nor disarm conspirators, nor overcome the opposition of the Anglican clergy. The excitement of success may in some respects have obscured his judgment; but he could take no backward steps, and if he had waded through slaughter to a throne, his government, while he held it, must be vigorous, and this could be only as he made all the discordant elements in the State submissive to his power.

To accomplish this result, he must assure himself of the loyalty of them who influenced public opinion. He would have them on his own side, if it were possible; but, at least, where he could, he would silence his enemies. The outcry, which had been raised before and during the years of the civil war, against the incapacity and unworthiness of some of the clergy, gave him the opportunity he desired of effecting his purpose. That in some parts of the country the ministrations of religion had been negligent and scandalous, there can be no question. Historical evidence of the facts from perfectly unprejudiced witnesses is cumulative and irresistible. If occasionally a bishop was lax or perfunctory in his great duties, there can be no doubt but that some of the clergy may have been frequently or even habitually remiss in theirs; and in the smaller rural parishes —as has been shown in an earlier part of this narrative— there may have been curates and incumbents quite unfitted for the sacred offices to which they had been appointed. Cromwell's quick eye saw at once what advantage he might gain from such circumstances, and he determined to use it for the purpose of strengthening his power.

It has long been wisely held, that one of the chief duties of government is to provide for the highest interests of the people—to see that their churches and schools are duly used for the purposes for which they have been erected and endowed, and that a class so useful and therefore so powerful as the clergy are at least formally doing the work to which they have been appointed. The question has been much debated in our day; but, if it is fitting that the administration should watch over the lower interests of citizens, it may be asked why they should be indifferent to or incapable of providing for those which are higher. Cromwell had no scruples as to the direct right of the government to care for the condition of the religious life in England; and he saw how easily that which might improve it could be employed to strengthen his authority in the state. He announced, that his great object was to reform the ministry of religion, by first making inquiries into the qualifications and conduct of the clergy throughout the kingdom; and to accomplish his purpose, after the dissolution of the Westminster Assembly, he appointed a body of persons attached to his interests, some of them divines, and some of them laymen, to be called "The Triers." They were to sit in London, and to examine all ministers who were able to go to the metropolis. If the distance were too great, or if personal infirmity, or the difficulty of travelling, prevented aged or feeble persons from making the journey, they were to be examined by a local committee in the county in which each lived. So that, by these regulations, the whole body of persons ministering in religion would be brought under the review of the government, who would thus know who were well affected to it, and who were to be watched as probable malcontents. It is evident that such an examining body might easily become one of the most inquisitorial and tyrannical, and that it might be used at will by the administration as a powerful means of discovering, silencing, and punishing its enemies.

There is reason to believe that often the Triers were partial and harsh; and that in numerous cases the clergy were pronounced to be unfit for their office, and were summarily dismissed from it, more for their manly assertion of political opinion, and for refusal to acquiesce in despotical usurpation, than for lack of theological knowledge, of spiritual fitness for their duty, and of diligence in doing it. Some unworthy incumbents were ejected by them, and, although Baxter approved of their action in such cases,—for no one could blame them for condemning the indolent and vicious who were possessed of benefices,—yet is it impossible to doubt that, in the majority of their decisions, they acted rather as political agents than as Church-reformers. In the first part of his Autobiography, he says: "Because this assembly of Triers is most heartily accused and reproached by some men, I shall speak the truth of them, and I suppose my word will be rather taken, because most of them took me for one of their boldest adversaries, as to their opinions, and because I was known to disown their power; insomuch that I refused to try any under them upon their reference, except very few whose importunity and necessity moved me, they being such as for their episcopal judgment, or some such cause, the Triers were likely to have rejected. The truth is, that though their authority was mild, and though some few who were over-busy, and over-rigid Independents among them, were too severe against all that were Arminians, and too particular in inquiring after evidences of sanctification in those whom they examined, and somewhat too lax in their admission of unlearned and erroneous men, who favoured Antinomianism or Anabaptism; yet to give them their due, they did abundance of good to the Church. They saved many a congregation from ignorant, ungodly, drunken teachers; that sort of men who intended no more in the ministry than to say a sermon, as readers say their common prayers, and to patch up a few good words together, to talk the people asleep on Sunday; and all the rest of the week to go with them to the alehouse, and harden them in their sin; and that sort of ministers who either preached against a holy life, or preached as men that never were acquainted with it. All those who used the ministry but as a common trade to live by, and were never likely to convert a soul, they usually rejected, and in their stead they admitted persons of any denomination, who were able, serious preachers, and lived a godly life. So that, though many of them were somewhat partial to the Independents, Separatists, Fifth-Monarchy men, and Anabaptists, and against the Prelatists and Arminians, so great was the benefit above the hurt which they brought to the Church, that many thousands of souls blessed God for the faithful ministers whom they let in, and grieved when the Prelatists afterwards cast them out again."

Apart from the political considerations to which allusion has been made, and which no doubt greatly influenced Cromwell in his appointment of the Triers, the principle is in itself legitimate, that scandalous and incompetent priests should be dismissed from a church in which they are both a disgrace and a weakness; and if full legal evidence of their evil behaviour can be secured, their ejection can meet with no disapproval. For all will admit the propriety of the statement, that the poorest Christian people should not be left in bad hands when discovered to be bad. The clergyman, who is in fact a privileged man, to whom every house is open, who can reprove with an authority no one else has, and who is the mainspring of religious work generally, ought, as has been said, to be fit for his place. But, in many of the inquiries made by the Protector's agents, either political feeling or theological bias influenced the judges, so that some of their decisions were harsh, groundless, and unjust. A careful examination might enable the Triers to judge of a clergyman's critical skill, the extent of his knowledge of the facts of revealed and of historical Christianity, and of the development of doctrine or ritual; but who is capable of reading the heart, and of determining the reality or strength of spiritual life in another? Who knows what thoughts utterly inconsistent with the Christian state may be habitual to him? The charity which thinks no evil should prevent men from usurping the right of judging the thoughts and motives, which are open only to His eye to Whom all judgment is committed. It is given to no man to read the secrets of another's mind, or to decide upon the quality of his moral affections; and with the infinite variety of sentiments and tastes, and of mental constitution, to apply one crucial form of opinion, or one severe ethical test, to them whom nature and education have made to differ in so many, is to judge inequitably, and to pronounce with presumption. It is a usurpation of the

Divine prerogative to judge of the spiritual state of any man; for He only can estimate conscience. To examine character and opinion by one rigid theological rule, is in effect to act as if all men must necessarily be of one mind, on a subject upon which their opinions may be as diverse as their features.

Among associated religionists an approach to general agreement may justly be expected in their sentiments, which may be very far from unanimity in the expression of them; or, in an assembly there may be perfect concord as to the use of a form of words, with many differences in the minds of the components as to the exact meaning to be assigned to them. It may be easy to estimate the amount and correctness of a clergyman's knowledge of the truths committed to him to teach and to defend; but it is utterly impossible so to read his soul as to determine his spiritual qualifications for his office. John Howe—one of the most devout, as certainly he was one of the most philosophical of Baxter's theological contemporaries—says: "It is the easiest thing in the world, when any sort or party of men have got power into their hands, to saint themselves, and to unsaint all other men at their own pleasure." No human contrivance can so guard the entrance of the Church, that occasionally men of improper motives, or even of corrupt minds, may not enter it; and probably there is no sect or cohesion of religious men, in any country of the world, who do not number amongst them persons who have only just so much sympathy with goodness as will enable them, by making profession of it, to obtain the means of livelihood, or to hold some social position. If, among the twelve apostles of the Lord, one of them was essentially and irremediably wicked, how can any Church reasonably believe or hope that all, who bear the sacred vessels of its service, have pure hearts and clean hands, when its clergy may be numbered by thousands? It is possible that in the souls of some of them corruption may riot all unseen. They may proclaim the words of Divine mercy and forgiveness; they may utter the awful denunciations which the Hebrew lawgiver and the prophets were commissioned to pronounce against evil-doers; or they may chant the praises of the eternal King and Saviour, which for twenty centuries the thankful and rejoicing Church have offered as their daily tribute; and all of these—in relation to some of them who minister—with the unchastened thoughts and impure affections of men whose hearts have the constant indwelling of sin. How is it possible to avoid such intrusion, in the present state of human society, in which, even in the fairest fields of God, evil grows side by side with good; both of them receiving warmth and vital power from the same sun, both equally refreshed by the rain and the dew?

To demand of each candidate for service in the Church a particular account of his religious history; of the exact time and manner of his first having serious thought of the Divine requirement, and of his own duty and responsibility; and to make such confession a subject for the investigation of others, who are themselves liable to infirmity, and as a preliminary condition of admission to that service, may produce systematic hypocrisy and deception, but will not ensure the Church against the entrance into its ranks of them who are corrupt and unworthy. Baxter's sentiment, formerly quoted, expresses the practical wisdom which should be directive in all public acknowledgment of Christian character—"Every man's profession is the valid evidence of the thing professed in his heart." No one will question, that all care should be taken to secure for the ministry men who have themselves known the living power of the truth they are to explain and enforce, and of thorough devotedness to duty; but no strictness of requirement, ingenuity of regulation, and scrupulousness of examiners will be able to exclude the artful hypocrite, who by adroit speciousness and pious fluency is able to meet objection, overcome suspicion, and satisfy inquiry.

Cromwell's Triers ejected some dissolute and indolent priests; but by their minute and impertinent questions they perplexed and harassed many excellent clergymen, who were unversed in the peculiar phraseology and minute subdivisions of subtle controversialists, and who cared little for differences determined, or distinctions defined, at Geneva or at Dort. The difficulties, in such an investigation of clerical capacity and fitness, must have been as to the standard by which qualifications were to be estimated and decided. The Presbyterian would think ill of the Anglican, and the Independent would condemn both; and no doubt the inquisitive and unscrupulous Triers dismissed many excellent men from their cures, either from anger at their disapproval of the Protector's usurped authority, or from a desire to confer the vacated benefices upon his adherents. Some of the English clergymen, afraid of the insolent harshness of the Triers, sought advice and assistance from the chief Puritan divines. Among others, the witty historian, Dr. Thomas Fuller, said to John Howe: "You may observe, sir, that I am a somewhat corpulent man, and I am to go through a very strait passage; I beg you would be so good as to give me a shove, and help me through." Howe, who knew his danger at the hands of the prejudiced examiners, gave him suitable counsel. When Fuller was summoned before the inquisitors, he was asked the question, which was put without discrimination to each incumbent, "Whether he ever had any experience of a work of grace in his heart?" Fuller at once replied, "That he could appeal to the Searcher of hearts, that he made a conscience of his very thoughts." Calamy says: "With this answer they were satisfied, as indeed they might well be." Howe, who had heard what question was invariably asked by the presumptuous investigators, no doubt suggested to Fuller the reply, which secured him from further molestation.

The powers of the thirty-eight Triers were far beyond any which the Bishops had possessed; for, on their approval, an instrument in writing gave one of their nominees full possession of the benefice they conferred on him, more directly than in former days by episcopal institution and induction. They could easily refuse persons, if they held political opinions adverse to the existing government, and without doubt many worthy clergymen were expelled from their livings upon that ground alone. The decision of the Triers was final. No appeal against their determination could be made, nor could they be compelled to give any reason for their ejection of a clergyman from his cure. In his "Complete History" Bishop Kennet says: "This holy inquisition was turned into a snare to catch men of probity, sense, and sound divinity, and to let none escape but ignorant, bold, canting fellows; for these Triers asked few questions in knowledge or learning, but about conversation and the grace of God in the heart, to which the readiest answers would arise from infatuation in some, and the trade of hypocrisy in others. By this means the rights of patronage were at their pleasure, and the character and abilities of divines whatever they pleased to make them; and churches were filled with little creatures of the State." Their conduct towards the illustrious Pococke, Professor of Arabic in the University of Oxford, and rector of Childrey, is a sufficient evidence that they could act unjustly. They summoned him to appear before them at Abingdon, and they would have quickly ejected him, but for the interference of Dr. John Owen, the Independent divine, at that time Dean of Christchurch; who, to his lasting honour, hastened from Oxford to the rescue; and with passionate language endeavoured to make the inquisitors know that the contempt of all men would fall upon them if, on the ground of insufficiency, they ejected a scholar whom all Europe held in the highest regard. The Triers, irritated that their intention was resisted by so eminent a person as the Dean of Christchurch, with bad grace acquitted Dr. Pococke. If, in the instance of a scholar of such deserved fame, the Triers were with difficulty prevented from depriving him of his cure, it may be readily believed with what injustice many clergymen were expelled from their livings, and often simply because they refused to admit that the Protector had legal right to rule.

The necessities of the military despotism which Cromwell had established in England made his government increasingly oppressive. The severe discipline requisite for the management of the victorious army was applied to the civil administration; and merely by the publication of a decree, he restricted the personal liberty of a large number of his educated and most peaceable subjects. His object was to humble the clergy, and at the same time to make conspiracy on their part against his government almost impossible. In August, 1654, he published "an ordinance for ejecting scandalous, ignorant, and insufficient ministers and schoolmasters"; by which, under a show of zeal for the purity of the clerical character, and for the fulfilment of their duty, he could rid himself of any educated persons who were opposed to his government, by reducing them to a position of dependence, and therefore necessarily of submission. The Ordinance appointed lay-commissioners for every county, who were empowered to call before them any public preacher, lecturer, parson, vicar, or schoolmaster, who is or shall be reputed ignorant, scandalous, insufficient, or negligent. "Such ministers and schoolmasters were to be accounted scandalous, who maintained blasphemous or atheistical opinions, who were guilty of cursing and profanity, who held any popish opinions, who were guilty of adultery, fornication, drunkenness, haunting of taverns or alehouses, of quarrellings or fightings, playing at cards or dice, profaning the Sabbath, or who allowed or countenanced any of these in their parishes or families. Also, all such as have read or used the Common Prayer-Book in public since the preceding January, or who shall at any time hereafter do so; and such as have declared, or shall declare, by writing, preaching, or otherwise publishing their disaffection to the present government." Such ministers were to be "accounted negligent, who (unless hindered by necessary absence, or infirmity of body) omitted to preach and pray on the Lord's Day. Such schoolmasters were to be accounted negligent, who wilfully absent themselves from their schools, and neglect to teach their scholars." Cromwell did all this without the consent of any Parliament, acting in fact as Charles I. and his council had acted before the civil war, and thus justifying all their illegal proceedings; and so arbitrary were the powers of the commissioners, that they were empowered to eject upon the oath of one witness only.

They were instructed to rank the reading of the Common Prayer with the sins of swearing, drunkenness, and adultery; and thus they were to make a clergyman's performance of his duty the evidence of his scandalous life. The clergy who were ejected were forbidden to preach or to teach in any parish from which they had been expelled; but they were allowed for maintenance one-fifth of the income of their cures. Notwithstanding all these inquisitions and persecutions of the Anglican clergy, Cromwell was the patron of learning and of learned men. He partly endowed a Divinity professorship, and he gave twenty-four valuable manuscripts to the Bodleian Library. He founded and endowed a college at Durham, and he appointed both to Oxford and Cambridge some professors whose names are still famous in the literary history of our country. But his government could be maintained only by a series of tyrannical and violent actions, both against the Anglican clergy and the Roman Catholic emissaries and priests. Although Cromwell may have himself been willing to give as much public liberty as consisted with peace, and with the safety of his person and government; and although he may have persecuted the clergy only because many of them were Royalists, his Council suggested extreme measures, and urged him to remit no severity against his political adversaries. The Royalists, actively opposed to his domination, were keenly watched, and their plots were frequently discovered. Absolute government is ever in fear of disaffection and revolution; conspiracies are rare in the nation where freedom is assured to every orderly and peaceable citizen.

In November, 1654, Cromwell decreed, "That no persons, after January 1st, 1655, shall keep in their houses or families, as chaplains, or as schoolmasters for the education of their children, any sequestered or ejected minister, fellow of a college, or schoolmaster, nor permit their children to be taught by such; that no such person shall keep school either publicly or privately, nor preach in any public place, or private meeting, of any others than those of his own family; nor shall administer Baptism, or the Lord's Supper, or marry any persons; or use the Book of Common Prayer, or the forms of prayer therein contained, on pain of being prosecuted, according to the orders lately published by his Highness and Council, for securing the peace of the Commonwealth." It is said that no person was proceeded against under this decree,—a fact which must have been the result rather of accident than of intention on the part of the military government. The decree never had the sanction of Parliament, and it was therefore an illegal interference with the liberty of the Anglican clergy, many of whom must have suffered severely from its enforcement; for they were liable to arrest upon suspicion, and to be punished at the will of the Council. Cromwell had won liberty of conscience by his defeat of the Royalist armies, but the exigencies of his usurped authority made his rule as unjust as that of Charles I. had been in the worst days of Laud and of Strafford.

CHAPTER XIII.

1654—1658.

BAXTER had never been on terms of intimacy with Cromwell. The two men had so little in common, that unity of opinion or of purpose could hardly exist between them; but Baxter thoroughly understood his character, and he was no uninterested observer of the principles of his administration, and of the effects of it at home and abroad. He says: "When Cromwell was made Lord Protector, he had the policy not to detect and exasperate the ministers and others who consented not to his government." But his necessities led him to forgetfulness of the rights of conscience; for which so much had been ventured and so much endured by both the contending parties. Cromwell's plea against the charge of inconsistency with his professions was, that both Anglicans and Roman Catholics were the avowed enemies of his authority; and that to make administration possible, both of them must be held in subjection. They suffered severely; for a military despotism is not scrupulous as to its means. That which was established by the sword must in every case be maintained by the sword. He would readily have granted to the Anglicans that they should not be disturbed, if none of them would interfere in political affairs; but, as has been already stated, in every instance he was overruled by his Council, who regarded the English clergy as irreconcilable enemies. The universal toleration, which in effect had been promised upon his assumption of supreme power, was refused, so far as they were concerned; although the various sects seem to have had more freedom of worship under his reign than at any former period; for when the chief authority was conferred upon Cromwell, in 1653, all men were assured that liberty in religion would be fully accorded to them "who professed faith in God by Jesus Christ." The promise made to the ear was rudely broken in the act. In the spring, a proclamation was published, which declared the expediency of better executing the laws against Jesuits and priests, and for the conviction of all Roman Catholic persons disaffected to the government; and in the subsequent declaration which Cromwell and his Council made in the following autumn, some reason or explanation was attempted of this act of oppression: "Because it was not only commonly observed, but there remains with us somewhat of proof, that Jesuits have been found amongst discontented parties of this nation, who are observed to quarrel and fall out with every form of administration in Church and State." It soon followed upon this cruel proclamation, that John Southworth, a Roman Catholic priest, was put to death for the exercise of his office; and the sanguinary laws against his fellow-religionists were maintained with rigour. At the same time, as if with prominent inconsistency of policy, Cromwell attempted to show indulgence to the Jews, who asked him for permission to build synagogues, and to carry on their commerce in London. But the hatred of the unhappy Israelites was then so strong, that even Cromwell was not able by a simple decree to give them the freedom they sought. He found it necessary to summon a committee of divines, lawyers, and merchants to advise him what reply to make to the Jewish petition; and who were to report whether it could be granted conscientiously in respect to religion, legally in regard to existing enactments, and advantageously for the trade of England. The referees disagreed with one another, and the Jews failed to obtain their object. It remained for our century to remove the last of the restrictions upon their public liberty.

They who best knew Cromwell maintained that he always had regard to the monarchical form of government; that in his heart he preferred an Established Church and the parochial system; and that away from the heated passions of ambitious generals and angry parliaments, in his moments of reflection, he had no sympathy with the democratic levellers, who overturned everything and settled nothing. Circumstances had compelled him to think with Hobbes, that "a wise and just despotism is the perfection of political society, and that the sovereign alone is to judge whether religions are safely to be admitted or not;" but his sagacious mind must have been convinced that monarchy in matters of religion does not harmonize with the spirit of Christianity. His own experience of government taught him that a large assembly, ever giving way to passion and invective in their discussions, were utterly unfitted to rule a nation; but that the safest and happiest state in which men can live is, where an enlightened monarchy has the advantage of a council of the wisest and most prudent in the land.—After a time, some Jews crept into London, and were allowed to trade without molestation; and even the Quakers, whom every sect opposed and condemned, found rest from persecution under Cromwell's administration.

Month by month his severities towards the English clergy increased. They alone had no freedom of worship, while every sect was at liberty to hold meetings for prayer and preaching. The object of the government, by silencing its ministers, was to gradually draw the affection of the people from the Church, to accustom them to other forms of sacred service, and ultimately to destroy it. Some of the clergy, for whose exclusion it had been difficult to find a pretext, were allowed to retain their livings; but the use of the Prayer-Book was absolutely prohibited. Those supplications were forbidden to be said—some of which, nearly as old as Christianity itself, had been employed in their hours of prayer by forty generations of the best of mankind, and which, with wonderful concentration of revealed truth, were as household words among the people. Long extemporaneous effusions took their place, in which prolixity and repetition of phrases often wearied the ignorant, disgusted the educated, and perplexed the young. The sword was laid upon reading-desk and Bible. Sturdy Ironsides, vociferating in church, would tear the surplice from the minister, snatch the Liturgy from his hand, contradict his expositions of Scripture, and bid him give place to men who could pray without book, and preach without limit. Several of the clergy, when called upon to officiate, would say the forbidden prayers from memory. When Bull was asked to baptize the child of a dissenter, he was able to repeat the service by heart from the Prayer-Book, with which the people were well pleased. Churchmen generally had a hard time under the tyranny of the Protector. If some of their families met together, the vigilant eyes of agents of the government were upon them. Spies watched their movements, wrote down and carried to Whitehall hasty expressions; noted their expenditure, tracked them when journeying, stood near them at markets, and even followed them when hunting. If they met in each others' homes to pray, they were forbidden to use the familiar words of Litany and Collect, which their fathers had employed. Tyranny hindered even devotion. If the sick man in his last hours would refresh his soul, when offering thanksgiving, by the Commemoration of the death of his Lord, the government forbade the utterance of prayer and of dedication in the ancient forms, with which early Fathers and venerated martyrs had expressed their gratitude for spiritual food and sustenance, and for the pledges of their Saviour's love. The picture in Christchurch Hall, of the three who dared to worship in the manner disallowed by the ruler, who was enthroned upon the graves of Charles and of Laud, was no exaggerated representation of the sorrows, the courage, and endurance of the time. No men more deserve the admiration of mankind than they who calmly suffer for conscience' sake.

A few clergymen whom Cromwell favoured were allowed

to minister without disturbance or prosecution; but the greater number of them were compelled to silence. Informers were many; spies infested every place where churchmen congregated, dogged the steps of prelate and priest; as eager in observation as they were infamous in conduct. Every churchman was considered a Royalist, and every Royalist was regarded as an enemy by the government. Some of the clergy took refuge in the houses of peers and country gentlemen, devoted themselves to study, or applied themselves to those early investigations in physical science, which led afterwards to the formation of the Royal Society. Although he was forbidden to continue the English service in his parish-church, Pococke, deprived of his canonry of Christchurch, without further fear of the Triers, devoted himself to the study of Aramaic and Arabic literature; Wilkins, Wallis, and Goddard pursued science at Oxford; Evelyn, Boyle, and Wren, with clergymen prohibited from their duties in church and cottage, gave themselves to the study of philosophy; and renowned Brian Walton, with the assistance of Edmund Castell, and the other Oriental scholars, the conspicuous constellation of the time, prepared under the patronage of Cromwell his Polyglott Bible, which, unequal in some respects to the Complutensian, Antwerp, and Paris Polyglotts, exceeds them all in direct usefulness to the biblical student. To have materially assisted Walton, and the eminent men who worked with him in this, which has been justly termed "the glory of that age and of the English Church," is a bright gleam in the darkness of the Protector's tyrannical administration.

The clergy were often forbidden to take shelter in the houses of country gentlemen. Hales, of Eton, and King, of Chichester, among many others, were driven from such places of refuge by the "Declaration." Others, expelled from house to house, often plundered of their furniture and of their books, reduced to poverty, were exposed to frequent persecutions. John Evelyn, certainly one of the most honourable and trustworthy witnesses in any cause, gives many instances, in his Diary, of the desolation of the Church, and of the silence and suffering of its ministers generally. As early as in March, 1649, he writes: "Mr. Owen, a sequestered and learned minister, preached in my parlour, and gave the blessed Sacrament, now wholly out of use in the parish-churches, which the Presbyterians and fanatics had usurped." . . . "I heard the Common Prayer (a rare thing in these days) in St. Peter's, at Paul's Wharf, London; and in the morning, the Archbishop of Armagh, that pious person and learned man, Ussher, in Lincoln's Inn Chapel." At Christmas, 1652, he writes: "Christmas Day, no sermon anywhere, no church being permitted to be open, so observed it at home." In January, 1653: "At our parish church a stranger preached. There was now and then an honest, orthodox man got into the pulpit, and though the present incumbent was somewhat of the Independent, yet he ordinarily preached sound doctrine, and was a peaceable man, which was an extraordinary felicity in this age." December 4th, of the same year: "Going this day to our church, I was surprised to see a tradesman, a mechanic, step up; I was resolved yet to stay and see what he would make of it. His text was from 2 Sam. xxiii. 20: 'And Benaiah went down also and slew a lion in the midst of a pit in the time of snow;' the purport was, that no danger was to be thought difficult when God called for a shedding of blood, inferring that now the saints were called to destroy temporal governments, with such feculent stuff; so dangerous a crisis were things grown to." Christmas Day: "No churches, or public assembly. I was fain to pass the devotions of that blessed day with my family at home." Ash Wednesday: "In contradiction to all custom and decency, the usurper Cromwell feasted at the Lord Mayor's." "There being no such thing as Church-anniversaries in the parochial assemblies, I was forced to provide at home for Whitsunday." 1654, December 25th: "No public offices in churches, but penalties on observers, so I was constrained to celebrate it at home." 28th: "A stranger preached. I understood afterwards that this man has been both chaplain and lieutenant to Admiral Pen, using both swords; whether ordained or not, I cannot say; unto such times were we fallen!" November 27th: "This day came forth the Protector's Edict or Proclamation, prohibiting all ministers of the Church of England from preaching, or teaching any schools, in which he imitated the Apostate Julian." December 25th: "There was no more notice taken of Christmas Day in churches. I went to London, where Dr. Wild preached the funeral sermon of preaching, this being the last day, after which Cromwell's Proclamation was to take place that none of the Church of England shall dare either to preach, or administer sacraments, teach schools, etc., on pain of imprisonment or exile. So this was the mournfullest day that in my life I had seen, or the Church of England itself since the Reformation; to the great rejoicing of both Papist and Presbyter. So pathetic was the discourse that it drew many tears from the auditory. Myself, wife, and some of our family received the Communion; God made me thankful, Who hath hitherto provided for us the food of our souls as well as bodies! The Lord Jesus pity our distressed Church, and bring back the captivity of Zion!" 1656, 3rd August: "I went to London to receive the blessed Sacrament, the first time the Church of England was reduced to a chamber and conventicle, so sharp was the persecution. The parish-churches were filled with sectaries of all sorts, blasphemous and ignorant mechanics, usurping the pulpits everywhere. Dr. Wild preached in a private house in Fleet Street, where we had a great meeting of zealous Christians, who were generally much more devout and religious than in our greatest prosperity." 25th December: "I went to London with my wife to celebrate Christmas Day. Mr. Gunning preached in Exeter Chapel. Sermon ended, as he was giving us the Holy Sacrament, the chapel was surrounded with soldiers, and all the communicants and assembly surprised and kept prisoners by them, some in the house, others carried away. It fell to my share to be confined to a room in the house, where yet I was permitted to dine with the master of it, the Countess Dorset, Lady Hatton, and some others of quality who invited me. In the afternoon, came Colonel Whalley, Goffe, and others from Whitehall, to examine us one by one; some they committed to the Marshall, some to prison. When I came before them, they took my name and abode, examined me why, contrary to an ordinance that none should any longer observe the superstitious time of the Nativity (so esteemed by them), I durst offend, and particularly be at Common Prayers, which they told me was but the mass in English, particularly pray for Charles Stuart, for which we had no Scripture. I told them we did not pray for Charles Stuart, but for all Christian kings, princes, and governors. They replied, in so doing we prayed for the King of Spain, too, who was our enemy and a papist, with other frivolous and ensnaring questions and much threatening; and finding no colour to detain me, they dismissed me with much pity of my ignorance. These were men of high flight, and above ordinances, and spake spiteful things of our Lord's Nativity. As we went up to receive the Sacrament, the miscreants held their muskets against us as if they would have shot us at the altar, but yet suffering us to finish the office of Communion, as perhaps not having instructions what to do in case they found us in that action. So I got home the next day, blessed be God!"

These instances will be enough to show how complete and violent was the suppression of the English Church, by them who boasted that they had done battle for freedom against the tyranny of their king; and it may be inferred how many and various were the indignities and sufferings of the ejected clergy. None of them was allowed to minister publicly within five miles of London. Their rectories and vicarages were occupied by men who had no respect for vested rights. They took possession by the command of the committee of the victorious Parliament, or at the will of the Protector; and they often allowed the buildings to be without repair; storing hay and corn in the chambers, and in some cases leaving the interiors open to the storms of winter. Sometimes, the new tenants declined to pay the stipulated one-fifth of the revenues of the livings to the families of the sequestrated clergy; and they sternly refused to administer the Sacrament in church to them who were not of their own party, and to baptize their children. The biographies of Hales of Eton, of Farindon, and of many more of them who were deprived of their livings by the decree of the Triers, may justly lead to the conclusion, that the action of the republican government in silencing the clergy, and in shutting up their churches, was done without pretext of law, by the hand of military authority. The ministers, thrown upon the charity of the world for their sustenance, were unceasingly harassed; always objects of suspicion to the generals commanding districts of the country, and to the officers who were placed over the garrisons in the towns. Their words in sermons, and even in social intercourse, spoken with no evil intention, were liable to the construction of treason under a government which daily violated the constitution. Their means of living were withdrawn; they were forbidden to teach the young; with the education and habits of clergymen, they could engage in no secular pursuits. Watched at home, and tracked abroad, they frequently relied for maintenance upon the donations of churchmen. When Farindon, suspended from his office, took leave of the congregation in his church in Milk Street, he received more than four hundred pounds by their contributions; so much they regarded his ministrations, and so strongly they protested against the senseless tyranny which deprived them of their clergyman. Many of his brethren, mercilessly and promptly ejected, were not equally fortunate in receiving timely and generous help in their distress. There is remarkable significance in the record in John Evelyn's Diary, under the date 23rd February, 1658: "There was now a collection for persecuted and sequestered ministers of the Church of England, whereof divers were in prison. A sad day! The Church now in dens and caves of the earth."

Nothing could justify these high acts of sovereignty, these outrages and oppressions on the part of Cromwell and his Council. That a Parliament should be violently dissolved, that the legal choice of the electors should be completely disregarded, that vested interests should be invaded, and that power should be exercised by the soldier's hand alone, may necessarily follow revolution, and the usurpation of authority; but that the whole body of the English clergy should be summarily commanded to pray, and preach, and to exercise their spiritual functions no more,—the many condemned and punished for the political hostility, or for the unworthiness, incompetence, and negligence of the few, can be defended on no principles of justice and equity. Such conduct would have been natural to the contemptible "Barebones' Parliament," whom the Protector expelled, and of whom Baxter says: "They intended to eject all the parish-ministers, and to encourage the gathering of Independent churches; that they cast out all the ministers in Wales, who, though bad enough for the most part, were yet better than none, or the few itinerants they set up in their room; and they attempted and had almost accomplished the same in England."

All power rested in the hands of Cromwell and his Council. Not only were the office and title of a king abolished, but the House of Lords was declared to be useless, and the government was proclaimed to be republican. The judges were appointed by authority of Parliament, or, if that assembly were prorogued, by that of the Protector. The coin current in the country bore the inscription of "The Commonwealth of England." The oath of allegiance, called the Engagement, was demanded of all the servants of the State. By his sagacity, tact, and determination, without consent of Parliament or of people, Cromwell had made himself the ruler of the nation. A series of successes confirmed that power, which, violently assumed, could be retained only by the sword. The Royalists, Presbyterians, and sectarian republicans were alike hostile to each other and to him. His spies revealed to him all their plots; and his real strength consisted not so much in the fidelity of the army, as in the fact that his enemies cordially hated one another. All the magistrates in counties and towns, holding their offices by his favour, were required to be constantly watchful each in his district. Cromwell could indeed publicly say: "How proper it is to labour for liberty, that men should not be trampled upon for their consciences. Is it ingenuous to ask for liberty, and not to give it? What greater hypocrisy than for those who were oppressed by the bishops to become the greatest oppressors themselves, so soon as their yoke is removed?" Although among his friends he allowed certain exemptions from the penalties declared in his decree, and connived at their use of the Common Prayer in their families; yet his hand continued to press heavily upon the Church of England, and he relaxed none of the restrictions upon the public use of the offices of its religion.

When Cromwell had dissolved the Parliament of 1654, in which for the first time in our history Irish and Scotch members sat with representatives of England, all really legal government came to an end. His rule became more and more despotism, and the people, conscious that they had lost their liberty, began to think of the possibility of restoring the young Prince Charles to the throne of his father. While the Protector governed, foreign affairs were managed by a vigorous hand. During the years of the English civil war, there had been great changes on the Continent of Europe, in which Britain in its state of distraction could take no part. The terrible Thirty Years' War was at an end, and if a firm religious peace had not been established, the Treaty of Westphalia had at least defined the frontiers of the Roman Catholic and Protestant powers. Cromwell's ambition was to be the acknowledged head of the Protestant League of Europe. In 1654, he urged the Parliament to act energetically for their brethren abroad, who often at great disadvantage struggled with the adherents of the Latin Church. He said to them: "You have on your shoulders the interest of all the Christian people of the world. I wish it may be written on our hearts to be zealous for that interest." Persecuted Protestants looked to him for help. The Duke of Savoy had resolved that his Protestant subjects should either enter the Roman Catholic Church or go into exile. To compel them, he poured large masses of troops into the Piedmontese valleys; for the Pope and the Italian princes had urged the Duke to get rid of his heretical subjects one and all. The troops were ordered to expel the inhabitants of the valleys from their homes, and to put to instant death them who dared to remain. Many of the unhappy Vaudois were massacred. In the spring of the year, as the snows melted and military operations became easier, the soldiers burned the villages in the valleys, driving the defeated peasants into the mountains, where many died miserably. The survivors sought pity and help from the Protestant powers. Their cry of agony was heard in England. The whole country was moved with indignation at the atrocity of the ruler, and with sympathy for his persecuted subjects. Milton embodied in immortal verse the prayers of thousands of the English people:—

> "Avenge, O Lord, Thy slaughtered saints, whose bones
> Lie scattered on the Alpine mountains cold!"

Early in May, Cromwell heard of the atrocious cruelties of the Duke of Savoy. Englishmen of all parties united their protests with his. The old Teutonic hate of wrong, and sympathy for oppressed brethren, gleamed out in the sudden anger of the land. The Protector never before appeared to use his great power so wisely. He quickly sent a messenger to the Duke of Savoy, demanding the immediate cessation of the persecution of the Vaudois. He threatened speedy vengeance. He appointed a day for a general fast; and he spoke and acted in the name of a people who have ever loathed and resisted oppression; and at his request then, as on many an occasion since, England opened her liberal hand, and in a very short time forty thousand pounds were collected, and remitted to the surviving peasants. Cromwell urged the Swiss cantons to invade Savoy; and he invited the Kings of Sweden and Denmark, with Holland and Switzerland, and the Reformed Churches throughout the world, to send contributions; they acquiesced with admirable liberality. He called upon the King of France and Cardinal Mazarin to unite with him in denouncing the wrongs of men, whose crime consisted in worshipping God after the custom of their fathers. He wrote to the Duke of Savoy, that "he was pierced with grief at the sufferings of the Vaudois, being united to them not only by the common ties of humanity, but by the profession of the same faith, which obliged him to regard them as his brethren; and he should think himself wanting in his duty to God, to charity, and to religion, if he should be satisfied with pitying them only, unless he also exerted himself to the utmost of his ability to deliver them out of it." He declared war against Spain, at that time the most intolerant of nations; and in 1656, he interfered with the French government on behalf of the Huguenots, who were persecuted and oppressed at Nismes. The wily Cardinal Mazarin, although he fretted under the peremptory demand of the Protector, that the outrages employed against the French Reformed Churches should immediately cease, dared not quarrel with a ruler who had helped France in her hour of need, who had a powerful navy, and whose infantry was the admiration of the world.

Cromwell well knew that his administration at home was tyrannical, but he found it necessary to act as if in conformity with law. In 1657, he summoned another Parliament. Many of the Irish and Scotch members of it were nominated by the government, and more than half of them held office under it. Neither Roman Catholics nor Royalists were allowed to vote. Even of them who were elected many were excluded, under the pretext of their disaffection. The

Protector boldly said, that his despotism had been "more effectual towards discountenancing vice, and settling religion, than anything done these fifty years. If it were to be done again, I would do it." It was proposed by a great majority to offer him the crown of England. He replied to them: "I cannot undertake the government with that title of king; and that is my answer to this great and weighty business." He had reached the height of power, and of such renown as might be obtained by a successful general who had possessed himself of supreme authority. Throughout Europe his administration was regarded with respect. His soldiers had won victory from the Spaniards on the sand-hills of France which look upon the Channel, and his ships had borne an expedition against them to the West Indies, which added Jamaica to the English dominions. Their cannon were feared in every harbour of the Mediterranean. His Admiral Blake, one of the British sea-kings, had found nothing too hard to conquer on that great water, which, for thousands of years, had been the place of battle between contending empires; forts, batteries, and enormous galleons yielded to the marine thunder of the republican Protector; who boasted, when he read to his Council the Admiral's despatches, he "hoped to make the name of an Englishman as great as ever that of a Roman had been."

During these years of Cromwell's military government, Baxter was passing what has been justly termed the Sabbath of his life at Kidderminster. Preaching and administering to his flock with no remission of his labour, he had that clear sunshine of peace, which he was never to see, or to see at long intervals only, in the gloomy and troubled future years. His heart prompted him to his work, and God strengthened him in it. The storms of the Commonwealth brought him no distress. He heard the thunder, but was unharmed by it. His duty was to meditate upon truth, to lessen suffering, to lead men to their Saviour, to diffuse the vital knowledge of His compassion, to comfort them who felt the thorn of grief, and to whisper the holy promises of pardon, hope, and peace in the ears of them whose feeble hearts were fluttering towards rest. With no wealth but that of a noble mind sanctified by the Spirit of his Lord; never absent when sufferers called for him in the huts of the poor; at all times ready to counsel and to cheer them; dismayed by no ghastly malady, fearing no contagion, forgetting no opportunity of charity,—earth had not anything to show more fair than the light of goodness, the patience, the hopefulness, with which Baxter ran his godly race. Beloved by his flock, reverenced by the town, men abstained from sin at his rebuke; rejoiced in the smile of his approval; felt the fragrance of holiness when he came to their homes; and crowded his church to listen to his declaration of the mercy which invited the diseased and the outcast to be healed, and to be restored to sanctity and bliss. From week to week, six hundred communicants continued the perpetual Memory of their Redeemer's death as their bounden duty and service. The people were temperate, peaceable, and devout at home; and they so thronged his church, that even the additional "five galleries" were insufficient to receive them who were eager to hear from their minister how they might be freed from the love and practice of iniquity. So that, rude and vicious at the first, under his fostering care they were educated to the Christian life, brought from impure and desolate darkness into a new day of fruitful goodness. They, who could not understand his syllogisms, yielded to his entreaties; wept when he convinced them of their evils and their remedy; and loved him with the gratitude of men who knew that they owed their best advantages to his toil and care.

From him they had learned not only that there is an unseen world, the noblest part of creation, but that they belonged to it, and were themselves beloved by its inhabitants, who had sympathy with them in the work, afflictions, and sorrows of life; who watched their course with the affections of brethren, to whose natures selfishness was impossible, and who would gladly welcome them to their fellowship of joy when the time of their departure should come. In such work, and among people he had so reformed and blessed, Baxter was happy. His successes soothed him in his often returning illnesses. The hands of them whom he had recovered to goodness ministered to him in his weakness. Some of them whom he had humanised sang him the hymns he loved, in the sad days when weakness confined him to his chamber. He saw the seed he had sown ripening to its harvest. There was often a bright, refreshing sun to shine upon the cloud of his personal suffering. Wonderful things had been done in his parish, surpassing all his expectation, and his heart overflowed with gladness.

During the intervals of his public work at Kidderminster, Baxter, who willingly wasted no hour of his life, wrote several quarto volumes, in addition to those formerly mentioned. Some of them were controversial, others of them theological and practical; and the substance of them may have formed parts of sermons preached in St. Nicholas' and St. Helen's churches in Worcester, where the services of so eminent a clergyman must have often been desired; in the neighbouring towns, and in St. Paul's Cathedral,—the noble structure which perished in the great fire of 1666. A few of these volumes are hardly remembered now, or are to be obtained with difficulty, found chiefly among the moths and dust of large libraries. Yet it is impossible to deny the usefulness of some of these treatises, although the subjects discussed in others of them have no more interest for mankind. Society has outgrown them, or forgotten them; even opinions have their fashion. Some of these small quartos, full of quotations from writers who are now as little recollected as the kings of the Goths, remind the reader of ancient arms, which are treasured in galleries and museums, formidable in their time, but cumbrous and useless since. His work on "Confirmation and Restauration," which appeared in 1658, is not without interest in our own day. It is not a defence of the Anglican rite of confirmation, although it contains much which is valuable in relation to it; but it is an attempt to prove, that all who are baptized in infancy should make a public profession of religion when they come to years of discretion; and that without such public profession they ought not to be admitted to the Supper of the Lord. His chief position is, that "as a personal faith is the condition before God of title to the privileges of the adult; so the profession of this faith is the condition of his right before the Church, and without this profession he is not to be taken as an adult member, nor admitted to the privileges of such." In 1658, Baxter published his "Universal Concord." For many years, he had fervently desired to obtain a union among Christians, based upon the acceptance of the ancient Creeds. This was perhaps one of the last of his works written during his ministry at Kidderminster. He says: "Having been desired to draw up those terms which all Christian Churches may hold communion upon, I published them, though too late for any such use (till God give men better minds), that the world might see what our religion and our terms of communion were; and that, if after ages prove more peaceable, they may have some light from those that went before them. It consisteth of three parts. The first containeth the Christian religion, which all are positively to profess; that is, either to subscribe the Scriptures in general, and the ancient creeds in particular, or at most the Confession or Articles annexed, *e.g.*, I do believe all the ancient canonical Scripture, which all Christian Churches do receive, and, particularly, I believe in God the Father Almighty, etc. The second part, instead of books of unnecessary canons, containeth seven or eight points of practice for Church-order. And here it must be understood, that these are written for times of liberty, in which agreement rather than force doth procure unity and communion. The third part containeth the larger description of the office of the ministry." Long afterwards, Baxter strove to attain the desirable end of the public concord of Christians. His hope was to accomplish the comprehension of Nonconformity by the Church, by some modification of terms, that secession might come to an end. If political opinions could have been separated from the chief subjects of ecclesiastical disagreement, there is every probability that he would have practically succeeded in making so large a fusion of them who held in common the chief truths of Christianity, that a large number of religious men in England would have welcomed his proposal; the Church would have escaped much agitation and hostility; and for all inimical purposes Nonconformity would have been reduced to very small proportions. Whenever it may again be attempted, the first step to such union will be, that each man shall cease to believe in the absolute infallibility of his own opinion. The statement is eminently true, that no religious union will be firm and lasting, the centre of which is a trifle, but it must be that rather which will attract and hold men strongly together. An agreement, based on the mutual acknowledgment of the vital truths of Christianity, would produce the firmest and best union among Christians, if each would show charity to the other in matters of less importance: in the admirable spirit of Cyprian, refusing "to break the Lord's peace for diversity of opinion."

CHAPTER XIV.

1658.

THE military government of Cromwell, often oppressive not only to clergymen, but also to judges and barristers, continued with no remission of its severity until the year 1658. The members who had been excluded from Parliament were again allowed to take their seats, after a long adjournment. Men began to hope that some relaxation of despotism was at hand; but the public discontent was not at an end. Plots were renewed, and the Protector began to find that his hand was not strong enough to hold the discordant parties in peace, and to maintain in its first vigour his own authority over the State. Men were really tired of the animosities which had continued for nearly twenty years, and a return to forbearance and mutual indulgence would have been gladly acquiesced in, except by the chief agitators, who had profited by civil discords. Even the most violent of the sectarians distrusted Cromwell. They had fought against the tyranny of the king. They had consented to his death. They had hoped that a strong and permanent republic would have been secured by the triumph of the parliamentary armies, and that prescription and inequality in the rights of citizenship would have ceased. But they found themselves under a government more exacting and repressive than that against which they had risen with the armed hand. Instead of a commonwealth, in which regard should have been had impartially to the rights of all citizens, they were living under a despotism painful to be endured, and too strong to be overthrown. Lord Clarendon relates, that some of the Baptists, who had been the most fanatical of all the adherents of the Parliament, enraged by their disappointment of a free, equable, and peaceful commonwealth, offered their services to Prince Charles to attempt the destruction of the Protector's power. They said they would give their lives and fortunes to him, if he would restore such a Parliament as his father had convoked; if he would give liberty of conscience; if he would abolish tithes, and would freely and fully pardon all who had been in arms against the crown. They called the Protector hypocrite, impostor, traitor, the curse of mankind, a sink of sin. In the address they sent to Prince Charles, they stated that "they took up arms in the late war for liberty and reformation, but assured His Majesty they were so far from entertaining any thoughts of casting off their allegiance, or extirpating the royal family, that they wished only to restrain those excesses of government, which were nothing but the excrescences of a wanton power, and were rather a burden than an ornament to the royal diadem."

It is not improbable that intelligence of this movement towards the exiled Charles, from the most violent of the sectaries, reached Cromwell, and as an additional evidence to him, that his tenure of authority rested on no goodwill or affection of the people generally, but only upon the strength and vigilance of his personal rule. So many years he had governed, and yet there seemed to be no real stability or permanence in his power. The surface was covered with herbage and flowers, but the fires of the volcano burned fiercely beneath it. The Anglican clergy were generally silenced, and their influence upon the public destroyed. He still repressed them with severity; and in the early summer of the year 1658, he had caused Dr. Hewitt, a rector of one of the city-parishes, to be beheaded on Tower Hill, for corresponding with Charles; but neither successive proclamations, nor the axe of the executioner, could kill the spirit of public liberty, nor give true strength to an administration which began in violence, and was maintained by injustice and fear. Such a state of things could not continue. There is a degree of endurance which is too much for nature. Constant dropping wears away even the rock; and perpetuated anxiety is destructive. Cromwell had become weary of his office. His age was not great, for he had not exceeded his sixtieth year; but he had had much toil both in the field and in the palace. His anxieties were more than could be numbered; his suspicions increased with his perplexities; every hour made watchfulness and precaution more necessary to him; there were few of them who had stood by his side in battle, or who sat with him at the council-table, whom he could really trust; every week brought him intelligence of renewed plots against his power, and even of conspiracies against his life; he knew the number and exasperation of his enemies; conscience, it may be, disturbed him, when he reflected how unjust he had been to the English Church, how cruelly his decrees had afflicted the most learned and godly of its clergy, and how many by his act alone had been deprived of the comforts of their fathers' religion in the last hours of decaying nature. The burden of governing men who knew not how to submit to his authority became too heavy to be borne. In a moment of irritation the great soldier said, "I would have been glad to have lived under my woodside, and to have kept a flock of sheep, rather than to have undertaken this government." The mind sometimes is too vigorous for the body in which it dwells, and the strongest frame bends and falls beneath the weight of hopeless care. In his Irish and Scotch campaigns Cromwell had repeatedly suffered from ague, a disease which made frightful havoc in the English life of the sixteenth and seventeenth centuries; and for some years his health had not been robust. At length his self-restraint and fortitude gave way, and he confessed to his Council and to Parliament that he had infirmities. On the fourteenth day of February, that Parliament was dissolved; and the

Protector issued orders to all the generals commanding in the counties, "to be most vigilant for the suppressing of any disturbance which may arise from any party whatsoever." He summoned to a council those officers on whom he thought he could rely. They promised to defend him with their lives. The plots of the malcontents, quickly discovered, were soon formed again; they took new shapes, and the designs imputed to the conspirators were desperate and sanguinary. Colonel Hutchinson told him of a plan to seize him at Whitehall, and to throw him into the Thames. The Royalist agents in London were unceasingly active; and among other evil tidings which reached him of the determination of his enemies to destroy his government, Cromwell received information, of the truth of which he could make no question, that the Marquis of Ormonde had come to the metropolis to incite and head an insurrection against him. On the fifteenth day of May a rising was to take place in the city. The Protector knew all—for his spies discovered every plot. The apprentices burst out in rebellion, but the artillery swept away the ill-guided youths who filled the streets, and the executioner completed what the cannon began. Just as long afterwards, by similar means, Napoleon destroyed Lepelletier's insurrection, and gave peace to distracted Paris. A gleam of victory once more brightened Cromwell's sky, before darkness covered it. On the twenty-fifth day of May, the English force under Lockhart, in union with a French army, overthrew the Spaniards commanded by Don John of Austria and the great Condé. The English infantry carried all before them; and the Dukes of York and Gloucester, the sons of Charles I., who were in the field with the Spanish general, saw with dismay how heroically their fellow-countrymen could fight. In consequence of the victory, gained chiefly by the valour of his troops, Dunkirk was placed in the Protector's hands. It was his last ray of success before night fell.

Cromwell became more and more conscious of failing health. Stern on the field of battle, severe in his method of government, terrible in his punishment of detected conspirators, Cromwell had the tenderest affections as a son, husband, and father; and he was intensely beloved by his family. Through the summer his darling daughter, Lady Claypole, was slowly dying. The Protector, unable to attend to any public business, watched for fourteen days by her bedside—for her agony was prolonged—wearied and broken by his grief. He asked an attendant in the chamber of his departing child to read him the words of the everlasting Truth, which had formerly comforted him in the depths of sorrow. He said: "This Scripture did once save my life, when my eldest son died, which went as a dagger to my heart, indeed it did." One of his attendants read those expressions of perfect resignation to the Divine will: "I have learned in whatsoever state I am to be therewith content. I know how to be abased, and how to abound: everywhere and in all things I am instructed both to be full and to be hungry, both to abound and to suffer need. I can do all things through Christ which strengtheneth me." Thus he waited until his loved daughter passed away. Troubles follow troubles: the dark stream flows on from yesterday and into the morrow. It is true, they sometimes come not single spies, but in battalions. Just before his daughter's death, Cromwell had lost his son-in-law, Rich, and the old Earl of Warwick, who had been the Protector's unchanging friend. His sorrows overbore his heart: his strength began to fail. He looked coldly upon the emblems of his power, and he turned wearily from the evils of his government, to ponder over the sorrows which darkened the happy light of his home, and which bent down the strong man. The depression produced by the decease of his daughter rendered him the more liable to the absorption of germs of disease. In the hot days of August he was seized with violent fever, which his physicians declared to be tertian ague. For some time he resisted its poison, and was able to walk in the gardens of his palace. The Quaker George Fox, who visited him at the time, says: "Taking boat, I went to Kingston, and from thence to Hampton Court, to speak with the Protector about the sufferings of the Friends. I met him riding into Hampton Court Park; and before I came to him, as he rode at the head of his life-guards, I saw and felt a waft of death go forth against him; and when I came to him, he looked like a dead man. After I had laid the sufferings of Friends before him, and had warned him, according as I was moved to speak to him, he bade me come to his house. So I returned to Kingston; and the next day, went up to Hampton Court to speak further with him. But when I came, Harvey, who was one that waited on him, told me the doctors were not willing that I should speak further with him. So I passed away, and never saw him more." The fever became stronger and stronger, and it was determined to remove him to Whitehall. In a few days his physicians declared him to be in great danger, and they informed him of it. He knew that his departure would put an end to the Commonwealth, and he said to them: "Do not think I shall die. Say not I have lost my reason, I tell you the truth. I know it from better authority than any you can have from Galen or Hippocrates. It is the answer of God Himself to our prayers." Much has been stated of his illness, which was either the imagination of a dreamer or the invention of an enemy; but, men wrote at the time, that when he asked Dr. Goodwin, who was at his bedside, if a man could fall from grace, and when he heard, on the authority of that divine, that it was impossible, he replied, "I am safe, for I am sure I was once in a state of grace." It was said by them who were not ashamed to whisper far and wide the secrets of a dying man's chamber, and to which Christian charity might fittingly have closed the ear, that Dr. Goodwin prayed, in language not unusually adopted by his fellow-religionists at that day, "Lord, we beg not for his recovery, for that Thou hast already granted and assured us of; but for his speedy recovery." During the ten days in which he suffered, London was agitated by the tidings of his danger. Who was to carry on the government when the great soldier should be at rest? Who would be able to satisfy the demands of the army? His son was known to be a man of easy life, and without capacity, quite unable to hold his father's sword. So citizens questioned with each other, as they heard each hour the last tidings from the physicians, or as they anxiously watched the windows of the room in which it was known that the Protector lay. The generals debated as to his successor, and at length they resolved that inquiry should be made of Cromwell on that important matter of state, before it became too late to interrogate him. Secretary Thurloe went softly to the pillow of the dying Protector, and asked him whom he would appoint to succeed him. In the interval of delirium, he muttered "Richard," and then, on the return of reason, all his serious thoughts had rest in heaven. The night before he died, he said, "I should be willing to live to be further serviceable to God and His people; but my work is done. Yet God will be with His people." Early in the morning of the third day of September, 1658, when the fierceness of the fever seemed to have abated, and that calm came which sometimes comes before the light of life is about to fade away, Major Butler, waiting upon the Protector, heard him slowly and gently offering his last prayer: "Lord, I am a poor, foolish creature; this people would fain have me live; they think it best for them, and that it will redound much to Thy glory, and all the stir is about this. Others would fain have me die: Lord, pardon them, and pardon Thy foolish people, forgive their sins, and do not forsake them, but love, and bless, and give them rest, and bring them to a consistency, and give me rest, for Jesus Christ's sake. Amen." Since the 30th of August, a storm had been passing over England. The tempest, of unusual fury, darkened and deepened more and more, until the third day of September, the anniversary day of Cromwell's victories at Dunbar and Worcester. He saw no rush of fire from the sky, he heard no crash of thunder, as the storm swept far and wide, over wood and hill and northern harvest-fields.

In complete unconsciousness he continued weakening, until, in the afternoon of the day, his mighty heart was still.

No tumults followed upon his death. On the 4th of September, Richard Cromwell was proclaimed Protector. Mrs. Hutchinson describes him "as a peasant in his nature, yet gentle and virtuous; but became not greatness." The people seemed to acquiesce in his assumption of the government; and the court of Charles were disappointed at the tranquillity. In the winter of the year, they complained, "We have not found that advantage by Cromwell's death as we reasonably hoped; nay, rather, we are the worse for it, and the less esteemed, people imagining by the great calm that has followed that the nation is united, and that the king has very few friends." Richard's pressing danger was from the utter want of money to carry on the administration. Oliver Cromwell accumulated no wealth, and his son had scarcely sufficient means to provide for his father's funeral, which, for that reason probably, was deferred until the end of November. We know, from the Diary of John Evelyn, of the unwise splendour and expense of that interment. He says: "November 22nd, I saw the superb funeral of the Protector. He was carried from Somerset House in a velvet bed-of-state drawn by six horses, housed with the same; the pall held up by his new lords; Oliver lying in effigie in royal robes, and crowned with a crown, sceptre, and globe, like a king; the pendants and guidons were carried by the officers of the army, and the imperial banners, achievements, etc., by the heralds in their coats; a rich caparisoned horse embroidered all over with gold; a knight of honour, armed cap-à-pied; and, after all, his guards, soldiers, and innumerable mourners. In this equipage they proceeded to Westminster; but it was the joyfullest funeral I ever saw, for there were none that cried but dogs, which the soldiers hooted away with a barbarous noise, drinking and taking tobacco in the streets as they went."

Baxter, perhaps with some prejudice, has drawn the character of Cromwell, but it may be taken generally as a sketch of him by an observer singularly truthful, and well able to delineate it: "I come now to the end of Cromwell's reign, who died of a fever before he was aware. He escaped the attempts of many who thought to have dispatched him sooner, but could not escape the stroke of God when his appointed time was come. Never man was higher extolled, and never man was baselier reported of and reviled, than this man. No mere man was better and worse spoken of than he, according as men's interests led their judgments. The soldiers and sectaries most highly magnified him, till he began to seek the crown and the establishment of his family; and then there were so many who would be half-kings themselves, that a king did seem intolerable to them. The Royalists abhorred him as a most perfidious hypocrite, and the Presbyterians thought him little better, in his management of public affairs. If, after so many others, I may speak my opinion of him, I think that having been a prodigal in his youth, and afterwards changed to a zealous religionist, he meant honestly in the main, and was pious and conscientious in the chief course of his life, till prosperity and success corrupted him. At his first entrance into the wars, being but a captain of horse, he took special care to get religious men into his troop. These were of greater understanding than common soldiers, and therefore were more apprehensive of the importance and consequence of the war; and, making not money, but that which they took for the public felicity, to be their end, they were the more engaged to be valiant,—for he that maketh money his end, doth esteem his life above his pay, and therefore is likely enough to save it by flight, when danger comes, if possibly he can. But he that maketh the felicity of Church and State his end, esteemeth it above his life, and, therefore, will the sooner lay down his life for it. Men of parts and understanding know how to manage their business. They know that flying is the surest way to death, and that standing to it is the likeliest way to escape; there being many that usually fall in flight, for one that falls in valiant fighting. These things, it is probable, Cromwell understood; and that none could be engaged, such valiant men as the religious. Yet, I conjecture that at his first choosing such men into his troop, it was the very esteem and love of religious men that principally moved him, and the avoiding of those disorders, mutinies, plunderings, and grievances of the country, which debauched men in armies are commonly guilty of. By this means he indeed sped better than he expected. Aires, Desborough, Berry, Evanson, and the rest of this troop did prove so valiant, that as far as I can learn, they never once ran away before an enemy. Hereupon he got a commission to take some care of the associated counties, where he formed this troop into a double regiment of fourteen troops, and all these as full of religious men as he could get. These having more than ordinary wit and resolution, had more than ordinary success; first in Lincolnshire, and afterward in the Earl of Manchester's army at York fight. With their successes, the hearts both of captains and soldiers secretly rose both in pride and expectation; and the familiarity of many honest, erroneous men, as Anabaptists, Arminians, etc., withal, began quickly to corrupt their judgments. Hereupon Cromwell's general religious zeal gave way to the power of that ambition which increased as his successes increased. Both piety and ambition concurred in countenancing all whom he thought godly, of what sort soever; piety pleaded for them as godly, and charity as men; and ambition secretly told him what use he might make of them. He meant well in all this at the beginning, and thought he did all for the safety of the godly, and the public good; but not without an eye to himself. When success had broken down all considerable opposition, he was then in the face of his strongest temptations, which conquered him when he had conquered others. He thought that he had hitherto done well, both as to the end and means,—that God, by the wonderful blessing of His providence, had owned his endeavours, and that it was none but God Who had made him great. He thought that if the war was lawful, the victory was lawful; and that if it were lawful to fight against the king, and to conquer him, it was lawful to use him as a conquered enemy, and a foolish thing to trust him when they had so provoked him. He thought that the heart of the king was deep, that he had resolved upon revenge, and that if he were once king, he would easily at one time or other accomplish it; that it was a dishonest thing of the Parliament to set men to fight for them against the king, and then to lay their heads upon the block, and be at his mercy; and that if this must be their case, it was better to flatter or please him than to fight against him. He saw that the Scots and Presbyterians in the Parliament did, by the covenant and the oath of allegiance, find themselves bound to the person and the family of the king; and that there was no hope of changing their minds in this. Hereupon he joined with that party in the Parliament who were for the cutting off of the king, and trusting him no more; and consequently he joined with them in raising the Independents to make a faction in the Synod at Westminster and in the City, in strengthening the sectaries in the army, city, and country, and in rendering the Scots and ministers as odious as he could, to disable them from hindering the change of government.

"In the doing all of this, which distrust and ambition persuaded him was well done, he thought it lawful to use his wits, to choose each instrument, and suit each means unto its end; and accordingly he modelled the army, and disbanded all other garrisons, forces, and committees, which were likely to have hindered his design. As he went on, though he had not resolved into what form the new Commonwealth should be modelled, he thought it but reasonable that he should be the chief person who had been chief in their deliverance; for the Lord Fairfax, he knew, had but the name. At last, as he thought it lawful to cut off the king because he thought he was lawfully conquered, so he thought it lawful to fight against the Scots that would set him up, and pull down the Presbyterian majority in the

Parliament, which would else, by restoring the king, undo all which had cost them so much blood and treasure. He accordingly conquered Scotland, and put down the Parliament; being the easier persuaded that all this was lawful, because he had a secret bias and eye towards his own exaltation. For he and his officers thought that, when the king was gone, a government there must be, and that no man was so fit for it as he himself; yea, they thought that God had called them by successes, to govern and take care of the Commonwealth, and of the interest of all His people in the land; and that if they stood by and suffered the Parliament to do that which they thought was dangerous, it would be required at their hands, whom they thought God had made the guardians of the land. Having thus forced his conscience to justify all his cause, cutting off the king, setting up himself and his adherents, putting down the Parliament and the Scots, he thought that, the end being good and necessary, the necessary means could not be bad. He accordingly gave his interest and cause leave to tell him how far sects should be tolerated and commended, and how far not; how far the ministry should be owned and supported, and how far not; yea, and how far professions, promises, and vows should be kept or broken; and therefore the covenant he could not away with, nor the ministers, further than they yielded to his ends, or did not openly resist them. He seemed exceedingly open-hearted, by a familiar, rustic, affected carriage, especially to his soldiers in sporting with them; but he thought secrecy a virtue, and dissimulation no vice; and simulation—that is, in plain English, a lie—or perfidiousness, to be a tolerable fault in a case of necessity; being of the same opinion with the Lord Bacon, who was not so precise as learned, 'that the best composition and temperature is to have openness in fame and opinion, secrecy in habit, dissimulation in seasonable use, and a power to feign if there be no remedy.' He, therefore, kept fair with all, saving his open or irreconcilable enemies. He carried it with such dissimulation, that Anabaptists, Independents, Antinomians did all think he was one of them; but he never endeavoured to persuade the Presbyterians that he was one of them, but only that he would do them justice and preserve them, and that he honoured their worth and piety; for he knew that they were not so easily deceived."

In November, a Parliament was summoned, elected upon the old system of representation, and moderate men were returned to it; but anarchy soon began to prevail. The directing mind had been taken away, and the whole body of the government lost its cohesion. There was confusion in every department of the State. The army and the citizens of London alike felt that the strong hand which had once held power was irrecoverably gone. There was neither wisdom to counsel nor force to control the discordant factions in the kingdom; but all men felt that Richard Cromwell was unequal to the office of a ruler, and that his early withdrawment from it was inevitable. Baxter briefly records the course of events by which the young Protector was compelled to return to private life: "The army set up Richard Cromwell, it seemed, upon trial, resolving to use him as he behaved himself; for though they swore fidelity to him, they meant to keep it no longer than he pleased them. When they saw that he began to favour the sober people of the land, to honour Parliaments, and to respect the ministers whom they called Presbyterians, they presently resolved to make him know his masters, and that it was *they*, and not *he*, who were called by God to be the chief protectors of the interest of the nation. He was not so formidable to them as his father had been, and therefore every one boldly spurned at him. The Fifth-monarchy men followed Sir Henry Vane, and raised a great, violent, and clamorous party against him among the sectaries in the city. Rogers, Freake, and such-like firebrands, preached them into fury, and blew the coals; but Dr. Owen and his assistants did the main work. The Wallingford-house party, consisting of the active officers of the army, determined that Richard's Parliament must be dissolved, and then he quickly fell himself. Though he never abated their liberties or their greatness, he did not sufficiently befriend them. Though Colonel Ingolsby and some others would have stuck to the Protector, and have ventured to surprise the leaders of the faction, and the Parliament would have been true to him, Berry's regiment of horse and some others were ready to begin the fray against him. As he sought not the government, he was resolved it should cost no blood to keep him in it; but if they would venture for their parts to new confusions, he would venture his part by retiring to privacy. And so to satisfy these proud, distracted tyrants, who thought they did but pull down tyranny, he resigned the government by a writing under his hand, and left them to govern as they pleased. His good brother-in-law Fleetwood, and his uncle Desborough, were so intoxicated as to be the leaders of the conspiracy; and when they had pulled him down, they set up a few of themselves under the name of a Council of State. So mad were they with pride, as to think the nation would stand by and reverence them, and obediently wait upon them in their drunken giddiness, and that their faction in the army was made by God an invincible terror to all that did but hear their names. The core of the business also was, that Oliver had once made Fleetwood believe that he would be his successor, and had drawn an instrument to that purpose; but his last will disappointed him. And then the sectaries flattered him, saying that a truly godly man, who had commanded them in the wars, was to be preferred before such an one as they censured to have no true godliness. I have no doubt that God permitted all this for good, and that, as it was the treason of a military faction to set up Oliver and destroy the king, so it was their duty to have set up the present king (Charles II.), instead of Richard. Thus God made them the means to their own destruction, contrary to their intentions, to restore the monarchy and family which they had ruined. But all this is no thanks to them; but that, which with a good intention had been a duty, as done by them was as barbarous perfidiousness as most history ever did declare. That they should so suddenly, so scornfully and proudly pull him down whom they had so lately set up themselves, and sworn allegiance to; that they should do this without being able to tell themselves why they did it; and that they should do it while a Parliament was sitting, which had so many wise and religious members, and accomplish it not only without the Parliament's advice, but in spite of it; that they should proudly despise not merely the Parliament, but all the ministers of London and of the land; yea, and act against the judgment of most of their own party (the Independents) is altogether wonderful."

The public distrust and confusion were so great that several of the chief men in London, who were skilled in affairs, wrote to General Monk, who commanded the northern army, inviting him to march into England, to confirm the authority of Parliament, and to give established order and a peaceful settlement to the state. On all sides men demanded a free Parliament. Fairfax, who commanded in Yorkshire, the inhabitants of the larger towns, the sailors on the Thames and in the chief havens of the country, were unanimous in making this request. Monk's course was clear before him, and he resolved to proceed at once. He collected money; increased the number of his troops; told them that the army in England was in opposition to the Parliament, whom all troops were bound to respect, obey, and defend, as receiving their pay from them; and that the civil authority ought to be supreme in the country. He moved quickly, crossing the Scottish border, and Lambert, who commanded in the North of England, retired before him. The fleet unanimously resolved to receive direction from the Parliament only, and to place themselves at their discretion. At York, Fairfax added largely to Monk's forces, who was profuse in his professions of loyalty to the Legislature; and thus he was able to march into London without encountering opposition. Before approaching the

15

Metropolis, he persuaded the government to remove their troops, quartered in the home-counties, into other parts of the country; so that the veterans, who had gained so many fields under Cromwell's command, were no longer in hand to resist the forces which Monk was leading towards the city. The people were utterly wearied by agitations and changes of administration; and they argued that it was for the advantage of all classes that a strong and settled government should be formed with good hope of permanence. Richard Cromwell had retired, and no general was competent to assume the authority which for many years Oliver had maintained. Mutual jealousy and suspicion prevented any effectual union of his officers for the management of public affairs; and men began seriously to think that the only solution of the difficulty would be in the immediate restoration of King Charles. The Royalists were unanimously prepared to receive their prince, who had been so long in exile; and the Presbyterians were willing to co-operate heartily with them; more from their intense hatred of the Independents, than from regard for the claims of the king; for if the Presbyterians feared and disliked the bishops, they detested both the principles and practices of the Independents in a much greater degree.

During the short period of Richard Cromwell's rule, Baxter published the "Holy Commonwealth; a Plea for the Cause of Monarchy, but as under God, the Universal Monarch:" one of the most remarkable of his books, and which had no slight influence upon his subsequent course. The chief principle he sought to maintain was, that the laws are above the king; that Parliament is the highest court in the country; and that power was given to the monarch solely for the common good. According to modern English ideas, the book is temperate in its advocacy of what is known to us as constitutional government, and against that which is despotical, whether under a king or under a Protector; but it was entirely opposed to the method of ruling which the Stuarts one and all adopted, and the obstinate maintenance of which, happily for the liberties and fortunes of Great Britain, expelled their family from the throne. Baxter wrote more directly and forcibly as a theologian than as a politician; but in this volume there was nothing which in an age of equal rights and of public freedom would have subjected him to censure, much less to prosecution. He gives an account of the origin and purpose of the work: "The book, which hath furnished my enemies with matter of reviling, which none must dare to answer, is my 'Holy Commonwealth.' The occasion of it was this: when our pretorian sectarian bands had cut all bonds, pulled down all government, and after the death of the king had twelve years kept out his son, few men saw any probability of his restitution, and every self-conceited fellow was ready to offer his model for a new form of government. Mr. Hobbes' 'Leviathan' had pleased many. Mr. Thomas White, the great Papist, had written his 'Politics' in English, for the interest of the Protector, to prove that subjects ought to submit and subject themselves to such a change. Mr. James Harrington (they say, by the help of Mr. H. Neville) had written a book in folio for a democracy, called 'Oceana,' seriously describing a form near to the Venetian, and setting the people upon the desires of a change. After this Sir H. Vane and his party were about their sectarian democratical model, which Stubbs defended. Rogers, Needham, and Mr. Bagshaw had also written against monarchy before. In the end of an epistle before my book on 'Crucifying the World,' I had spoken a few words against this innovation and opposition to monarchy; and having especially touched upon 'Oceana' and 'Leviathan,' Mr. Harrington seemed in a Bethlehem rage; for by way of scorn he printed half a sheet of foolish jests, in such words as idiots or drunkards use, railing at ministers as a pack of fools and knaves; and by his gibberish derision persuading men that we deserve no other answer than such scorn and nonsense as beseemeth fools. With most insolent pride he carried it, as if neither I nor any ministers understood at all what policy was, but prated against we knew not what, and had presumed to speak against other men's art, which *he* was master of, and his knowledge, to such idiots as we, incomprehensible. This made me think fit, having given that general hint against his 'Oceana,' to give a more particular charge, and withal to give the world and him an account of my political principles, and to show what I held as well as what I denied; which I did in that book called 'Holy Commonwealth,' as contrary to his heathenish Commonwealth. In which I pleaded the cause of monarchy as better than democracy and aristocracy, but as under God the Universal Monarch. Here Bishop Morley hath his matter of charge against me, of which one part is that I spake against unlimited monarchy, because God Himself hath limited all monarchs. If I had said that laws limit monarchs, I might amongst some men be thought a traitor and inexcusable; but to say that God limiteth monarchs, I thought had never before been chargeable with treason, or opposed by any that believed there is a God. If they are indeed unlimited in respect of God, we have many gods or no god. But now it is dangerous to meddle with these matters, most men say, 'Let God defend Himself.'"

Baxter gave this account of his book many years subsequently to its publication, after he had suffered much and long under the rule of Charles II. If some of his propositions would be condemned in our day of religious and civil liberty, as hardly consistent with the modern theory of constitutional government; yet his principles generally are those which harmonize with that conservative moderation of opinion, which, with very few exceptions, has been distinctive of the ablest men of all parties, who in our time have had share in the administration of public affairs. The following passages may show the general principles of the work, and when the temper of the days succeeding the Protectorate is duly considered, they may reveal the causes of the indignation this book produced against him: "The laws in England are above the king; because they are not his acts alone, but the acts of king and parliament conjunctly, who have the legislative, that is, the sovereign power. The king was to execute judgment according to these laws, by his judges in his courts of justice; and his parliament was his highest court, where his personal will and word were not sufficient authority to suspend or cross the judgment of the court, except in some particular cases submitted to him. The people's rights were evidently invaded; ship-money and other impositions were without law, and so without authority. The new oath imposed by the convocation and the king, the ejecting and punishing ministers for not reading the Book of Sports, for not bowing towards the altar, for preaching lectures, and twice on the Lord's Day, with many the like, were without law, and so without authority. The Parliament did remonstrate to the kingdom, the danger of the subversion of its religion and liberties, and of the common good and interest of the people, whose trustees they were, and we were obliged to believe them both as the most competent witnesses and judges, and the chosen trustees of our liberties. We are ourselves incapable of a full discovery of such dangers till it be too late to remedy them; and therefore the constitution of the government, having made the Parliament the trustees of our liberties, had made them our eyes by which we must discern our dangers, or else they had been useless to us. The former proceedings afforded us so much experience as made the Parliament's remonstrance credible. We saw the king raise forces against the Parliament, having forsaken it, and first sought to seize upon its members in a way which he confessed a breach of its privilege. All the king's counsellors and soldiers were subjects, and legally under the power of the Parliament. It had power to try any subject, and adjudge them to punishment for their crimes. The offenders, whom it would have judged, fled from justice to the king, and there defended themselves by force. When the Parliament commanded us to obey them, and not resist them, I knew not how to resist and disobey them without violation of the command of God, 'Let every soul be subject to the higher power,' etc., and without incurring the danger of the condemnation there threatened to resisters. I think none doubts but that command obliged Christians to obey the senate as well as the emperor. When it was confessed by the king that the legislative power was in the three estates conjunct, and the estate was mixed, and consequently that the Parliament had a part in the sovereignty, I thought it treason to resist them as the enemy did, apparently in order to their subversion; and unlawful to disobey their just commands such as I thought these were. I had great reason to believe that if the king had conquered the Parliament, the nation had lost all security of their liberties, and been at his mercy, and not merely under his government; and that if he had conquered them by such persons as he then employed, it had not been in his power to have preserved the Commonwealth if he would. His impious and popish armies would have ruled him, and used him as other armies have done those that trusted them. I knew that the Parliament was the representative body of the people of the Commonwealth, who are the subject of the common good; that the common good is the essential end of government, and, therefore, that it cannot be a just war that by their king is made against them, except in certain excepted cases; and that the end being more excellent than the means is to be preserved by us, and by no means to stand in competition with the end. And therefore if I had known that the Parliament had been the beginners, and most in fault, yet the ruin of our trustees and representatives, and so of all the security of the nation, is a punishment greater than any fault of theirs against a king can deserve, and that their faults cannot disoblige me from defending the Commonwealth. I owned not all that ever they did; but I took it to be my duty to look to the main end. I knew that the king had all his power for the common good, and therefore that no cause can warrant him to make the Commonwealth the party which he shall exercise hostility against. War against the Parliament, especially by such an army, in such a cause, is hostility against them, and so against the Commonwealth. All this seemed plain to me; and especially when I knew how things went before, and who were the agents, and how they were minded, and what were their purposes against the people. I shall continue with self-suspicion to search, and be glad of any information that may convince me if I have been mistaken, and I make it my daily earnest prayer to God that He will not suffer me to live or die impenitently, or without the discovery of my sin, if I have sinned in this matter. Could I be convinced of it, I would as gladly make a public recantation as I would eat or drink; and I think I can say that I am truly willing to know the truth. But yet I cannot see that I was mistaken, in the main cause, or dare repent of it, nor forbear the same, if it were to do again in the same state of things. I should do all I could to prevent such a war, but if it could not be prevented, I must take the same side as then I did. And my judgment tells me that if I should do otherwise, I should be guilty of treason or disloyalty against the sovereign power of the land, of perfidiousness to the Commonwealth, of preferring offending subjects before the laws and justice, the will of the king above the safety of the Commonwealth, and consequently above his own welfare; and that I should be guilty of giving up the land to blood, or to much worse, under pretence of avoiding blood in a necessary defence of all that is dear to us."

If judgment is to be made according to the results of it, the publication of this work was one of the chief mistakes of Baxter's literary life. Political questions had not been the subjects of his special study, and his opinions were necessarily affected by the furious passions of the time. This book may have been written more hastily than his other works; and when the evident inadequacy of Richard Cromwell to his office kindled hope or excited fear for the future of the country, the work exposed him to great censure. Men of all opinions assailed or reviled him, not only Harrington and the malignant Pettit, but Morley, and especially L'Estrange and Long. Afterwards, the University of Oxford condemned it to be burned; and Baxter had such consolation as might be gained from the fact that his book was consumed at the same time with those of John Owen, who had been Cromwell's Dean of Christchurch, and of one since held in repute throughout the civilized world, John Locke, the philosopher and patriot. Yet unbroken prosperity fell not to all Baxter's revilers, whose bitterness was extreme, and their language often resembling the angry imprecations of the inhabitants of the lanes which bordered the Thames, or of the profligates of Whetstone Park. Some of them learned to repent of their unreasonable malignity; and the inevitable retribution visited others when seeking the high places of the world, where they who fell never rose again. Baxter relates an anecdote of South, who when very young had been mentioned to him as well qualified to help him as his curate at Kidderminster, but who afterwards sought to gain the favour of them who were able to promote him by assailing the author of the "Holy Commonwealth." South had been appointed to preach before Charles II., and he determined to ingratiate himself with the monarch by publicly attacking Baxter's book. A great congregation assembled to hear him, and to see the king and his court. Baxter says: "When South had preached a quarter of an hour, he was utterly at a loss, and so unable to recollect himself that he could go no further, but cried, 'The Lord be merciful to our infirmities!' and hurried out of the pulpit. About a month after, they were resolved that Mr. South should preach the same sermon before the king, and not lose his expected applause; and preach it he did, little more than half an hour, with no admiration at all of the hearers; and, for his encouragement, the sermon was printed. When it was printed, many desired to see what words they were that he was stopped at the first time, and they found in the printed copy all that he had said first, and one of the next passages that he was to have delivered, was against me for my 'Holy Commonwealth.'" For ten years Baxter allowed the vituperation to continue, and at last it became more than even his long-suffering nature could bear, and he took the singular course of recalling the book, and of asking the public to consider it as not written. In the preface to the "Life of Faith," long afterwards, in expressing his regret that he published "The Holy Commonwealth," he says: "Let the reader know that, whereas a bookseller hath in his catalogue of my books named my 'Holy Commonwealth,' I do hereby recall the said book, and profess my repentance that ever I published it, and that not only for some bye-passages—though the first part of it, which is the defence of God and reason, I recant not. But this revocation I make with these provisions: that I reverse not all the matter of the book, nor all that that more than one have accused; that I make not this recantation to the military fury and rebellious pride and tumult against which I wrote it; that though I dislike the Roman clergy's writing so much of politics, and I detest ministers meddling in state matters, yet I hold it not simply unbecoming a clergyman to expound the fifth commandment, nor to show the dependence of human powers on the Divine, nor to instruct subjects to obey with judgment and for conscience' sake; that I protest against the judgment of posterity, and all others that were not of the same time and place, as to the mental censure either of the book or revocation, as being ignorant of the true reasons of them both. Which things provided, I hereby under my hand, as much as in me lieth, reverse the book, and desire the world to take it as *non scriptum.*" "Ever since the king came in, that book of mine was preached against before the king, spoken against in the Parliament, and wrote against by such as desired my ruin. Morley, Bishop of Worcester, and many after him, branded it with treason, and the king was still told that I would not retract it, but was still of the same mind, ready to raise another war, and a person not to be endured. New books every year came out against it, and even men that had been taken for sober and religious, when they had a mind for preferment, and to be taken notice of at court, and by the prelates, did fall on preaching or writing against me, and especially against this book, as the most probable means to accomplish their ends. When I had endured this ten years, and found no stop, but that still they proceeded to make me odious to the king and kingdom, and seeking my utter ruin this way, I thought it my duty to remove this stumbling-block out of their way, and without recanting any particular doctrine in it, to revoke the book and disown it, desiring the reader to take it as *non scriptum*, and telling him that I repented of the writing of it. The incessant bloody malice of the reproaches made me heartily wish, on two or three accounts, that I had never written it; because it was done just at the fall of the government, and was buried in our ruins, and never that I knew did any great good; because I find it best for ministers to meddle as little as may be with matters of polity, how great soever their provocations may be; and therefore I wish that I had never written on any such subject. I repented also that I meddled against Vane and Harrington, which was the second part in defence of monarchy, seeing that the consequents had been no better, and that my reward had been to be silenced, imprisoned, turned out of all, and reproached implacably and incessantly as criminal, and never like to see an end of it. He that had wrote for so little, and so great displeasure, might be tempted, as well as I, to wish he had sat still, and let God and man alone, with matters of evil polity. Though I was not convinced of many errors in that book, so called by some accusers, yet I repented the writing of it as an infelicity, and as that which did no good, but hurt."

CHAPTER XV.

1659—1660.

WHEN General Monk entered London, he was at the head of an army of thirty thousand men, whose confidence he had completely gained. Quartered at Whitehall, power was in his hands. A new Parliament was summoned, and the majority of the members elected to it were Presbyterians, who appointed Monk to be Commander-in-chief, and they set aside all officers who were known to be Republicans. In the meantime Charles, at Breda, was eagerly watching the course of events, where large numbers of the exiled noblemen had resorted to him. Expectant clergymen flocked to his court, hoping to be restored to the rectories and vicarages from which Cromwell's Triers had ejected them. Charles's course seemed beset with difficulties. The Parliament and many of the soldiers belonged to the powerful Presbyterian body, and large numbers of their ministers were in possession of English parishes. These men were much disturbed by the reports which were brought to England of Charles's frivolous and dissolute life, and of the character of those whom he had chosen as his friends and companions. In June, 1654, Charles had abjured the Protestant religion, and had been received, at St. Germains, into the Roman Catholic communion. This fact was not altogether unknown to some of the Anglican clergy. Bishop Burnet, in the "History of his Life and Times," while recording the fact that the king had changed his religion during his exile, declares at the same time that only two noblemen knew it; but the historical witnesses to the transition are numerous. That change was not unnatural; a son for the most part inherits some of the mental and moral qualities of his mother; and Henrietta Maria of France had all the religious and political antipathies which prevailed in the Bourbon Court in which she had been educated. So that it is easy to understand that, in the years of exile, she persuaded all her children to make profession of the religion of the Latin Church. To Charles himself, during the greater part of his life, it is probable that Christianity and Protestantism were equally matters of indifference, for he continually neglected the precepts of the one, and much of his administration was carried on without regard for the other. The practical difficulty before him was how to declare himself the zealous head of the Anglican Church, without being in open hostility to the dissidents, who, if combined, would be formidable opponents to his restoration. The dexterous duplicity inherited from his parents availed him on this as on many subsequent occasions. His first object was to gain Monk to his side, and he secretly despatched a letter to him by the hand of that general's cousin, Sir John Grenville. Monk dared not write anything in reply to it, but he verbally requested the messenger to inform the king that he would serve him faithfully; and he advised that Charles should declare a general pardon for all who had been in arms against the crown; that he should promise liberty of conscience, and unrestricted religious privileges; and that no persons who had acquired confiscated estates should be disturbed in the possession of them. The Presbyterians, who must have had a secret understanding with Monk, sent a deputation to Charles, who welcomed them with the gentle kindness and affability he could so well assume; listened patiently to their representations; deceived them first, and persecuted them afterwards. They proposed to him that Parliament should direct the naval and military forces of the country, and that an amnesty should be declared, so that no man might suffer for the part he had taken in the civil war. Charles, in repeating to his friends that which occurred at the interview, ridiculed these suggestions, adding, "They little think General Monk and I are on such good terms."

The Commonwealth daily grew more and more into disfavour with the public, who felt that they could breathe more freely now that the military despotism was at an end, and with but little thought that, in the history of a state, a change in the form of its government seldom makes any beneficial alteration in the social condition of the people. The national feeling, especially in the larger towns, changed with remarkable rapidity. They who had lately been popular idols were thrown down and dishonoured. Oliver and his saints became objects of derision. They who had mourned at his burial, now drank with exulting joy the health of the king. Even the ballad-singers in the streets, drunken and ragged, sang songs in contempt of the great soldier and his son. The taverns should be opened to all comers; the conduits should spout wine; feasting and merriment should follow fasting and gloom; they would laugh without censure, and riot with no fear of constables and justices; the reign of precisians and pietists was at an end; no one should hinder the people's joy,—the player and the morris-dancer, the bull-baiting and the prize-fighting, should again enliven holidays, and revive old British sports, and encourage manliness of spirit; for the king would bring back all the long-forbidden enjoyments, and Englishmen should be themselves again.

The Parliament met on the 26th of April, 1660; and Sir John Grenville openly placed in Monk's hands a letter which Charles commanded him to present, addressed to the Speaker of the House of Commons. It contained the famous Declaration of Breda; in this the king invited the House to return to their allegiance and their duty to their Sovereign, and he promised that the past should be forgiven and forgotten, and all the rights of Parliament should be maintained for the future. In the Declaration Charles promised to give "a general pardon to all his loving subjects who should lay hold of it within forty days, except such who should be excepted by Parliament. These only excepted, let all our subjects how faulty soever rely upon the word of a king solemnly given, that no crime committed against us or our royal father shall ever be brought into question, to the prejudice of their lives, estates, or reputation. We do also declare a liberty to tender consciences, and that no man shall be disquieted or called in question for differences of opinion in matters of religion, which do not disturb the peace of the kingdom. And we shall be ready to consent to such an Act of Parliament, as upon mature deliberation shall be offered to us, for the full granting that indulgence."

The House of Commons resolved, that "according to the ancient constitution, the government of this kingdom is and ought to be by King, Lords, and Commons." They voted a gift of fifty thousand pounds to Charles,—four thousand five hundred pounds in gold, and a draft for twenty-five thousand pounds. Pepys writes, that when Grenville brought the money to the king, he "was so joyful that he called the Princess Royal and the Duke of York to look upon it as it lay in the portmanteau before it was taken out." Richard Cromwell, wisely distrusting Charles's word, at once resigned his Chancellorship of the University of Oxford, and went to the Continent, where he might be secure from the revenge of the Stuarts.

Charles quickly accepted the invitation of the House of Commons. On the 26th of May, he landed at Dover, and, on the 29th of that month, he rode with his two brothers through the streets of London to Whitehall. Arthur Jackson, a noted Presbyterian minister, presented him with a Bible, as he passed to the Palace. The king said: "It is the thing that I love above all things in the world." The streets were strewed with the fresh flowers of the spring, then reigning in all its glory over English fields and homesteads, "With yellow cowslip and with pale primrose." Carpets or banners were hung from every house. The conduits ran with wine, and the citizens, as if exulting in the prospect of a settled and peaceful government, shouted joyful welcome to the king. Charles laughed at the easy rapidity by which he had passed from exile to a throne; and as he saw the submission of the people, the universal festivity, the garlands and banners, and as he received the salutations of the thousands who lined the streets, he said: "It is my own fault that I had not come back sooner; for I find nobody who does not tell me that he has always longed for my return."

The accession of Charles II. changed the character of the social life of England, almost as quickly as tropical storms affect the face of the country over which they pass. Puritanism had not been without signal advantage to all classes of people. It has left its mark upon the noble theological literature, much of which remains as gold which is buried in the earth. The accumulations and the neglect of ages have left large portions of it almost unknown, and generally unread; but the treasure exists to enrich and reward the diligent seeker. Feebler modern writers have incorporated parts of it in their ephemeral books; just as Roman princes have built their palaces with stones taken from the shattered temples of the gods, the glorious remains of art and its great masters. Nothing written since is to be compared with its nobler works, and certain of the authors in the succeeding generations who have attained to fame, as Bishop Butler, Paley, and the Apologists, owe to it occasionally not only their better thoughts, but sometimes the very line of their arguments. In literature and in the higher class of theology, Bacon, Shakespeare, Bishop Hall, Milton, John Howe, Baxter, Manton, Bunyan, and the starry host, the grandeur of whose thoughts is the true glory of their age, grew with the growth of Puritanism, and were in every case influenced by the healthful quickening it produced in the minds of men. So that the works of the modern exponents of theology, and often of practical religion, seem dwarfed, weak, and ineffectual, when compared with the wider range of sacred truth, the deeper thinking, and the larger conceptions of the writers of that older time. It is impossible to doubt that Puritanism produced the freedom, strength, and activity of modern British and American life. We owe our liberty, our power of social organization, our ideas of the propriety and dignity of public virtue and of private purity, to the resistance our forefathers made to the tyranny and immorality of the Stuart dynasty; and to their remonstrance against the insufferable principle, that the will of one fallible and frail man is to be the law for the abject obedience of millions. Puritanism, which was really only the demand of men for liberty of thought, was marred by the violence of the sectarian revolters in the civil war, and by the military severity of Cromwell's administration; but much of its moral effect was good, and had it been more moderate, it had not lost visible form and power when the Protector passed away. The Puritan idea of government was that of a Church-state, in which the Revealed Will of God should control all affairs, and religion be the condition upon which public service and private duty must rest; and that all human law should be enacted in the spirit of that which is Divine. Such an administration would necessarily frame penal statutes against vicious practices; and the consequent danger would be that its strictness should produce either hypocrisy or superstition. It is easy therefore to understand that, under the Protector's rule, the tolerated religion would be severe in its requirements and observances; and that outwardly the mass of the people would be abstinent from those indulgences which law forbade, but of which at heart they had no disapproval. Acts of Parliament cannot make men virtuous, and public enjoyment and festive merriment cannot be restrained by statute.

On the return of Charles II. there was a rapid moral reaction in a considerable portion of English social life. Men felt that an enforced prohibition of what are deemed personal pleasures was both unnatural and unwise; and they found that if the new government sought to restrict liberty of speech and of political action, they allowed full freedom to sensuality. By his contemporaries Charles was regarded as one of the most dissolute of men. Hitherto poverty had placed the only limit to the self-indulgence of a prince whose misfortune it was to have had weak principles with strong passions. He was surrounded in Breda by needy flatterers, abundant in vices; and the associates of his long exile there and in Paris would have corrupted a hermit. He had learned in their school of vicious profanity, and he had learned willingly and well. When he returned to England as its king, he brought with him as his friends and courtiers some of the most profligate men at that time in Europe. Their dress was gaudy, their minds depraved, their talk blasphemous, and their habits dissolute. They laughed at religion, rioted in debauchery, were quick of quarrel, obscene and drunken. The evil flood which these men let in spread far and wide. The moral example of the king, who was openly profligate, and of his brother the Duke of York, who was secretly immoral, was pernicious to every national interest. Literature was defiled by coarse language, indecent wit, and foul allusions. Plays, fitted only to be burned by the hand of the hangman, were the amusement of the monarch and of the lewd women in whose society he delighted. In every rank men suffered from the contagion of immorality. Each day the town heard of some new adultery; or listened to the horrid recital of seductions, succeeded by duels; of estates lost by gamblers, whose suicides quickly followed; of watchmen beaten by the fine gentlemen; and of peaceable citizens returning to their homes at nightfall assailed and maimed by some of the nobles of the court. In a year or two, the former public restraints of vice were practically removed. The king seemed to have become absolutely abandoned to a profligate life. He was perhaps the most thoroughly vicious man in London. His own chaplains remarked that he came directly from the chambers of his mistresses to the celebration of Holy Communion at church. For many years he acted as if he were utterly without a conscience, and as if life had no higher aim, no nobler destiny than to be a continuous revel of impurity. His language was often profane, and indecent wit was his delight. Bishop Burnet and others, who so describe him, and who were in frequent association with the king, were not likely either to misjudge his manner of life, or wilfully to misrepresent it. He rejoiced in impure plays, and in his heart he loved the revelry, intrigues, and vices which those mischievous compositions represented. His example diffused its baneful influence on every side. Men, who in Cromwell's day were outwardly decorous, gave themselves up to habits of depravity, and ridiculed the religion they had once professed. Some even of the clergy forgot their recent calamities, and the decorum which became them. Baxter says of this time: "Every week produced reports of one or other clergyman, who was taken up by the watch, drunk at night, and mobbed in the streets. Some were taken with lewd women, and one was reported to be drunk in the pulpit." These were no doubt the few exceptions to the general conduct of the restored clergy. Every age of the Church has had to deplore some who were faithless and profligate in their ministry; but all classes of society in a nation are necessarily vitiated, when the king is depraved and dissolute.

In 1660, the Parliament determined to provide so liberally for Charles, that he should have no occasion to raise money by unconstitutional means. When thanking them he said, with his usual disregard of truth: "I promise you, I will not apply one penny of that money to my own particular occasions, till it is evident to me that the public will not stand in need of it." In a very short time more than two millions of money had been lavished upon his excesses, and the money voted to provide a fleet had mostly been squandered upon the king's mistresses, whose extravagance was as great as their impurity. Pepys, who was not unfriendly to

Charles, says that when the House of Commons required to inspect the accounts, the very notion of such a demand "made the king and court mad; the king having given orders to my Lord Chamberlain to send to the playhouses and brothels, to bid the Parliament men that were there to go to the Parliament presently."

Charles remembered that the indignities and sufferings of his father were unavenged. To forget no injury received, and to punish it without mercy, was the attribute of all his family. To them and to him revenge was sweet, and the death of enemies a delightful recompense for anxiety or peril endured on their account. Before his restoration, the House of Commons resolved to except seven persons from the benefit of any amnesty. The king thought the number by far too small. Some of them fled in time; others were arrested, who had been so unhappy as to deceive themselves by the hope that there could be any clemency in Charles's heart. Of them who had sat as judges of his father, twenty-five were dead, and nineteen had escaped to the Continent. Twenty-nine who were apprehended were tried as traitors, nineteen of them were sentenced to be imprisoned for life, with the severest punishment, and ten of them were sentenced to death. The king heard with undisguised joy of their conviction and sentence; and he determined to feast his eyes with the sight of the last agonies of his father's judges. Their prolonged sufferings gave him unfeigned pleasure. His friend John Evelyn writes in his Diary of 17th of October, 1660, but with no expression of disgust at the revolting cruelty of Charles, and of his indecency in witnessing their sufferings: "Scot, Scroope, Cook, and Jones suffered for reward of their iniquities at Charing Cross, in sight of the place where they put to death their natural prince, and in the presence of the king his son, whom they also sought to kill. I saw not their execution, but met their quarters mangled, and cut, and reeking, as they were brought from the gallows in baskets on the hurdle. Oh the miraculous providence of God!" Bishop Burnet says: "The trials and executions of the first that suffered were attended by vast crowds of people. All men seemed pleased with the sight; but the firmness and show of piety of the sufferers, who went out of the world in a sort of triumph, in the cause for which they suffered, turned the minds of the populace, insomuch that the king was advised to proceed no farther." But, on 30th of January, 1661, the king had a sight still more gratifying to him, and which he would remember with delight on every anniversary-day of his father's execution. Evelyn records: "This day (Oh the stupendous, inscrutable judgments of God!) were the carcases of those arch-rebels Cromwell, Bradshaw (the judge who condemned His Majesty), and Ireton (son-in-law to the usurper), dragged out of their superb tombs in Westminster among the kings, to Tyburn, and hanged on the gallows there, from nine in the morning till six at night, and then buried under that fatal and ignominious monument in a deep pit; thousands of people who had seen them in all their pride being spectators." This was done by special command from the king to the Dean of Westminster. and he ordered the body of the illustrious Admiral Blake to be removed from the Abbey on the same day to St. Margaret's Church. Even the frivolous Pepys was shocked at the fiendish vengeance of the king upon the decaying remains of Cromwell; for he says: "Which, methinks, do trouble me, that a man of so great courage as he was should have that dishonour." But Charles came of a race who never forgave nor forgot, and to whom revenge was inexpressibly sweet; and it was to such a king for twenty-five dreadful years the government of England, and, what was infinitely more disastrous, the headship of the Anglican Church, were to be entrusted.

Before he could have peaceful possession of his throne, Charles had many difficulties to encounter. The Presbyterian party had been mainly the instruments of his restoration, and he could not at once forget his indebtedness, nor take measures for their repression. He remembered with unfailing bitterness what he had suffered at their hands, in the unhappy days which preceded the defeat at Dunbar. He abhorred the strictness of their principles, ridiculed their conscientiousness of conduct, the independence of their character, and the mode of their religious worship. He never forgot the length of their prayers, and his weariness under their sermons. Charles knew their general integrity of character, how strong they were in numbers and in influence; and acting with his usual duplicity, he received their ministers with emphatic expressions of respect, and appointed some of them to be his chaplains. Among these were Baxter, Calamy, and Reynolds. Baxter's position was peculiar and painful. An ordained clergyman of the Church of England, he had held his office at Kidderminster for fourteen years, during the period of republican rule, without the license or sanction of a bishop, and during that time he naturally felt more and more his freedom from supervision and control; and to some extent, isolated from his Anglican brethren, he sympathized with the Presbyterians, his neighbours, who belonged to the most powerful body of religionists, during the repression and persecution of the Anglican clergy: so that Baxter was considered to be the chief man of that party, although he never renounced his connection with the Church into which he had been received in Worcester Cathedral. His love of discussion led him by degrees to entertain objections to certain expressions in the Book of Common Prayer, objections indeed which many excellent men have made since his day, but to which they have not been able to give practical effect; and easy to be raised, for there is scarcely anything advantageous to mankind to which some exception may not be taken. His peculiar position at Kidderminster may have inclined him to scrupulousness, and the lack of all episcopal supervision and association gave him that habitual personal independence which makes deference to the opinions of another difficult, if not impossible. The enforced silence of the Royalist Anglican clergy threw him into the society of Presbyterians, and probably he learned from them to question the propriety of certain expressions in the Prayer-Book. He came at length to be considered the leader of that party, and certainly to some extent he justified that opinion. During several years, he had laboured in the production of numerous books in doctrinal and practical theology. His large mind embraced many subjects,—not merely the success of the Church at home, but also its extension abroad. They are generally the most zealous in their advocacy and support of Christian missions to foreign lands, who are the most strenuous for the Church at home; and while Baxter worked energetically in his own parish, he was thoughtful of the want and miserable ignorance of them who were living in the midnight of heathenism; and he was employed, during the latter part of Richard Cromwell's government, in arranging a plan for the propagation of the Gospel among the North American Indians, in whose tribes successful missions had been conducted chiefly by Eliot, often called the Apostle of the Indians; and which subsequently were continued by Brainerd, of whom Jonathan Edwards, the President of Princeton College, New Jersey, wrote a well-known biography. Cromwell, when Protector, had directed that a collection should be made in every parish in England to provide Eliot and others with funds. Enough was contributed to produce an investment of about eight hundred pounds a year. After the restoration of Charles II., the person who had originally sold the land in which the investment was made, possessed himself of it again, on the plea that the sale was void, because it had not received the sanction of the king. Baxter, Robert Boyle, and the other trustees of the purchased estate applied to the Lord Chancellor, who settled the dispute in their favour. Baxter consequently was brought into frequent correspondence with Eliot; and the extract given below is interesting from the fact, that Baxter's efforts to promote Christian missions to foreign lands are said to have produced the first plan, upon which the well-known Society for the Propagation of the Gospel was founded long afterwards.

Alluding to his own ejection from his ministry, he says: "Though our sins have separated us from the people of our love and care, and deprived us of all public liberty of preaching the Gospel of our Lord, I greatly rejoice in the liberty, help, and success which Christ has so long vouchsafed you in this work. There is no man on earth, whose work I think more honourable and comfortable than yours; to propagate the Gospel and Kingdom of Christ into those dark parts of the world is a better work than our hating and devouring one another. There are many here who would be ambitious of being your fellow-labourers, but that they are informed you have access to no greater number of the Indians than you yourself and your present assistants are able to instruct. An honourable gentleman, Mr. Robert Boyle, the governor of the corporation for your work, a man of great learning and worth, and of a very public universal mind, did mention to me a public collection in all our churches, for the maintenance of such ministers as are willing to go hence to you, partly while they are learning the Indian language, and partly while they labour in the work, as also to transport them. There are many here, I conjecture, who would be glad to go anywhere, to the Persians, Tartarians, Indians, or any unbelieving nation, to propagate the Gospel, if they thought they would be serviceable; but the difficulty of their languages is their greatest discouragement. The universal character that you speak of, many have talked of, and one hath printed his essay, and his way is only by numerical figures, making such and such figures to stand for the words of the same signification in all tongues; but nobody regards it. I shall communicate your motion here about the Hebrew, but we are not of such large and public minds, as you imagine; every one looks to his own concernment, and some to the things of Christ that are near them at their own doors. But if there be one Timothy that naturally careth for the state of the Churches, we have no man of a multitude more like-minded; but all seek their own things. Good men who are wholly devoted to God, and by long experience are acquainted with the interest of Christ, are ready to think all others should be like them, but there is no hope of bringing any more than here and there an experienced, holy, self-denying person, to get so far above their personal concernments and narrowness of mind, and so wholly to devote themselves to God. The industry of the Jesuits and friars, and their successes in Congo, Japan, China, etc., shame us all save you; but yet, for their personal labours in the work of the Gospel, here are many that would be willing to lay out, where they have liberty and a call, though scarce any that will do more in furthering great and public works. I should be glad to learn from you how far your Indian tongue extendeth; how large or populous the country is that useth it, if it be known; and whether it reach only to a few scattered neighbours, who cannot themselves convey their knowledge far, because of other languages. We very much rejoice in your happy work, the translation of the Bible, and bless God that strengthened you to finish it. If anything of mine may be honoured to contribute in the least measure to your blessed work, I shall have great cause to be thankful to God."

Baxter and the representatives of the Presbyterian party who associated themselves with him energetically promoted the return of the king, which they knew would be very repugnant to the Independents: for between these sects there was no cordiality. He hoped that the Restoration would lead to a permanent settlement of religious difficulties. The Earl of Manchester presented him, Reynolds, and Calamy to the king, in hope that, as they had been appointed Royal Chaplains, they would have a favourable opportunity of acquainting the monarch with their opinions. Baxter says: "We exercised more boldness at first than afterwards would have been borne. When some of the rest had congratulated His Majesty's happy restoration, and declared the large hope which they had of a cordial union among all dissenters by his means, I presumed to speak to him of the concernments of religion, and how far we were from desiring the continuance of any factions or parties in the Church, and how much a happy union would conduce to the good of the land and to His Majesty's satisfaction. I assured him that though there were turbulent, fanatic persons in his dominions, those whose peace we humbly craved of him were no such persons; but such as longed after concord, and were truly loyal to him, and desired no more than to live under him a quiet and peaceable life in all godliness and honesty. But as there were differences between them and their brethren about some ceremonies or discipline of the Church, we humbly craved His Majesty's favour for the ending of those differences; it being easy for him to interpose, that so the people might not be deprived of their faithful pastors, and ignorant, scandalous, and unworthy ones obtruded on them. I presumed to tell him that the people we spoke for were contented with an interest in heaven, and the liberty and advantages of the gospel to promote it; and that if these were taken from them, and they were deprived of their faithful pastors and liberty of worshipping God, they would take themselves as undone in this world, whatever else they should enjoy: that thus the hearts of his most faithful subjects, who hoped for his help, would even be broken; and that we doubted not but His Majesty desired to govern a people made happy by him, and not a broken-hearted people. I presumed to tell him that the late usurpers so well understood their own interest, that, to promote it, they had found the way of doing good to be the most effectual means; and had placed and encouraged many thousand faithful ministers in the Church, even such as detested their usurpation; and that so far had they attained their ends hereby, that it was the principal means of their interest in the people; wherefore, I humbly craved His Majesty that, as he was our lawful king, in whom all the people were prepared to centre, so he would be pleased to undertake this blessed work of promoting their holiness and concord; and that he would never suffer himself to undo the good which Cromwell or any other had done, because they were usurpers that did it; or discountenance a faithful ministry, because his enemies had set them up,—but that he would rather outgo them in doing good, and opposing and rejecting the ignorant and ungodly of what opinion or party soever,—that the people whose cause we recommended to him had their eyes on him as the officer of God, to defend them in the possession of the helps of their salvation; which if he were pleased to vouchsafe them, their estates and lives would cheerfully be offered to his service. I humbly besought him that he would never suffer his subjects to be tempted to have favourable thoughts of the late usurpers, by seeing the vice indulged which they suppressed, or the godly ministers or people discountenanced whom they encouraged; and that all his enemies' conduct could not teach him a more effectual way to restore the reputation and honour of the usurpers than to do worse than they, and destroy the good which they had done. And again I humbly craved that no misrepresentations might cause him to believe, that because some fanatics have been factious and disloyal, therefore the religious people in his dominions, who are most careful of their souls, are such, though some of them may be dissatisfied about some forms and ceremonies in God's worship, which others use; and that some of them might go under so ill a character with him by misreports behind their backs. I further humbly craved that the freedom and plainness of these expressions to His Majesty might be pardoned, as being extorted by the present necessity, and encouraged by our revived hopes. I told him also that it was not for Presbyterians or any party as such, that we were speaking, but for the religious part of his subjects in general, than whom no prince on earth had better. The king gave us not only a free audience, but as gracious an answer as we could expect; professing his gladness to hear our inclinations to agreement, and his resolution to do his part to bring us together; and that it must not be by bringing one party over to the other, but by abating somewhat on both sides, and meeting in the midway; and that if it were not accomplished, it should be owing to ourselves and not to him. Nay, that he was resolved to see it brought to pass, and that he would draw us together himself; with some more to that purpose. Insomuch that old Mr. Ash burst out into tears of joy, and could not forbear expressing what gladness this promise of His Majesty had put into his heart."

The king's great difficulty in relation to the Church continued. For nearly twenty years the bishops had been in silence and obscurity, and only nine of them survived. The mass of the citizens of London had become wholly indifferent to them; the elder of them remembered their former splendour, and their severity towards the clergy who resisted the domination of Archbishop Laud; but the younger knew nothing of episcopal action, nor of cathedral service. When, after the Restoration, the bishops in their robes assembled in Westminster Abbey, Pepys says: "But oh! at their going out, how people did most of them look upon them as strange creatures, and few with any kind of love or respect." Generally, the citizens of London had no friendly feeling towards the prelates. They had learned from the Puritan clergy, whom they regarded as the interpreters to them of the Word of God, the immense importance of personal religion; that a man is just so much, and no more, as he is in the sight of God; that the Old Testament ideas of the priesthood are not to be applied to the Christian ministry; that differences among Christians may be—as indeed has been repeated since—only as the broken rays of light all coming from one centre; that in prayer, whether in public or in private, God hears not the voice but the heart; that the great principle taught in the New Testament is the unfolding of the kingdom of God from within, from the union with Christ by faith; and that men are to be recovered from sinfulness of mind and of conduct not in masses, nor necessarily as they are components of any religious organization, but as each one receives the sanctifying influences of holy truth in his heart. These were the principles which the Puritan clergy had successfully taught them. The citizens generally heard with indifference of the restoration of the bishops; they were devoted to the mode of Divine worship to which they had been accustomed during the years of parliamentary victory and of Oliver's government; and many of them firmly believed with Sir Henry Vane, that "the province of the magistrate in this world is man's body; not his conscience, nor the concerns of eternity."

But the Court felt the necessity of taking some decided step, and of putting an end to incessant contention in religion. The bishops urged the king to compel submission to their demands. Charles had promised to grant liberty of conscience; but it was clearly impossible to allow the Presbyterian system, which he utterly hated, to continue in prominence. He would gain by temporising, and until men were more accustomed to the new administration, and to the revival in the churches of the Anglican service. He invited Baxter and his associates to prepare some practicable scheme of Church-order and government. They submitted to him a plan of Church-reform based upon Archbishop Ussher's "Reduction of Episcopacy": in which it was proposed, that the bishop in each see should be the president of a diocesan board of presbyters, and that the Prayer-Book should be accepted with a few verbal alterations, and with the disuse of what in the disputations of the time were called "superstitious practices." The king, who saw the wisdom of composing the differences by a compromise, which has been for ages the peculiarly English method of settling many disputes, published a Declaration. Bishoprics were offered to some of the Presbyterians, and many eminent Nonconformists were admitted into the ministry of the Anglican Church. Among other amendments, Charles promised, that "no bishop should exercise any arbitrary power, nor impose anything but according to law, and that a Commission should be appointed to review the Liturgy, and to make additional forms." Baxter says: "When we went to the king, and expected there to meet the divines of the other party, according to promise, with their proposals also, containing the lowest terms which they would yield to for peace; we saw not a man of them, nor any papers from them of that nature, no, not to this day. His Majesty very graciously renewed his professions that he would bring us together, and see that the bishops should come down and yield on their part. Yet was not Bishop Ussher's model the same in all points that we could wish; but it was the best that we could have the least hope, I say not to obtain, but acceptably to make them any offers of. Before this time, by the king's return many hundred worthy ministers were displaced, and cast out of their charges because they were in sequestrations, where others had been by the Parliament cast out. Our earnest desires had been that all such should be cast out as were in any benefice formerly belonging to a man that was not grossly insufficient or debauched, but that all who had succeeded these scandalous ones should hold their places. These wishes being vain, and all the old ones restored, the king promised that the places where any of the old ones were dead, should be confirmed to the possessors—but we were all of us to be endured but a little longer." Charles II. may have desired to make a compromise between the contending religionists, and he offered bishoprics to Baxter, Reynolds, and Calamy. Reynolds accepted the bishopric of Norwich, Baxter refused that of Hereford, and Calamy declined to accept that of Coventry and Lichfield. Baxter says of this offer of the king: "A little before the meeting about the King's Declaration, Colonel Birch came to me as from the Lord Chancellor, to persuade me to take the bishopric of Hereford; and I perceived that Colonel Birch came privately, that a bishopric might not publicly be refused, for he told me they would not bear such a repulse. I told him that I was resolved never to be bishop of Hereford; but I could give no positive answer till I should see the king's resolutions about the way of Church government. At last the day that the King's Declaration came out, when I was with the Lord Chancellor, he asked me if I would accept of a bishopric. I told him, if his lordship would procure us the settlement of the matter of that Declaration by passing it into a law, I promised him to take that way in which I might most serve the public peace. I doubted not but the laws would prescribe such work for bishops, in silencing ministers, and troubling honest Christians for their conscience, and ruling the vicious with greater lenity, as that I had rather have the meanest employment among men. To Mr. Calamy I would give no counsel, but for Dr. Reynolds I persuaded him to accept it, so be he would publicly declare he took it on the terms of the king's Declaration. When I came to the Lord Chancellor, I the next day put a letter into his hand, which he took in good part." The letter expresses Baxter's conscientiousness and his simplicity of mind: "My Lord, your great favour and condescension encourage me to give you more of my sense of the business which your lordship was pleased to propound. Being raised to some joyful hopes of seeing the beginning of a happy union, I shall crave your lordship's pardon for presuming what further endeavours will be necessary to accomplish it. If your lordship will endeavour to get the Declaration passed into an Act—if you will procure a commission to review the Common Prayer-Book, according to the Declaration—if you will further effectually the restoration of able ministers to a settled station of service in the Church—if you will open some way for the ejection of the insufficient, scandalous, and unable—if you will put as many of our persuasion as you can into bishoprics, if it may be, more than three—if you will desire the bishops to place some of them in inferior places of trust, especially rural deaneries. For my own part, I hope by letters this very week to disperse the seeds of satisfaction into many counties of England. I must confess to your lordship that I am utterly against accepting of a bishopric, because I am conscious that it will overmatch my sufficiency, and affright me with the thought of my account for so great an undertaking. Especially, because it will very much disable me from an effectual promoting of the Church's peace. I therefore humbly crave that your lordship will put some able man of our persuasion into the place you intend for me, though I now think that Dr. Reynolds and Mr. Calamy may better accept of a bishopric than I. That you will believe I as thankfully acknowledge your lordship's favour as if I were by it possessed of a bishopric: and if your lordship continue in those intentions, I shall thankfully accept it in any other state or relation that may further my service to the Church and to His Majesty. But I desire that it may not be a cathedral relation. And whereas the vicar of the parish where I have lived will not resign, but accept me only as his curate, if your lordship would procure him some prebendary or other place of competent profit, for I dare not mention him to any pastoral charge, or place that requireth preaching, that so he might resign that vicarage to me, without his loss, according to the late Act before December; for the sake of that town of Kidderminster, I should take it as a very great favour. But if there be any great inconvenience or difficulties in the way, I can well be content to be his curate."

CHAPTER XVI.

1660—1661.

THE bishops would have nothing to do with a plan of Church reform founded on Archbishop Ussher's model of government. They began to feel they were recovering their power, and they resolved to adopt Strafford's policy of "Thorough," and to revive the doctrine of passive obedience and non-resistance to the will of the sovereign, which had been fatal to Charles I. They who were ready to enforce it were appointed to vacant sees; and for their losses in their long-continued deprivation, the prelates were soon enriched by the enormous sums of money they demanded for renewal of leases. Bishop Burnet says: "What the bishops did with their great fines was a pattern to all their lower dignitaries, who generally took more care of themselves than of the Church; the men of service were loaded with many livings and many dignities. With this accession of wealth, there broke in upon the Church a great deal of luxury and high-living, on pretence of hospitality; and with this overset of wealth and pomp that came upon men in the decline of their age, they who were now growing into old age became lazy and negligent in all the true concerns of the Church." It was necessary to proceed step by step in avenging the sufferings of the clergy under the despotism of the Protector. Spies were sent out into every part of the country, to mark and to report how the return of the bishops was received by the Presbyterian congregations. Restored to their seats in the House of Lords, while every Member of Parliament was compelled to receive the Holy Communion, according to the Anglican rite, as a condition of holding his seat; and while many of the clergy, who had formerly been ejected for the alleged cause of scandalous living, were now restored to their benefices; the bishops felt that, as the King and the Chancellor were on their side, they might venture to go further. The books of John Milton, late Latin secretary to Cromwell, and of John Goodwin, were called in by royal proclamation, or burned by the hangman; and this and similar proceedings would familiarize the citizens of London with the change of public affairs. But with the Presbyterians the bishops, or the majority of them, were resolved to make no compromise. Nothing should be yielded, even in the least degree, to their demands. The forms and phrases to which they objected should be retained with obstinate refusal of change. In vain Stillingfleet pleaded, that "the Saviour, Who took away the yoke of Jewish ceremonies, did never intend to gall the necks of His disciples with another instead of it. Why should not such things be sufficient for communion with the Church, which are sufficient for eternal salvation? What charter hath Christ given the Church to bind men up to more than Himself hath done, or to exclude those from her society who may be admitted into heaven? Will Christ ever thank men at the Great Day for keeping such out of communion with His Church, whom He will vouchsafe not only crowns of glory to, but it may be aureolæ too, if there be such things there? In the Primitive Church, it was never thought worth while to make any standing laws for rites and customs that had no other original but tradition, much less to suspend men from her communion for not observing them." But the temper of the victorious royalists, and of the prelates who had recovered their dignities and emoluments, was against any concession to the remnant of their former conquerors.

At the opening of the session, the king announced to the Parliament, that "he valued himself much upon keeping his word, and upon making good whatsoever he had promised to his subjects." But the government immediately brought in and carried the Test and Corporation Act, which was intended to destroy the power of Nonconformists in the cities and towns, where generally they were strong in numbers and in property. The Act required, that everyone holding any municipal office should receive the Holy Communion, according to the rites of the Anglican Church, and should declare it was unlawful on any grounds to take up arms against the sovereign. Thus all Nonconformist magistrates and town-councillors were by it rendered incapable of doing the state any public service. This Act was followed by an order in Council declaring that all religious meetings were illegal, if held outside the walls of parish-churches. The king's Declaration, however, had promised that a commission should be appointed of twelve bishops and twelve Puritan divines, to review the Book of Common Prayer, and to make such alterations in it as should be thought necessary to restore and continue peace and unity in the churches, under His Majesty's government.

On the side of the Anglican Church, Sheldon, bishop of London, Cozins, bishop of Durham, Morley of Worcester, Sanderson of Lincoln, Walton of Chester, and others of repute among the scholars of the time, were appointed; and on the side of the Puritan, or, more strictly defining it, of the Presbyterian party, were Baxter, Calamy, Manton, Newcomen, Spurstow, Dr. Lightfoot, and others, who were well known as able defenders of their principles. They were appointed to assemble on the fifteenth day of April, 1661, at the lodgings of the Bishop of London, in the Savoy, and the Commission was to continue in force until the twenty-fifth day of July. Baxter in his Autobiography gives a full account of the discussion. He says: "A meeting was accordingly appointed, and the Savoy named by them for the place. The Commission being read, the Archbishop of York, Dr. Frewen, a peaceable man, spake first, and told us that he knew nothing of the business, but perhaps the

Bishop of London knew more of the king's mind in it, and therefore was fitter to speak on it than he. The Bishop of London told us that it was not they, but we, that had been the seekers of this conference, and who desired alterations in the Liturgy; and therefore, they had nothing to say or do, till we brought in all that we had to say against it in writing, and all the additional forms and alterations which we desired. Our brethren were very much against this motion, and urged the king's Commission, which required us to meet together, advise, and consult. They told him, that by conference we might perceive as we went on what each would yield to, and might more speedily dispatch, and probably obtain our end; whereas writing would be a tedious, endless business, and we should not have that familiarity and acquaintance with each other's minds which might facilitate our concord. But the Bishop of London resolutely insisted on not doing anything till we brought in all our exceptions, alterations, and additions at once. In this I confess, above all things else, I was wholly of his mind, and prevailed with my brethren to consent; but I conjecture for contrary reasons. For I suppose he thought we should either be altogether by the ears, and be of several minds among ourselves, at least in our new forms; or that when our proposals and forms came to be scanned by them, they should find as much matter of exception against ours as we did against theirs; or that the people of our persuasion would be dissatisfied or divided about it. So I told the bishops that we accepted of the task which they imposed on us. On the fourth day of May we had a meeting with the bishops, where we gave in our paper of exceptions to them, which they received. The seventh was a meeting at Sion College of all the London ministers, for the choice of a president and assistants for the next year; where some of the Presbyterians, upon a petty scruple, absenting themselves, the diocesan party carried it, and so got the possession and rule of the college. As I foresaw what was likely to be the end of our conference, I desired the brethren that we might draw up a plain and earnest petition to the bishops, to yield to such terms of peace and concord as they themselves did confess to be lawful to be yielded to; for though we were equal in the king's commission, yet we are commanded by the Holy Ghost if it be possible, and as much as in us lieth, to live peaceably with all men. If we were denied, it would satisfy our consciences, and justify us before all the world, much more than if we only disputed for it. This motion was accepted, and I was desired to draw up the petition, which I did, and being examined was, with a word or two of alteration, consented to. When we met with the bishops, to deliver in these papers, I was required to deliver them; and, if it were possible, to get audience for the petition before all the company. I told them that though we were equals in the present work, and our appointed business was to treat, yet we were conscious of our place and duty, and had drawn up a petition to them, which, though somewhat long, I humbly craved their consent that I might read. Some were against it, and so they would have been generally, if they had known what was in it; but at last they yielded to it, but their patience was never so put to it by us as in hearing so long and ungrateful a petition. When I had read it, Dr. Gunning began a long and vehement speech against it, to which, when he came to the end, I replied; but I was interrupted in the midst of my reply, and was fain to bear it, because they had been patient with so much ado so long before. I delivered them the petition when I had read it, and with it a fair copy of our reformed Liturgy, called additional forms and alterations of theirs. They received both, and so we departed. After this, when the bishops were to have sent us two papers, one of their concessions, how much they would alter of the Liturgy as excepted against, and the other of their acceptance of our offered forms or reasons against them; instead of both these, a good while after, they sent us such a paper as they did before, of their reasonings against all our conceptions, without any abatements or alterations at all that are worth the naming. Our brethren, seeing what they were resolved to bring it to, and how unpeaceably they managed the business, did think best to write them a plain answer to their paper, and not to suppress it, as we had done by the first. This task also they imposed on me. I went out of town, to Dr. Spurstow's house in Hackney for retirement, where, in eight days' time, I drew up a reply to their answer to our exceptions. This the brethren read and consented to. By this time our commission was almost expired, and therefore our brethren were earnestly desirous of personal debates with them upon the papers put in, to try how much alteration they would yield to. We therefore sent to the bishops to desire it of them, and at last they yielded to it, when we had but ten days more to treat. When we met them, I delivered the answer to their former paper, the largeness of which I saw displeased them; but they received it. We earnestly pressed them to spend the little time remaining in such pacifying conference as tended to the ends which are mentioned in the king's Declaration and Commission; and told them that such disputes which they had called us to by their manner of writing, were not the things which we desired, or thought most conducing to those ends.

I have reason to think that the generality of the bishops and doctors present never knew what we offered them in the reformed Liturgy, nor in this reply, nor in any of our papers, save those few which we read openly to them, for they were put up, and carried away. So that, it seems, before they knew what was in them, they resolved to reject our papers right or wrong, and to deliver them up to their contradictors. When we came to our debates, I first craved of them their animadversions on our additions and alterations of the Liturgy, which we had put in long before; and that they would tell us what they allowed or disallowed in them, that we might have the use of them, according to the words in the King's Declaration and commission. But they would not by any importunity be entreated at all to debate that, or to give their opinions about those papers. Our next business was to desire them by friendly conference to go over the particulars which we excepted against, and to tell us how much they would abate, and what alterations they would yield to. This Bishop Reynolds oft pressed them to, and so did the rest of all of us that spake. They said no alterations were necessary, but they would yield to all that we proved so. Here we were left in a very great strait; if we should enter upon a dispute with them, we gave up the end and hope of our endeavours; if we refused it, we knew that they would boast that, when it came to the setting-to, we would not so much as attempt to prove anything unlawful in the Liturgy, nor dare dispute it with them. We spoke to the deaf; they had other ends, and were other men, and had the art to suit the means unto their ends. For my part, when I saw they would do nothing else, I persuaded our brethren to yield to a disputation with them, and let them understand that we were far from fearing it, seeing they would give us no hopes of concord." They arranged at last, that Doctors Pearson, Sparrow, and Gunning should debate against Baxter, Jacomb, and Dr. Bates. Baxter says of it: "The Bishop of London, Dr. Sheldon, since Archbishop of Canterbury, only appeared the first day of each conference, which, beside that before the king, was but twice in all, as I remember, and meddled not at all in any disputations; but all men supposed that he and Bishop Morley, and next Bishop Hinchman, were the doers and disposers of all such affairs. The Archbishop of York (Frewen) spake very little, and came but once or twice in all. Bishop Morley was often there, but not constantly, and with free and fluent words, with much earnestness, was the chief speaker of all the bishops, and the greatest interrupter of us; vehemently going on with what he thought serviceable to his end, and bearing down our answers by the said fervour and interruptions. Bishop Cosins was there constantly, and had a great deal of talk with so little logic, natural or artificial, that I perceived no one much moved by anything he said. But two virtues he showed, though none took him for a magician; one was, that he was excellently well versed in canons, councils, and fathers, which he remembered, when by citing of any passages we tried him. The other was, that he was of a rustic wit and carriage, so he would endure more freedom of discourse with him, and was more affable and familiar than the rest. Bishop Hinchman, since Bishop of London, was of the most grave, comely, reverend aspect of any of them, and of a good insight of the fathers and councils. Cosins, and he, and Dr. Gunning being all that showed any considerable skill in them among us; in which they were all three of very laudable understandings, and better than any other of either of the parties that I met with. Bishop Hinchman spake calmly and slowly, and not very often, but was as high in his principles and resolutions as any of them. Bishop Sanderson of Lincoln was sometimes there, but never spake that I know of, except a very little; but his great learning and worth are known by his labours, and his aged peevishness not unknown. Bishop Gauden was our most constant helper; he and Bishop Cosins seldom were absent. And how bitter soever his pen might be, he was the only moderator of all the bishops, except our Bishop Reynolds. He showed no logic, nor meddled in any dispute or point of learning; but he had a calm, fluent, rhetorical tongue, and if all had been of his mind, we had been reconciled. But when by many days' conference in the beginning, we had got some moderating concessions from him, and from Bishop Cosins by his means, the rest came in the end, and brake them all. Bishop Lucy of St. David's spake once or twice a few words calmly; and so did Bishop Nicholson of Gloucester, and Bishop Griffiths of St. Asaph's, though not Commissioners. King, Bishop of Chichester, I never saw there. Bishop Warner of Rochester was once or twice. Lany of Peterborough was once or twice there, and Walton, Bishop of Chester, but neither of them spake much. Among all the bishops there was none that had so promising a face as Dr. Sterne, Bishop of Carlisle. He looked so honestly, gravely, and soberly that I scarce thought such a face could have deceived me. When I was entreating them not to cast out so many of their brethren through the *nation*, he turned to the rest of the reverend bishops, and said, 'He will not say in the *kingdom*, lest he own a *king*.' This was all I ever heard that worthy prelate say. I told him with grief that half the charity which became so grave a bishop might have helped him to a better exposition of the word nation. Bishop Reynolds spake much the first day, for bringing them to abatements and moderation, and afterwards he sat with them, and spake now and then a word for moderation. He was a solid, honest man, but through mildness and excess of timorous reverence for great men, altogether unfit to contend with them. Mr. Thorndike spake once a few impertinent, passionate words, confuting the opinion which we had received of him from his first writings, and confirming that which his second and last writings had given us of him. Dr. Earle, Dr. Heylin, and Dr. Barwick never came. Dr. Hacket, since Bishop of Coventry and Lichfield, said nothing to make us know anything of him. Dr. Sparrow said but little, but that little was with a spirit enough for the imposing dividing cause. Dr. Peirce and Dr. Gunning did all their work, beside Bishop Morley's discourses, but with great difference in the manner. Dr. Peirce was their true logician and disputant, without whom, as far as I could discern, we should have had nothing from them, but Dr. Gunning's passionate invectives, mixed with some argumentations. He disputed accurately, soberly, and calmly, being but once in any passion; breeding in us great respect for him, and a persuasion that if he had been independent, he would have been for peace, and that if all had been in his power, it would have gone well. He was the strength and honour of that cause, which we doubted whether he heartily maintained. He was their forwardest and greatest speaker, understanding well what belonged to a disputant; a man of greater study and industry than any of them; well read in fathers and councils, and of a ready tongue; I hear and believe, of very temperate life also, as to any carnal excesses whatsoever; but so vehement for his high, imposing principles, and so over zealous for Arminianism, and formality, and church pomp, and so very eager and fervent in his discourse, that I conceive his prejudice and passion much perverted his judgment. I am sure they made him lamentably overrun himself in his discourses. Of Dr. Peirce I will say no more, because he hath said so much of me. On our part, Dr. Bates spake very solidly, judiciously, and pertinently, when he spake. As for myself, the reason why I spake so much was, because it was the desire of my brethren, and I was loath to expose them to the hatred of the bishops; but was willing to take it all upon myself, they themselves having so much wit as to be therein more sparing and cautious than I. I thought also that the day and cause commanded me those two things, which then were objected to me as my crimes, viz., speaking too boldly and too long. I thought it a cause that I could comfortably suffer for, and should as willingly be a martyr for *charity* as for *faith*."

Bishop Burnet says of the Conference: "The two men that had the chief management of the debate, were the most unfit to heal matters, and the fittest to widen them that could have been found out. Baxter was the opponent, and Gunning was the respondent, who was afterwards advanced, first to Chichester, and then to Ely. He was a man of great reading, and noted for a special subtlety of arguing. All the arts of sophistry were made use of by him on all occasions, in as confident a manner as if they had been sound reasoning. Baxter and he spent some days in much logical arguing, to the diversion of the town, who thought here were a couple of fencers engaged in disputes that could never be brought to an end or have any good effect." Baxter and his party objected to the sign of the cross in baptism, to the use of the surplice at all services, to compulsory kneeling for all who are admitted to Holy Communion, to the administration of it to persons morally unfitted for it, to some terms in the Absolution and in the

Burial Service, and to the requirements of subscription to the Thirty-Nine Articles before permission could be had to preach. These objections have been repeated many times since the Savoy Conference, and they are still advanced by some devout persons, who make them their excuse for not worshipping in the Church of their fathers.

The bishops, who had resolved to concede nothing, and whose intention, it cannot be doubted, was to expel all objecting clergymen from the Church, were angered by the persistent arguments of Baxter and his associates; and the more so from the fact, that he was so ill advised by his friends as himself to compose and to present a liturgy, and which with his almost incredible industry he had completed in a fortnight,—a work with many scriptural and pious expressions, but, as all men admitted, inferior to that which the Anglican Church had formed to a large extent from ancient uses, and adopted as its own. Men wrote at the time, that the friends of the bishops crowded the hall, and that their angry shouts and invectives put a violent end to the Conference, and with many unseemly reflections upon Baxter's clouded mind and scholastic method of reasoning. Bishop Sanderson, who was chairman,—and to hear whom, when preaching, Charles I. used to say, he carried his conscience,—declared that Gunning had the best of the debate. Bishop Morley was especially severe against Baxter, and the bitterness seems never to have been mitigated. The bishops unanimously declared that they knew of no necessity for making alterations in the Prayer-Book, nor could they consent to give up the use of the least ceremony, nor to heed the objections which had been offered. The Presbyterian party sent an account to the king of all that had been debated at the Conference; but no reply was made to their communication. The time allotted for the commission was at an end, and no approach to a peaceful settlement of the disputed questions had been made; but subsequently the bishops consented to some insignificant alterations, which were entirely unsatisfactory to their opponents, and on both sides the debate ended in exasperation and unseemly anger. Bishop Burnet says of it: "No alterations were made in favour of the Presbyterians; for it was resolved to gratify them in nothing." The bishops were entirely guided by Sheldon, under the counsel of Lord Clarendon, who had the bitterest hatred of Nonconformists of all degrees; and his influence is to be traced in the whole course of the discussion. Bishop Burnet says of Sheldon, that "he was a dexterous man in business, had a great quickness of apprehension, a very true judgment. He was a generous and charitable man. He had perhaps too great pleasantness of conversation. He had an art, that was peculiar to him, of treating all that came to him in a most obliging manner, but few depended much on his professions of friendship. He seemed not to have a deep sense of religion, if any at all; and spoke of it most commonly as of an engine of government, and a matter of policy." The practical advantages of such a conference may justly be questioned. The objection which the theologian of the Eastern Church, Gregory of Nazianzus, had to every Council convened for the purpose of religious disputation, must still have force with them who know the temptations and dangers of such an assembly. Neither the awful subjects of Divine Revelation, nor the proprieties in the conduct of public worship can be matters suitable, for debate in a large assembly of men who are irritated by social or political grievances; and when argument is often interrupted by expressions of displeasure, and conclusions are arrived at from a desire rather for victory than for truth. In such a scene it often happens, that that which is most conspicuous to the unprejudiced observer is the moral infirmity of man's nature, warped by prejudice, or swayed by passion. In regarding the Savoy Conference, in relation to the subsequent history of English religion, there are those who regret that a few concessions in form and phrase were not made at it, which some devout men within the Church and separated from it have desired, and which they hoped would either have prevented, or have lessened permanent schism. The opportunity for making the proposed changes may never occur again; in our own day any compromise of the kind would seem to be almost impossible.

After the failure of the Savoy Conference, the king declared to Parliament: "I know you will not take it unkindly, if I tell you I am as zealous for the Church of England as any of you can be. I am as much in love with the Prayer-Book as you can wish, and have prejudices enough against those who do not love it, who I hope in time will be better informed, and change their minds." He commanded the Convocation, on 20th of November, to look carefully through the Book of Common Prayer, and to make such amendments and additions to it as might be thought necessary. On 20th of December, the alterations made were approved and signed by both Houses. The amendments introduced, and the additions to it, made the book more exceptionable than before to the Presbyterians; and the bishops rejoiced that they had not only triumphed over objections, but had made the continuance in the Anglican Church of the opposing clergy utterly impossible. The fierce passions of the time; the bitter recollections of their persecutions, first by the Parliament, and afterwards by the Protector; the gladness of them who had been so long exiled that they had recovered station, emolument, and power by the restoration of the English Church, and the quickening excitement of success, prompted the bishops to revenge, made them refuse every proposal for conciliation, and resolve upon speedy coercion. No wonder, if the thoughtful men, whom John Locke represented, remarked that episcopal hands again drew the sword of St. Peter; and that they who held it heeded not the command of the Prince of Peace to sheathe it, to avenge not themselves, and to be gentle towards all men. For at that time, they were maddened by the recollection of the sufferings of nearly twenty years, by their degradation, and their enforced silence; and the bishops perhaps were especially indignant, that so large a number of the clergy had been ejected by the Triers on the damaging charge of profligate and scandalous living. The Court and the Episcopate agreed in their hatred of Puritanism, and in the determination to overcome it, not by persuasion and conviction, but by the use, under forms of law, of the power of the crown.

In the autumn of this year, Charles II. proceeded to avenge himself further upon his enemies by unseemly acts, which in our day perhaps an African chieftain, far from a missionary station, might not be ashamed to perpetrate. The king issued a warrant to the Dean and Chapter of Westminster, to take up the bodies of all persons who had been unwarrantably buried in Henry VII.'s Chapel, since the year 1641, and to inter them in the neighbouring churchyard. The remains of about twenty persons were cast out of their graves. Those of Cromwell's mother, his daughter Lady Claypole, Pym, Dr. Dorislaus, Dr. William Twisse, who had been the prolocutor of the Westminster Assembly, and of others, were thrown together in one pit in St. Margaret's Churchyard. In the meantime, the agents of the court had imprisoned more than four thousand Quakers, for refusing to take an oath which was opposed to their religious convictions. In one prison sixty of them were confined in a small room. Some prisons were so crowded that the captives could not sit down. In others they were refused even straw to lie upon, torn from their comfortable homes, from their shops and looms, harassed, plundered, and treated with barbarity. Crowded, ill-fed, unwashed, deprived of healthy air, many of them died miserably in the jails; undeserved cruelties, inflicted upon some of the most peaceful, orderly, and industrious subjects of the king. To him who observed the state of society in London within two years after Charles's restoration, religion seemed to have passed out of public regard. It was ridiculed in comedies patronised by the king, and laughed at in festivities. All over the country, the Puritan clergy were suspended, and sometimes ejected, on slight pretexts. The profligacy of the Court had so infected public morals, that, in order to hush the remonstrances of the faithful few who had not forgotten God, the sovereign was advised to say, when he prorogued the Parliament: "I cannot but observe that the whole nation seems to be a little corrupted in their excess of living. I hope it has been only the excess of joy after so long suffering, that has transported us to these excesses. I do believe I have been faulty myself. I promise you I will reform." But there was no amendment either in the Court or in society. If the king ever had an honest intention of living less viciously, his resolution was soon forgotten. The Parliament professed great zeal for the Church; but Pepys says, "The new members were for the most part young men, and the most profane, swearing fellows that I ever heard in my life." The immorality of the palace corrupted all classes of the people, and vice rioted where, three years since, virtue seemed to reign. Nothing could be more painful to the moralist, than to mark the social life of England, during the period of transition from the rigour of Cromwell's government, to the relaxation of morality which Charles II. and his associates produced throughout the country, in a tide of profligate debauchery. Bishop Burnet says, that great offence was given to many devout churchmen by the new epithet, "our most religious King," which the flattery or the gratitude of the bishops had applied to Charles in the collect for the Parliament; a title which, in the common meaning of the word in our language, could not in any sense be true of him. Use at length made it familiar; but, at first, it so shocked whatever decency remained among the less profligate courtiers, that some of them would venture to ask Charles in his revels, "What must all his people think, when they heard him prayed for as their most religious king?" Lord Clarendon, the Chancellor, remonstrated with him on his immoralities. If the bishops had done so too, how strong a protest might they have made against an example which corrupted the English nation, and which must have been eminently pernicious to the Church of which he was the head! The Church could hardly have had a more terrible enemy than the "most religious king," unless it were his brother and successor; and nothing more attests its inherent spiritual strength, than the fact that it survived its disastrous connection with such successive monarchs.

The country was becoming demoralised. Drunkenness in a short time was habitual to large classes of the people. Some of the vices of Constantinople seemed to have been suddenly transferred to London. The language of men became foul with obscenity and blasphemy. The fine gentleman never spoke but with many imprecations on his head, his heart, his soul. The king was a profuse swearer, and he who was loyal must imitate his sovereign. Charles drank deeply, and gambled constantly; and the peers and country gentlemen must follow their prince's example. English ladies sitting in the theatres listened to foul expressions which, if uttered in any assembly of peasant women in our day, would cause an outcry of indignant shame; and they saw their sovereign surrounded by painted and bedizened courtesans, whose common language no virtuous mother or daughter could hear without a shudder, and of whose life they could not think without a prayer to be kept from the paths of the destroyer. So the attempt of the Protector's government to compel a nation to be religious had thus ended, by the willing help of Charles, in a reaction of loathsome impurity.

Notwithstanding these and other tolerated depravities, the administration in all its departments was terribly severe, and the punishments it inflicted for trifling offences were cruel. Women convicted of crime were burned alive, and for lesser offences were mercilessly flogged through the streets. A wretched girl, who had lost her virtue, was hunted from town to town, if she had no means of living, that her offspring might not be chargeable to the place of her domicile; happy if she escaped frightful scourging. Beggars when apprehended were first flogged, and then driven to their own parishes. Even tender children for their slight offences underwent the lash. When farmers met to sell their cattle or wheat, the business was occasionally enlivened by the burning of a witch in the market-place; and shouting thousands, adding to her sufferings by their filthy revilings, thronged to witness the dreadful death of a spiteful or decrepit neighbour, convicted on the testimony either of knaves or of madmen. Wizards and witches were sought for far and wide by informers, who were paid upon their conviction; and, during trial, they were often indecently examined in court by persons who pretended to be able to find the devil's tokens upon them. The discovery of a mole, or other unusual mark, upon the skin, tended directly to the conviction of the accused, who was tied hand and foot, and thrown into a river or pond to test her innocency—the survival of the cruel water-ordeal of our Saxon ancestors, established for the trial of the poor when charged with the commission of offences. If the person suspected of practising witchcraft floated on the surface of the water, without the movement of swimming, the fact was taken to be clear evidence of her guilt; but if she sank, she was acquitted, and generally drowned. The fire-ordeal was retained for the rich, the water-ordeal for the poor man; or as Glanville expresses it, *Si fuerit rusticus.* In some districts of the country, where teachers and the taught were alike superstitious and ignorant, a woman of weak intellect, or of remarkable deformity of body, was always in danger of accusation. If she muttered in her feebleness and derangement of mind, she was suspected of conversing with malignant spirits who cruelly afflicted her. If she roamed alone in the cooler evening air, after the heat of a day in August, she was thought to be waiting for the sabbath of the fiends, when Satan assembled his servants for horrid revelry. If she gathered herbs, from which she might make a decoction to lessen the cramps of rheumatism caused by the clay floor of her cottage, or to strengthen her against the chills of the ague, she was charged with seeking poisons for the destruction of infants. She was said sometimes to take the form of a hare, to conjugate with cats, to bark like a dog, to feed on toads in the moonlight, or to lurk in the shape of a goat under her neighbours' windows, in order that she might torture them with pains, frighten them by nightmares, afflict them with melancholy, confuse their understandings, terrify them by noises in the darkness, curdle the milk in their dairies, spoil their brewages of ale, make their chairs and tables move about their rooms, shake them in their beds, stop up their chimneys, or kindle a fire in their roofs. The mass of the people, ignorant and superstitious, miserable in their homes, rude in their habits, depraved in their tastes, hopeless of improvement in their prospects, utterly disregarded by the fine gentlemen of the court, were glad when winters were mild, harvests plentiful, and ale cheap; and they gave little heed to the rumours which reached them, of the Protector's death, and of the restoration of the merry king, who swore like a dragoon, drank like a toper, and was clever at the card-table; who sang love-songs with women from France, went oftener to the theatre than to church, and rioted in luxurious profusion at Whitehall.

CHAPTER XVII.

1661—1662.

AFTER the failure of the Savoy Conference, from which some of the Puritan clergy had unwisely hoped for advantages to themselves, Baxter returned to Kidderminster; wearied, it may be thought, by the strife of tongues, and glad to receive the welcome of the people who loved him, and to whom for sixteen years he had been a wise teacher, a faithful counsellor, and a constant friend. Bishop Morley, his antagonist at that Conference, had lately been appointed to the diocese of Worcester, and from him Baxter could expect little generous consideration; for that prelate had entirely agreed with Sheldon and Gunning in the determination to expel all clergymen from ministration in the Anglican Church, who publicly objected to a word in the Liturgy, or to any part of the accustomed ceremonial. Baxter had long and well ministered in the parish, and his affections centred in its people. He was beloved and revered by them as no successor could hope to be. His service had been of the utmost advantage to the town. He was an ordained English clergyman, and he had nothing in common with them who had shut up the churches and murdered the king; he had been energetic in promoting the restoration of Charles II.; he believed that the episcopal form of church-government was the most ancient, and he held the not unreasonable or traitorous opinion, that the bishop should govern with the help of presbyters. The king had already offered him the bishopric of Hereford; but he would sacrifice promotion, dignity, and whatever these might bring, if he might be permitted to return permanently to his work in the Church at Kidderminster. He had suggested that the aged vicar of the town, who was legally in possession of the parish and its emoluments, might be preferred to some other office in the Church; and the Lord Chancellor Clarendon had offered to provide for the vicar out of his own income, until a vacancy should occur to which he might be appointed. Baxter was willing to continue his ministrations there without receiving any stipend; and it rested with the bishop, as the legal authority, whether his request should be granted. He was ready to conform, or he would not have applied to the bishop for a license; and he argued that his long-continued service in the town, the great affection of the parishioners towards him, the evident success of his ministry, the crowded church, and the increasing number of communicants, were valid reasons for his retaining the office. Burnet says that Morley, Bishop of Worcester, was a pious and charitable man, of a very exemplary life, but extremely passionate, and very obstinate. Hating Presbyterians, and fearing Baxter, Morley replied, that he had been for years only an intruder in the parish, with no episcopal license, and therefore with no legal right to his position. When men determine on a cruel or vindictive action, they can easily devise or discover reasons which may appear to warrant it; and to enable him to stand well with the world, even if he failed also to satisfy the requirements of his own conscience, he gave out that he refused to license Baxter to Kidderminster on account of the sentiments in his book, "The Holy Commonwealth." An excuse is not always a reason; the fact was, that Morley disliked Baxter with all the intensity of an obstinate opponent, who had been angered and perplexed by his arguments at the Savoy Conference, in which he was thought to have been sorely pressed by his antagonist; and he was resolved, whether for good or for evil, to make use of his episcopal irresponsibility to prevent Baxter from ever preaching again in the diocese of Worcester. So much he feared the true-hearted, ardent man, whom an evil accident had put in his power, that Morley refused even to admit him to an interview, unless some one were present as a witness, and if need be as a defender. So conscience ever makes the evil-doer a coward. According to the maxim of the ancients, quoted by Cicero, that the utmost rigour of the law is the utmost injustice, Morley was legally right, but morally wrong, in his harsh retaliation upon Baxter; requiting the devout, industrious, and successful labours of sixteen years by exclusion from the parish. Upon him rests the shame of using his power tyrannously against the ablest clergyman in his diocese, whom forbearance would have gained to the service of the English Church; and of putting an end in the harshest manner to duties, which for devotion, integrity, and success have never been surpassed in ecclesiastical history. The deed is to be classed with other wrongs, which sometimes have been done by them, to whom either ancient law, or the customs or indifference of society, have unwisely given irresponsible authority, with which few men can be trusted, and which no man should be permitted to have, excepting in circumstances of unusual public difficulty or danger. The King and the Lord Chancellor wished that Baxter should return to Kidderminster; but Bishop Morley would not consent to it, fearing the terrible opponent who had given him trouble in the Savoy Conference. Baxter says of his difficulties with Morley: "When I had refused a bishopric, I did it from such reasons as offended not the Lord Chancellor; and therefore instead of it I presumed to crave the favour to restore me to preach to my people at Kidderminster again, from whence I had been cast out, when many hundreds of others were ejected, upon the restoration of all those who have been sequestered. It was but a vicarage, and the vicar was a poor, unlearned, ignorant, silly reader, who little understood what Christianity and the articles of his Creed did signify. Once a quarter he said something which he called a sermon, which made him the pity or the laughter of the people. This man, being unable to preach himself, kept always a curate under him for that purpose. Before the wars, I had preached there only as a lecturer, and he was bound to pay me sixty pounds per annum; my people were so dear to me, and I to them, that I would have been with them upon the lowest lawful terms. Some laughed at me for refusing a bishopric, and petitioning to be a reading vicar's curate; but I had little hopes of so good a condition, at least for any considerable time. The ruler of the vicar and all the business was Sir Ralph Clare, an old man, and an old courtier, who carried it towards me, all the time I was there, with the greatest civility and respect, and sent me a purse of money, when I went away, which I refused. He was the principal cause of my removal. I suppose he thought that when I was far enough off, he could so far rule the town as to reduce the people to his way. Openly, he seemed to be for my return at first, that he might not offend the people; and the Lord Chancellor seemed very forward in it, and all the difficulty was to provide some other place for the old vicar, Mr. Dance, that he might be no loser by the change. The king himself must be engaged in it; the Lord Chancellor earnestly presseth it; Sir Ralph is willing, and very desirous of it; and the vicar is willing, if he may but be recompensed with as good a place, from which I had received but ninety pounds a year. But the hindrance was, that among all the livings and prebendaries of England, there was none fit for the poor vicar. A prebend he must not have, because he was incompetent, and yet he is still thought competent to be the pastor of near four thousand souls. The Lord Chancellor, to make the business certain, engages himself for a valuable stipend to the vicar, and his own steward shall be commanded to pay it for him. What could he desire more? But the poor vicar was to answer him that this was no security to him; his lordship might withhold that stipend at his pleasure, and then where was his maintenance? Give him but a legal title to anything of equal value, and he would resign. The patron also was my sure and intimate friend. But no such thing was to be had, and so Mr. Dance must keep his place. Though I requested not any preferment but this, yet even for this I resolved I would never be importunate. I only nominated it as the favour which I desired, when their offers in general invited me to ask more; and then I told them if it were any way inconvenient to them, I would not request it. In the end it appeared that two knights of the county, Sir Ralph Clare and Sir John Packington, who were very great with Dr. Morley, newly-made Bishop of Worcester, had made him believe that my interest was so great, and I could do so much with ministers and people in that county, that unless I would bind myself to promote their cause and party, I was not fit to be there." The Lord Chancellor was so anxious for Baxter's appointment to the vicarage of Kidderminster, that he wrote to Sir Ralph Clare: "I am a little out of countenance, that after the discovery of such a desire in His Majesty, that Mr. Baxter should be settled in Kidderminster, as he was heretofore, and my promise to you, by the king's direction, that Mr. Dance should very punctually receive a recompense by way of a rent upon his or your bills charged here upon my steward, Mr. Baxter hath yet no fruit of this His Majesty's good intention towards him; so that he hath too much reason to believe that he is not so frankly dealt with in this particular as he deserves to be. I do again tell you that it will be very acceptable to the king if you can persuade Mr. Dance to surrender that charge to Mr. Baxter, and in the meantime, and till he is preferred to as profitable an employment, whatever agreement you shall make with him for an annual rent, it shall be paid quarterly upon a bill from you charged upon my steward, Mr. Clutterbucke; and for the exact performance of this, you may securely pawn your full credit. I do most earnestly entreat you, that you will with all speed inform me what we may depend upon in this particular, that we may not keep Mr. Baxter in suspense, who hath deserved very well from His Majesty, and of whom

His Majesty hath a very good opinon." "Can anything," says Baxter, "be more serious, cordial, and obliging than all this? For a Lord Chancellor, that hath the business of the kingdom upon his hand, and lords attending him, to take upon his time so much and often about so low a vicarage or a curateship, when it is not in the power of the king and the Lord Chancellor to procure it for him, though they so vehemently desire it? But, oh! thought I, how much better life do poor men live, who speak as they think, and do as they profess, and are never put upon such shifts as these for their present conveniences. Wonderful, thought I, that men who do so much overvalue worldly honour and esteem, can possibly so much forget futurity, and think only of the present day, as if they regarded not how their actions be judged by posterity. Notwithstanding all his extraordinary favour, since the day the king came in, I never received as his chaplain, or as a preacher, or on any account, the value of one farthing of public maintenance. So that I, and many a hundred more, had not had a piece of bread, but for the voluntary contribution, whilst we preached, of another sort of people; yea, while I had all this excess of favour, I would have taken it indeed for an excess, as being far beyond my expectations, if they would but have given me liberty to preach the gospel without any maintenance, and leave me to beg my bread. I wrote a letter at this time to my mother-in-law, containing nothing but our usual matter, even encouragements to her in her age and weakness, fetched from the nearness of her rest, together with the report [of Venner's insurrection], and some sharp and vehement words against the rebels. By means of Sir John Packington or his soldiers the post was searched, and my letter intercepted, opened, and revised; and by Sir John sent up to London to the bishops and the Lord Chancellor. It is a wonder that, having read it, they were not ashamed to send it up; but joyful would they have been could they but have found a word in it which could possibly have been distorted to an evil sense, that malice might have had its prey; I went to the Lord Chancellor and complained of this usage, and that I had not the common liberty of a subject to converse by letters with my own family. He disowned it, and blamed men's rashness, but excused it from the distempers of the times; yet he and the bishops confessed they had seen the letter, and that there was nothing in it but what was good and pious. Two days after came the Lord Windsor, Lord-Lieutenant of the county and Governor of Jamaica, with Sir Charles Littleton, the king's cup-bearer, to bring me my letter again to my lodgings. Lord Windsor told me the Lord Chancellor appointed him to do it; so after some expression of the abuse, I thanked him for his great civility and favour. But I saw how far that sort of men was to be trusted."

For some time after his refusal by the Bishop of Worcester, Baxter preached once a week in London, at Dr. Bates's Church, St. Dunstan's-in-the-West, where the people gave him a stipend. He says: "The congregation being crowded provoked envy to accuse me: and one day the crowd did drive me from my place. It fell out that at St. Dunstan's Church, in the midst of a sermon, a little lime and dust, and perhaps a piece of brick or two, fell down in the steeple or belfry near the boys: so that they thought the steeple and church were falling, which put them all into so confused a haste to get away, that the noise of their feet in the galleries sounded like the falling of the stones. The people crowded out of doors, the women left some of them a scarf, and some a shoe behind them, and some in the galleries cast themselves down upon those below, because they could not get down the stairs. I sat down in the pulpit, seeing and pitying their vain distemper, and as soon as I could be heard, I entreated their silence, and went on. The people were no sooner quieted and got in again, and the auditory composed, but some who stood upon a wainscot-bench near the communion table, brake the bench with their weight, so that the noise renewed the fear again, and they were worse disordered than before. One old woman was heard at the church-door asking forgiveness of God for not taking the first warning, and promising, if God would deliver her this once, she would take heed of coming hither again. When they were again quieted I went on; but the church having before an ill name as very old, rotten, and dangerous, it put the parish upon a resolution to pull down all the roof, and build it better; which they have done with so great reparation of the walls and steeple, that it is now like a new church, and much more commodious for the hearers. While the church was repairing, I preached out of my quarter at St. Bride's at the other end of Fleet Street, where the common prayer being used by the curate before sermon, I occasioned abundance to be at common prayer, who before avoided it: and yet my accusations still continued. On the week-days, Mr. Ashurst with about twenty citizens desired me to preach a lecture in Milk Street; for which they allowed me forty pounds per annum, which I continued nearly a year, till we were all silenced. At the same time, I preached every Lord's Day at Blackfriars, where Mr. Gibbons, a judicious man, was minister. In Milk Street I took money, because it came not from the parishioners, but from strangers, and so was no wrong to the minister, Mr. Vincent, a very holy, blameless man. But at Blackfriars I never took a penny, because it was the parishioners who called me, who would else be less able and ready to help their worthy pastor, who went to God by a consumption, a little after he was silenced and put out. At these two churches I ended the course of my public ministry, unless God cause an undeserved resurrection. Before this I resolved to go to the Bishop of London, to ask him for his license to preach in his diocese. Soon after my return to London, I went into Worcestershire, to try whether it were possible to have any honest terms from the reading vicar there, that I might preach to my former flock; but when I preached twice or thrice, he denied me liberty to preach any more. I offered then to take my lecture, which he was bound to allow me, under a bond of £500; but he refused it. I next offered to be his curate, and he refused it. I then offered to preach for nothing, and he refused it: and lastly, I desired leave but once to administer the Sacrament to the people, and preach my farewell sermon to them; but he would not consent. At last, I understood he was directed by his superiors to do what he did. I then went to the Bishop of Worcester, and reminded him of his promise to grant me his license; but he refused me liberty to preach in his diocese, though I offered to preach only on the Creed, the Lord's Prayer, and the Ten Commandments—catechistical principles, and only to such as had no preaching. Bishop Morley told me when he silenced me, that he would take care that the people should be no losers, but should be taught as well as they were by me. When I was gone, he got awhile a few scandalous men, with some that were more civil, to keep up the lecture, till the paucity of the auditors gave them a pretence to put it down. He came himself one day and preached a long invective against them and me as Presbyterians, and I know not what; so that the people wondered a man would venture to come up into a pulpit and speak so confidently to those he knew not, the things which they commonly knew to be untrue. But this sermon was so far from winning any of them to the estimation of their new bishop, or curing what he called the admiration of my person, which was his great endeavour, that they were much confirmed in their former judgments. But still the bishop looked at Kidderminster as a factious, schismatical, Presbyterian people, that must be cured of their overvaluing of me, and then they would be cured of all the rest. Whereas if he had lived with them the twentieth part so long as I had done, he would have known that they were neither Presbyterians, nor factious, nor schismatical, nor seditious; but a people that quietly followed their hard labour, learned the Holy Scriptures, lived a holy, blameless life, in humility and peace with all men, and never had any sect or separated party among them, but abhorred all faction and sidings in religion, and lived in love and Christian unity. When the bishop was gone, the Dean, Dr. Warmestry, came and preached about three hours to cure them of the admiration of my person; and a month after, came again and preached over the same, persuading the people that they were Presbyterians, and schismatical, and were led to it by their overvaluing of me. The people admired the temerity of these men, and really thought that they were scarce well in their wits, who would go on to speak things so far from truth of men whom they never knew, and that to their own faces. For there was but one, if one, Presbyterian in the town; the plain, honest people minding nothing but piety, unity, charity, and their callings. This dealing, instead of winning them to the preacher, drove them from the lecture, and then, as I said, they accused the people of deserting it, and put it down. In place of this ordinary preacher, they set up one of the best parts they could get, who was far from what his patrons spake him to be; he was quickly wearied, and went away. They next set up a poor dry man, who had been a schoolmaster near us, and after a little time, he died. They then took another course, and set up a young man, the best they could get, who took the contrary way to the first, over applauded me in the pulpit, spoke well of themselves, and used them kindly. They were naturally glad of one that had some charity. Thus the bishop used that flock, who say that till then they never knew so well what a bishop was, or were before so guilty of that dislike of episcopacy, of which they were so frequently and vehemently accused. Having parted with my dear flock, I need not say with mutual sense and tears, I left Mr. Baldwin to live privately among them, and oversee them in my stead, and visit them from house to house; advising them, notwithstanding all the injuries they had received, and all the failings of the ministers that preached to them, that they should keep to the public assemblies, and make use of such helps as might be had in public, together with their private helps."

The exclusion from the parish where he had laboured so long was a sore affliction to Baxter. His heart was all but broken by the harsh and unnecessary severance made by the bishop. To his quick bosom quietude was an impossible condition; and a renewed application, on his return to Kidderminster, to Bishop Morley was again refused. In the church there his voice was never to be heard again. One of his latest friends says of him: "It was his meat and drink, the life and joy of his life, to do good to souls." This delight was to be his no more, except in peril of fines and imprisonment. But he was not left to mourn alone. Provision of happiness had been made for him, a sweet solace for many griefs. All London was moved by tidings that the great divine of Kidderminster, the eloquent preacher, the author read by thousands, the eager disputant at the Savoy Conference, and but lately angrily ejected by his bishop, was about to be married. Baxter says: "It was rung about everywhere, partly as a wonder, partly as a crime; and the king's marriage was scarcely more talked of than mine." He had himself, as was well known, often expressed doubt as to the expediency of the marriages of clergymen. He was then forty-six years of age, and it was reported that he had many bodily infirmities, which rendered him an object rather of pity than of affection. Men ridiculed the old student. They laughed at the sudden amorousness of the great preacher. They questioned if he were not turning an eye to the pomps and vanities he had decried. They professed to wonder that any one could be willingly troubled with so great a burden, as the care of a clergyman whose youth was passed, whose health was feeble, and who had been summarily deprived, however unjustly, of his calling. The wits in the coffee-houses had pleasant half-hours in discussing the last news of him, in mocking him as a lover and a bridegroom, and in laughing at the tidings which had so excited the town. They professed wondrous pity for the lady who had consented to be the wife of the preaching exile from Kidderminster; and they said it was passing strange that, as only just come of age, she could consent to share the lot of life with the sharp debater of the Savoy, so thin, so old, and so frail. But it is not for the frivolous mind to understand, nor for the ribald tongue to tell, the resolution, strength, and beauty of virtuous love, nor the immeasurable and immovable constancy of the pure woman's heart, who has set her affections on goodness which ever attracts and delights the gentle soul. It was nothing to him that they laughed; nor to her that they frowned. She said, as the lady, whom Philip Henry was about to marry, replied to the officious friends who told her they did not even know where her lover came from: "True; but I know where he is going, and I should like to go with him." "There is a comfort in the strength of love;" and none were ever better assorted than Richard Baxter and Margaret Charlton, and no life was happier than that which their marriage consecrated and blessed. Reserved and kindly, carefully educated in the culture which became a young gentlewoman of the time, in her heart she passionately loved the great preacher, who had carefully watched over her earlier days, prayed with her in illness, comforted her in sorrow, trained her to holy thought and dedication, and guided her in the way which all the good have gone who are resting in peace. She had made him her earthly example of goodness, and in the morning of her lovely life, she gave herself to him, feeble, poor, and persecuted. She heard the sarcasm of the flippant, and the censure of the old and stern; she bore meekly the ready disapproval of them of her own companions whose charms had no adorers, and whose blame was not unmingled with envy; unmoved from her purpose, and with undiminished affection. Baxter was supremely happy in the faithful love of so true a friend, who brought the light of peace into his dwelling; soothed his irritation by her graceful gentleness; even counselled him in difficulty by that wisdom which is instinctive in some of her sex; nursed him in sickness; tended him in prison; comforted him when wounded by the arrows of slander; in the gloomy days of seclusion, when the hand of man was against him, she sang him the melodies he loved, read him the comfortable words of Divine consolation, and lived as an angel of goodness in his uncertain home, until she passed away. He loved her with all the pure passion of a soul nourished by heavenly truth and chastened by affliction. The storms which raged around his habitation, broke on his threshold, but had no entrance there so long as his wife remained to shed upon it the warm light of her affection. Afterwards, when left alone in his suffering in the winter-time of life, all his pleasant places of memory were fragrant with thoughts of her tender love and care, until upon him also the day broke, and the wicked ceased to trouble, and the weary one had rest. In the period of persecution which followed their marriage, Baxter and his wife had no certain dwelling-place. "They first had a house in Moorfields; then they removed to Acton; after that to another there; after that to one of the former again; after that to divers others in another place and county. The women have most of that sort of trouble, but my wife easily bore it all." The narrative of their love and marriage was written, towards the close of his career, in a work which Baxter called "A Breviate of her Life." He says: "We were born in the same county, within three miles and a half of each other; but she of one of the chief families of the county, and I but of a mean freeholder, called a gentleman, for his ancestors' sake. Her father, Francis Charlton, Esq., was one of the best justices of the peace in that county, a grave and worthy man who did not marry till he was aged and grey, and died while his children were very young. There were three of them, of which the eldest daughter and the only son are yet alive. He had one surviving brother, who, after the father's death, maintained a long and costly suit about the guardianship of the heir. This uncle Robert was a comely, sober gentleman, but the wise and good mother, Mary, durst not trust her only son in the hands of one that was his next heir; and she thought that nature gave her a greater interest in him than an uncle had. Her house, being a sort of small castle, was then garrisoned for the king. At last, Robert procured it to be besieged by the

Parliament's soldiers, stormed and taken; where the mother and children saw part of the buildings burnt, and some lie dead before their eyes; and so Robert got possession of the children. Afterwards, however, she by great wisdom and diligence surprised them, secretly conveyed them to Mr. Bernard's in Essex, and secured them against all his endeavours. The wars being ended, and she, as guardian, possessing her son's estate, took him to herself, and used his estate as carefully as for herself; but out of it conscientiously paid the debts of her husband, repaired some of the ruined houses, and managed things faithfully according to her best discretion, until her son marrying took his estate into his own hands. She, being before unknown to me, came to Kidderminster, desiring me to take a house for her alone. I told her I would not be guilty of doing anything which should separate a mother from an only son. She went home, but shortly came again, and took a house without my knowledge. When she had been there alone awhile, her unmarried daughter Margaret, then about seventeen or eighteen years of age, came after her from her brother's, resolving not to forsake the mother, who deserved her dearest love; though sometimes she went to Oxford to her eldest sister, wife to Mr. Ambrose Upton, then canon of Christchurch. At this time the good old mother lived as a blessing among the honest poor weavers of Kidderminster, strangers to her, whose company for their piety she chose before all the vanities of the world. The unsuitableness of our age, and my former known purposes against marriage, and against the conveniency of ministers marrying, who have no sort of necessity, made ours the matter of much public talk and wonder. But the true opening of her case and mine, and the many strange occurrences which brought it to pass, would take away the wonder of her friends and mine that knew us. Both in her case and mine there was much extraordinary, which it doth not concern the world to be acquainted with. From the first thoughts of it, many changes and stoppages intervened, and long delays, till I was silenced and ejected; and so being separated from my old pastoral charge, which was enough to take up all my time and labour, some of my dissuading reasons were then over. At last, on September 10th, 1662, we were married in Bennet-Fink church by Mr. Samuel Clark, having been before contracted by Mr. Simeon Ash, both in the presence of Mr. Henry Ashurst and Mrs. Ash. She consented to these conditions of our marriage: first, that I should have nothing that before our marriage was hers,—that I, who wanted no earthly supplies, might not seem to marry her for covetousness; secondly, that she would so alter her affairs, that I might be entangled in no lawsuits; thirdly, that she would expect none of my time which my ministerial work should require. When we were married, her sadness and melancholy vanished; counsel did something to it, and contentment something; and being taken up with our household affairs did somewhat. We lived in inviolated love and mutual complacency, sensible of the benefit of mutual help, nearly nineteen years. I know not that ever we had any breach in point of love, or point of interest, save only that she somewhat grudged that I had persuaded her for my quietness to surrender so much of her estate, to the disabling her from helping others so much as she earnestly desired. But that even this was not from a covetous mind is evident by these instances. Though her portion, which was two thousand pounds, beside what she gave up, was by ill debtors two hundred pounds lost in her mother's time, and two hundred pounds after, before her marriage; and all she had, reduced to about one thousand six hundred and fifty pounds, yet she never grudged at anything that the poverty of debtors deprived her of."

CHAPTER XVIII.

1662—1663.

IN the springtime of the year, Bishops Sheldon and Morley, prompted probably by Lord Clarendon, resolved to take such action as would free the Anglican Church from the last vestige of Puritanism. They would tolerate no difference of opinion in matters ecclesiastical, and every clergyman who had the least scruple of objection should be compelled to leave the Church. They urged Chief-Justice Keeling to frame an Act, which should embody the principle of the statute made in the reign of Queen Elizabeth, for one uniform order of common service and prayer, to be used by authority of Parliament, and which should compel the adoption of the Prayer-Book recently amended by Convocation. The new measure, called the Act of Uniformity, enjoined that all ministers should be bound to use and say the morning prayer, evening prayer, and all other common prayers, in such form and order as are mentioned in the book; and that every clergyman, before the feast of St. Bartholomew, 1662, should openly and publicly, in the presence of the congregation assembled for religious worship, declare his unfeigned assent and consent to the use of all things contained and prescribed in the same book. The penalty for neglecting or refusing to make this declaration was to be deprivation, *ipso facto*, of all his spiritual promotions. Clergymen of all ranks, fellows, tutors, professors, every one keeping a private or public school, and all persons teaching in private families, before the feast of

St. Bartholomew, 1662, were required to state their abhorrence of taking up arms against the king, and that they would conform to the Liturgy of the Church of England. The clergy, who refused to make such a declaration, were to be immediately deprived; schoolmasters and tutors who failed to do so were to be imprisoned for three months, and to be fined five pounds. It was further enacted, that no person should hold any benefice, or administer Holy Communion, before he be episcopally ordained a priest, on pain of forfeiting one hundred pounds for each offence. No one was to be permitted to lecture, preach, or read in any church or chapel, unless licensed by a bishop, under the penalty of three months' imprisonment for each offence. In every church and college-hall in which there was not in use a copy of the amended Prayer-Book, the person presiding over or otherwise responsible for the building should be liable to a fine of three pounds a month, so long as such church or college-hall was unprovided with it. By this Act every Presbyterian in possession of a living was required to be ordained by a bishop, and to make the prescribed declarations, or to be ejected from it. When this Act was brought into Parliament, many of the more moderate members expressed great disapproval of its severity. To meet this objection, the government caused reports to be spread, for which there was no shadow of truth, that plots were being formed in many counties by the Presbyterians; and they, who hesitated to vote for the injury of their neighbours and friends, were constrained to do so by fear of insurrection. Great resistance, however, was made in the Houses to the passing of the Act, but it was carried in both of them by small majorities.

The Act of Uniformity was intended by its promoters to be cruel. Some of the restored clergy were said to be anxious to obtain possession of the rich livings held by the Puritans; and all agreed in their hatred of the men whose party had triumphed in the civil war, who had killed the king, and silenced the English Church. A few of the

Presbyterian clergy conformed, and, with gentler treatment of them, there is little doubt but that the greater number would have made the required declarations. The bishops feared that a large number of the Puritan divines would consent to the provisions of the Act, and would thus retain their livings; but that would have been contrary to the wishes of the passionate men, eager for revenge, who, unhappily for its best interests, had in their hands at that time the control of the fortunes of the Anglican Church. While the Bill was being debated in Parliament, Lord Manchester told the king that he was afraid none of the Presbyterian ministers would comply with the hard terms of it. Sheldon, Bishop of London, one of its chief promoters, said: "I am afraid they will. Now we know their minds, we'll make them knaves if they conform." Dr. Allen remarked, "It is a pity the door is so strait." Sheldon replied, "It is no pity at all; if we had thought so many of them would have conformed, we would have made it straiter." Nature is stronger than institutions, and the anger and hatred of numerous churchmen, who had suffered grievous wrongs under the Protector's government, made them revengeful when power returned to their hands. They thought that the interests of the Church required not only the humiliation, but the complete suppression of them who differed from it. The republicans might recover their strength, they argued; stability of opinion is uncertain; the throne and the Church might again be in danger; better to make certain of present advantages, than to allow any form of opposition to remain. The king, who really cared for neither party, pretended to favour the severity of the bishops, in hope that the strength of the Protestant bodies might be so weakened by the existence of a permanent confederation of Nonconformists, that the toleration which must ultimately follow, would make it the more easy for him to bring in the Latin Church.

The provisions of the Act of Uniformity were cruel. "It was to have effect," says Bishop Burnet, "on the twenty-fourth day of August, in order that the deprived clergy might lose the tithes for the year, which are commonly due at Michaelmas. No provision whatever was made for the maintenance of any who might be ejected. When, by the original Act of Queen Elizabeth's reign, many clergymen were deprived of their livings, and when they who were Royalists were driven out by Cromwell, a fifth part of the proceeds of the benefices was reserved for their support. The Presbyterians remembered what a Bartholomew's day had been held at Paris ninety years before, which was the day of that massacre, and did not stick to compare the one with the other. The Book of Common Prayer with the new corrections was that to which they were to subscribe. But the corrections were so long a preparing, and the vast number of copies that were to be wrought off for all the parish-churches of England made the impression go on so slowly, that there were few books set out to sale when the day came. So many that were well affected to the Church, but that made conscience of subscribing to a book that they had not seen, left their benefices on that very account. Some made a journey to London on purpose to see it. With so much precipitation was that matter driven on, that it seemed expected that the clergy should subscribe implicitly to a book they had never seen. This was done by too many, as I was informed by some of the bishops. About two thousand of them fell under the Parliamentary deprivation, as they gave out. This raised a grievous outcry over the whole nation. Baxter told me that had the terms of the king's Declaration been stood to, he did not believe but that above three hundred of them would have been so deprived. Here were many men much valued, some on better grounds, others on worse, who were now cast out ignominiously, reduced to great poverty, provoked by much spiteful usage, and cast upon those popular practices, that both their principles and their circumstances seemed to justify, of forming separate congregations, and of dissenting from the public worship. The blame of all this fell heaviest on Sheldon." It was impossible for all the clergy to read the alterations in the Prayer-Book within the specified time. The Dean and Chapter of Peterborough declared they could not read the new book before the twenty-fourth day of August, and they were obliged to ask the Bishop "to dispense with the default." If the Act had been only perspective in its operation, much of the cruelty attending it might have been averted; but John Locke says: "So great was the zeal in carrying out this affair, and so blind was the obedience required, that if you compute the time of passing this Act with the time allowed for the clergy to subscribe the Book of Common Prayer thereby established, you shall plainly find it could not be printed and distributed, so as one man in forty could have seen and read the book they did so perfectly assent and consent to."

The bishops were determined to enforce the Act to the very letter of it. On St. Bartholomew's Day, one-fifth of the English clergy were driven from their parishes,—a great religious expulsion. It originated, was arranged and completed by Lord Clarendon and Bishops Sheldon and Morley; who thought thereby to root up noxious weeds from their pastures. If they removed any who were evil, they ejected the good with them; for in one day they expelled the most able and energetic of them who were possessed of parishes, and who had the greater number of the larger livings in their hands. No one acquainted with the history of the time, and with the scholarship and worth of many of them who were ejected, will hesitate to question the wisdom of the enactment, which at once destroyed so great a force in the religious life of England, and which prevented the public from having the advantage which undoubtedly must have resulted from the regular religious teaching of men so eminent as Howe, Baxter, John Owen, Calamy, Bates, and others, whose names are still held in veneration in Great Britain and in America, and whose works have long usefully outlived the names of their persecutors. No subject of the king was at that time superior to John Howe as an accurate theologian and a profound philosophical thinker, the associate and friend of some of the purest of the nobility and of the scholars of his day; a man of the highest refinement of mind, and well worthy, in the opinion of them best able to estimate his power, to receive the title of "the English Plato," with which posterity have requited the evil accident of his ejection from the parish of Great Torrington. Baxter had not his equal as a preacher, and he had already acquired great fame as an energetic parish-priest, and as an admirable writer on doctrinal and practical religion. With them were many others, who from that St. Bartholomew's day ceased to deepen religious thought, and to shed by their public exhortations and instructions a healthful influence upon their age.

Between the Anglican and the Latin Churches the Reformation had made an impassable gulf; and the Act of Uniformity completely severed the English Church from every other Protestant religious community, and created the immense disadvantage of a permanent form of Dissent, which wise concession might either have lessened, or have entirely prevented. Experience has shown that the effect of the Act has been especially injurious to the Anglican Church, and, among other evil results, by preventing any expansion in its service—except when commanded by vote of Parliament—and any adaptation to new modes of thought, and to the requirements of a race ever advancing in civilization, in commercial progress, in social improvement, and in national and political power. After the passing of the Act all internal reform was impossible, and any modification of the public service was prohibited. New religious organizations were formed, noble societies to propagate Christian truth, to lessen ignorance and misery, and to promote the higher interests of mankind. Hospitals and charitable institutions were founded, and which called for the help and prayers of the clergy; education was demanded by English artisans for their children; the farmers and producers asked that, in the autumn of the year, they might offer special thanksgiving for the crops and fruits of field and of orchard: but to meet these wise requirements of a people growing in devout feeling, and in affection for their fathers' Church, the Act of Uniformity gave constant prohibition and restriction. With alleged doubtful legality, bishops have from time to time written or sanctioned forms of prayer, to meet some of the wants of the increasing religious life in English churchmen, and often peculiarly and remarkably inferior in phrase and structure to the nervous and condensed English of the Prayer-Book; but by the instinctive demand for them, testifying to the unwisdom of an Act, which, designed to produce uniformity, lessened the vital powers of the Church, and for many years reduced its movements to the precision and rigidity of those of a machine. The action of the bishops was that of misdirected zeal, with a determination to punish the seceders: for they not only ejected them, but persecuted them after their expulsion; and thus by forcing all the sects into a compact union, they gave a permanent form to dissent; so that discordant dissidents, too numerous to be crushed, have become by degrees a powerful organization, always in sympathy with each other, and in active enmity to the Church, which happily they have not been able a second time to overthrow.

The number of the Puritan and Presbyterian clergy who were deprived of their cures, after the investigation of all trustworthy evidence, may be estimated at little less than two thousand. Many of them who were driven out deserved well of the king; for they had actively promoted his restoration, and they were among the most devout, loyal, and peaceful of his subjects. Some of them after ejection attended the parish churches, and received the sacraments according to the Anglican rite. The sudden withdrawment of so large a number of eminent public teachers produced, for many years, a disastrous diminution in the spiritual life and active power of the Church. Able successors to such men as Manton, Bates, Baxter, Owen, Clarkson, Calamy, Poole, Caryl, Philip Henry, Charnock, Howe, Flavel, and many more, could not easily be found. The author of the "Five Groans of the Church," a rigid Anglican, and hostile to the Puritans, complains of the impossibility of filling the pulpits vacated by men of such power and reputation. He laments that "above three thousand ministers were admitted into the Church, who were unfit to teach because of their youth; of fifteen hundred debauched men ordained, of the ordination of many illiterate men, of one thousand three hundred and forty-two factious ministers, a little before ordained, and that, of twelve thousand church-livings or thereabouts, three thousand or more being impropriate, and four thousand one hundred and sixty-five sinecures, there was but a poor remainder left for a painful and honest ministry." The expulsion of the Puritan and Presbyterian clergy was undoubtedly effected under a form of law, insomuch as the Houses of Parliament had passed an Act to procure it. Legally considered, many of them were simply intruders into parishes from which good and zealous clergymen had been ejected by the Triers, because they would not renounce their fidelity to the king, nor consent to the usurpation of Cromwell. Others of them, without episcopal license, and in violation of the requirements of ecclesiastical rule, had ministered in parishes which pertained to the English Church. If the Anglican Church was that which the state adopted, and whose endowments were secured by Civil Law; and if in the Book of Common Prayer were the regulations prescribed for the conduct of public worship by its ministers; the requirement by the Government, or by the bishops acting under its authority, for uniformity in its services, was not unjust. The victories gained by the Parliamentarian armies had led to the expulsion and persecution of many of the Anglican clergy, and to the occupation of their parishes by persons who were nominated to them by the republican rulers. When those rulers fell, and the death of Oliver led to the return of Charles II. as sovereign, the benefices would necessarily revert to the Church restored by the re-establishment of the monarchy.

Nothing could justify the tyrannical deprivation of any clergymen by the Protector, only on the ground that they were Royalists; and many of them whom he placed in their cures were not in a true sense ministers of the English Church. Upon their restoration to power, the bishops therefore were legally right in recovering the benefices for those surviving Anglican clergymen who had been unlawfully and violently thrust out; but they were morally wrong in doing it vindictively, and with a determination to have no compromise with men who, in numerous instances, had done good service in the parishes to which they had been appointed either by the Parliament or by the Protector, and whose former incumbents in many cases were dead; and especially were the prelates culpable in sanctioning their persecution for many years after their deprivation; and in bringing terrible sufferings upon their wives and children. The ejection and oppression of the Anglican clergy by the government of Cromwell can in no sense justify the persecution and frequent imprisonment of the deprived Puritans and Presbyterians by the government of Charles II. Both administrations in this respect acted cruelly and unwisely, and the adherents of each of them suffered in turn from that justice which avenges oppression, and which helps them to right who suffer wrong. It is unquestionable that the Anglican Church has been far more injured by the Act of Uniformity, than were the Puritans and Presbyterians against whom it was framed. The profligacy of the king and his court had evil effect on the lives of many churchmen. The rapid enrichment of the bishops by their receipt of enormous fines on the renewal of leases, and the luxury which increase of wealth often produces, were detrimental to personal religion and to devotion to duty. Corruption began to revive in the exercise of patronage. The nepotism, which down to our own day has been a frequent cause of injury to parishes, and of injustice to laborious clergymen, often caused incumbents to be appointed to cures, who did not promote the higher interests of the Church. The restored clergy in many cases became rapacious pluralists. In the days of his exile they had done service for the king, and some of them, whom he was not too indolent to remember, he rewarded with accumulated benefices. Shortly after the passing of the Act of Uniformity, as if in practical irony of his religious faith, whose chief principle is self-denial, Dr. Ryves, one of Baxter's persecutors, was at the same time "Rector of Acton, Rector of Hadley, Dean of Windsor and of Wolverhampton, and Chaplain in Ordinary to the king." No doubt he would have welcomed more preferments had they been attainable, and he deemed it bliss that in most of those he held, he could do his duty by deputy. At Acton "a raw and ignorant curate" tilled the field; but, as a less fortunate labourer, he was not allowed to possess the harvest. The happily renewed and invigorated Church of our day, rejoicing to visit and befriend the poor, to care equally for all the flock, and to be a living witness for truth, is less and less likely to be bound and enfeebled by regulations which diminish energy, impede progress, and prevent success; and will gradually become freed from unworthy customs, and from whatever abuses may exist, inherited from evil years, when selfishness degraded and avarice marked the lives of ecclesiastics favoured by the crown.

Many of the Presbyterian clergy conformed for the sake of their families. Some of them applied themselves to the study of medicine, and became eminent as physicians; and others were received into the houses of noblemen and gentlemen, who pitied their calamities, and abhorred the profligacy of the king and his court, which every day became more puplic and more shameless. Some of them became chaplains in country-houses; others went to the Continent, or found a welcome and a home among their expatriated brethren in New England, where the seeds of freedom had already been largely sown, and where the foundations had been laid of that vast, powerful, and magnanimous English-speaking State, which seems to be destined to take the lead in all that can promote the civilization and happiness of mankind. Some of the Puritan clergy had means of livelihood, which enabled them to bear the sudden loss of their stipends with equanimity; but many of them who were summarily deprived had large families and scanty resources. Collections were made for them in various towns and districts of the country, and it is alleged, as a singular fact in their sufferings after ejectment, that none of them in all their poverty were ever imprisoned for debt. Bishop Burnet says of them: "They cast themselves upon the providence of God and the charity of their friends. This begot esteem, and raised compassion." Baxter, who well knew the circumstances of some of the deprived Puritans and Presbyterians, says: "Many hundreds of them with their wives and children had neither house nor bread; the people they left were not able to relieve them, nor durst they if they had been able, because it would have been called a maintenance of schism or faction. Many of the ministers, afraid to lay down their ministry after they had been ordained to it, preached to such as would hear them in fields and private houses, till they were apprehended and cast into jails, where many of them perished. The people were no less divided; some conformed, and others were driven to a greater distance from the Church, and resolved to abide by their faithful pastors at all events: they murmured at the government, and called the bishops and conforming clergy cruel persecutors, for which, and for frequenting the private assemblies of their ministers, they were fined and imprisoned, till many families left their native country, and settled in the plantations." On the return of the king, Lord Clarendon had resolved on restoring the Anglicans to the dignities and emoluments from which Cromwell had expelled them, and that the Puritan clergy should not only be ejected from their livings, but also be forbidden to exercise their ministry. In carrying out the plan he had formed, he found ready assistants in Bishops Sheldon, Morley, Gunning, and others. All means which the government could command were employed to accomplish the result. The Act of Uniformity, they said, should be applied with unsparing exactness and severity, and others should be proposed, if the former were found insufficient to put an end to the preaching of the expelled divines. The Puritan ministers were soon placed in circumstances of increasing misery. They were attacked by some of the younger Anglican clergy in their sermons on Sundays. They were ridiculed in comedies. Profligate men, and the still more abandoned women, who crowded the benches of the new theatres, to see the king and the wanton ladies who wasted his money, degraded his dignity, and injured his reputation, laughed at the clever mimicry upon the stage of the tones in which it was said the Puritans prayed and preached; were infinitely amused at their imaginary temptations to vice, and at the hypocrisy they were charged with assuming; at the goblets they drained in the houses of citizens, and at the fair cheeks they kissed in secret. The king was not ashamed to hear some of his most loyal and peaceable subjects ridiculed and dishonoured by false representations, amid the uproarious laughter and the frightful blasphemies of the foulest and vilest of mankind. The rabble swarmed from cellars and garrets to insult the Puritans in the streets, and threatened them with violence, which a mob is always quick to employ. So that the unhappy ministers were compelled to lay aside the clothing peculiar to their profession, and to walk in secluded streets, and in the shades of evening. Baxter suffered with his friends, but he had at once the attraction and consolation of the Divine philosophy with whose truths he had for many years nurtured his soul. He comforted himself by the assurance, which was an anchor of security in the fury of the storm, that the Everlasting Wisdom was reigning over all the disordered and confused human society; that He had not given up His own world and them who loved Him to the disposal and government of the devil; that He would not leave His servants remedilessly to be stricken and to perish; and that the seeming success and triumph of evil would precede the final victory of goodness and truth. It was recorded at the time: "Such magistrates were put into commission as executed the penal laws with severity. Informers were encouraged and rewarded. It is impossible to relate the sufferings both of ministers and people; the great trials, with hardships upon their persons, estates, and families by uncomfortable separations, dispersions, disgraces, imprisonment, expenses in law, tedious sicknesses, and incurable diseases ending in death. Though they were as frugal as possible, they could hardly live: some lived on little more than brown bread and water; many had but eight pounds or ten pounds a year to maintain a family, so that a piece of flesh has not come to one of their tables in six weeks' time: their allowance would scarcely afford them bread and cheese. One went to plough six days and preached on the Lord's Day. Another was forced to cut tobacco for a livelihood."

To guard himself from the publications of remonstrance against the tyranny of his government, and of his gambling, drunkenness, and immorality, the king had provided that an Act should be passed forbidding any person to print books or pamphlets, unless these were first licensed by authorised persons. Law-books were to be licensed by the Lord Chancellor; books on history by a Secretary of State; novels, romances, fairy tales, books of divinity, of physic, and of love by the Archbishop of Canterbury, or the Bishop of London. Three days after the passing of the Act of Uniformity, Drs. Manton, Bates, and Calamy petitioned the king for toleration, and he is said to have proposed to his Council some relaxation of the severity of the law. The Earl of Manchester suggested that the more eminent Puritan divines should be allowed to retain their livings for the rest of their lives, and that curates should be appointed to the churches to read the required service. This proposition was strenuously opposed by Lord Clarendon, who demanded the strict application of the law; and by Bishop

Sheldon, who declared if the Act were suspended he could not maintain his episcopal authority, and that this would render the legislature ridiculous, and be the occasion of endless distractions. The law was therefore allowed to take effect, and there was no prospect of alleviation of the intolerable hardships of the ejected Puritans. Baxter says of his own sufferings at the time: "As we were forbidden to preach, so we were vigilantly watched in private, that we might not exhort one another, or pray together; and as I foretold them oft, how they would use us when they had silenced us, every meeting for prayer was called a dangerous meeting for sedition, or a conventicle at least. I will now give but one instance of their kindness to myself. One Mr. Beale in Hatton Garden, having a son, his only child, who being long sick of a dangerous fever, was brought so low that the physicians thought he would die, desired a few friends, of whom I was one, to meet at his house, to pray for him. Because it pleased God to hear our prayers, and that very night to restore him, his mother shortly after falling sick of a fever, we were desired to meet to pray for her recovery, the last day when she was near to death. Among those who were to be there, it fell out that Dr. Bates and I did fail them, and could not come; but it was known at Westminster that we were appointed to be there, whereupon two justices of the peace were procured from the distant parts of the town, one from Westminster, and one from Clerkenwell, to come with the Parliament's sergeant-at-arms to apprehend us. They came in the evening, when part of the company were gone. There were then only a few of their kindred, besides two or three ministers to pray. They came upon them into the room, where the gentlewoman lay ready to die, drew the curtains, and took some of their names; but missing their prey, returned disappointed. What a joy would it have been to them that reproached us as Presbyterian, seditious schismatics, to have found but such an occasion as praying with a dying woman, to have laid us up in prison! Yet that same week, there was published a witty, malicious invective against the silenced ministers, in which it was affirmed that Dr. Bates and I were at Mr. Beale's house, such a day, keeping a conventicle. The liar had so much extraordinary modesty as within a day or two to print a second edition, in which those words so easy to be disproved were left out. Such eyes were everywhere then lifted upon us."

The prisons were fast filling with Puritans and Quakers. Of the latter sect, misunderstood or misrepresented by nearly all the religionists of the time, more than four thousand were in gaol, and in a few years the number was increased to twelve thousand. Both Presbyterians and Quakers were fined again and again, for absenting themselves from church. Informers watched them, detected their times of meeting, and appeared against them in the magistrates' courts. Numbers of them languished in the filthy prisons. Alleyne, who wrote the "Alarm to the Unconverted," once a book of great popularity, perished in the gaol at Taunton; and Powell, one of the most famous of the Welsh preachers, transferred from dungeon to dungeon, after suffering terrible imprisonment for eleven years, died in the Fleet prison. John Bunyan, author of the "Pilgrim's Progress," and whose name is a household-word wherever the English language is spoken, committed on a charge of preaching in unlicensed conventicles, was confined for eleven years in the gaol at Bedford. The imprisonment of such persons for such a cause well illustrates the reign of one of the most corrupt of men, the most faithless of husbands, and the worst of kings. Everywhere impurity prevailed. Charles corrupted his kingdom in its whole extent. His money was profusely lavished on various forms of vice. The younger courtiers endeavoured to imitate him in depravity; and many of the clergy, who grieved when they saw the gradual rising of the flood of iniquity which they were unable to stem, began to feel that they had fallen on evil days.

The numerous mistresses of the king, the most of whom had one or more other admirers, interfered in the distribution of patronage; trafficked in the sale of places; shameless and abandoned, they impoverished the ambitious, and contaminated the young; they gambled and revelled; fickle in their favours, and false in their promises. Few persons who have acquainted themselves with trustworthy records of Charles II.'s court will disagree with the historian Hallam, who says: "We are much indebted to the memory of Barbara, Duchess of Cleveland, Louisa, Duchess of Portsmouth, and Mrs. Eleanor Gwyn. We owe a debt of gratitude to the Mays, Killigrews, the Chiffinches, and the Grammonts. They played a serviceable part in ridding the kingdom of its besotted loyalty. They saved our forefathers from the Star Chamber and the High Commission Court; they laboured in their vocation against standing armies and corruption; they pressed forward the great ultimate security of English freedom, the expulsion of the House of Stuart."

CHAPTER XIX.

1663—1665.

IN June, 1663, Juxon, Archbishop of Canterbury, died, who had attended Charles I. at his execution; and Sheldon, Bishop of London, was appointed to succeed him. He immediately projected new measures, which he erroneously thought would completely repress, if not destroy, Puritanism. A Bill was brought into Parliament, continuing in full force the Act of Elizabeth, which after their conviction condemned all persons peremptorily refusing to come to church, to banishment, and in case of their return, to death; and it further enacted, that "if any person above the age of sixteen years, after the 1st of July, 1664, shall be present at any meeting, under colour or pretence of any exercise of religion, in other manner than is allowed by the Liturgy or practice of the Church of England, where shall be five or more persons than the householder, shall for the first offence suffer three months' imprisonment, or pay a sum not exceeding five pounds; for the second offence, six months' imprisonment, or pay a sum not exceeding ten pounds; and for the third offence, the offender to be banished to some of the American plantations for seven years, excepting New England or Virginia, or pay one hundred pounds; and in case they return or make their escape, such persons are to be adjudged felons, and suffer death. Sheriffs or justices of peace are employed to dissolve, dissipate, and break up all unlawful conventicles, and to take into custody such of their number as they think fit.

They who suffer conventicles in their houses or barns are liable to the same forfeitures as other offenders. The prosecution is to be within three months. Married women taken at conventicles are to be imprisoned for twelve months, unless their husbands pay forty shillings for their redemption." The Act of Uniformity was directed against the Puritan and Presbyterian clergy; the Conventicle Act struck at the laity, who adhered to them, and who could be convicted on the oath of one informer before a single magistrate, and without the verdict of a jury. A more terrible instrument of social tyranny could hardly be devised or employed; but it was in an age when men's minds were familiar with ecclesiastical cruelties. In Spain and Italy the Inquisition was then in all its vigorous activity. In France Louis XIV. was harassing his Huguenot subjects with ceaseless ferocity, and strengthening one religious party in his kingdom by murdering many of the other; and that, not because he hated either Protestants or Jansenists, but because he regarded all who were alienated from the Latin Church in his dominion as enemies to his authority. In Scotland shocking cruelties and barbarities were being daily perpetrated against all who differed from the dominant religious party. There was a vindictive and ruthless spirit in the world, so that the policy of Clarendon and of Archbishop Sheldon was quite in harmony with the general temper of the time. In England liberty had not yet fully come, and toleration was not understood. The Conventicle Act soon overcrowded the gaols in every county. Occasionally, a Puritan clergyman, who attended the church of the parish in which he lived, would preach in his own dwelling to his adherents after the public service was over. Informers made the fact known to the magistrate, who ordered the house to be broken open, and the congregation to be arrested. The preacher, if convicted, was fined twenty pounds; the same sum was charged upon the place of meeting, and five shillings upon each of the hearers. If payment of the fine was not made upon conviction, immediate distraint followed on furniture and goods. The Diary of Philip Henry repeatedly records the seizure of his own property, and that of his neighbours, under this Act; which entirely forbade social prayer, however grievous the affliction of families might be, who, suffering in their households from some of the frequent diseases of the time, were threatened with the horrors of a crowded and noisome prison, if they asked their neighbours, in accordance with ancient custom, to come and pray with them for the recovery of a sick wife or of a feverish child. Of these events Baxter says: "About these times the talk of liberty to the silenced ministers, for what end I know not, was revived again; and we were blamed by many that we had never once petitioned the Parliament; for which we had sufficient reasons. It was said that they were resolved to grant us either an indulgence by way of dispensation, or a comprehension by some additional act, taking in all that could conform in some particular points. For my own part, I meddled but little with any such business, since the failing of that which occasioned so much displeasure; and the rather, because though the brethren commissioned with me stuck to me as to the cause, yet they were not forward enough to bear their part of the ungrateful management, nor of the consequent displeasure. But yet when an honourable person was earnest with me to give him my judgment, whither the way of indulgence or comprehension was the more desirable, that he might discern which way to go in Parliament himself, I gave him my mind, though I thought it was to little purpose. Instead of indulgence and comprehension, on the last day of June, 1663, the Bill against private meetings for religious exercises passed the House of Commons, and shortly afterwards was made a law. The calamity of the Act, beside the main matter, was that it was made so ambiguous, that no man that ever I met with could tell what was a violation of it, and what not; not knowing what was allowed by the Liturgy or practice of the Church of England in families, because the Liturgy meddleth not with families; and among the diversity of family practice, no man knoweth what to call the practice of the Church. Too much power was given to the justices of the peace to record a man an offender without a jury, and if he did it carelessly, we were without any remedy, seeing he was made a judge. According to the plain words of the Act, if a man did but preach and pray, or read some licensed book, and sing psalms, he might have more than four present, because these are allowed by the practice of the Church in the church; and the Act seemeth to grant an indulgence for place and number; which must be meant publicly, because it meddleth with no private exercise. But when it came to the trial, these pleas with the justices were vain; for if men did but pray, it was taken for granted that it was an exercise not allowed by the Church of England, and to jail they went. And now came the people's trial as well as the ministers'. While the dangers and sufferings lay on the ministers alone, the people were very courageous, and exhorted them to stand it out and preach till they went to prison. But when it came to be their own case, they were venturous till they were once surprised and imprisoned; but then their judgments were much altered, and they that censured ministers before as cowardly, because they preached not publicly, whatever followed, did now think that it was better to preach often in secret to a few, than but once or twice in public to many; and that secrecy was no sin when it tended to the furtherance of the Gospel, and to the Church's good. The rich, especially, were as cautious as the ministers. But yet their meetings were so ordinary, and so well-known, that it tended greatly to the jailers' commodity. The people were in a great strait, those especially who dwelt near any busy officer or malicious enemy. Many durst not pray in their families, if above four persons came in to dine with them. In a gentleman's house, where it was ordinary for more than four visitors, neighbours, messengers, or one sort or other, to be at dinner with them, many durst not then go to prayer, and some scarcely durst crave a blessing on their meat, or give

God thanks for it. Some thought they might venture if they withdrew into another room, and left the strangers by themselves; but others said, it is all one if they be in the same house, though out of hearing, when it cometh to the judgment of the justices. In London, where the houses are contiguous, some thought if they were in several houses, and heard one another through the wall or a window, it would avoid the law; but others said, it is all in vain whilst the justice is judge whether it was a meeting or no. Great lawyers said, if you come on a visit or business, though you be present at prayer or sermon, it is no breach of the law, because you met not *on pretence of a religious exercise:* but those that tried them said, such words are but wind, when the justices come to judge you. And here the Quakers did greatly relieve the sober people for a time; for they were so resolute, and so gloried in their constancy and sufferings, that they assembled openly at the Bull and Mouth, near Aldersgate, and were dragged away daily to the common jail; and yet desisted not, but the rest came the next day, nevertheless: so that the jail at Newgate was filled with them. Abundance of them died in prison, and yet they continued their assemblies still. They would sometimes meet only to sit still in silence, when, as they said, the Spirit did not move them; and it was a great question, whether this silence was a religious exercise not allowed by the Liturgy, etc. Once, upon such reasons as these, when they were tried at the sessions, in order to a banishment, the jury acquitted them; but were grievously threatened for it. After that, another jury did acquit them, and some of them were fined and imprisoned for it. But thus the Quakers so employed Sir K. B., and the other searchers and prosecutors, that they had the less leisure to look after the meetings of soberer men, which was much to their present ease. The divisions or rather the censures of the nonconforming people, against their ministers and one another, began now to increase; which was long foreseen, but could not be avoided. I that had incurred so much the displeasure of the prelates and all their party, for pleading for the peace of the Nonconformists, did fall under more of their displeasure than any one beside, as far as I could learn. With me they joined Dr. Bates, because we went to the public assemblies, and also to the common prayer, even to the beginning of it. Not that they thought worse of us than of others, but that they thought our example would do more harm; for I must bear them witness, that in the midst of all their censures of my judgment and actions, they never censured my affections and intentions, nor abated their charitable estimation of me in the main. Of the leading prelates, I had so much favour in their hottest indignation, that they thought what I did was only in obedience to my conscience. So that I see by experience, that he who is impartially and sincerely for truth, and peace, and piety, against all factions, shall have his honesty acknowledged by the several factions, whilst his actions, as cross to their interests, are detested; whereas, he that joineth with one of the factions shall have both his person and actions condemned by the other, though his party may applaud both."

Under this Act a series of persecutions began by which many families were sorely afflicted. No one, who was not often seen at church, was safe from the vigilance of spies, who watched the door of every house in which a prosperous Puritan lived. The vilest of mankind hired themselves to men in authority to learn the art of detection, and to practise it by means which Englishmen have ever held in abhorrence. The condition of the country was utterly wretched: dissipation and impurity were gradually infecting all classes of the people. Charles's government became unwisely embroiled with that of Holland. Under the guidance of some of the ablest statesmen in Europe, that small republic, with an inferior land-force, was powerful at sea. Its merchant-vessels visited every shore. Its harbours were crowded by the ships of all civilised nations. The warehouses of Amsterdam and of Rotterdam were filled with the silks and spices, and the richest produce of the East. The citizens were prudent, thrifty, and brave, and their marine boldly, and sometimes with success, encountered the men whom Blake had led to victory over the fleets of Spain. Charles wasted life and treasure in making war upon the people with whom, of all others, his interest should have induced him to have formed a firm and enduring alliance. He had received many kindnesses at their hands; but it was natural to him to have a feeble or imperfect recollection of them who had helped him in the days of adversity. He had the reward of them who ill requite their benefactors; for, in the course of hostilities, the Dutch not only burned his ships in the Thames, but also put London in fear. Pepys says of the disasters recurring in that unnatural and impolitic war: "Everybody nowadays reflects upon Oliver and commends him, what brave things he did, and made all the neighbour princes fear him." During these troubles, Baxter, seldom able to preach, was not inactive. Since his ejection from Kidderminster, he had written controversial works, and treatises on practical religion, and none of them without value: "The Life of Faith," "The Successive Visibility of the Church," "The Last Work of a Believer," "The Mischiefs of Self-Ignorance," his "Controversy with the Bishop of Worcester on the Causes of his leaving Kidderminster," "Saint or Brute," "Now or Never," and "The Divine Life." Wearied by the unceasing observation of spies, he took up his abode at Acton. He says: "Having lived three years and more in London, and finding it neither agree with my health nor studies, the one being brought very low and the other interrupted, and all public service being at an end, I betook myself to live in the country at Acton, that I might set myself to writing, and do what service I could for posterity, and live as much as possibly I could out of the world. Thither I went on the 14th of July, 1663, where I followed my studies privately in quietness, and went every Lord's Day to the public assembly, when there was any preaching or catechising, and spent the rest of the day with my family, and a few poor neighbours that came in; spending now and then a day in London. The next year, 1664, I had the company of divers godly, faithful friends that tabled with me in summer, with whom I solaced myself with much content. Having almost finished a large treatise called, 'A Christian Directory, or Sum of Practical Divinity,' that I might know whether it would be licensed for the press, I tried the licensers with a small treatise, the 'Character of a Sound Christian, as differenced from the weak Christian and the Hypocrite.' I offered it Mr. Grig, the Bishop of London's chaplain, who had been a Nonconformist, and professed an extraordinary respect for me; but he durst not license it Yet after, when the Plague began, I sent three single sheets to the Archbishop of Canterbury's chaplain, without any name, that they might have passed unknown; but accidentally they knew them to be mine, and they were licensed. The one was Directions for the .sick; the second was Directions for the conversion of the ungodly; and the third was Instructions for a holy life: for the use of poor families that cannot buy greater books, or will not read them. March 26th, 1665, being the Lord's Day, as I was preaching in a private house, where we received the Lord's Supper, a bullet came in at the window among us, passed by me, and narrowly missed the head of a sister-in-law of mine that was there, but hurt none of us. We could never discover whence it came. In June following, an ancient gentlewoman with her son and daughter came four miles in her coach to hear me preach in my family, as out of special respect to me. It fell out, contrary to our custom, that we let her knock long at the door, and did not open it; and so a second time, when she had gone away and come again; and the third time she came when we had ended. She was so earnest to know when she might come again to hear me, that I appointed her a time; but before she came, I had the secret intelligence from one that was nigh her, that she came with a heart exceeding full of malice, resolving if possible to do me what mischief she could by accusation; and so that danger was avoided." The number and value of his works, his great success as a preacher, the well-known purity of his life, and the report of his undeserved sufferings, caused his fame to extend to the Netherlands, to Germany, and to Switzerland. Eminent professors and divines read his books, admired his character, and desired to form friendship with him. Letters came to him repeatedly from Switzerland, and especially from Saumur, where Amyraut, the author of one of the best works extant upon the Psalms, was professor of theology. He was one of the ablest of those French Protestant divines who were the glory of the declining Reformed Church in that country; and his writings are unworthy of modern neglect. But Baxter was every day under observation so keen and unremitting, and the watch kept by the Government at that time over all correspondence upon which it was possible to lay their hands was so close and constant, that he was afraid to send any reply to the letters of the scholars and theologians who admired his power as a controversialist, and chiefly as a writer in practical divinity, in which, it has been happily said, there is a vigorous pulse that keeps the reader awake. "The vigilant eye of malice that some had upon me," says Baxter, "made me understand that though no law of the land was against literary persons' correspondences beyond the seas, nor had any divines been hindered from it, yet it was likely to have proved my ruin, if I had but been known to answer one of their letters, though the matter had been ever so much beyond exception. So that I neither answered this nor any other, save only by word of mouth to the messenger, and that but in small part. Our silencing and ejection they would quickly know by other means, and how much the judgment of the English bishops did differ from theirs about the labours and persons of such as we. About this time, I thought to meet the case with some learned and moderate ejected ministers of London, about communicating sometimes at the parish-churches in the Sacrament; for they that came to common prayer, came not yet to the Sacrament. They desired me to bring in my judgment and reasons in writing, which being debated they were all of my mind in the main, that it is lawful and a duty where greater accidents preponderate not. But they all concurred unanimously in this, that if we did communicate at all in the parish-churches, the sufferings of the Independents, and those Presbyterians that could not communicate there, would certainly be very much increased; which now were somewhat moderated by our concurrence with them. I thought the case very hard on both sides, that we who were so much censured by them for going somewhat further than they, must yet omit that which else must be our duty, merely to abate their sufferings who censure us; but I resolved to forbear with them awhile rather than any Christian should suffer by occasion of an action of mine, seeing God will have mercy and not sacrifice; and no duty is a duty at all times."

Terrible calamities were near at hand to disturb the king and his courtiers in their vicious indulgences. At intervals, since the beginning of the seventeenth century, pestilence, produced in the filthy cities of the East, had appeared in various towns of the Continent, and had again and again destroyed large numbers of persons in England. People never heard of its approach without a shudder; but no one is known to have suggested to them that freer ventilation, purer water, and a system of drainage would lessen the ravages of epidemical diseases; and would give the citizens of London some security against the danger, which might come to them from contact with the unhealthy crews of Italian and Greek ships, however few in number, unloading on the Thames. The memory of the awful Black Death of 1348 still lingered among men. They told their families by their winter-fires of that dreadful pestilence, recorded in their ancient chronicles, and terrible as the angel who in one night left destruction and silence in the camp of the Assyrian enemy of the people of God, and the history of which they heard read in churches, not without fear. They remembered that historians related that the mysterious disease came slowly from Egyptian and Syrian towns, floating as clouds float from land to land; long remaining in the filthy streets, from which in earlier times fever and leprosy were never absent, until at length it reached England; destroying, as tradition said, far and wide in city and town, in village and farm; more than fifty thousand dying in and around Norwich; desolating Bristol and other cities, and sweeping like a destructive flood throughout the country, until few were left to bury the unnumbered dead, and to till the ground. So that, even with the imperfect memory of such horrors, the very name of pestilence was dreadful to the English people. At the end of 1664, there had been rumours in London that the plague was causing many deaths in the seaports of the Continent; but no police existed to recommend and to enforce cleanliness of home and street, and there was no knowledge of what in our day is termed sanitary regulation. The streets in London and in the chief towns were narrow, the roofs overhanging them on each side; the gutters in the middle of the public way, obstructed by filth, which seethed in the warm rays of summer, and rotted under winter-rain. The houses, without proper accommodation for ventilation and health, undrained and unclean, were fitting places to attract pestilence, and to retain it when it had come. The winter and spring of 1665 had been unusually mild and dry. There was an entire lack of the rains which generally restore the verdure of the world in April and May. The sun gave forth excessive heat from a cloudless sky. Bishop Burnet says: "A great comet raised the apprehensions of those who did not enter into just speculations concerning those matters." Pepys writes: "The 7th of June was the hottest day that I ever felt in my life. This day, much against my will, I did in Drury Lane see two or three houses marked with a red cross upon the doors, and 'Lord, have mercy upon us' writ there; which was a sad sight to me, being the first of the kind that to my remembrance I ever saw." The pestilence spread rapidly. The great heat of the air, the impure water, the gutters black with accumulated filth, the narrow and close streets, the absence of all rain and of refreshing wind, and especially the dread which filled the hearts of the citizens, made London an easy and quick prey to the plague. All who were able to escape hastened from the city. The streets were thronged by the carriages and waggons bearing away families and such of their effects as could be readily removed. Panic reigned throughout the land. Each borough made regulations for preventing the entrance of strangers, and for the general security. Every inn was shut against the travellers. The gates of towns were barricaded against them, and they were driven back with blows and execrations from villages they attempted to pass through. They whose callings or other circumstances compelled them to remain in London were terrified by almanacs and "predictions," which foretold horrors to come, and by fanatics and madmen, who shrieked, as they ran through the streets at night, horrible announcements of the judgments of heaven against a city doomed to destruction. On all sides quacks proclaimed their unfailing cures, the miserable race who live upon the sufferings, the weaknesses, and the fears of mankind. Enormous quantities of "plague-water" were given to the poor by the charitable, or were sold by the vociferating impostors, who, smitten by the pestilence, sometimes died while extolling and offering their remedies. The king and his court fled before the plague to Oxford, which by wise precaution of cleansing and draining remained free from contagion. Pepys writes early in August: "The people die so that now it seems they are fain to carry the dead to be buried by daylight, the night not sufficing to do it in." All through that month, the great heat of the air continued, with a cloudless sky by day, and with a peculiarly oppressive atmosphere at night; and the citizens died by thousands. Thomas Vincent, a man worthy to be everlastingly remembered, one of the Puritan clergy, who remained in the city all through the deadly time, to pray with the dying, and to preach to the living, in his book published two years afterwards, says of that woeful August: "Now people fall as thick as the leaves in autumn, when they are shaken by a mighty wind. Now there is a dismal solitude in London streets, every day looks with the face of a Sabbath-day, observed with a greater solemnity than it used to be in the city. Now shops are shut in, people rare and very few that walk about, insomuch that the grass begins to spring up in some places, and a deep silence in every place, especially within the walls. No prancing horses, no rattling coaches, no calling in customers and offering wares, no London cries sounding in the ears. If any voice be heard, it is the groans of dying persons breathing forth their last, and the funeral knells of them that are ready to be carried to their graves. Now shutting up of visited houses (there being so many) is at an end, and most of the well are mingled among the sick, which otherwise would have got no help. Not one house in a hundred but what is affected; and in many houses half the family is swept away, in some from the eldest to the youngest; few escape but with the death of one or two. Never did so many husbands and wives die together; never did so many parents carry their children with them to the grave, and go together into the same house under earth, who had lived together in the same house upon it. Now the nights are too short to bury the dead; the whole day, though at so great length, is hardly sufficient to light the dead that fall thereon into their graves." The plague continued through September, a month which is often peculiarly fatal in seasons of pestilence. Great fires were ordered to be kept burning in every street, in hope that they might purify the polluted air. Towards the end of the month, the rain which had long been withheld fell heavily and continuously. As the days became cooler and shorter, the plague gradually decreased. One by one dwelling-houses and shops were opened, which had been shut up through the summer. Trade slowly revived, the citizens ventured to greet one another again. Travellers from the country came into the town. The plague had wrought frightful havoc; nearly one hundred thousand of the inhabitants of London had died. They who returned to the city often sought in vain for kinsmen and friends; for one inhabitant of it out of every three had perished. Baxter records some of the events of the disastrous year: "And now, after the breaches on the churches, the ejection of the ministers, and impenitency under all, wars and plague and danger of famine began at once on us. War with the Hollanders, which yet continueth; and the driest winter, spring, and summer that ever man alive knew, or our forefathers mention of late ages; so that the grounds were burnt like the highways, where the cattle should have fed. The meadow-grounds where I lived, bare but four loads of hay, which before bare forty; the plague hath seized on the famousest and most excellent city of Christendom, and at this time nearly 8,300 die of all diseases in a week. It hath scattered and consumed the inhabitants, multitudes being dead and fled. The calamities and cries of the diseased and impoverished are not to be conceived by those who are absent from them. Every man is a terror to his neighbour and himself; and God for our sins is a terror to us all. Oh, how is London, the place which God has honoured with His Gospel above all places of the earth, laid low in horrors, and wasted almost to desolation by the wrath of that God Whom England hath contemned! A God-hating generation are consumed in their sins, and the righteous also are taken away as from greater evils yet to come. Yet under all these desolations the wicked are hardened, and cast all on the fanatics; the true dividing fanatics and sectaries are not yet humbled for former miscarriages, but cast all on the prelates and imposers; and the ignorant vulgar are stupid, and know not what use to make of anything they feel. But thousands of the sober, prudent, faithful servants of the Lord are mourning in secret, and waiting for His salvation; in humility and hope they are staying themselves upon God, and expecting what He will do with them. From London the plague is spread through many counties, expecially next London, where few places, especially corporations, are free: *which makes me oft groan; and wish that London, and all the corporations of England, would review the Corporation Act, and their own Acts, and speedily repent.*

"Leaving most of my family at Acton, compassed about with the plague, at the writing of this, through the mercy of my dear God and Father in Christ, I am hitherto in safety and comfort in the house of my dearly beloved and honoured friend, Mr. Richard Hampden, of Hampden, in Buckinghamshire, the true heir of his famous father's sincerity, piety, and devotedness to God; whose person and family the Lord preserve; honour them that honour Him, and be their everlasting rest and portion! The number that died in London, besides all the rest of the land, was about a hundred thousand, reckoning the Quakers, and others that were never put in the bills of mortality. The richer sort removing out of the city the greatest blow fell on the poor. At first so few of the more religious sort were taken away that, according to the mode of too many such, they began to be puffed-up, and boast of the great difference which God did make; but quickly after they all fell alike. Yet not many pious ministers were taken away. I remember only three, who were all of my acquaintance. It is scarcely possible for people who live in a time of health and security to apprehend the dreadful nature of that pestilence. How fearful people were thirty or forty, if not a hundred miles from London, of anything they bought from mercers' or drapers' shops, or of goods that were brought to them: or of any person who came to their houses! How they would shut their doors against their friends; and if a man passed over the fields, how one would avoid another as we did in the time of the wars; how every man was a terror to another! Oh, how sinfully unthankful are we for quiet societies, habitations, and health! Not far from the place where I sojourned, at Mrs. Fleetwood's, three ministers of extraordinary worth were together in one house—

Mr. Clarkson, Mr. Samuel Cradock, and Mr. Terry, men of singular judgment, piety, and moderation. The plague came into the house where they were, and one person dying of it caused many that they knew not of earnestly to pray for their deliverance; and it pleased God that no other person died. One great benefit the plague brought to the city, it occasioned the silenced ministers more openly and laboriously to preach the Gospel, to the exceeding comfort and profit of the people; insomuch that to this day the freedom of preaching which this occasioned cannot by the daily guards of soldiers, nor by the imprisonment of multitudes, be restrained. The ministers that were silenced for nonconformity had ever since 1662 done their work privately, and to a few; not so much through their timorousness, as their loathness to offend the king, and in hope that their forbearance might procure them some liberty, and through some timorousness of the people that would hear them. When the plague grew hot, most of the conformable ministers fled, and left their flocks in the time of their extremity; whereupon divers Nonconformists, pitying the dying and distressed people, who had none to call the impenitent to repentance, or to help men to prepare for another world, or to comfort them in their terrors, when about ten thousand died in a week, resolved that no obedience to the laws of mortal men whatsoever could justify them in neglecting men's souls and bodies in such extremities. They therefore resolved to stay with the people, and to go into the forsaken pulpits though prohibited, and to preach to the poor people before they died; also to visit the sick and get what relief they could for the poor, especially those that were shut up. Those who set upon this work were Mr. Thomas Vincent, late minister in Milk Street, with some strangers that came thither after they were silenced; as Mr. Chester, Mr. Janeway, Mr. Turner, Mr. Grimes, Mr. Franklin, and some others. Often those heard them one day who were sick the next, and quickly dead. The face of death did so awaken both the preachers and the hearers, that preachers exceeded themselves in lively, fervent preaching, and the people crowded constantly to hear them. All was done with great seriousness, so that through the blessing of God abundance were converted from their carelessness, impenitence, and youthful lusts and vanities; and religion took such a hold on many hearts as could never afterwards be loosed."

Many of the physicians, distrusting their own means of cure, and afraid of the terrible pestilence, had fled before it. Pepys, who in his Diary gives that priceless gossip which brings the year vividly before the reader, says: "January 22nd. The first meeting of Gresham College since the plague. Dr. Goddard did fill us with talk, in defence of his and his fellow-physicians going out of town in the plague time; saying that their particular patients were most gone out of town, and they left at liberty, and a great deal more." "February 4th. Lord's Day: and my wife and I the first time together at church since the plague, and now only because of Mr. Mills his coming home to preach his first sermon; expecting a great excuse for his leaving the parish before anybody went, and now staying till all are come home: but he made a very poor and short excuse, and a bad sermon." Bishop Burnet alludes to the flight of some of the clergy in the time of peril: "A great many of the ministers of London were driven away by the plague, though some few stayed. Many churches being shut up, when the inhabitants were in a more than ordinary disposition to profit by good sermons, some of the Nonconformists upon that went into the empty pulpits and preached; and it was given out, with very good success; and in many other places they began to preach openly, not without reflecting on the sins of the court, and on the ill-usage that they themselves had met with. This was represented very odiously at Oxford."

CHAPTER XX.

1665—1668.

GREAT anger was expressed by the court at Oxford that the deprived Puritans had dared, during the ravages of the plague, to reflect upon the virtue of the king; and Archbishop Sheldon, and Ward, lately appointed to be Bishop of Salisbury, were determined to provide some more stringent means of repressing them. On the thirty-first day of October, 1665, before the pestilence had ceased, an Act was passed, "To restrain Nonconformists from inhabiting corporations." It was enacted that all Nonconformist ministers should take the oath, that it is not lawful on any pretence to take arms against the king, and that each of them should depose that "I will not at any time endeavour any alteration of government either in Church or State. And all such Nonconformist ministers shall not after 24th of March, 1666, unless in passing the road, come or be within five miles of any city, town, corporation, or borough that sends burgesses to Parliament; or within five miles of any city, town, or place, wherein they have since the act of oblivion been parson, vicar, or lecturer; or where they have preached in any conventicle on any pretence whatsoever, before they have taken and subscribed the aforesaid oath—upon forfeiture for every such offence of the sum of forty pounds, one third to the king, one third to the poor, and a third to him that shall sue for it; and such as shall refuse the oath aforesaid shall be incapable of teaching any public or private schools, or of taking any boarders or tablers to be taught or instructed, under pain of forty pounds, to be distributed as above. Any two justices of the peace, upon oath made before them, of any offences against this Act, are empowered to commit the offender to prison for six months." Many peers, and one or two of the wiser and more temperate bishops, opposed this Act, well knowing how injurious it must ultimately prove to the Church, which unhappily at that time had furious and indiscreet defenders; but Clarendon urged on Archbishop Sheldon and others to carry the Bill, and it became law. Bishop Burnet states that Sheldon and Ward were the bishops that argued most for the Act, which came to be called the Five Mile Act. "All that were secret favourers of popery promoted it; their constant maxim being, to bring all the sectaries into so desperate a state, that they should be at mercy, and forced to desire a toleration on such terms as the king should think fit to grant it on."

To save themselves from utter ruin, some of the Puritan clergy, among them John Howe and Dr. Bates, took the oath, but many others could not, and either they went at once to prison, or they wandered forth without a dwelling, or they heard at home with anguish of heart the cries of hungering children. Many of them lived upon charity, "some with difficulty getting, and others (educated to modesty) with greater difficulty begging their bread." Of these exiled clergymen, Bishop Burnet says: "Many were put to hard shifts to live, being so far separated from the chief places from which they drew their chief subsistence. Yet as all this severity in a time of war, and of such a public calamity, drew very hard censures on the promoters of it, so it raised the compassions of their party so much, that I have been told they were supplied more plentifully at that time than ever." The historian Hallam, with that philosophical discrimination which distinguishes him, says of this Act: "The Church of England had doubtless her provocations; but she made the retaliation more than commensurate to the injury. No severity comparable to this cold-blooded persecution had been inflicted by the late powers, even in the ferment and fury of a civil war." Clarendon, Sheldon, and Ward, Bishop of Salisbury, promoted the Act; and, when it had passed, Sheldon as Archbishop determined to apply it completely. On the seventh day of July, 1665, when the Puritan clergy were laboriously ministering to the sick and dying in London, among the horrors of the plague, Sheldon directed the bishops in the province of Canterbury to make a return to him of the names of all ejected clergymen, with a statement of their places of abode, and of their means of livelihood. It is said that the returns are still to be seen in the library at Lambeth Palace. A churchman may hope that some succeeding archbishop, kinder in heart and wiser in his day, dropped a penitential tear upon these records of persecution, while praying the true Head of the Anglican Church both to pardon the intemperate zeal of them who were irreligious for religion, and to avert its consequent retribution. It is probable that some of the ejected clergymen, half maddened by oppression, were fanatical plotters against the Government, and that laws were necessary to coerce them; but Lord Clarendon and his episcopal allies treated all of them indiscriminately, as persons whom it was necessary not only to restrain, but to punish. Even the most moderate of them were more rigorously treated than were the men who ridiculed the Prayer-Book, and were insolent to the bishops: no exception was made, even with respect to Baxter, who was himself an English clergyman, frequent in his attendance at the Sacrament, and sometimes preaching in the pulpits of the parish-churches. But no circumstances mitigated the severity which was exercised against all the Puritan clergy; they must either relinquish their few and inconsiderable objections, or be compelled to submission. Many of them, sorely pressed, agreed together that they could not take the oath; and that it were better for them to abandon home, and friends, and means of subsistence, than to do what conscience forbade. They felt the inward voice could not deceive them, and must not be disregarded. Some of them who possessed property, went to live in small towns and villages, where, if they were destitute of many of the comforts and consolations of friendship, they might hope to be without molestation; but oftentimes, when they fled before the persecutor, their adherents, in dread of the vengeance of the government, refused to receive them into their houses.

The year 1666, John Dryden's *annus mirabilis*, brought to England no alleviation of trouble and disaster. The war with Holland gave no great victory to the English fleet, sufficient to ensure peace; for Opdam, Van Tromp, and Ruyter were no unworthy antagonists of the royal admirals. John Evelyn mourns over what he saw at Sheerness: "The sad spectacle, more than half the gallant bulwark of the kingdom miserably shattered; hardly a vessel entire, but appearing so many wrecks and hulls, so cruelly had the Dutch mauled us; and none knew for what reason we first engaged in this ungrateful war." But other calamities were approaching: the city which had been smitten by the plague was now to be given to the flames. Men disagreed as to the cause of so terrible a visitation. Some attributed it to the Dutch, in retaliation for fishing villages which had been burned by English squadrons; others accused the Jesuits as the authors of the conflagration. One unhappy lunatic, a Huguenot from Rouen, whose mind was probably disordered by the sight of a city in flames, asserted that he had himself kindled the fire, and he was speedily executed upon his own confession. The summer of 1666 was very hot, and with less rain than for many years before. The Thames was low in its bed, and there was scarcely water enough to supply the daily wants of the citizens. The houses in London to a large extent were built of timber filled up with plaster, and the overhanging roofs were mostly thatched. Warehouses for oil, spirits, turpentine, and other inflammable materials, were intermingled with the dwellings, excepting in Thames Street, where were the larger store-rooms of the merchants who traded with Northern Germany,

France, and Holland. Pepys and Evelyn in their Diaries, and Baxter in his Autobiography, have left trustworthy accounts of one of the most terrible calamities which has ever visited the metropolis of a civilised nation. On Sunday, the second day of September, when the heat was great and the sky cloudless, and with a violent east wind blowing upon the city, a fire broke out in a small shop in a lane near the place upon which the Monument was afterwards built. Pepys was awakened by the cries of citizens running to give help; and later in the morning, as the fire was quickly driven to other streets, he rowed up the river in order that he might note and report upon the extent of the conflagration. He saw the houses, dried by the unusually great heat of a long summer, kindled with frightful rapidity. He hastened to Whitehall to inform the king. For once, Charles was thoroughly frightened. He directed Pepys to order the Lord Mayor to have intervening houses pulled down, to stay the progress of the fire. One record he makes in his Diary attests the love of music among the citizens at that time, and which no civil strife nor tyrannical government had lessened. He says: "The river was full of lighters and boats taking in goods; and good goods swimming about in the water; and I observed that hardly one lighter or boat in three that had the goods of a house in, but there was a pair of virginals in it." He saw—as in our day men saw in the burning of Chicago—large masses of ignited roofs driven by the wind, and falling upon other roofs, which immediately they kindled. As night drew on, Pepys saw the fire sweep with a roar like that of a great tempest from street to street, lighting up the spires of churches, "in a most horrid, malicious, bloody flame, not like the fire-flame of an ordinary fire, and making an arch more than a mile long." The king rode with his brother through the streets, in fear and anxiety; doing all he could, and commanding what he thought it expedient to be done; directing large supplies of provisions to be given to the homeless and hungering people, and sending all that could be obtained from his palace to feed the mothers and their children. Pepys adds characteristically: "None of the nobility came out of the country at all to help the king, or comfort him, or prevent commotions at this fire. Some of the courtiers said, 'Now the rebellious city is ruined, the king is absolute, and was never king indeed till now.'" Evelyn writes: "2nd Sept. This fatal night about ten, began that deplorable fire near Fish Street in London. 3rd. I had public prayers at home. The fire continuing, after dinner I took coach with my wife and son and went to the Bankside in Southwark, where we beheld the dismal spectacle, the whole city in dreadful flames near the water side; all the houses from the Bridge, all Thames Street, and upwards towards Cheapside, down to the Three Cranes, were now consumed. The fire having continued all this night (if I may call that night which was as light as day for ten miles round about, after a dreadful manner), when conspiring with a fierce eastern wind in a very dry season; I went on foot to the same place, and saw the whole south part of the city burning from Cheapside to the Thames, and all along Cornhill (for it likewise kindled back against the wind as well as forward), Tower Street, Fenchurch Street, Gracious Street, and so along to Bainard's Castle, and was now laying hold of St. Paul's Church, to which the scaffolds contributed exceedingly. The conflagration was so universal, and the people so astonished, that from the beginning, I know not by what despondency or fate, they hardly stirred to quench it, so that there was nothing heard or seen but crying out and lamentations, running about like distracted creatures, without at all attempting to save even their goods; such a strange consternation there was upon them, so as it burned both in breadth and length, the churches, public halls, exchange, hospitals, monuments, and ornaments, leaping after a prodigious manner from house to house and street to street, at great distances one from the other; for the heat with a long set of fair and warm weather had even ignited the air and prepared the materials to conceive the fire, which devoured after an incredible manner houses, furniture, and everything. Here we saw the Thames covered with goods floating, all the barges and boats laden with what some had time and courage to save, as, on the other, the carts, etc., carrying out to the fields, which for many miles were strewed with movables of all sorts, and tents erecting to shelter both people and what goods they could get away. Oh the miserable and calamitous spectacle! All the sky was of a fiery aspect, like the top of a burning oven, and the light seen above forty miles round about for many nights. God grant mine eyes may never behold the like, who now saw above ten thousand houses all in one flame; the noise and cracking and thunder of the impetuous flames, the shrieking of women and children, the hurry of people, the fall of towers, houses, and churches was like an hideous storm, and the air about all so hot and inflamed that at the last one was not able to approach it, so that they were forced to stand still and let the flames burn on, which they did for near two miles in length, and one in breadth. The clouds also of smoke were dismal, and reached, upon computation, near fifty-six miles in length. Thus I left it this afternoon burning, in resemblance of Sodom or the Last Day. It forcibly called to my mind that passage—'non enim hic habemus stabilem civitatem;' the ruins resembling the picture of Troy. London was, but is no more!

"Sept. 4th. The burning still rages, and it was now gotten as far as the Inner Temple; all Fleet Street, the Old Bailey, Ludgate Hill, Warwick Lane, Newgate, Paul's Chain, Watling Street now flaming, and most of it reduced to ashes; the stones of Paul's flew like grenados, the melting lead running down the streets in a stream, and the very pavements glowing with fiery redness, so as no horse nor man was able to tread on them, and the demolition had stopped all the passages, so that no help could be applied. The eastern wind still more impetuously driving the flames forward. Nothing but the almighty power of God was able to stop them, for vain was the help of man. It crossed towards Whitehall; but, oh! the confusion there was then at that court!—the blowing up of houses made a wider gap than any that had yet been made by the ordinary method of pulling them down with engines; this some stout seamen proposed early enough to have saved nearly the whole city, but this some tenacious and avaricious men, aldermen, etc., would not permit, because their houses must have been of the first. It now pleased God by abating the wind, and by the industry of the people, when almost all was lost, infusing a new spirit into them, that the fury of it began sensibly to abate about noon, so as it came no further than the Temple westward, nor than the entrance of Smithfield north. The coal and wood wharves, and magazines of oil, rosin, etc., did infinite mischief. The poor inhabitants were dispersed about St. George's Fields, and Moorfields, as far as Highgate, and several miles in circle, some under tents, some under miserable huts and hovels, many without a rag or any necessary utensils, bed or board, who from delicateness, riches, and easy accommodations in stately and well-furnished houses were now reduced to extremest misery and poverty. I was infinitely concerned to find that goodly church, St. Paul's, now a sad ruin, and that beautiful portico (for structure comparable to any in Europe, as not long before repaired by the late king) now rent in pieces, flakes of vast stone split asunder, and nothing remaining entire but the inscription in the architrave, showing by whom it was built, which had not one letter of it defaced. It was astonishing to see what immense stones the heat had in a manner calcined, so that all the ornaments, columns, friezes, capitals, and projectures of massy Portland stone flew off, even to the very roof, where a sheet of lead covering a great space was totally melted. It is also observable that the lead over the altar at the east end was untouched, and among the divers monuments, the body of one bishop remained entire. Thus lay in ashes that most venerable church, one of the most ancient pieces of early piety in the Christian world, besides near a hundred more. I then went towards Islington and Highgate, where one might have seen some two hundred thousand people of all ranks and degrees dispersed and lying along by their heaps of what they could save from the fire, deploring their loss, and though ready to perish for hunger and destitution, yet not asking one penny for relief; which to me appeared a stranger sight than any I had yet beheld."

The account of the great fire which Baxter gives supplies another glimpse of one of the most woeful disasters which Europe had known, since that sacking of Rome by the barbarians, and which occasioned Augustine's great work, *De Civitate Dei;* ever strengthening and refreshing to them who delight, above all other sources, to go to the uncorrupted fountains of Truth. Baxter writes: "On the second of September, 1666, after midnight, London was set on fire; next day the Exchange was burnt, and in three days almost the whole city within the walls, and much without them. The season had been exceeding dry before, and the wind in the east when the fire began. The people, having none to conduct them aright, could do nothing to resist it, but stand and see their houses burn without remedy, the engines being presently out of order, and useless. The streets were crowded with people and carts, to carry away what goods they could get out; they that were most active, and befriended by their wealth, got carts and saved much, and the rest lost almost all. The loss in houses and goods is scarcely to be valued, and among the rest the loss of books was an exceeding great detriment to the interests of piety and learning. Mostly all the booksellers in St. Paul's Churchyard brought their books into vaults under St. Paul's Church, where it was thought almost impossible that fire should come. But the church itself taking fire, the exceeding weight of the stones falling down did break into the vault, and let in the fire, and they could not come near to save the books. The library of Sion College was burned, and most of the libraries of ministers conformable and unconformable in the city; with the libraries of many nonconformists of the country, which had lately been brought up to the city. I saw the half-burnt leaves of books, near my dwelling at Acton, six miles from London; but others found them near Windsor, twenty miles distant. At last the seamen taught them to blow up some of the houses with gunpowder, which stopped the fire, though in some places it stopped as wonderfully as it had proceeded, without any known cause. It stopped at Holborn Bridge, and near St. Dunstan's Church in Fleet Street; at St. Sepulchre's Church, when the church was burnt; at Christ Church, when it was burnt; and near Aldersgate and Cripplegate, and other places at the city wall. In Austin Friars, the Dutch Church stopped it, and escaped; in Bishopsgate Street, and Leadenhall Street, and Fenchurch Street, in the midst of the streets it stopped short of the Tower: and all beyond the river escaped. Thus was the best and one of the fairest cities of the world turned into ashes and ruins in three days' space, with many scores of churches, and the wealth and necessaries of the inhabitants. It was a sight which might have given any man a lively sense of the vanity of this world, and of all its wealth and glory, and of the future conflagration, to see the flames mount towards heaven, and proceed so furiously without restraint; to see the streets filled with people so astonished that many had scarcely sense left them to lament their own calamity; to see the fields filled with heaps of goods, costly furniture, and household stuff, while sumptuous buildings, warehouses, and furnished shops and libraries, etc., were all on flames, and none durst come near to secure anything; to see the king and nobles ride about the streets, beholding all these desolations, and none could afford the least relief; to see the air, as far as could be beheld, so filled with the smoke, that the sun shined through it with a colour like blood; yea, when even it was setting in the west, it so appeared to them that dwelt on the west side of the city. But the dolefullest sight of all was afterwards to see what a ruinous, confused place the city was, by chimneys and steeples only standing in the midst of cellars and heaps of rubbish; so that it was hard to know where the streets had been; and dangerous for a long time to pass through the ruins, because of vaults and fire in them. No man that seeth not such a thing can have a right apprehension of the dreadfulness of it."

Time brings its revenges, and the ejected Puritans may have been convinced of the fact, when this eventful year saw the disgrace and fall of their persecutor, Lord Clarendon. The victories of Ruyter and De Witt over the English fleet; their burning Sheerness; their capture of some of the finest vessels in the Royal Navy; the consternation of the people, unaccustomed to hear the roar of the conqueror's cannon on their shores, raised a storm against the Chancellor which he could not brave. The Dutch fleet closely blockaded the river, and London could receive no supplies from the sea—"a dreadful spectacle," says Evelyn, "as no Englishman ever saw, and a dishonour never to be wiped off." Hated by the dissolute women of the court, who ruled the king, Clarendon had not only counselled Charles to virtuous living, but he had resisted his attempt to make himself an absolute monarch. The king, who had often fretted at the counsel of Clarendon, that he should abandon immoralities, after the instinct of his race neither forgave nor forgot the admonition. The disasters to the English fleet, and the rumour that Clarendon had enriched himself by appropriating moneys which belonged to the Treasury, gave the king an excuse which he deemed sufficient to dismiss a man from his service, who had been his faithful friend and counsellor in days both of adversity and of prosperity. John Evelyn, who visited the fallen earl, says: "I found him in his bedchamber, very sad; he had enemies at court, especially the buffoons and ladies of pleasure, because he thwarted some of them, and stood in their way." An Act was passed to banish him for life; and at the end of the year, he retired to Rouen, where he spent his last years, in reading Livy,

Tacitus, and all that remained to the world of Cicero, and in writing his "History of the Rebellion." To some extent, he had resisted the despotism of Charles II.; and his opposition was afterwards rewarded by the passing of the Habeas Corpus Act, which prevented the king from imprisoning any subject without trial; and especially by the termination of the arbitrary Licensing Act, which removed some restriction upon the freedom of the press in England, and without personal danger gave a certain limit to the temperate discussion of public affairs.

Baxter says of the disgrace of Lord Clarendon: "The Parliament at last laid all upon the Lord Chancellor Hyde; and the king was content it should be so. Whereupon many speeches were made against him, and an impeachment or charge brought in against him, and vehemently urged. Among other things it was alleged that he counselled the king to rule by an army, which many thought, bad as he was, he was the chief means of hindering. To be short, when they had first sought his life, at last it was concluded that his banishment should satisfy for all; and so he was, by an Act of Parliament, banished for life. The sale of Dunkirk to the French, and a great comely house which he had newly built, increased the displeasure that was against him; but there were greater causes which I must not name. It was a notable providence that this man who had been the great instrument of state, and had dealt so cruelly with the Nonconformists, should thus by his own friends be cast out and banished, while those he had persecuted were the most moderate in his cause, and many of them for him. It was a great ease that befell good people throughout the land by his dejection. For his way had been to decoy men into conspiracies, or to pretend plots, upon the rumour of which the innocent people of many countries were laid in prison; so that no man knew when he was safe. Since then the laws have been made more and more severe, yet a man knoweth a little better what to expect, when it is by a law he is to be tried. It is also notable that he, who did so much to make the Oxford law for banishing ministers from corporations who took not that oath, doth in his letter from France since his banishment say that he never was in favour since the Parliament sat at Oxford."

After the fall of Clarendon, the Government for a time became less severe to the ejected clergy. The policy of the king had been to use so much severity towards them, that they might petition for a toleration, which should be extended equally to his Roman Catholic subjects; and in his speech at the opening of Parliament, Charles said: "I hold myself obliged to recommend to you that you should seriously think of some course to beget a better union and composure in the minds of my Protestant subjects, in matters of religion, whereby they may be induced not only to submit quietly to the Government, but also cheerfully give their assistance to the support of it." Bishop Burnet remarks, that "the king was highly offended at the behaviour of most of the bishops. Archbishop Sheldon and Morley lost his favour. When complaint was made to him of some disorders and conventicles, the king said the clergy were chiefly to blame, for if they had lived well, and gone about their parishes, and taken pains to convince the Nonconformists, the nation might have been well settled; but they thought of nothing but to get good benefices, and keep a good table. If the clergy had done their parts, it had been easy to run down the Nonconformists; but they will do nothing, and will have me do everything; and most of them do worse than if they did nothing. I have a very honest chaplain, to whom I have given a living in Suffolk; but he is a very great blockhead, and yet has brought all his parish to church. I cannot imagine what he could say to them, for he is a very silly fellow; but he has been about from house to house, and I suppose his nonsense has suited their nonsense, and in reward of his diligence I have given him a bishopric in Ireland." "At this time," the Bishop adds, "the court fell into much extravagance in masquerading: both king and queen and all the court went about masked, and came into houses unknown, and danced there, with a great deal of wild frolic. They were carried about in hackney-chairs. Once the queen's chairmen, not knowing who she was, went from her: so she was alone, and was much disturbed, and came to Whitehall in a hackney-coach; some say it was in a cart. The Duke of Buckingham proposed to the king, that he would give him leave to steal her away, and send her to a plantation, where she could be well and carefully looked to, but never heard of any more: so it should be given out she had deserted: and upon that it would fall in with some principles to carry an Act for a divorce. The king himself rejected this with horror. He said it was a wicked thing to make a poor lady miserable, only because she was his wife." It was one of the remarkable coincidences, which are sometimes found in the great story of the world, that a man so utterly profligate as the king was, should have been also the director of the religious observances of his people; and that he, who was himself perfectly destitute of any good guiding principles, should have moved actively in restraining the zeal of his bishops; and while professing to pity the Nonconformists, should have purposed that their sufferings should be his argument for giving a toleration, which should be extended to all the adherents of the Latin Church in his dominions.

Baxter explains the method adopted: "When the Duke of Buckingham came first into high favour, he was looked on as the chief minister of State, instead of the Chancellor, and showed himself openly for toleration, or liberty for all parties, on matters of God's worship. Others also then seemed to look that way, thinking the king was for it. Whereupon those who were most against it grew into seeming discontent. The Bishop of Winchester, Morley, was put out of his place, as Dean of the Chapel Royal, and Bishop Crofts of Hereford was put into it. At the same time the ministers of London, who had ventured to keep open meetings in their houses, and preached to great numbers contrary to the law, were by the king's favour connived at; so that the people went openly to hear them without fear. Some imputed this to the king's own inclination to liberty of conscience; some to the Duke of Buckingham's prevalency; and some to the Papists' influence, who were for liberty of conscience for their own interest. But others thought that the Papists were really against liberty of conscience, and did rather desire that the utmost severities might ruin the Puritans, and cause discontents and divisions among ourselves, till we had broken one another all into pieces, and turned all into such confusion as might advantage them to play a more successful game than ever toleration was likely to be. Whatever was the secret cause, it is evident that the great visible cause was the burning of London, and the want of churches for the people to meet: it being, at the first, a thing too gross, to forbid an undone people all public worship with too great rigour; and if they had been so forbidden, poverty had left so little to lose as would have made them desperately go on. Therefore some thought all this was to make necessity seem a favour."

The negotiations, however, for securing toleration had no result; but Baxter affirms that fourteen hundred at least of the Puritan ministers would have accepted the terms proposed, if they had been certain of them. While recording the failure of the attempted agreement, Baxter relates an incident which casts no little light upon the temper and habits of the time. "In April, 1668, Dr. Creighton, Dean of Wells, the most famous, loquacious, ready-tongued preacher of the Court, who was used to preach Calvin to hell and the Calvinists to the gallows, and by his scornful revilings and jests to set the Court on a laughter, was suddenly in the pulpit, without any sickness, surprised with astonishment, worse than Dr. South, the Oxford orator, had been before him. When he had repeated a sentence over and over, he was so confounded that he could go no further at all, and was fain to all men's wonder to come down. His case was more wonderful than almost any other man's, being not only a fluent extempore speaker, but one that was never known to want words, especially to express his satirical or bloody thoughts."

The proceedings against the Puritans, under the Conventicle Act, were continued with vigour. Many of the ejected clergy were imprisoned for teaching the sons of gentlemen, and for receiving pupils into their houses. The Bishop of Hereford sent several of them to gaol for disobeying the Five Mile Act, where they had long-continued punishment. They who had suffered much under Cromwell's persecutions, when the Anglican clergy were forbidden to be tutors in families, or to occupy any public position in which they might teach other than republican principles, retaliated upon the offending Puritans. The kingdom was full of faction and discontent. The Plague and the Great Fire had caused much misery. The trade of the country, injured by these calamities, and by the strict blockade of the Thames by the Dutch fleet, was almost at an end. The negotiations attempted with the Nonconformists alarmed the bishops, who were resolved upon applying the recent Acts with more severity. In June, Archbishop Sheldon requested the prelates of his province to give him an exact account of the conventicles in their dioceses, and to report upon the probability of their speedy and complete suppression by the magistrates; but he found that while individuals were imprisoned, and subjected to much suffering, the mass of the Nonconformists still remained disaffected to the Church, and they were the more firmly united with each other as their persecution became more rigorous.

CHAPTER XXI.

1668—1670.

IN his withdrawment from London to Acton, Baxter had hoped he should be free from the intrusion of spies. He says: "While I lived at Acton, as long as the Act against conventicles was in force, though I preached to my family, few of the town came to hear me; partly because they thought it would endanger me, and partly from fear of suffering themselves, but especially because they were an ignorant poor people, and had no appetite for such things. When the Act expired, they came so many that I wanted room; and when once they had come and heard, they afterwards came constantly, insomuch that in a little time there was a great number of them, who seemed very seriously affected with the things they heard, and almost all the town and parish, besides abundance from Brentford and the neighbouring parishes came; and I knew not of three in the parish that were adversaries to us or our endeavours, or wished us ill." In that place he formed a friendship with Judge Hale, one of the ablest of them who have presided over English courts of justice, and who delighted to argue with the astute clergyman, his neighbour, on the more difficult questions of religion and philosophy. The most enduring memorial of that eminent judge is that which was written by the hand of Baxter. In 1670, the Conventicle Act was renewed, and in effect it set aside trial by jury, inasmuch as the power of a single magistrate was made sufficient for all the purposes of the law. It provided that the husband should be punished if his wife went to a conventicle; and the magistrate was empowered to break open the doors of any house of which there might be suspicion that religious assemblies were being held in it. Any person preaching in such conventicle was held liable to a fine of twenty pounds for the first, and of forty pounds for every subsequent offence; and if the offender took to flight, his goods and chattels were to be seized. This renewed Act was rigidly applied in all the dioceses. Ward, Bishop of Salisbury, has the unenviable fame of having been one of the chief instigators of it. Many families were ruined by the arrest and imprisonment of them upon whom their means of subsistence depended. In the city of London the law was so strictly enforced, that some of the merchants made arrangements to remove, if necessary, into Holland. Informers were diligent in their infamous calling, gaining large sums from the preachers and from their congregations. Houses were broken open, when suspected of being places for preaching, furniture carried away, the tradesman's coffers robbed; and men spoke of the peculiar hardships of some of the sick, whose "beds were taken from under them, and themselves laid on the floor." Some of the bishops, and many of the more generous clergy, deplored these severities, as surpassing even those which had been borne under the tyranny of Cromwell; but these gentler spirits had no power to quench the unwise ardour of others. Parker, Archbishop Sheldon's chaplain, and whose zeal obtained for him the mitre of Oxford, declared "that tender consciences, instead of being complied with, must be restrained with more peremptory and unyielding rigour than naked and unsanctified villainy." In May, 1670, Archbishop Sheldon directed ecclesiastical judges and officers "to take notice of all Nonconformists, holders, frequenters, and maintainers of conventicles, especially of the preachers or teachers in them; ever keeping a more watchful eye over the cities and greater towns, from whence the mischief is for the most part derived unto the lesser villages and hamlets. And wheresoever they find such offenders, they do address themselves to the civil magistrates, imploring their help and assistance for preventing and suppressing the same. And what the success may be, we must leave to God Almighty. I have this confidence, under God, that if we do our parts seriously by God's help, and the assistance of the civil power, we shall in a few months see a great alteration,—the seduced people returning from their seditious teachers to the unity of the Church, and uniformity of God's worship." Every incumbent received a copy of this letter. Bishop Ward hurried from house to house to arrest offenders. On one occasion, Bishop Gunning, unable to enter a house where he thought a sermon was being preached, sent for a constable to break down the door with a sledge-hammer. The fines and imprisonments were many and grievous. The court favoured the persecution, in hope that so much suffering might make toleration indispensable, and in the benefit of which Roman Catholics should have part. Many of the persons fined and imprisoned were tradesmen, mechanics, and farmers. In the hot days of August, when in country-places reapers were busy in harvest-fields, and the citizens of London were glad when evening fell to cool their heated, dusty streets, the Quaker William Penn and his companions, finding their meeting-house in Gracechurch Street closed, and with soldiers before the door, preached to the crowd outside. He was at once arrested and tried. The jury acquitted him, in spite of the censures and threats of the judge; for the citizens sympathized with him in his patience, and admired his calm endurance under persecution and suffering. In the meantime, the dissipations of the king and his companions increased. Days and nights in succession were spent in shameful excesses. Vice reigned at Whitehall, and John Evelyn was grieved, as he wrote, to see "the jolly blades racing, dancing, feasting, and revelling, more resembling a luxurious and abandoned rout than a Christian court."

In his home at Acton, Baxter was not permitted to be in peace. He fretted at the enforced silence which the late

Acts compelled, and he could not refrain from preaching when he had opportunity. Writing of this year, he says: "The parson of this parish was Dr. Ryves, Dean of Windsor and of Wolverhampton, parson of Hasely and of Acton, chaplain in ordinary to the king, etc. His curate was a weak young man, who spent most of his time in the ale-houses, and read a few dry sentences to the people once a day. Yet, because he preached true doctrine, and I had no better to hear, I constantly heard him when he preached, and went to the beginning of the common-prayer. As my house faced the church-door, and was within hearing of it, those that heard me before, went with me to the church; scarcely three that I know of in the parish refusing. When I preached, after the public exercise, they went out of the church into my house. It pleased the doctor and parson that I came to church, and brought others with me, but he was not able to bear the sight of people crowding into my house, though they heard him also; so that, though he spake me fair, and we lived in seeming love and peace while he was there, yet he could not long endure it. When I had brought the people to church to hear him, he would fall upon them with groundless reproaches; as if he had done it purposely to drive them away, and yet he thought that my preaching to them, because it was in a house, did all the mischief; though he never accused me of anything that I spake, for I preached nothing but Christianity and submission to our superiors, faith, repentance, hope, love, humility, self-denial, meekness, patience, and obedience. He was the more offended, because I came not to the Sacrament with him; though I communicated in the other parish churches in London and elsewhere. I was loth to offend him by giving him the reason; which was, that he was commonly reputed a swearer, a curser, a railer, etc." Proceedings were to be taken against Baxter under the Conventicle Act. He was arrested at the instigation of Dr. Ryves, the rector of Acton, now to be remembered rather as a greedy pluralist than as the author of "Mercurius Rusticus," long since unheeded of mankind. He was the more embittered against Baxter, because he had himself suffered with many other clergymen under the persecutions and oppressions of the government of Cromwell. He urged the magistrates to commit Baxter to gaol. The people of the village were indignant, and his friend, Judge Hale, was grieved that their virtuous and revered neighbour should by the malice of their rector be incarcerated with cutpurses and felons. His faithful wife insisted on sharing his bondage with him. He vividly describes his sufferings: "They would have given me leave to stay till Monday before I went to gaol, if I would have promised them not to preach, the next Lord's Day, which I refused. This was made a heinous crime against me at the court, and it was also said that it could not be out of conscience that I preached, else why did not my conscience put me on it so long before? Whereas I had ever preached to my own family, and never once invited any one to hear me, or forbade any. The whole town of Acton was greatly exasperated against the Dean, when I was going to prison; so much so, that ever after they abhorred him as a selfish persecutor. Nor could he have devised more to hinder the success of his seldom preaching there; but it was his own choice, 'Let them hate me, so they fear me.' Thus I finally left that place, being grieved most that Satan had prevailed to stop the poor people in such hopeful beginnings of a common reformation, and that I was to be deprived of the exceeding grateful neighbourhood of the Lord Chief Baron Hale, who could scarce refrain tears when he heard of the first warrant for my appearance. As I went to prison, I called on Sergeant Fountain, my special friend, to take his advice; for I would not be so injurious to Judge Hale. He perused my mittimus, and in short advised me to seek for a *habeas corpus*, but not in the usual court (the King's Bench), for reasons known to all that knew the judges; nor yet in the Exchequer, lest his kindness to me should be an injury to Judge Hale, and so to the kingdom; but at the Common Pleas, which he said might grant it, though it is not usual. My greatest doubt was, whether the king would not take it ill, that I rather sought to the law than to him. My imprisonment was at present no great suffering to me, for I had an honest jailer, who showed me all the kindness he could. I had a large room, and the liberty of walking in a fair garden. My wife was never so cheerful a companion to me as in prison, and was very much against my seeking to be released. She had brought so many necessaries, that we kept house as contentedly and as comfortably as at home, though in a narrower room, and had the sight of more of my friends in a day, than I had at home in half a year. I knew also if I got out against their will, my sufferings would be never the nearer to an end. But yet, on the other side, it was the extreme heat of summer, when London was wont to have epidemical diseases. The hope of my dying in prison, I have reason to think, was one great inducement to some of the instruments to move to what they did. My chamber being over the gate, which was knocked and opened with noise of prisoners, just under me, almost every night, I had little hope of sleeping but by day, which would have been likely to have quickly broken my strength, which was so little that I did but live. The number of visitors daily put me out of hope of studying, or of doing anything but entertain them. I had neither leave at any time to go out of doors, much less to church on the Lord's Days, nor on that day to have any come to me, or to preach to any but my family. Upon all these considerations, the advice of some was I should petition the king. To this I was averse, and my counsellor Sergeant Fountain advised me not to seek it, nor yet to refuse their favour if they offered at it, but to be wholly passive as to the court, and to seek my freedom by law, because of my great weakness, and the probability of future peril to my life: and this counsel I followed. My *habeas corpus* being demanded at the Common Pleas was granted, and a day appointed for my appearance. When I came, the judges, I believe, having not before studied the Oxford Act, when Judge Wild had first said, 'I hope you will not trouble this court with such causes,' asked whether the king's counsel had been acquainted with the case, and seen the order of the court; which being denied, I was remanded back to prison, and a new day set. They suffered me not to stand at the bar, but called me up to the table, which was an unusual respect; and they sent me not to the Fleet, as is usual, but to the same prison, which was a greater favour. Being discharged from my imprisonment, my sufferings began, for I had there better health than I had for a long time before or after. I had now more exasperated the authors of mine imprisonment. I was not at all acquitted as to the main cause. They might amend their mittimus, and lay me up again. I knew no way how to bring my main cause, whether they had power to put the Oxford oath on me to a legal trial, and my counsellors advised me not to do it, much less to question the judges for false imprisonment, lest I were borne down by power. I had now a house of great rent on my hands, which I must not come to, and had no other house to dwell in. I knew not what to do with all my goods and family. I must go out of Middlesex; I must not come within five miles of a city or corporation, etc. Where to find such a place, and therein a house, and how to remove my goods thither, and what to do with my house till my time expired, were more trouble than my quiet prison by far, and the consequents yet worse. Gratitude commandeth me to tell the world who were my benefactors in my imprisonment, and calumny as much obligeth me, because it is said amongst some that I am enriched by it. Sergeant Fountain's general counsel ruled me. Mr. Wallop and Mr. Offley lent me their counsel, and would take nothing. Of four sergeants that pleaded my cause, two of them, Sergeant Windham, afterwards Baron of the Exchequer, and Sergeant Sise, would take nothing. Sir John Bernard, a person I never saw but once, sent me no less than twenty pieces; the Countess of Exeter, ten pounds; and Alderman Bard five. I received no more, but I confess more was offered me, which I refused;

and more would have been given, but that they knew I needed it not: and this much defrayed my law and prison charges. When the same justices saw that I was thus discharged, they were not satisfied to have driven me from Acton, but they made a new mittimus by counsel, as for the same supposed fault, naming the fourth of June as the day on which I preached; and yet not naming any witness, though the Act against conventicles was expired long before. This mittimus they put in an officer's hand in London to bring me, not to Clerkenwell, but among the thieves and murderers to the common gaol at Newgate; which was, since the fire which burnt down all the better rooms, the most noisome place that I have heard of, of any prison in the land, except the Tower dungeon. The next habitation which God's providence chose for me was at Totteridge, near Barnet, where for a year I was fain with part of my family, separated from the rest, to take a few mean rooms, which were so extremely smoky, and the place withal so cold, that I spent the winter in great pain, one quarter of a year by a sore sciatica, and seldom free from much anguish."

During these weary years of ejectment, observation, and imprisonment, Baxter wrote some of his most valuable works. "The Reasons of the Christian Religion" is one of the most remarkable of these books, and not the less so from its containing two dedications, one addressed to the "Christian reader," and the other to the "hypocrite reader." The book appeared as a thick quarto volume, in 1667, and Baxter states that in writing it he desired to excite Christians to attempt the conversion of the heathen. It grieved him that the Church possessed so small a portion of the world, that "five parts of it were still heathens and Mahometans, and that Christian princes and preachers did no more for their recovery." It has been already stated in this history that, in 1663, united with his friend Ashurst, and with the illustrious Robert Boyle, Baxter obtained a charter of incorporation for the Society for the Propagation of the Gospel in New England, and the parts adjacent in America. This was a revival of the Society which had been first formed in 1646, by authority of an Act of Parliament. Baxter's name should ever be associated with its renewal. The well-known Society of our own day is of later date. It is said by Sir James Stephen to be "founded on the model of that for the establishment of which Baxter laboured." The second part of this book is of considerable importance to attainment in doctrinal theology, from the fact that it contains a clear analysis of the evidences of revealed Christianity; and on the argument especially of its adaptation to our mental and moral constitution, and to the necessities of our nature. This is followed by a remarkable discussion of the testimony which Revelation gives to the authority of the Redeemer, and it anticipated some of the abler works of our century, written by German and English theologians. There is much logical directness in the method of this treatise, which presents the subject in four parts:—the Prophetical testimony to the Saviour, and the Divinity of His life and teaching; the miracles of the Redeemer and His Apostles; and the effect of His Truth on human life and character. The book contains one remarkable paragraph, which like certain choice passages of Hooker, Jeremy Taylor, Milton, and John Howe, is one of the gems of the literature of the seventeenth century, which they who have once seen, desire to retain in vivid recollection. It is an invocation of the Sacred Spirit, the Author of Truth,—the rapturous expression of a soul whose fervour had been kindled, as was the Hebrew seer's, by the touch of hallowed fire—"As Thou art the Agent and Advocate of Jesus my Lord, O, plead His cause effectually in my soul against the suggestions of Satan and my unbelief; and finish His healing, saving work, and let not the flesh or world prevail. Be in me the resident Witness of my Lord, the Author of my prayers, the Spirit of adoption, the seal of God, the earnest of mine inheritance. Let not my nights be so long and my days so short, nor sin eclipse those beams which have often illuminated my soul. Without Thee books are senseless scrawls, studies are dreams, learning is a glowworm, and wit is but wantonness, impertinence and folly. Transcribe those sacred precepts on my heart, which by Thy dictates and inspirations are recorded in Thy Holy Word. I refuse not Thy help for tears and groans,—but O, shed abroad that love upon my heart, which may keep it in a continual life of love. Teach me the work which I must do in heaven; refresh my soul with the delights of holiness, and the happiness which arises from the believing hopes of the everlasting joys. Exercise my heart and tongue in the holy praises of my Lord. Strengthen me in sufferings, and conquer the terrors of death and hell. Make me the more heavenly, by how much the faster I am hastening to heaven; and let my last thoughts, words, and works on earth be likest to those which shall be my first in the state of glorious immortality, where the kingdom is delivered up to the Father, and God will for ever be All and in all; of Whom, and through Whom, and to Whom are all things, to Whom be glory for ever. Amen."

The sermon, entitled the "Life of Faith," and which he preached before the king, in July, 1660, Baxter published, in 1670, enlarged into a quarto volume. It may be wondered how Charles II. patiently listened to a discourse of such length, which could not easily have been spoken in much less than two hours, and so remarkably full of theology. Barrow is said to have preached for three hours at one time. How sermons of such length were endured by the frivolous ladies and gentlemen sunning themselves at Whitehall, may well exercise the judgment of them who to-day are satiated with the effusion for half-an-hour of the feebler modern declamation, in which sometimes the theological element is of the nature of a vanishing fraction. It is fair, however, to add that the original sermon was only fifty pages in length: the quarto into which it was expanded has more than five hundred pages. Many modern readers would prefer the original publication to the enlargement of it. The book, which contains much that is excellent, is dedicated to

Richard Hampden, the son of the great patriot who fell in battle on Chalgrove Field.

Liberated from prison, Baxter retired to the pleasant village of Totteridge, where he might hope for peace. Situated on an eminence, and with an invigorating atmosphere, it might enable him to regain health; and if he could not continue that work of preaching to which he had consecrated his life, he might at least, as opportunity offered, do good by stealth, and might produce more of those quarto volumes which had already made his name famous among European theologians. It is probable that there in the smoky chamber, in which it was his misery to live, he finished his "Christian Directory," which he called "A Sum of Practical Theology and Cases of Conscience: directing Christians how to use their knowledge and faith; how to improve all helps and means, and to perform all duties; how to overcome temptations, and to corrupt or mortify every sin." It was published in folio, in 1673. He says of it: "I must do myself the right to notify the reader, that this treatise was written, when I was, for not subscribing, forbidden by the law to preach; and when I had been long separated far from my library and from all books, saving an inconsiderable parcel that wandered with me where I went. It is likely that the absence of books will appear to the reader's loss in the materials of the treatise; but I shall have this advantage of it, that he will not accuse me as a plagiary." In his defence against the charge that he had written many and large books, and which afterwards was repeated to his injury on one of the most painful days of his troubled life, he says: "As to the number and length of my writings, it is my own labour that maketh them so, and my own great trouble, that the world cannot be sufficiently instructed and edified in fewer words. Are not the works of Augustine and Chrysostom much longer? Who yet hath reproached Aquinas or Suarez, Calvin or Zanchy, for the number and greatness of the volumes they have written? When did I ever persuade any one of you to buy or read any book of mine? What harm will they do to those that let them alone? Or what harm can it do to you for other men to read them?" During Baxter's retirement at Totteridge, the Earl of Lauderdale, who was then on his way to Scotland to regulate the affairs of the Church in that kingdom, at the request of the king sent for Baxter to the neighbouring town of Barnet, that he might consult him on the work proposed to be done; and he was commanded to offer him a bishopric, or the presidency of one of the universities, if he would accompany the Earl to that country. Baxter declined the honour offered him, in which probably there was no sincere or kind intention on the part of Charles, and he wrote a letter to Lauderdale, a portion of which may be introduced here, in evidence of his prudence and dignity in dealing with so clever and unscrupulous a negotiator. "My Lord,—Being deeply sensible of your lordship's favours, and especially for your liberal offers for my entertainment in Scotland, I humbly return you my very hearty thanks, but the following considerations forbid me to entertain any hopes, or further thoughts of such a removal. The experience of my great weakness and decay of strength, and particularly of this last winter's pain, and how much worse I am in winter than in summer, fully persuade me that I should live but a little while in Scotland, and that in a disabled, useless condition, rather keeping my bed than the pulpit. I am engaged in writing a book, which, if I could hope to live to finish, is almost all the service I expect to do God and His Church more in the world—a Latin *Methodus Theologiæ*. Indeed I can hardly hope to live so long, as it requires yet nearly a year's labour more. Now if I should spend that half year or year, which should finish this work, in travel, and the trouble of such a removal, and then leave it undone, it would disappoint me of the ends of my life. I live only for work, and therefore should remove only for work, and not for wealth and honours, if ever I remove. If I were there, all that I could hope for were liberty to preach the Gospel of salvation, and especially in some university among young scholars. But I hear that you have enough already for this work, who are likely to do it better than I can. I have a family, and in it a mother-in-law of eighty years of age, of honourable extract and great worth, whom I must not neglect, and who cannot travel. To such an one as I it is so great a business to remove a family, with all our goods and books so far, that it deterreth me from thinking of it, especially having paid so dear for removals these eight years as I have done; and being but yesterday settled in a house which I have newly taken, and that with great trouble and loss of time. And if I should find Scotland disagree with me, which I fully conclude it would, I must remove all back again. When I am commanded 'to pray for kings and all in authority,' I am allowed the ambition of this preferment, which is all that ever I aspired after, 'to live a quiet and peaceable life in all godliness and honesty.' *Diu nimis habitavit anima mea inter osores pacis.* I am weary of the noise of contentious revilers, and have oft had thoughts to go into a foreign land, if I could find where I might have healthful air and quietness, but to live and die in peace. When I sit in a corner, and meddle with nobody, and hope the world will forget that I am alive, court, city, and country are still filled with clamours against me. When a preacher wanteth preferment, his way is to preach or write a book against the Nonconformists, and me by name. Never did my eyes read such impudent untruths, in matter of fact, as such writings contain. They cry out for answers and reasons of my nonconformity, while they know the law forbiddeth me to answer them unlicensed. If I might but be heard speak for myself, I would request that I might be allowed to live quietly, to follow my private studies, and might once again have the use of my books, which I have not seen these ten years. I pay for a room for their standing in at Kidderminster, where they are eaten by worms and rats; having no sufficient security for my quiet abode in any place to encourage me to send for them. I would also ask that I might have the liberty every beggar hath, to travel from town to town. I mean but to London, to oversee the press, when anything of mine is licensed for it. If I be sent to Newgate for preaching Christ's Gospel (for I dare not sacrilegiously renounce my calling, to which I am consecrated *per sacramentum ordinis*), I would request the favour of a better prison where I may but talk and write. I have a license to preach publicly in London diocese, under the Archbishop's own hand and seal, which is yet valid for occasional sermons, though not for lectures or cures; but I dare not use it, because it is in the bishop's power to recall it. Would but the bishop, who, one should think, would not be against the preaching of the Gospel, not recall my license, I could preach occasional sermons, which would absolve my conscience from all obligation to private preaching. For it is not maintenance that I expect. I never received a farthing for my preaching, to my knowledge, since May 1st, 1662. I thank God that I have food and raiment, without being chargeable to any man, which is all that I desire, had I but leave to preach for nothing, and that only where there is a notorious necessity. I humbly crave your lordship's pardon for the tediousness of this letter."

"In the year 1671," writes Baxter, "the diocese of Salisbury was more fiercely driven on to conformity by Dr. Seth Ward than any place else, or than all the bishops in England did in theirs. Many hundreds were prosecuted by him with great industry; and among others, that learned, humble, holy gentleman, Mr. Thomas Grove, an ancient Parliament man, of as great sincerity and integrity as almost any man I ever knew. He stood it out awhile in a lawsuit, but was overthrown, and fain to forsake his country, as many hundreds more are likely to do. His name remindeth me to record my benefactor. A brother's son of his, Mr. Robert Grove, was one of the Bishop of London's chaplains, and the only man that licensed my writings for the press, supposing them not to be against law, in which case I should not expect it. Beside him, I could get no licenser to do it.

And as being silenced, writing was the far greatest part of my service to God for His Church, and without the press my writings would have been in vain, I acknowledge that I owe much to this man, and one Mr. Cook, the Archbishop's chaplain, that I lived not in vain. While I am acknowledging my benefactors, I add that this year died Sergeant John Fountain, the only person from whom I received an annual sum of money; which though, through God's mercy, I needed not, yet I could not in civility refuse; he gave me ten pounds per annum, from the time of my being silenced till his death. When he lay sick, which was almost a year, he delivered to the judges and lawyers that sent to visit him such answers as these, 'I thank your lord or master for his kindness; present my service to him, and tell him, it is a great work to die well; his time is near, all worldly glory must come down; entreat him to keep his integrity, overcome temptations, and please God, and prepare to die.' He deeply bewailed the great sins of the times, and the prognostics of dreadful things which he thought we were in danger of; and though in the wars he suffered imprisonment for the king's cause, towards the end he abandoned that party."

CHAPTER XXII.

1671—1676.

THE year 1672 began in gloom and in much public distress, resulting from an arbitrary act of Charles II., and one of the most infamous in his reign. The king's debts were large and ever increasing, for his profligacy had hardly any limit; and he had from time to time induced bankers in the city to advance money to the Exchequer, receiving as their security certain parts of the revenue, which were set aside to pay the principal and interest of the sums thus borrowed from them. The king paid at the rate of eight per cent. for the money they advanced him, and he had given frequent assurances that all received should be fully and punctually returned to them; and the bankers on their part paid at the rate of six per cent. to the citizens who entrusted them with the funds they lent to the king. Charles owed them nearly a million and a half, and acting, it is said, on the advice of Lord Shaftesbury, who took care beforehand to withdraw his own money from the bankers, he issued a proclamation, that for a year he would give no more interest for the moneys he had borrowed of his subjects, but that at the end of that time he hoped he might resume his payments of it. He accordingly ordered that the Exchequer should be shut up.

Many persons had entrusted their savings to the bankers, relying on the word of their "most religious king" that interest would be regularly paid them. A great panic at once possessed the minds of men, and all who had deposited their money with the bankers and goldsmiths hurried to them to demand its return. Many honourable merchants and tradesmen became bankrupt. John Evelyn says that "widows and orphans were ruined" by this perfidious dishonesty of Charles, who paid no interest for many years. He and his Ministers, alarmed at the public outcry and denunciation of their tyranny, resolved to obtain ready money by seizing in time of peace the Dutch merchant-fleet of sixty vessels passing up the Channel; but that fleet was so strongly protected by an armed convoy that the English admiral, unaccustomed to the work of a buccaneer, was able to possess himself of only four of them, and his sailors were indignant that their monarch compelled them to be pirates. Charles's attack upon the merchant-fleet was speedily followed by a declaration of war against Holland. Of his own losses by the shameful act of the king, Baxter says: "In the beginning of the year 1671-2 the king caused his exchequer to be shut; so that whereas a multitude of merchants and others had put their money into the bankers' hands, and the bankers lent it to the king, and the king gave orders to pay out no more of it for a year, the murmur and complaint in the city were very great, that their estates should be, as they called it, so surprised. This was the more complained of because it was supposed to be in order to assist the French in a war against the Dutch; they therefore took a year to be equal to perpetuity, and the stop to be a loss of all, seeing wars commonly increase necessities but do not supply them. Amongst others, all the money and estate that I had in the world was there, of my own, except ten pounds per annum, which I enjoyed for eleven or twelve years. Indeed it was not my own, which I will mention to counsel those that would do good, to do it speedily and with all their might. I had got in all my life the net sum of one thousand pounds. Having no child, I devoted almost all of it to a charitable use, a free school; I used my best and ablest friends for seven years, with all the skill and industry I could, to help me to some purchase of house or land to lay it out on, that it might be accordingly settled. But though there were never more sellers, I could never by all these friends hear of any that reason could encourage a man to lay it out on as secure, and a tolerable bargain; so that I told them I did perceive the devil's resistance of it, and did suspect that he would prevail, and I should never settle it, but it would be lost. So hard it is to do any good when a man is fully resolved. Divers such observations verily confirm me that there are devils that keep up a war against goodness in the world."

In March, 1672, Charles issued a Declaration of Indulgence, in which it was declared "That his majesty, by virtue of his supreme power in matters ecclesiastical, suspends all penal laws thereabout, and that he will grant a convenient number of meeting-places to men of all sorts that conform not: provided the persons are approved by him, that they only meet in places sanctioned by him with open doors, and do not preach seditiously, nor against the Church of England." The Court attempted to bribe the prominent Puritan clergymen into acknowledgment of the king's dispensing power by offering each of them a small pension, but which Baxter refused to receive. The object of the king was to enable his Roman Catholic subjects to open churches, and to celebrate without offence or molestation the rites of their religion. The immediate result of the Declaration was to release many thousands of Quakers and of other Nonconformists from their imprisonment. John Bunyan, after a confinement of twelve years in Bedford gaol, and with his "Pilgrim's Progress" completed, went forth to freedom, and, it is said, owing to the intervention in his favour of the Bishop of Lincoln. The Presbyterian ministers were licensed to preach. They gathered large numbers of adherents, and it became clear to the bishops that if the Declaration were not withdrawn, the Acts of repression which had been in force would be of no avail for the future, should a change of policy be determined on. After recovering from an unusually painful attack of illness, Baxter says: "I had till now forborne, for several reasons, to seek a license for preaching from the king upon the toleration, but when all others had taken theirs, I delayed no longer, but sent to seek one. The 19th of November, my baptism-day, was the first day after ten years of silence that I preached in a tolerated public assembly, though not yet tolerated in any consecrated church, but only against law, in my own house. Some merchants set up a Tuesday's lecture in London, to be kept by six ministers at Pinner's Hall, allowing them twenty shillings apiece each sermon, of whom they chose me to be one. But when I had preached there only four sermons, I found the Independents so quarrelsome with what I said, that all the city did ring of their backbitings and false accusations; so that had I but preached for unity, and against division or unnecessary withdrawment from each other, or against unwarrantable narrowing of Christ's Church, it was said abroad that I preached against the Independents. Especially if I did but say that man's will had a natural liberty, though a moral thraldom to vice; that men might have Christ and life, if they were truly willing; and that men have power to do better than they do, it was cried abroad among all the party that I preached up Arminianism and free will and man's power; and, oh! what an odious crime was this! On January, the 24th, 1672-3, I began a Tuesday lecture at Mr. Turner's church in New Street, near Fetter Lane, with great convenience and God's encouraging blessing: but I never took a penny of money for it from any one. The Parliament met again in February, and voted down the king's Declaration as illegal. The king promised them that it should not be brought into precedent, and thereupon they consulted of a bill for the ease of Nonconformists or Dissenters. On February the 20th, I took a house in Bloomsbury in London, and removed thither after Easter with my family; God having mercifully given me three years of great peace among quiet neighbours at Totteridge, and much more health or ease than I expected, and some opportunity to serve Him."

The Declaration produced a ferment throughout the

country. All parties agreed that it was an attempt of the king to obtain absolute power; and the House of Commons, in resolving "that penal statutes in matters ecclesiastical cannot be suspended but by consent of Parliament," went so far as to threaten to refuse supplies of money until the Declaration was withdrawn. The necessities of the king obliged him to consent to their resolution. The Parliament immediately passed the Test Act, which required that "all persons bearing any office of trust or profit shall take the oaths of supremacy and allegiance in public and open court, and shall also receive the sacrament of the Lord's Supper, according to the usage of the Church of England, in some parish-church on some Lord's Day immediately after Divine service and sermon—also declaring their belief that there is no transubstantiation in the sacrament of the Lord's Supper, or in the elements of bread and wine, or after the consecration of it by any person whatsoever." The penalty for breach of this Act was, that the offender could not sue in any court of law, nor be executor of the will of a friend, nor receive a legacy, nor hold any public office; and, in addition to all these deprivations, that he should be fined five hundred pounds. This was the last of the six penal laws against Puritans and Nonconformists passed in Charles II.'s reign. These laws had been executed with severity, reducing many families to poverty, casting many excellent men for years into prison among thieves, compelling others to emigrate to New England; and they were measures of no real advantage to the Anglican Church, neither increasing its efficacy, nor improving the character, nor adding to the social influence of the clergy. The Church is weak so far and so long as it relies for its enlargement and material success upon the help and protection of the secular power; but it is a mighty force for propagating truth, for recovering men to righteousness, and for honouring its glorious Head and Lord, only as it depends for its strength and growth upon the spirit of the living God, Who was given at its foundation to be with it until the world shall have been gained and blessed. "At this time," writes Baxter, "April, 1674, God so much increased my languishing, and laid me so low by an incessant inflation of my head, and translation of my great flatulency thither to the nerves and members, increasing for ten or twelve weeks to greater pains, that I had reason to think that my time on earth would not be long. And, oh! how good hath the will of God proved hitherto to me; and will it not be best at last? Experience causeth me to say to His praise, 'Great peace have they that love His law, and nothing shall offend them; and though my flesh and heart do fail, God is the rock of my heart, and my portion for ever.' Taking it to be my duty to preach while toleration continued, I removed the last spring to London, where, my diseases increasing, for about half a year constrained me to cease my Friday's lecture, and an afternoon sermon on the Lord's Day in my own house, to my grief; and to preach only one sermon a week at St. James's market-house, where some one had hired an inconvenient place. But I had great encouragement to labour there, because of the notorious necessity of the people; while the greatness of the parish of St. Martin made it impossible for the tenth, perhaps the twentieth, person in the parish to hear in the parish-church; and the next parishes, St. Giles and Clement Danes, were almost in the like case. On July 5th, 1674, at our meeting over St. James's market-house, God vouchsafed us a great deliverance. A main beam, weakened before by the weight of the people, so cracked, that three times they ran in terror out of the room, thinking it was falling, but remembering the like at St. Dunstan's-in-the-West, I reproved their fear as causeless. But the next day, taking up the boards, we found that two rends were so great, that it was a wonder of providence the floor had not fallen, and the roof with it, to the destruction of multitudes. The Lord make us thankful! It pleased God to give me marvellous encouragement in my preaching at St. James's. The crack having frightened away most of the richer sort, especially the women, most of the congregation were young men of the most capable age, who heard with very great attention, and many that had not come to church for years received and manifested so great a change as made all my charge and trouble easy to me."

When the Indulgence was revoked, the king became violent in his anger against the Puritans and Nonconformists. He said they had joined the Parliament in passing the Test Act, in order to exclude Roman Catholics from places of trust, and to prevent that public exercise of their religion, to secure which was the great object of his policy; for the future he would show them no pity; and he smiled with satisfaction, when they told him that a clergyman preached before the House of Commons, that "the Nonconformists ought not to be tolerated, but to be cured by vengeance; fire should be set to the faggot, and they should be taught by scourges or scorpions, and their eyes opened with gall." Charles loved revenge, and he directed that the Nonconformists who had objected to his dispensing power should be proceeded against rigorously under the penal laws. Baxter records some of the severities which he was one of the first to suffer from the anger of the king: "I was the first that was apprehended by warrant, and brought before the justices as a conventicler. One, Keeling, an ignorant fellow, had got a warrant as bailiff and informer to search after conventiclers, Papists, and Protestants, which he prosecuted with great animosity and violence. Having then left St. James's, the lease of the house being out, I preached only on Thursdays, at Mr. Turner's. By the Act it was required I should be judged by a justice of the city or division or county where I live. So that, the preaching-place being in the city, only a city justice might judge me. Keeling went to many of the city justices, but none of them would grant him a warrant against me; he therefore went to the justices of the county, who lived near me, and Sir John Medlicot and Mr. Bennet, brother to Lord Arlington, ignorant of the law herein, gave their warrant to apprehend me, and bring me before them. The constable or informer gave me leave to choose what justices I would go to. I therefore went with them to seek divers of the best justices, but could find none of them at home, and so spent that day in a state of pain and great weakness, being carried up and down in vain. But I used the informer kindly, and spake that to him which his conscience, though a very ignorant fellow, did not well digest. The next day I went with the constable and him to Sir William Pulteney. Sir William showed from the Act that none but a city-justice had power to judge me for a sermon preached in the city, and so the informer was defeated. As I went out of the house I met the Countess of Warwick and Lady Lucy Montague, and told them of the case and warrant, who assured me that he whose hand was at it knew nothing of it, and some of them sent to him, and Keeling's warrant was called in within two or three days. It proved that one Mr. Barwell, sub-bailiff of Westminster, set Keeling on work, and told him what a good service it was to the Church, and what he might gain by it. Lord Arlington most sharply chid his brother for granting his warrant; and within a few days, Mr. Barwell riding the circuit was cast by his horse, and died in the very fall. Sir John Medlicot and his brother a few weeks after lay both dead in his house together. Shortly after Keeling came several times to have spoken with me to ask my forgiveness, and not meeting me, went to my friends in the city with the same words; though a little before he boasted how many hundred pounds he should have of the city-justices for refusing him justice. At last he found me within, would have fallen down on his knees to me, and asked me earnestly to forgive him. I asked him what had changed his mind; he told me that his conscience had no peace from the hour he troubled me, and that it increased his disquiet that no justice would hear, nor one constable of forty execute the warrant, and all the people cried out against him; but that which set it home was Mr. Barwell's death, for of Sir John Medlicot's he knew not. I exhorted the man to universal repentance and reformation of life. He told me he would never meddle in such businesses, or trouble any man more, and promised to live better himself than he had done."

The continued persecution against them who dissented from the Church began to produce sympathy in their favour, and among citizens who had no accord with their principles. It was grievous, they said, to see from week to week men carried to prison, who were upright in their transactions, unblamable in their lives, and held in respect by the bankers and merchants, and that it were every way better that the bishops adopted persuasion rather than force to induce agreement in religious opinions. Some of the magistrates, who much disliked Nonconformity, endeavoured to absent themselves from court, on the days when they expected the Puritan or Presbyterian clergy would be brought before them to be punished for unlicensed preaching; and on one occasion, long remembered by them who were liable to arrest for praying with their acquaintances, and for exhorting them to amendment of life, when twelve of the bishops came into the city to dine with Sir Nathaniel Herne, the sheriff, he told the prelates, that for himself and others they could not trade with their fellow-citizens one day and put them in prison the next. Baxter lived in daily dread of incarceration, distressed in mind that he could no more reason with men of their sins, nor by his voice protest against the abounding wickedness of the time; and he so diseased and feeble, that even continued existence seemed both to himself and to others almost miraculous. His books were bought and read by multitudes who differed from him in some of his opinions, but who admired the purity of his life, his patience under suffering, his laborious and successful service at Kidderminster, the earnestness and power of his preaching, and the excellence of his theological and practical works. Even they who persecuted him admitted his goodness and unselfish devotedness as a clergyman. Bishop Burnet said, he ever held Baxter in great esteem, and that "if he had any acquaintance with serious, vital religion, it was owing to his reading Baxter's practical works in his younger days." Constantly harassed by informers, many of whom received large sums of money for the successful prosecution of their infamous calling, suspected and watched by the Government, and scarcely for a single day free from pain, Baxter had much distress and affliction. The description which Tacitus gives of the insecurity of life and property from such men, in the days of Tiberius and of his cruel successors, would well apply to the state of the ejected clergy after the passing of the penal Acts in the reign of Charles II. The calling most hateful to Englishmen of every rank is that of the spy. Men of that infamous class abounded in the years when the Conventicle Act and the Five Mile Act were put in force against the Puritans and Presbyterians. They wore disguises, they attended religious meetings, and with sanctimonious looks and words they crept into families, whispering to servants, bribing housemaids, listening at doors, and sometimes incurring heavy castigation when suddenly detected. Some of them pretended to belong to the number of the elect, to delight in pious conversation, and to be thankful for their religious privileges. Especially vigilant on Sundays, they mingled with the crowds going to the churches, closely followed any one suspected of Puritanism, tracked him if he went to a conventicle, then hastened to the magistrates for authority to burst open the door, and to seize the offender. If soldiers were quartered in a town, they were commanded to go with the informer, to seize the preacher, to disperse the congregation, and to arrest any prominent members of it. The hearer who possessed property was generally selected for apprehension. He was dragged before the magistrate and fined; and should the unhappy delinquent not have money in his pocket at the time sufficient to pay the fine and the attendant costs, the informer and his accomplices hastened to his dwelling, broke open drawers and coffers, stole rings, lace, money, or books, and anything which could be conveniently carried away. Such men were the offscouring of mankind. They were profligates of the lowest class, living generally in filthy taverns, and expending their shameful gains in gambling and vice. Honest men shunned them, even thieves were ill at ease in their company; and when toleration put an end to their disgraceful service, few persons were willing to employ them; they lived in poverty, and died in want and misery. Baxter was for years pestered by such men. He says of some of them: "Keeling the informer, being commonly detested for persecuting me, was cast into gaol for debt, and wrote to me to endeavour his deliverance, which I did. A while before, another of the chief informers of the city and my accuser, Marshall, died in the Compter, where his creditors laid him to keep him from doing more harm; yet did not the bishops change or cease. Two more informers were set on work, who first assaulted Mr. Case's meeting, and next got in as hearers into Mr. Reid's meeting, where I was preaching. When they would have gone out to fetch justices, for they were known, the doors were locked to keep them in till I had done; and one of them, supposed to be sent from Fulham, stayed weeping. Yet went they straight to the justices, and the week following heard me again as informers at my lectures. Sir Thomas Davis, notwithstanding all his warnings and confessions, sent his warrants to a justice of the division where I dwelt, to distrain upon me on two judgments for fifty pounds, for preaching my lecture in New Street. When the warrants were issued, my wife did, without any repining, encourage me to undergo the loss, and did herself take the trouble of removing and hiding my library awhile (many scores of books being so lost), and after to give it away, *bonâ fide*, some to New England, and the most at home, to avoid distraining on them. Some Conformists are paid to the value of twenty pounds a sermon for their preaching, and I must pay twenty pounds and forty pounds a sermon for preaching for nothing. Oh, what pastors hath the Church of England, who think it worth their unwearied labours, and all the odium which they contract from the people, to keep such as I am from preaching the Gospel of Christ, and to undo us for it as far as they are able; though these many years they do not, for they cannot, accuse me for one word that ever I preached, nor one action else that I have done; while the greatest of the bishops preach not three a year themselves! The dangerous crack over the market-house at St. James's put many upon desiring that I had a larger and safer place for meeting; and though my own dulness, and great backwardness to troublesome business, made me very averse to so great an undertaking, judging that it being in the face of the court it would never be endured, yet the great and incessant importunity of many, out of a fervent desire of the good of souls, did constrain me to undertake it." Baxter's wife, who had remarkable energy in all that would make him more useful in his public service, or happy in their home, by the help of her friends, the Countesses of Clare, Warwick, and Tyrconnel, Ladies Armine, Hollis, Richards, Clinton, Fitzjames, and many others, raised a new building in Bloomsbury, in hope that there might be some lull in the storm of persecution, which had beat upon him so pitilessly and so long; and that he might be enabled to teach the truths of religion to them who revered his character and delighted in his instruction. But he had no rest from threats of violence, from dread of imprisonment, and from the offensive observations of informers.

"I was so long wearied," he says, "with keeping my doors shut against them that came to distrain on my goods for preaching, that I was fain to go from my house, and to sell all my goods, and to hide my library first, and afterwards to sell it; so that if books had been my treasure (and I valued little more on earth), I had now been without a treasure. For about twelve years I was driven a hundred miles from them; and when I had paid dear for the carriage, after two or three years, I was forced to sell them. The prelates, to hinder me from preaching, deprived me also of these private comforts; but God saw that they were my snare. We brought nothing into this world, and we must carry nothing out. The loss is very tolerable. I was the more willing to part with goods, books, and all, that I might have nothing to be distrained, and so go on to preach; and accordingly removing my dwelling to the new chapel which I had built, I purposed to venture to preach in it, there being forty thousand persons in the parish, as is supposed, more than can hear in the parish-church, who have no place to go to for God's public worship; so that I set not up church against church, but preached to those that must else have had none. When I had preached there but once, a resolution was taken to surprise me the next day, and send me for six months to the common gaol, upon the Act for the Oxford oath. Not knowing this, it being the hottest day of the year, I agreed to go for a few weeks into the country, twenty miles off; but the night before I should go, I felt so ill, that I was fain to send to disappoint both the coach and my intended companion, Mr. Sylvester. When I was thus fully resolved to stay, it pleased God after the ordinary coach-hour, that three men from three parts of the city met at my house accidentally, just at the same time almost to a minute; of whom if any one had not been there, I had not gone; viz., the coachman again to urge me, Mr. Sylvester, whom I had put off, and Dr. Cox, who compelled me, and told me he would else carry me into the coach. It proved a special, merciful providence of God; for after one week of languishing and pain, I had nine weeks' greater ease than ever I expected in this world, and greater comfort in my work. For my good friend, Richard Beresford, Esq., clerk of the Exchequer, whose importunity drew me to his house, spared no cost, labour, or kindness for my health or service. Being driven from home, and having an old license yet in force, by the countenance of that, and the great industry of Mr. Beresford, I had leave and invitation for ten Lord's Days, to preach in the parish-churches round about. The first parish that I preached in, after thirteen years' ejection and prohibition, was Rickmansworth, after that at Sarrat, at King's Langley, at Chesham, at Chalford, at Amersham, and that often twice a day. Those heard who had not come to church for seven years; and two or three thousand heard, where scarcely a hundred were wont to come, and with so much attention and willingness as gave me very great hopes that I never spake to them in vain; thus soul and body had these special mercies. But the censures of men pursued me as before; the envious sort of the prelatists accused me, as if I had intruded into the parish-churches too boldly and without authority. The quarrelsome sectaries or separatists did in London speak against me for drawing people to the parish-churches and the Liturgy. All my days, nothing has been charged on me as crimes, so much as my costliest and greatest duties. But the pleasing of God and saving souls will pay for all. The country about Rickmansworth abounding with Quakers, because W. Penn, their captain, dwelleth there, I was desirous that the poor people should once hear what was to be said for their recovery, which coming to Mr. Penn's ears, he was forward to a meeting, where we continued speaking to two rooms full of people, fasting from ten o'clock till five. One lord, two knights, and four conformable ministers, besides others, being present; some all the time, some part. The success gave me cause to believe that it was not labour lost; an account of the conference may be published ere long, if there be cause. While this was my employment in the country, my friends at home had got one Mr. Seddon, a Nonconformist, of Derbyshire, lately come to the city as a traveller, to preach the second sermon in my new-built chapel; he was told and over-told all the danger, and desired not to come if he feared it. I had left word that if he would but step into my house through a door, he was in no danger, they having no power to break open any but the meeting-house. While he was preaching, three justices, supposed of Secretary Coventry's sending, came to the door to seize the preacher. They thought it had been I, and had prepared a warrant upon the Oxford Act to send me for six months to the common gaol. The good man and two weak honest persons, entrusted to have directed him, left the house where they were safe, and thinking to pass away, came to the justices and soldiers at the doors, and there stood by them till some one said, 'This is the preacher'; and so they took him, blotted my name out of the warrant, and put in his; though almost every word fitted to my case was false of his. To the Gate-House he was carried, where he continued almost three months of the six: and being earnestly desirous of deliverance, I was put to charges to accomplish it, and at last having righteous judges, and the warrant being found faulty, he had an *habeas corpus*, and was freed upon bonds to appear again the next term."

CHAPTER XXIII.

1676—1681.

DURING many years of the government of Charles II., Baxter patiently bore persecution, imprisonment, and the seizure of his property. He grieved most for the loss of the library he had carefully collected. Some of his books, saved from distraint by the adroitness of his wife, were sent to America, where they rest in Harvard University; to which his "most entire friend," Henry Ashurst, bequeathed a considerable sum; and among a free and generous people, the descendants of them who were driven away by the storms of persecution, to form the foundation of the great State, in which the rights of each citizen are equitably regarded, and where liberty is universal. At Whitehall, the dissipation of the king was excessive; his court was perhaps more generally vicious than that of the contemporary Sultan. His heartlessness, perfidy, and frivolity were shocking even to some of the profligate men by whom he was surrounded. He seems not to have had the least regard for truth and honesty, if, in addition to other evidence, reliance can be placed upon the statement, that when once in a discussion before the Council, Coventry told him that he was supporting a vile cause which was essentially unjust and corrupt, the king replied, "I have got good money for doing it." To them who knew him best he appeared to have no sense of religion, nor any controlling thought of his own great responsibility. He had inherited the belief that he reigned by Divine right, and that his people were necessary to his authority; conceptions which appear to be entirely out of favour with the modern world.

Flattered and encouraged in depravity by the parasites who were nourished upon his profligacy, he seems to have given no practical heed to the reasonableness of public liberty; and he had so taught his courtiers the evil principles which had guided him in all his administration, that they used to say, "We are the finest flour, and the people are the coarsest bran." In one of the conversations which Burnet, afterwards Bishop of Salisbury, had with the king, Charles replied to his remonstrances against his constant immoralities, that "he thought God would not damn a man for a little irregular pleasure." The daily life of the king could not but injuriously influence the social state of London; for the sovereign is the example to the nation he governs. Charles had a graceful bearing, and that unfailing courtesy which attracted men to him; he had a keen sense of the ludicrous; a ready expression of humour, sometimes almost amounting to wit; a discernment of character, to which experience gave a certain exactness; an habitual fondness for pleasure and frivolity, and a constant dislike of business, and of anything which could disturb the calm of an indolent life. He was affable, and occasionally profuse in gifts to his friends. But naturally he was false and perfidious, and he belonged to a race who could neither forget an injury nor forgive an enemy. His gross neglect, after his restoration, of many of them who in the days of his adversity had given him their all; and his wasting large sums of money, which might have removed their distresses, upon harlots and spies, present him in a lurid light to them who seek to have a glimpse of that mournful time, when public liberty was becoming more and more restricted, and when the supremacy of vice was complete. It was impossible that any people could live in contented happiness under the government of such a king, at once heartless, frivolous, and abandoned. Their best interests were disregarded, and there were no means of producing improvement either in public virtue or in social happiness. The purpose of the monarch was to gain despotic authority, and although often successfully opposed by the Houses of

Parliament, who had some recollection of their former power and freedom, he kept this object ever in view. Ministers and Parliaments succeeded each other; something of the ancient virtue survived in the state; but patriot peers and commoners were marked men at Whitehall, and reserved for certain vengeance, whenever their words or conduct should give the least legal pretext for proceeding against them; for they had given unpardonable offence either by their daring opposition to the will of their sovereign, or by their public advocacy of thorough reform in the habits of the court, and in the administration of affairs.

In 1677, Sheldon, the Archbishop of Canterbury, died, and the ejected Puritans and Presbyterians hoped to have in consequence some relaxation of the penal laws. Baxter, who lived in constant peril from enemies, had lost his constant friend and counsellor, Chief Justice Hale, who had held him in the highest regard. In his will he left Baxter a sum of money, with which, he says, "I purchased the largest Cambridge Bible, and put his picture before it as a monument to my house. But waiting for my own death, I gave it to Sir William Ellis, who laid out about ten pounds to put it into a more curious cover, and keep it for a monument in his honour." Even when retired from public service, after the withdrawment of his license, and while engaged in the labour of composing his treatises, Baxter had the daily misery of insecurity. He completed one of his chief works, "The Catholic Theology," a folio of seven hundred pages, full of discussions, after the manner of the earlier schoolmen, of the most abstruse and difficult questions which the human mind can treat of, and which can have few attractions for any whose professions or inclinations do not lead them to the study of those subjects which relate to Divine Sovereignty, to the origin of evil and the responsibility of man, to the relation of liberty and necessity to human conduct, and, above all, to the progressive development of our race towards that period when, as Lessing long afterwards wrote, men will do good because it is right, and not because of rewards for it. But in all his controversy Baxter shows the vigour and generosity of his nature; he has no narrow views, no acrimony, no bitterness of censure. The goodness which possessed his soul moderated his ardour, and prevented the envenomed word. The work composed in such a spirit seems to have raised up no adversary against him, and no man, then or since, has ventured to controvert his conclusions on those awful subjects, upon which many may dare to speculate, but on which no one can decide with certainty. He states what was his design in writing the book: "My mind being these many years immersed in studies of this nature, and also having long wearied myself in searching what Fathers and Schoolmen have said of such things before us, and my genius abhorring confusion and equivocals, I came by many years' longer study to perceive that most of the doctrinal controversies among Protestants are far more about equivocal words than matter; and it wounded my soul to perceive what work both tyrannical and unskilful, disputing clergymen had made, these thirteen hundred years, in the world. Experience, since the year 1643, till this year 1675, hath loudly called me to repent of my own prejudices, sidings, and censurings of causes and persons not understood, and of all the miscarriages of my ministry and life which have been thereby caused; and to make it my chief work to call men that are within my hearing to more peaceable thoughts, affections, and practices. And my endeavours have not been in vain—but the sons of the cowl were exasperated the more against me, and accounted him to be against every man, that called all men to love and peace, and was for no man in a contrary way." His unhappiness from continual liability to arrest increased, and he found it to his sorrow necessary to take less part in the public ministry. Spies ceased not to watch his steps; the Government were prepared to treat him with great severity, if he gave them opportunity; his feeble health added daily to his sufferings; and in his anger Charles had no relenting.

"When I had been kept a whole year from preaching,"

says Baxter, "in the chapel which I built, I began in another in a tempestuous time, on account of the necessity of the parish of St. Martin, where about sixty thousand souls had no church to go to, nor any public worship of God! How long, Lord! About February and March, 1676, it pleased the king importunately to command and urge the judges and London justices to put the laws against Nonconformists in execution; but the nation was backward to it. In London they were often and long commanded to it; till at last, Sir Joseph Sheldon, the Archbishop of Canterbury's near relation, being Lord Mayor, on April 30th, the execution began. They were required especially to send all the ministers to the common gaols for six months, on the Oxford Act, for not taking the oath, and dwelling within five miles. This day Mr. Joseph Read was sent to gaol, being taken out of the pulpit, preaching in a chapel in Bloomsbury, in the parish of St. Giles. He did so much good to the poor ignorant people who had no other teacher, that Satan owed him a malicious disturbance. He had built the chapel in his own house (with the help of friends), in compassion to those people who, as they crowded to hear him, so did they follow him to the justices, and to the gaol, to show their affection. It being the place where I had been used often to preach, I suppose was somewhat the more maliced. The very day before, I had new secret hints of men's desires of reconciliation and peace, and motions to offer some proposals towards them, as if the bishops were at last grown peaceable. To which, as ever before, I yielded and did my part, though long experience made me suspect that some mischief was near, and some suffering presently to be expected from them. Mr. Jane, the Bishop of London's chaplain, preaching to the Lord Mayor and aldermen in the month of June, turned his sermon against Calvin and me. My charge was that I had sent as bad men to heaven as some that be in hell; because in my book called 'The Saint's Rest' I had said that I thought of heaven with the more pleasure, because I should there meet with

Peter, Paul, Austin, Chrysostom, Jerome, Wickliff, Luther, Zwinglius, Calvin, Beza, Hooper, Latimer, Reynolds, Preston, Sibbes, Brooke, Pym, Hampden. Which of these the man knew to be in hell I cannot conjecture: it is likely those who differed from him in judgment; but till he proves his revelation, I shall not believe him. Being denied forcibly the use of the chapel which I had built, I was obliged to let it stand empty, and pay thirty pounds per annum for the ground-rent myself, and glad to preach for nothing near it, at a chapel built by another for gain in Swallow Street. It was among the same poor people who had no preaching, the parish having sixty thousand souls in it more than the church could hold. When I had preached there a while, Justice Parry, with one Sabbes, signed a warrant to apprehend me, and on the 9th of November six constables, four beadles, and many messengers were set at the chapel doors to execute it. I forbore that day, and afterwards told the Duke of Lauderdale of it, and asked him what it was that occasioned their wrath against me. He desired me to go and speak with the Bishop of London. I did so, and he spake fairly, and with peaceable words. I offered also to resign my chapel in Oxenden Street to a Conformist, if so he would procure my continual liberty in Swallow Street, for the sake of the poor multitudes that had no church to go to. He did as good as promise me, telling me that he did not doubt to do it; but instead of that the constables' warrant was continued, though some of them begged to be excused; so I came near the bishop no more, when I had tried what their kindness and promises signify. When Dr. William Lloyd became pastor of St. Martin's-in-the-Fields, upon Lamplugh's preferment, I was encouraged by Dr. Tillotson to offer my chapel in Oxenden Street for public worship, which he accepted to my great satisfaction; and now there is constant preaching there; be it by Conformists or Nonconformists. I rejoice that Christ is preached to the people in that parish, whom ten or twenty such chapels cannot hold."

The remaining years of Charles's reign were some of the most unhappy which the English people had known since the years when, by the advice of Philip II., Queen Mary endeavoured to have absolute rule in affairs of Church and State. The peace concluded with the Dutch did but little to allay popular discontent, and plots against the king and his Government were frequent. Oates, Dangerfield, Bedloe, and others invented conspiracy, and lived luxuriously upon the gains of their pretended revelations. The Roman Catholics were often pursued to the death by these and other infamous informers, who were approved and bribed by men of power in the country; and distrust and apprehension possessed society, for no man felt himself to be secure against the accusations of men, whose revelations induced the citizens of London to believe that, under the influence of the Jesuits, Papist and Presbyterian would unite to destroy the Monarchy, and to deliver the kingdom to the despotism of the Pope and of the French king. Nothing was too absurd to be credited upon the oaths of them whose imagination and rapacity were alike unbounded; and, as under every tyrannical and corrupt administration, witnesses could readily be found who would swear to the truth of anything which Oates and his associates pretended to reveal. Of these woeful days Baxter writes: "My unfitness, and the torrent of late matter here, stop me from proceeding to insert the history of this age. It is done, and likely to be done so copiously by others, that these shreds will be of small signification. Every year of late hath afforded matter for a volume of lamentations. But that posterity may not be deluded by credulity, I shall truly tell them that lying most impudently in print against the most notorious evidence of truth, in the vending cruel malice against men of conscience and the fear of God, has become so ordinary a trade that it is likely with men of experience to pass ere long for a good conclusion, *dictum vel scriptum est a malignis, ergo falsum est.* Many of the malignant clergy and laity, especially L'Estrange, 'The Observator,' and such others, do with so great confidence publish the most notorious falsehoods, that I must confess it hath greatly depressed my esteem of most history and of human nature. If other historians be like some of these times, their assertions, whenever they speak of such as they distaste, ought to be read like Hebrew, backward; and are so far from signifying truth, that many for one are downright lies. It is no wonder perjury hath grown so common, when the most impudent lying hath so prepared the way."

More and more the clouds were darkening upon Baxter. Enfeebled by disease, pursued by relentless enemies, deprived of the books which had been one of the delights of his life, unable to preach of the compassionate goodness of his Redeemer, falsely accused of actions which were hateful to his soul, the waves of trouble beat heavily upon him. One by one his friends and counsellors departed, and he remained to mourn that he could no more be cheered and advised, in the calamities of his ejectment and persecution, by the good and the wise who esteemed him. He says: "Near the same time died my father's second wife, Mary, the daughter of Sir Thomas Hunks, and sister to Sir Fulke Hunks, the king's governor of Shrewsbury in the wars. Her mother, the old Lady Hunks, died at my father's house, between eighty and one hundred years old; and my mother-in-law died of a cancer at ninety-six, in perfect understanding, having lived from her youth in the greatest mortification and austerity to her body, and constancy of prayer and all devotion of any one that ever I knew. She lived in the hatred of all sin, strictness of universal obedience, and for thirty years longing to be with Christ; in constant acquired infirmity of body, got by avoiding all exercise, and long secret prayer in the coldest seasons. Being of a constitution naturally strong, she was afraid of recovering whenever she was ill. For some days before her death she was so taken with the 91st Psalm, that she would get those who came near her to read it over and over, which Psalm also was a great comfort to Beza even against his death." The storm, which had long been raging around him, and striking down his relatives and friends, fell at last upon his home, and swept away the strength and prop of his existence, the dear and unselfish companion in his years of exclusion, imprisonment, and silence. It is not said from what disease she suffered during the early days of that summer, and Baxter tells but little of her affliction; as though he felt that on the sacredness of the last agony and departure of the sweet and gentle lady the eye of man should not look; but on the fourteenth day of June, 1681, at the age of forty, she passed to her rest, leaving him as his stay and comfort the sure and certain hope of her bliss. "Her image would survive among his thoughts," until they were united again in the unsuffering kingdom, where the Eternal Goodness would receive him, and wipe the tears for ever from his eyes. In the lonely misery of his diseased and weary life, he would never forget the pure kindness of her soul, her tender care, her constant love, the gladness with which her presence had soothed his heart and brightened his home. John Howe preached "her funeral sermon," where she had been accustomed to pray, to a large assembly who well knew her virtues and her charities, and who were the better for her example. The sermon, in the style and length customary at the time, and dedicated to Baxter, is worthy of its great author's power and reputation. In it Howe speaks of Mrs. Baxter's "strangely vivid and great wit and very sober conversation. She gave proof of the real greatness of her spirit, and how much she disdained to be guided by their vulgar measures that have not wit and reason and religion enough to value the accomplishments of the mind and inner man, and to understand that knowledge, holiness, a heavenly heart, entire devotedness to the Redeemer, a willingness to spend and be spent in the service of God, are better and more valuable things than so many hundreds or thousands a year. She knew how to make her estimate of the honour of a family and a pedigree, as things valuable in their kind, without allowing herself so much vanity as to reckon they were things of the most excellent kind, and to which nothing personal could be equal.

Her life might teach all those especially of her own sex, that a life's time is for some other purpose than to indulge and trim and adorn the body." Baxter buried her in her mother's tomb, on the seventeenth day of June, in Christchurch, which had been left in ruins by the great fire of 1666. He says: "The grave was the highest, next the old altar, or table, in the chancel, on which her daughter had caused a very fair, rich, large marble stone to be laid about twenty years ago, on which I caused to be written her titles, and some Latin verses, and these English ones:—

"Thus must thy flesh to silent dust descend,
Thy mirth and worldly pleasure thus will end;
Then, happy, holy souls!—but woe to those
Who heaven forgot, and earthly pleasures chose.
Hear now this preaching grave—without delay,
Believe, repent, and work while it is day.

But Christ's Church on earth is liable to those changes to which the Jerusalem above is in no danger. In the doleful flames of London, 1666, the fall of the church broke the marble all to pieces, so that it proved no lasting monument. I hope this paper monument, erected by one who is following even at the door, in some passion indeed of love and grief, but in sincerity of truth, will be more publicly useful and durable than that marble stone was." The verses are representative of Baxter, who would lose no opportunity of uttering salutary truth or kindly warning, to strengthen the good or reclaim the sinning; for it was truly said of him, the passion of his nature was love to the souls of men. With all regard for the exaggeration which affection might produce, in that memorial which he called the "Breviate of her Life," he has drawn the lines of a noble character, which we can reverently look back upon amid the worthies of that time, who enriched their age with thoughts of beauty and words of goodness, and who are gone, as the sorrowing preacher wrote, "to that blessed society above, where light, life, and love, and therefore harmony, concord, and joy, are perfect and everlasting." Nature renews her decaying powers; they have not altogether perished who are departed—"Not without hope we suffer and we mourn."

It is only just to his memory to quote a few sentences from the memorial of his affection and sorrow: "As to religion, we were so perfectly of one mind, that I know not that she differed from me in any one point or circumstance, except in the prudential management of what we were agreed in. She was for universal love of all true Christians, and against appropriating the Church to a party, and against censoriousness and partiality in religion. She was for acknowledging all that was of God in Conformists and Nonconformists, but she had much more reverence for the elder Conformists than for most of the younger ones, who ventured upon things which Dissenters had so much to say against, without weighing or understanding the reasons on both sides. The nature of true religion, holiness, obedience, and all duty to God and man was printed in her conceptions in so distinct and clear a character, as made her endeavours and expectations still look at greater exactness than I and such as I could reach. She was very desirous that we should all have lived in a constancy of devotion and a blameless innocency; and in this respect she was the meetest helper that I could have had in the world, that ever I was acquainted with. For I was apt to be over careless in my speech, and too backward to my duty, and she was still endeavouring to bring me to greater readiness and strictness in both. If I spoke rashly and sharply, it offended her. If I carried it (as I am apt) with too much neglect of ceremony or humble compliment to any, she would modestly tell me of it. If my very looks seemed not pleasant, she would have me amend them, which my weak, pained state of body indisposed me to do. If I forgot any week to catechise my servants, and familiarly instruct them personally, besides my ordinary family duties, she was troubled at my remissness. And whereas of late years, my decay of spirits, and diseased heaviness and pain, made me much more seldom and cold in profitable conference and discourse in my house than I had been when I was younger, and had more care and spirits and natural vigour, she much blamed me, and was troubled at it, as a wrong to herself and others."

Widowed and distressed, Baxter returned from his wife's grave to his desolated home, to strengthen himself to meet the troubles which he foresaw must soon come to him. He must bear his burden alone. He felt no more the touch of the gentle hand which had ministered to him in patient affection and skilful tenderness. He heard no more the voice which had spoken to him words of love and comfort in many days of anguish and perplexity. The persecution became more severe during the last years of Charles's reign than at any former period of it. Baxter withdrew into the country after his great sorrow, but he returned to London in August. His own narrative will best explain the cause of his renewed afflictions. "I was able to preach only twice, of which the last was my usual lecture in New Street, and which fell out to be the 24th of August, just that day twenty years that I and near two thousand more had been by law forbidden to preach. I was sensible of God's wonderful mercy that had kept so many of us twenty years in so much liberty and peace, while so many severe laws were in force against us, and so great a number were round about us who wanted neither malice nor power to afflict us. I took that day my leave of the pulpit and public work in a thankful congregation; and it was like indeed to be my last. But after this, when I had ceased preaching, and was newly risen from extremity of pain, I was suddenly surprised by a poor, violent informer and many constables and officers, who rushed in, apprehended me, and served on me one warrant to seize my person for coming within five miles of a corporation, and five more warrants to distrain for a hundred and ninety pounds for five sermons. They cast my servants into fears, and were about to take all my books and goods, when I contentedly went with them towards the justice to be sent to jail, and left my house to their will. But Dr. Thomas

Cox meeting me forced me in again, to my couch and bed, and went to five justices, and took his oath without my knowledge, that I could not go to prison without danger of death. On that the justices delayed a day till they could speak with the king, and told him what the doctor had sworn; so the king consented that for the present imprisonment should be forborne, that I might die at home. But they executed all their warrants on my books and goods, even the bed that I lay sick on, and sold them all. Some friends paid them as much money as they were prized at, which I repaid, and was fain to send them away. But though I sent the justice the written deeds, which proved that the goods were none of mine, nor ever were, and sent two witnesses whose hands were to those conveyances, and offered their oaths of it, and also proved that the books I had many years ago alienated to my kinsman, this signified nothing to them; they seized and sold all nevertheless, and both patience and prudence forbade us to try the title at law, when we knew what charges had lately been given to justices and juries, and how others had been used. If they had taken only my cloak, they should have had my coat also, and if they had smitten me on one cheek, I would have turned the other; for I knew the case was such, that he that will not put up with one blow, one wrong, or slander, shall suffer two; yea, many more. But when they had taken and sold all, and I had borrowed some bedding and necessaries of the buyer, I was never the quieter; for they threatened to come upon me again, and take all as mine, whosesoever it was, which they found in my possession. So that I had no remedy, but utterly to forsake my house and goods and all, and take secret lodgings at a distance in a stranger's house; but having a long lease of my own house, which binds me to pay a greater rent now than it is worth, wherever I go I must pay that rent. The separation from my books would have been a greater part of my small affliction, but that I found I was near the end both of that work and that life which needeth books, and so I easily let go all. Naked came I into the world, and naked must I go out; but I never wanted less what man can give, than when man had taken all away. My old friends and strangers were so liberal that I was fain to restrain their bounty. Their kindness was a surer and larger revenue to me than my own. But God was pleased quickly to put me past all fear of men, and all desire of avoiding suffering from them by concealment, by laying on me more Himself than man can do. Then imprisonment with tolerable health would have seemed a palace to me; and had they put me to death for such a duty as they persecute me for, it would have been a joyful end of my calamity; but day and night I groan and languish under God's just-afflicting hand. The pain, which before only tried my reins, tore my bowels, and scarce any part or hour is free. As waves follow waves in the tempestuous seas, so one pain followeth another in this sinful, miserable flesh. I die daily, and yet remain alive. God in His great mercy, knowing my dulness in health and ease, doth make it much easier to repent and hate my sin, loathe myself, contemn the world, and submit to the sentence of death with willingness, than otherwise it was ever likely to have been. Oh, how little is it that wrathful enemies can do against us, in comparison of what our sin and the justice of God can do! and oh, how little is it that the best and kindest of friends can do for a pained body, or a guilty, sinful soul, in comparison of one gracious look or word from God! Woe be to him that hath no better help than man; and blessed be he whose hope and help are in the Lord!"

In 1681, Baxter published the only book he wrote in the Latin language, "Methodus Theologiæ Christianæ," a great folio of nine hundred pages; a large part of it, as he told the Earl of Lauderdale, had been written at Totteridge, "in a troublesome, smoky, suffocating room, in the midst of daily pains of sciatica, and many worse." He toiled over it for several years, declaring, in this arsenal of argument and refutation, all the known relations between God and man, with all the obligations which result from them; and endeavouring to prove that the fact of the Trinity is universal, and that it exists not only in the Great Creator, but in everything which He has made. Thus he maintains that there the Father, the Redeemer, and the Holy Spirit form the Trinity of the Godhead. Power, mind, and will are the trinity in man; nature, grace, and glory are the trinity in the Divine Kingdom; and light, heat, and motion are the trinity in the economy of our earthly kingdom. The Father as Ruler, the Son as Saviour, the Holy Spirit as Sanctifier, are the Trinity in the government of the Church. Faith, hope, and love are the Trinity in the Christian life. This folio is a work of vast labour, and of great subtlety and ingenuity; and even if no modern student reads it, the book remains as a memorial of Baxter's wonderful skill and labour, and of his right to be ranked with John Howe, More, Cudworth, Bramhall, and others of the philosophers and Platonists who were among the great thinkers of the seventeenth century on subjects which can never be alien to human life, thought, and destiny.

CHAPTER XXIV.

1682—1685.

THE year 1682 brought no alleviation either of public discontent or of religious persecution. The king aimed at the possession of absolute government; and his unforgiving heart revealed itself in the prosecution and condemnation of men who were convicted of feigned offences by the perjury of abandoned witnesses, and by the subserviency of judges and of bribed or intimidated juries. Charles had gained some signal political victories, and had gradually rid himself of them who were unwilling to place English liberty under the feet of an unscrupulous, sanguinary, and perfidious king. Men generally feared that his debauchery and tyranny would bring on public calamities. John Evelyn, one of the wisest gentlemen of the time, "looking out of his chamber-window towards the west, saw a meteor of an obscure bright colour, very much in shape like the blade of a sword. What this may portend," he says, "God only knows. But such another phenomenon I remember to have seen in 1640, about the trial of the great Earl of Strafford, preceding our bloody rebellion. I pray God avert His judgements." After telling his Parliament that "nothing should ever alter his affection to the Protestant religion as established by law, nor his love to Parliament, for he still would have frequent Parliaments," Charles dissolved it, and for the rest of his reign never summoned another. The apprehension which disquieted Evelyn, possessed the minds of thousands. No man felt himself to be secure, and there was no guarantee for the continuance of public liberty. The king, who had never forgiven the ejected Puritans for resisting him in his attempt to bring in the religion of the Latin Church, was determined to harass them with the utmost severity. One after another, men of virtue and honour were hurried to the scaffold. Charles rioted in shedding blood. Accusations against patriotic and virtuous citizens were easily made, and under his corrupt administration, judges and jurymen would seldom hesitate to convict him who was charged with being an enemy to the throne. Liberty lay bleeding at the feet of a frivolous, voluptuous, and utterly cruel king. The Earl of Essex was murdered when a prisoner in the Tower; Lord Russell and Algernon Sidney, two of the most virtuous living Englishmen, were beheaded. Warrants were issued for the arrest of many more, who, happily forewarned, escaped to the Continent from the vindictive anger of their sovereign. In the meantime, the king's brother, the Duke of York, afterwards James II., who governed Scotland, delighted in the cruelty he naturally loved. He applied the torture without pity to unhappy religionists who fell into his hands. He watched with emotions of pleasure their pallid faces, while they were enduring the agony caused by the thumbscrew, as the terrible instrument crushed muscle and bone. When the Cameronians, who were dragged before him, were put to the question by having their legs beaten in the iron boot, and when his council one by one, sickening at the ghastly sight, fled from the room, James remained alone to see the limbs smashed by the mallet and steel wedge, with the calm satisfaction of one who makes a scientific investigation of the tissues and nerves of the human body, while being prepared for anatomical demonstration. These were the two princes whose flatterers, some of whom held preferments in the Anglican Church, assured them in fervid language that they ruled their people by a Divine right.

During this and the following year, Baxter lived in retirement and in suffering. With little strength for public duties, he had leisure to write "The True History of Councils enlarged and defended," smaller works on "The Immortality of the Soul," "On the Nature of Spirits," "Compassionate Counsel to Young Men," "How to do Good to Many," "A Family Catechism," "Obedient Patience," and his "Farewell Sermon to his Hearers at Kidderminster." During this year he published one very useful book, of perpetual freshness and beauty, his "Dying Thoughts;" especially consoling to the revered patriot Lord William Russell before his execution; whose noble wife, when he perished by the scourge of the anger of the king, John Howe comforted in her deep grief, by the assurance, that the rewards of the other state will be sufficiently ample for all the sufferings and sorrows wherewith sincerity is often attended in this. Bishop Burnet states, that "Lord Russell from the time of his imprisonment looked upon himself as a dead man, and turned his thoughts wholly to another world. He read much in the Scriptures, particularly in the Psalms, and read Baxter's "Dying Thoughts." This work of Baxter has comforted the souls of many others in those days of weakness and pain, while they were waiting for the coming of the Angel, to whose hand the Lord of life intrusts the key which opens for His servants the gate of bliss. Baxter wrote this book for his own use; and shortly before his departure he published it, that others also might have benefit from it, who, hoping for the "endless morn of light," prayed in the language recorded of the faithless seer, that they might have the death and the hereafter of the righteous. In the preface of the book, the reader is told that he wrote it for himself, "unresolved whether any one should ever see it, but at last inclined to leave that to the will of my executors, to publish or suppress it when I am dead as they saw cause. But my person being seized on, and my library and all my goods distrained on by constables and sold, I am constrained to relinquish my house (for preaching and being in London), I knew not what to do with multitudes of manuscripts that had long lain by me; having no house to go to, but a narrow hired lodging with strangers: wherefore I cast away whole volumes which I could not carry away, both controversies, and letters practical, and cases of conscience, but having newly lain divers weeks, night and day, in waking torments, nephritic and colic, after other long pains and languor, I took this book with me in my removal, for my own use in my further sickness. Three weeks after, falling into another extreme fit, and expecting death, where I had no friend with me to commit my papers to, merely lest it should be lost, I thought it best to give it to the printer. I think it is so much the work of all men's lives to prepare to die with safety and comfort, that the same thoughts may be useful for others that are so for me. If those men's lives were spent in serious, preparing thoughts of death, who are now studying to destroy each other, and tear in pieces a distressed land, they would prevent much dolorous repentance."

The publication of books so large and numerous led Baxter into difficulties, which the envy of some and the malice of others used to his disadvantage. They who hated his principles, and who had unremittingly persecuted him for many years, charged him with ruining his publisher. He says of the accusation: "But now comes a new trial; my sufferings are my crimes. My bookseller, Nevil Symmonds, is broken, and it is reported that I am the cause, by the excessive rates that I took for my books of him; and a great Dean, whom I much value, foretold that I would undo him. Of all the crimes in the world I least expected to be accused of covetousness. Satan being the master of this design to hinder the success of my writings when I am dead, it is part of my warfare under Christ to resist him. I tell you, therefore, truly all my covenants and dealings with booksellers to this day. When I first ventured upon the publication of my thoughts, I knew nothing of the art of booksellers. I did, as an act of mere kindness, offer my book called 'The Saint's Rest,' to Thomas Underhill and Francis Tyton to print, leaving the matter of profit, without any covenants, to their ingenuity. They gave me ten pounds for the first impression, and ten pounds apiece, that is, twenty pounds for every after impression, till 1665. I had in the meantime altered the book, by the addition of divers sheets. Mr. Underhill died; his wife became poor. Mr. Tyton had losses by fire in 1666. They never gave, nor offered me a farthing for any impression after that, nor so much as one of my books; but I was fain out of my own purse to buy all that I gave to any friends or poor person that asked it. This loosening me from Mr. Tyton, Mr. Symmonds stepped in, and told me Mr. Tyton said he never got three pence by me, and brought witness. Hereupon I used Mr. Symmonds only. When I lived at Kidderminster, some had defamed me of a covetous getting of many hundred pounds by the booksellers. I had till then taken of Mr. Underhill, Mr. Tyton, and Mr. Symmonds for all, save the 'Saint's Rest,' the fifteenth book, which I usually gave away; but if anything for second impressions were due, I had little in money from them, but in such books I wanted at their rates. But when this report of my great gain came abroad, I took notice of it in print, and told them that I intended to take more hereafter; and ever since I took the fifteenth book for myself and friends, and eighteen-pence more for every ream of the other fourteen which I destinated to the poor. With this, while I was at Kidderminster, I bought Bibles to give to all the poor families; and I got three hundred or four hundred pounds, which I destined all to charitable uses. At last at London it increased to eight hundred and thirty pounds, which, delivering to a worthy friend, he put it into the hands of Sir Robert Viner, with a hundred pounds of my wife's, where it lieth, settled on a charitable use after my death, as from the first I resolved. If it fails, I cannot help it. I never received more of any bookseller than the fifteenth book, and this eighteen-pence a ream. And if, for after impressions, I had more of these fifteenths than I gave away, I took about two-third parts of the common price of the bookseller, or little more, and oft less; and sometimes I paid myself for the printing many hundreds to give away; and sometimes I bought them of the bookseller above my number, and sometimes the gain was my own necessary maintenance; but I resolved never to lay up a groat of it for any but the poor. My own condition is this: of my patrimony or small inheritance I never took a penny to myself, my poor kindred needing it much more. I am fifteen or sixteen years divested of all ecclesiastical maintenance. I never had any church or lecture that I received wages from, but, within these three or four years, much against my disposition, I am put to take bounty of special particular friends; my wife's estate being never my property, nor much more than half our yearly expense. If then it be any way unfit for me to receive such a proportion as aforesaid, as the fruit of my own long and hard labour for my necessary and charitable uses; and if they that never took pains for it have more right than I, when every labourer is master of his own, or if I may not take some part with them, I know not the reason of any of this. Men grudge not a cobbler, or a tailor, or any day labourer, for living on his labours, and why an ejected minister of Christ, giving freely five parts to a bookseller, may not take the sixth to himself or to the poor, I know not. For divers impressions of the 'Saint's Rest' I have not had a farthing; for no book have I had more than the fifteenth book to myself and friends, and the eighteen-pence a ream for the poor and works of charity. Verily, since I devoted all to God, I have found it harder to give it when I do my best, than to get it; though I submit of late to Him partly upon charity, and am so far from laying up a groat, that (though I hate debt), I am long in debt."

The extract here made from the appendix to his Autobiography will shed light upon some of the literary arrangements of the time, and will indirectly deepen the bright lines of Baxter's character as a philanthropist, who had dedicated himself to the offices of religion, and whose conduct was in harmony with his profession; for, instead of injuring the bookseller, he had given him nearly a thousand pounds over and above the gains which the custom of his trade allowed him, for publishing the works placed in his hands. Viewed on every side, Baxter stands forth as one of the greatest of Englishmen, worthy to be remembered not only as one of the most successful of our preachers, one of the ablest of our writers on doctrinal and practical theology, with that philosophical power which made him worthily a successor of Francis Bacon, and a contemporary of Cudworth and Locke,—one of the immortal band who have resisted iniquity, borne persecution, and left to posterity the fragrant memory of holy self-denial, and of charity for the diseased and suffering; for his fellow-countrymen, whose minds had received no light of truth; for unregarded and untaught children; and for the heathen nations, who knew not the purifying influence of the Christian faith.

Through the gloomy years 1683 and 1684, unable to appear in public as a preacher, Baxter continued to write quarto volumes. Some of them, especially "Catholic Communion Defended," and "Catholic Communion doubly Defended," are not without interest in our day. But he was not yet outside the circle of the storm which had so long and terribly beaten upon him: for the Court was more and more resolved to punish the surviving Puritan clergymen, and if not to make their disagreement from any practice of the Church impossible, to prevent them from expressing an opinion hostile to the Government. "In 1684, while I lay in pain and languishing," says Baxter, "the justices of the sessions sent warrants to apprehend me, about a thousand more being in catalogue to be all bound to their good behaviour. I thought they would send me six months to prison for not taking the Oxford oath, and dwelling in London, and so I refused to open my chamber-door to them, their warrant not being to break it open; but they set six officers at my study door, who watched all night, and kept me from my bed and food, so that the next day I yielded to them, who carried me, scarce able to stand, to the sessions, and bound me in four hundred pounds' bond to my good behaviour. I desired to know what my crime was, and who were my accusers; but they told me it was for no fault, but to secure the Government in evil times, and that they had a list of many suspected persons that they must do the like with, as well as me. I desired to know for what I was numbered with the suspected, and by whose accusation; but they gave me good words, and would not tell me. I told them I would rather they sent me to gaol than put to wrong others, by being bound with me in bonds that I was likely to break to-morrow; for if there did but five persons come in when I was praying, they would take it for a breach of good behaviour. They told me not if they came on other business unexpectedly, and not to a set meeting, nor yet if we did nothing contrary to law and the practice of the Church. I told them our innocency was not now any security to us. If two beggar-women did but stand in the street, and swear that I spake contrary to the law, though they heard me not, my bonds and liberty were at their will; for I myself, lying on my bed, heard Mr. J. R. preach in a chapel on the other side of my chamber, and yet one Sibil Dash and Elizabeth Cappell, two miserable, poor women who made a trade of it, swore to the justices that it was another that preached, and they had thus sworn against many worthy persons in Hackney and elsewhere, on which their goods were seized for great mulcts or fines. To all this I had no answer, but that I must give bond, when they knew that I was not likely to break the behaviour, unless by lying in bed in pain. On the 11th of December, 1684, I was forced in all my pain and weakness to be carried to the sessions-house, or else my bonds of four hundred pounds would have been judged forfeit. The more moderate justices who promised my discharge, would none of them be there, but left the work to Sir William Smith and the rest; who openly declared that they had nothing against me, and took me for innocent, but that I must continue bound lest others should expect to be discharged also; which I openly refused. My sureties, however, would be bound against my declared will, lest I should die in gaol, and so I must continue. Yet they discharged others as soon as I was gone. I was told they did all by instructions from ——, and that the main end was to restrain me from writing; which now should I do with the greatest caution, they will pick out something that a jury may take for a breach of my bonds. January 17th, I was forced again to be carried to the sessions, and after divers good words, which put me in expectation of freedom, when I was gone, one Justice Deerham said that it was likely these persons solicited for my freedom that they might hear me in conventicles. On that they bound me again in a four hundred pound bond for above a quarter of a year; and so it is like it will be till I die or worse; though no one ever accused me for any conventicle or preaching since they took all my books and goods about two years ago, and I for the most part keep my bed."

Never was English liberty in greater danger than in the last year of the reign of Charles II. Apprehension and gloom prevailed among all classes, and some of the ablest men, the sons of them who had taken active part for and against the Crown in the last generation, now began to hold counsel on the state of public affairs. The utmost precaution was required, for a tyrannical Government is ever timid, suspicious, and watchful. But the king was resolved at all hazards upon an absolute rule. The charters of cities and towns one after another were taken away from them. The judges were the abject servants of the Court. The juries were either bribed or terrified; so that Charles could gain such verdicts as he wished against persons charged with opposition to his Government. The clergy, with all their great influence in the national life, were unable to resist the rapid progress of the king to a pure despotism; and there were among them some of the best of those able and eloquent men, whose names are precious in English memory. If they, on the one hand, had prudently abated something of their severity towards the Nonconformists, the Government, on the other, had relaxed or remitted none of those methods of repression which they had long adopted, and which modern opinion condemns as useless and unwise. Charles II., who had learned nothing from the adversities of his father, after gradually collecting a considerable number of troops in London, imagined that he was strong enough to possess himself of that absolute authority at the attainment of which he had long and craftily aimed. The freedom of Englishmen was never in more peril. His cruel brother, the Duke of York, was at hand to suggest or to help as occasion might require. The king had no Parliament to express opinion upon his designs, nor to control his movements; and men, who at every risk would have resisted his attempts, had died on the scaffold, or were imprisoned, or had fled the country to escape arrest and execution; but, as the hour of confident security often precedes the time of greatest hazard and danger, so a tempest suddenly burst from his summer's sky, and all was changed.

Through the winter of 1685, men said that the king was in more vigorous health than for many years past, and it was thought that his habit of passing much of the day in the open air would prevent the recurrence of gout, from which at intervals he had suffered; but the unexpected return of that insidious disorder had prevented him for some weeks from the exercise of rapid walking, to which he had long accustomed himself and his companions. Unequal to active exertion, he spent the greater part of each day in his laboratory; for he and Prince Rupert, to whom the invention of the beautiful art of mezzotint engraving has been ascribed, often amused themselves in making such experiments as the imperfect knowledge of chemistry at that time permitted. In his Diary, on Sunday, 25th of January, Evelyn writes: "Dr. Dove preached before the king. I saw this evening such a scene of profuse gaming, and the king in the midst of his three concubines, as I had never before seen. Luxurious dallying and profaneness." On the Sunday following, the first day of February, Evelyn again visited the court, and he writes of what he saw there: "I can never forget the inexpressible luxury and profaneness, gaming, and all dissoluteness, and, as it were, total forgetfulness of God (it being

Sunday evening), which I was witness of, the king sitting and toying with his concubines, Portsmouth, Cleveland, and Mazarine; a French boy singing love-songs in that glorious gallery, whilst about twenty of the great courtiers and other dissolute persons were at basset round a large table, a bank of at least 2,000 in gold before them, upon which two gentlemen who were with me made reflexions with astonishment. Six days after, all was in the dust!" On that Sunday, Charles felt himself out of health, his appetite had failed, and he took little food except a mouthful or two of soup, of which he complained it was too thick, and not to his taste. He passed a restless night, and in the morning Dr. King, who often assisted him in making chemical experiments, found that the king spoke confusedly and incoherently. Before he could examine him, Charles fell down, his face becoming swollen and black, and his eyes distorted. The physician promptly used his lancet, and with the flow of blood the king's consciousness was restored. On Tuesday he seemed to be recovering, but on Thursday another fit came on, and the physicians told the Duke of York that Charles could not live till the morrow. Sancroft, Bishop of London, and Ken, Bishop of Bath and Wells, exhorted him to repent and to prepare for another world; but he gave no heed to their renewed entreaties. His concubine, the Duchess of Portsmouth, sat on the bed, nursing him as a wife would nurse her husband. James whispered in his brother's ear, and Charles immediately requested all persons who were present, except two of his attendants, to leave the room, and James brought in Huddlestone, a Roman Catholic priest, who was said to have saved the king's life at the battle of Worcester. The door of the bedroom was doubly locked, and it was opened only when Lord Faversham called for a glass of water. It was said afterwards at Rome, that the king, when receiving the Sacrament from the priest's hand, was unable without water to swallow what was administered to him; but the priest gave the king extreme unction, and absolution, of which assuredly he had great need. All was very hurriedly done, the door was opened, and the Anglican bishops and others were re-admitted, in utter ignorance of all that which had taken place in their absence. The pious Ken again exhorted the king, and seven times urged him in vain to receive the Sacrament; but the king replied that he had no strength for it. Ken gave him absolution, and then, it was said, the two bishops and the others, with the concubine, kneeled down, and the king gave all of them his blessing. Apprehensive that he was drawing near to his end, Charles formally placed the government in the hands of his brother, and he again urged the duke, "not to let poor Nelly starve," referring to his mistress, Eleanor Gwyn; saying, "he had always loved her, and he loved her now to the last." The unhappy and long-neglected queen sent in to "ask his pardon for any offence she might have committed." Charles, with some approach to penitence, as charity would hope, replied, "It is I that ought to ask her pardon." So far as men knew, he spoke no word of religion, nor of special regret for his sins, nor for the innocent blood he had shed, nor of his large debts; but he painfully lingered on with a flickering light of life, until shortly after eleven o'clock on the morning of Friday, the sixth day of February, 1685, when the awful darkness fell, and he passed away from the scene of his injustice, revelry, and wasted existence. He had reached only his fifty-fourth year, and after a reign over Great Britain of nearly twenty-five years. Some of his physicians not unreasonably suspected that the king had died from poison, as men generally at that time believed his sister, the Duchess of Orleans, had died; but the truth cannot in either case be determined. His death caused great surprise in London, and the citizens lamented it; not so much from their regard for the monarch, as from their fear of his successor, who was well known to be hostile to their religion, and unfavourable to their liberty. Charles, just after his accession, had violated the graves of the republicans; and men reported that his own funeral was singularly mean, and that in the arrangements of it which related to his state and dignity, the king had deserved better treatment at the hands of his brother than to have been hurried to his tomb without the ceremonies which befitted his rank. John Evelyn remarks of it: "Feb. 14th. The king this night was very obscurely buried in a vault under Henry VII.'s chapel at Westminster, without any manner of pomp, and soon forgotten after all this vanity."

Few kings had seen greater changes of fortune than Charles II., and few ever learned so little the practical wisdom which adversity teaches. He was faithfully followed by a large number of men, who expended in his service all their available means, and many of whom he forgot or neglected when prosperity came to him. He seems to have had little taste for literature, although the discoveries and investigations of awakening science amused him; and to have manifested some of the worst vices without compensating virtues. He had a cheerful affability and courtesy, but little kindness of nature; for he never forgave an injury, nor showed compassion to an enemy when he fell into his power. He hated the restraints of religion, and his example of frivolity and debauchery ruined many, who were attached to him by his gentle bearing and urbanity. Bishop Burnet's observation appears to be correct, that there are some points of resemblance between his reign and that of Tiberius, more perhaps in the artfulness with which he promoted his cruel and arbitrary designs, than in any other quality; and Burnet even imagines that the king resembled that ferocious emperor in the features of his face. But that which is most repulsive in his life is the constant hypocrisy of his declared zeal for the Anglican Church, while throughout his reign he was really a Roman Catholic; dexterously concealing the fact even to the last.

The Duke of York, who, by the death of Charles, had become king, with the title of James II., at the first meeting of his Council, promised that he would maintain and defend the Church of England, as it was established by law; intending, as it then seemed, to please or pacify the citizens of London; and people foolishly used a phrase, which was repeated throughout the country, "We have now the word of a king, and a word never yet broken." Dr. Sharp, Archbishop of York, so thoroughly believed in James's promise, that, when preaching at the time at St. Lawrence, Jewry, he said: "As to our religion, we have the word of the king, which, with reverence be it spoken, is as sacred as my text." James soon gave practical proof of his sincerity; for, on the first Sunday after his accession, he went publicly to Roman Catholic mass. He began his reign with the determination to be an absolute monarch, and he commanded the duties of excise and customs to be levied, which were given to Charles only for his life. To the Scottish Parliament the king wrote: "I am resolved to maintain my power in its greatest lustre, that I may be better able to defend your religion against fanatics;" and he induced them to increase the existing cruel laws against the Covenanters. These unhappy zealots were threatened with death if they went to a conventicle, or even if they listened to a preacher on a hill-side, or in a market-place. The royal soldiers were quartered on them, with free license to plunder and harass their families. James was eager to emulate the persecution of the French Protestants by Louis XIV. The miseries of the Huguenots in France were equalled by those of dissident Protestants in Scotland; and there is no darker page in all the history of the northern kingdom, than that which relates the ferocity of the government of James, and the sufferings of the weak and helpless, who were punished for virtuously adhering to their particular form of religion. In England, the new king expressed his determination to enforce the laws for the suppression of differences in public worship, which had been passed during his brother's reign, and permission was given to apply them universally. All the chapels in which Puritans and Nonconformists assembled were immediately closed; informers were again employed in their iniquitous work; and grave citizens were watched and harassed, and many of them arrested on false accusations. Soldiers were directed to aid the civil power in dispersing assemblies, and in seizing the preachers, who, if taken with the richer persons in their congregations, were hurried before the magistrates, heavily fined, or summarily imprisoned. Many of them were arrested or incarcerated upon suspicion of being associated with conspirators, or merely on the plea of public security. Philip Henry relates his repeated confinements in Chester Castle, although he lived as a peaceful country-gentleman,—one of the most loyal and religious subjects of the crown, and abundant in charities. If the soldiers at any time surprised an assembly in a preacher's house, and he escaped capture at their hands, they searched his dwelling throughout, rifled his coffers, burst open his cellars, ravaged his library, turned the sick out of their beds, treated the women of the family with indecent violence, and left their home robbed and wasted; as in Germany the pikemen of Tilly devastated the dwellings of the inhabitants of towns they stormed in the Thirty Years' War. The preachers were often compelled to lurk in villages distant from their homes, or to go out only at nightfall stealthily and in disguise.

Baxter did not continue the memorial of his life beyond the year 1685. The great severity of the Government, his inability to preach in safety, and his increasing disease, made it necessary for him to withdraw from public ministration. Only a few of the ejected clergy who then survived were his trusted friends. Although he was generally considered to be the leader of the Presbyterian party, it is doubtful if he ever in heart seceded from the English Church. The effect of his early education, and especially of his study of Hooker's "Ecclesiastical Polity," with the experience of a conscientious, varied, and long investigation, convinced him that the Anglican Church was based upon Holy Scripture and upon the doctrines and practice of the earlier Fathers. So that he never forgot his original position as one of its clergy; and in his later years he often went to its services, as a man returns to the home of his youth, joined in its prayers, and kneeled at its Sacrament. He would include within the Church all who believed in the truths contained in the Apostles' Creed, the Lord's Prayer, and the Ten Commandments. He held that a true Catholic's chief work was to be a peace-maker, and that it should be the aim of a Christian's life to seek peace and to maintain it, placing the unity of the Church upon that which is essential to the Church. In one of his later writings on the sense of the Articles of the Anglican Church, he says: "If I have hit on the true meaning, I subscribe my assent, and I thank God that this national Church hath doctrine so sound." Many events and reflections of his later years were left unwritten, and the student of history must regret that his Autobiography ends before some of the most painful portions of his career were reached. It may be conjectured, that the Baxter-manuscripts contain much which would throw light upon years of which the published records are few and indistinct. We owe it chiefly to Calamy and Sylvester that anything has been made known of the last period of his life. They had frequent association with him; but no record they have left has the originality, vigour, and freshness of his own narrative. The lover of art may look with pleasure at the works of men who were pupils in the schools of the great masters of painting in Italy, Holland, and Britain; but at the very best they are only the shadows of the glories which remain to us of Raffaelle and Guido, of Rembrandt, and of Gainsborough and Reynolds. Baxter's own narrative of his life and times, as it is the most interesting, is certainly one of the fullest memorials of the evil days of the reigns of the later Stuarts. This work, entitled "Reliquiæ Baxterianæ," was printed after his death by his friend Sylvester, who seems not to have acted as an editor, but simply to have published it in the unarranged state in which the writer left it. Baxter has artlessly narrated the events of his life and times from the year of his birth, 1615, to 1684, dividing the book into three parts—the first, from his birth to the Commonwealth; the second contains some account of the Westminster Assembly, and of the civil wars; and the third brings the memorial down to 1684. Parts of this Autobiography have necessarily been used in the present narrative, because the book contains some of the best sources of information, and the facts are recorded with guileless simplicity, and in vigorous language. Sylvester, in attempting to explain the occasional incoherence in the history, states that Baxter wrote it as his other works and studies and frequent infirmities permitted; that he was more intent upon the matter than the method; and finding his evening shadows growing long, as the presage of his own approaching and expected change, he was willing that the work should be done somewhat imperfectly than not at all. In "His Own Life," Dr. Calamy says of this long-expected and much-desired book, that "Baxter left it with his other manuscripts to the care of his beloved friend Mr. Sylvester, who was chary of it to the last degree, and not very forward to let it be seen. I found the good man counted it a sort of sacred thing to have any hand in making alterations of any sort, in which I could not but apprehend he was cramped by a sort of superstition." The historical student, when so fortunate as to obtain the original folio edition of this book, will find that he has not only a faithful record of the days in which tyranny grew stronger, reached its summit, and was overthrown, and the foundation of English freedom strongly laid, but also the delineation of one of the most remarkable of our countrymen; all his heart, his opinions, his public work, his religious difficulties, his many sorrows, his ardent love of truth and freedom, his holy living, his lifelong charities, described by a hand which erred, if at all, from inadvertence; and the whole forming one of the important parts of the national literature.

CHAPTER XXV.

1685—1686.

AFTER the accession of James II. to the throne, he followed his brother's example in avenging himself upon his enemies. The character of this monarch presents an instructive study to the philosophical historian. He had inherited the imperfections of James I. and of Charles I.; he had all the obstinacy of the former, and the determination to be despotic, which ruined the latter; with a natural cruelty of disposition, and a passion for revenge, which united made him one of the worst of men and one of the most merciless of kings. He promised, on attaining supreme power, to maintain the Church as established by law, to govern justly, and to abandon his course of adultery with Mrs. Sedley and others; but with the innate duplicity of his race, he said one thing while intending another. Exerting all his power to destroy the integrity of the Church, from the beginning of his reign he attempted to establish a tyranny. Vicious habitually, he appointed unprincipled judges; he relied upon packed or intimidated juries; he punished the convicted by death, if it were possible; or by hurtful imprisonment, and ruinous fines and confiscations. Heartless, superstitious, and licentious; endeavouring to make everything subservient to his will; a cruel persecutor, to whose nature moderation was impossible; he left unemployed no method of violence and of corruption to attain his ends. It was whispered at Court that his reign began with bad omens, which were much considered in that age, when the human mind was not yet freed from slavish fears; and it was long remembered that at his coronation, on the Feast of St. George, when he refused to follow the example of all his predecessors since the Reformation, in receiving the Sacrament according to the Anglican rite, that his crown proved larger than his head could bear; that the canopy over him fell down; and that his illegitimate son by Mrs. Sedley died on that day.

When James had been only a few weeks upon the throne, he resolved upon the public prosecution of two men, differing immensely in character, but representing parties in the State who were equally hostile to his principle of arbitrary government. By punishing the one he would gratify his own malignant passion, and the revenge of the Roman Catholics, who had suffered much both for the exercise of their religion, and from false charges of disloyalty to the crown. By the second prosecution he would strike terror into the Puritans, whom James never forgot as the successful opponents of his father, and who were known to advocate the widest freedom both in religious and in civil affairs. He determined therefore that he would inaugurate his government by the prosecution of Titus Oates on the one hand, and of Richard Baxter on the other. A judge was selected to give sentence in these two cases, upon whom the king could rely for unscrupulousness and severity in his conduct towards them who were to be brought to trial. Judge Jeffries was a man after James's own heart; and among all the lawyers who had ever presided in Westminster Hall, through ages of darkness and wrong, no one could have been found who would more naturally and willingly adjudicate in accordance with the wishes of a cruel king. Dr. Titus Oates, who had long been in prison, was brought to his trial, on May 7th, 1685. He was assailed with bitter and unseemly language by the judges who tried him. From Jeffries, directed by the king, Oates could expect no mercy. That ferocious servant of the Crown sentenced him to be stripped of his priestly clothing, to be put in the pillory in Palace Yard and at the Royal Exchange, to be whipped through the streets, on one day from Aldgate to Newgate, and the next day from Newgate to Tyburn. He was to be imprisoned as long as he lived, and to be placed in the pillory five times in every year. The sentence was illegal, and shockingly cruel; the secular court had really no power to deprive him of his office as a priest, nor to condemn him to perpetual imprisonment. The intention of the judges no doubt was that Oates should be flogged to death. James heard of the sentence with joy; for the race he came of delighted to reflect upon the sufferings of their enemies. The flogging on the first day was so severe, that Oates was taken back to prison nearly dead. Some persons pleaded with the king that the rest of the sentence should be remitted, as, men said, the unhappy man's back had the appearance of having been flayed, and was horribly swollen. The king replied to the entreaty for mercy, "He shall go through with it, if he has breath in his body." Oates, on the second day, was placed on a sledge, because unable to walk in consequence of the dreadful previous scourging. He received in all seventeen hundred stripes, and he gained the admiration of many persons from the patient fortitude with which he bore the terrible infliction of the long-designed cruelty of the king; who was so much pleased by the exact account he received of Oates's suffering, that he resolved to make use of severe public flogging, on every occasion in which fortune should permit him to have the pleasure of avenging himself on them who were convicted of plotting against his government; for it were better to torture them than to kill them. In such manner this "most religious king," as he was entitled in the solemnities of public prayer, used his brief authority.

His success in the conviction and punishment of Oates determined James to hasten the trial of Baxter, who was loyal to the sovereign, esteemed even by his enemies as a man of unstained life, and of eminent ability; but he was held to be the representative of a party who must be terrified into submission to the throne. Before his accession, James had hinted that, when power came to his hand, he would punish him. In the early part of the year, Baxter had published a "Paraphrase of the New Testament," which James had been persuaded was a seditious and dangerous book. Roger L'Estrange, who had for years pursued Baxter with malignant hostility, is said to have suggested the passages in the book upon which prosecution might be founded, and the king's desire gratified. A warrant was issued for his arrest, and, on the 28th day of February, he was committed to the King's-Bench prison. His acute suffering from illness made it necessary for him to apply for a *habeas corpus*, and obtaining it, he went into the country till term began. On the 14th of May, he pleaded not guilty to the information which had been laid against him; and on the 18th of May, his counsel moved the court that the trial might be for a short time postponed, on account of Baxter's ill-health. Jeffries roared out in a half-drunken rage: "I will not give him a minute's time more to save his life. We have had to deal with other sorts of persons, but now we have a saint to deal with, and I know how to deal with saints as well as sinners. Yonder stands Oates in the pillory, and he says he suffers for the truth, and so says Baxter; but if Baxter did but stand on the other side of the pillory with him, I should say two of the greatest rogues and rascals in the kingdom stood there." The biographers, who were eyewitnesses of the trial, supply its chief incidents, which Lord Macaulay and others have verbally reproduced in their narratives of it. One trustworthy account of it is that which Calamy gives; but Mr. Orme, the laborious editor of the last complete English edition of Baxter's Practical Works, gives, in an extract from the Baxter-manuscripts, a vivid relation of the occurrences in court, written by one who was present there. The charge specifically brought against Baxter was, that he reflected on the bishops of the Anglican Church in a manner which legally was seditious. A few of the passages to which objection was made may be referred to here:—Mark iii. 6,

"It is little folly to doubt there be devils, while devils incarnate dwell among us. What else but devils, sure, could ceremonious hypocrites consult with politic royalists to destroy the Son of God for saving men's health and lives by miracle?" Mark ix. 39, "Men that preach in Christ's name, therefore, are not to be silenced, though faulty; if they do more good than harm, dreadful then be the case of them that silence Christ's faithful ministers." Mark iv. 31, "These persecutors and the Romans had some charity and consideration, in that they were restrained by the fear of the people, and did not accuse and fine them as for routs, riots, and seditions." Luke x. 2, "Priests now are many, but labourers are few. What men are they that hate and silence the faithfullest labourers, suspecting that they are not for their interest?"—The quotations from "The Paraphrase" are sufficiently harmless, and in our time they would pass without censure. But in the days of the Tyranny, the government of James saw enmity in opinions which did not admit the Divine right of the king to rule, and the perfectness of his administration of affairs. The indictment against Baxter has been preserved, and is worthy in part of being transferred to these pages:—"Quod Richardus Baxter, nuper de, &c., Clericus existens person' seditiosa et factiosa, pravæ mentis, impiæ, inquietæ, turbulent' disposition' et conversation', ac machinans, practicans, et intendens, quantum in ipso fuit, non solum pacem et communem tranquillitat' dict' Dom' Regis infra, hoc regnum Angl' inquietare, molestare, et perturbare ac seditionem, discord' et malevolent' int' ligeos et fideles subdit' dict' Dom' Regis movere, p'curare, et excitare, verum etiam sinceram, piam, beatam, et pacificam Protestant' Religion' infra hoc regn' Angl' usitat', ac Prelat', episcopos, aliosq: Clericos in ecclesia Anglicana legibus hujus regni Angl' stabilit', ac Novum Testamentu' Dom' Salvator' nostri Jesu Christi in contempt' et vilipend' inducere et inutile reddere; quodq: p'd R. B. ad nequissimas, nefandissimas et diabolicas intention' suas, pred' perimplend' perficiend' et ad effect' redigend' 14 die Febr', anno regni dict Dom' Jacobi Secundi, &c., primo, vi et armis, &c., apud, &c., falso illicite, injuste, nequit', factiose, seditiose et irreligiose fecit, composuit, scripsit, impressit, et publicavit, et fieri, componi, scribi, imprimi, et publicari causavit, quendam falsum, seditiosum, libellosum, factiosum, et irreligiosum librum, intitulat' A Paraphrase on the New Testament, with Notes doctrinal and practical. In quo quidem falso, seditioso, libelloso, factioso et irreligioso libro int' al' content' fuer' hœ falsæ, factiosæ malitiosæ scandalosæ et seditiosæ sententiæ de eisdem Prelat' Episcopis, aliisq : Clericis ecclesiæ hujus regn' in his Angl' verbis sequend' videl't. Note, Are not these preachers and prelates (Epòs aliosq : clericos præd' Ecclesiæ hujus regn' Angl' innuend') then the least and basest that preach and tread down Christian love of all that dissent from any of their presumptions, and so preach down not the least but the great command ? Et ult' idem altoru' dict' Dom' Regis nunc general' pro eodem Dom' Rege dat cur', hic intelligi et informari, quod in al' loco in p'd' falso, scandaloso, seditioso, et irreligioso libro, int' al' content' fuer' hæ al' falsæ, libellosæ, scandalosæ, seditiosæ, et irreligiosæ sentent' sequent' de Clericis Ecclesiæ hujus regn', videl't. Note, It is folly to doubt whether there be Devils, while Devils incarnate live here amongst us (Clericos pred' hujus regni Angl' innuendo); what else but Devils, sure, could make ceremonious hypocrites (Clericos pred' innuendo) consult with politic royalists (ligeos et fidel' subdit" dict' Dom' Regis hujus regni Angl' innuendo) to destroy the Son of God for saving men's health and lives by miracle ?" &c., &c., &c.

His friend, Sir Henry Ashurst, had retained the services of some of the ablest members of the English bar in defence of Baxter, and who rose to eminence in more peaceful times, when freedom had been restored to the country. After the counsel for the Crown had given reasons and details for the prosecution, Pollexfen addressed the court and the jury in Baxter's behalf. Judge Jeffries snorted and squeaked, urged by the king, it would seem, to spare nothing to gain the conviction of

Baxter; and half-maddened by brandy, and by the excitement of trying a man whose fame was in every town of the kingdom. The barrister temperately urged, that in preparing his defence he had found it necessary to consult some of the chief writers on the New Testament, who agreed with Baxter in many of the opinions he had expressed in his Paraphrase, beginning with Dr. Hammond; and, "Gentlemen," he said to the jury, "though Mr. Baxter made an objection against you, as not fit judges of Greek, which has been overruled, I hope you understand English, common sense, and can read." Jeffries roared in a hideous rage at the barrister, that "he should not sit there to hear him preach and cant to the jury beforehand." "No, my lord," he replied, "I am counsel for Mr. Baxter, and shall offer nothing but what is *ad rem.*" "Come, then," said Jeffries, "what do you say to this count? Read it, clerk, on Matt. xii. 38-40. Is he not an old knave to interpret this as belonging to liturgies?" "So do others of the Church of England," Pollexfen replied, "who would be loath so to wrong the cause of liturgies as to make them a novel invention, or not to be able to date them as early as the Scribes and Pharisees." Jeffries roared again, squeaked through his nose, mimicked the Puritan clergy, as the actors were accustomed to do in the comedies which pleased Charles II., ridiculing their supposed manner in praying; and he said, "No, no, Mr. Pollexfen, they were long-winded extempore prayers, such as they used to say when they appropriated God to themselves: 'Lord, we are Thy people, Thy peculiar people, Thy dear people.'" "Why, my lord," said the barrister, "some will think it hard measure to stop these men's mouths, and not let them speak through their noses." But Jeffries had taken brandy enough to rouse the brutal insolence of his nature, and he screamed out, "Pollexfen, I know you well. I will set a mark upon you; you are the patron of the faction. This is an old rogue, who has poisoned the world with his Kidderminster doctrine. Don't we know how he preached formerly, 'Curse ye Meroz; curse them bitterly that come not to the help of the Lord, to the help of the Lord against the mighty'? He encouraged all the women and maids to bring their bodkins and thimbles to carry on their war against the king of ever-blessed memory. An old schismatical knave, a hypocritical villain." Pollexfen replied, "I beseech your lordship suffer me a word for my client. It is well known to all intelligent men of age in this nation that these things do not apply to the character of Mr. Baxter, who wished as well to the king and the royal family as Mr. Love, who lost his head for endeavouring to bring in the son long before he was restored. And, my lord, Mr. Baxter's loyal and peaceable spirit King Charles would have rewarded with a bishopric, when he came in, if he would have conformed." Jeffries shouted, "Aye, aye, we know that; but what ailed the old blockhead, the unthankful villain, that he would not conform? Was he wiser or better than other men? He hath been, ever since, the spring of the faction. I am sure he hath poisoned the world with his linsey-woolsey doctrine." Then his face flamed with rage, and he raved and shouted again, "The conceited, stubborn, fanatical dog! Hang him! This old fellow hath cast more reproach upon the constitution and discipline of our Church than will be wiped off these hundred years; but I'll handle him for it; for, by G——, he deserves to be whipped through the city." Pollexfen replied, "My lord, I am sure these things are not *ad rem.* Some men think it very hard these men should be forced against their consciences from the Church. But that is not my business. I know not what reasons sway other men's consciences; my business is to plead for my client, and to answer the charge of dangerous sedition, which is alleged to be contained in the 'Paraphrase of the New Testament.'" Mr. Wallop, who followed for the defence, said the matter depending as a point of doctrine should be referred to his bishop, but that Baxter's book on the New Testament contained many eternal truths; and that the real libellers were the men who drew the information against him. "My lord," he added, "I humbly conceive the bishops Mr. Baxter speaks of, as your lordship, if you have read Church history, must confess, were the plagues of the Church and of the world." Jeffries said, "Mr. Wallop, I observe you are in all these dirty causes, and were it not for you gentlemen of the long robe, who should have more wit and honesty than to support and hold up these factious knaves by the chin, we should not be at the pass we are." Wallop replied, "My lord, I humbly conceive that the passages accused are natural deductions from the text. I am counsel for the defendant, and if I understand either Latin or English, the information now brought against Mr. Baxter upon such a slight ground is a greater reflection upon the Church of England than anything contained in the book he is accused for." "Sometimes," cried Jeffries, "you humbly conceive, and sometimes you are very positive. You talk of your skill in Church history, and of your understanding Latin and English. I think I understand something of them as well as you; but in short must tell you, if you do not understand your duty better, I shall teach it you." Another able barrister followed, and then Baxter ventured to say, "My lord, I have been so moderate with respect to the Church of England, that I have incurred the censure of many of the Dissenters on that account." "Baxter for bishops!" shouted the infuriated judge, "that is a merry conceit indeed. Turn to it, turn to it." Rotherham, the barrister, then turned to the passage, and read, that "great respect is due to those truly called to be bishops among us." "Aye, this is your Presbyterian cant," said Jeffries; "'truly called to be bishops'; that is, himself and such rascals, called to be bishops of Kidderminster and other such places. Bishops set apart by such factious, snivelling Presbyterians as himself; a Kidderminster bishop he means. According to the saying of a late learned author—and every parish shall maintain a tithe pig metropolitan." Baxter again tried to speak, and Jeffries, forgetting the dignity and decorum of the office he held, burst out into vulgar reviling: "Richard, Richard, dost thou think we'll hear thee poison the court? Richard, thou art an old fellow, an old knave; thou hast written books enough to load a cart, every one as full of sedition as an egg is full of meat. Hadst thou been whipped out of thy writing-trade forty years ago, it had been happy. Thou pretendest to be a preacher of the gospel of peace, and thou hast one foot in the grave; it is time for thee to think what account thou intendest to give. But leave thee to thyself, and I see that thou'lt go on as thou hast begun; but, by the grace of God, I'll look after thee. I know thou hast a mighty party; and I see a great number of the brotherhood in corners, waiting to see what will become of their might Don, a doctor of the party (Dr. Bates) at your elbow; but by the grace of Almighty God, I'll crush you all. Come, what do you say for yourself, you old knave?—come, speak up. What doth he say? I'm not afraid of you, for all the snivelling calves you have got about you." Baxter said, "Your lordship need not fear, for I'll not hurt you. But these things will surely be understood one day; what fools one sort of Protestants are made, to persecute the other. I am not concerned to answer such stuff, but I am ready to produce my writings for the confutation of all this, and my life and conversation are known to many in this nation." Attwood, another of Baxter's counsel, endeavoured by reading the text to meet the charges against him. Jeffries vociferated, "You shan't draw me into a conventicle, nor your snivelling parson neither." The barrister urged that he ought to be heard, that he might do the best for his client. The judge insolently ordered him again and again to sit down. The other counsel, Williams and Phipps, saw that it was useless to argue with a brutal judge, inflamed by brandy, and by his indecent excitement setting aside justice at the bidding of the king. The summing up was as flattering to James as it was unfair to Baxter, of whom Jeffries said, "It was notoriously known there was a design to ruin the king and nation. The old game had been renewed; and this person had been the main incendiary. He is as modest now as can be; but time was when no man was so ready at 'Bind your kings with chains, and your nobles with fetters of iron;'

and, 'To your tents, O Israel.' Gentlemen, for God's sake don't let us be gulled twice in an age." When the judge had ended his charge, Baxter exclaimed, "Does your lordship think that any jury will pretend to pass a verdict upon me upon such a trial?" Jeffries replied, "I'll warrant you, Mr. Baxter; don't you trouble yourself about that." The packed and bribed jury immediately gave a verdict of guilty against Baxter, who, referring to Chief-Justice Hale, said, "There was once a judge who had better thoughts of me." Jeffries answered, "There's not an honest man in England but takes you for a great knave." Sir Henry Ashurst carried Baxter in his carriage to his home, and the judge hastened to tell the cruel tyrant at Whitehall that the hated preacher was convicted. Had Jeffries been able to look forward only three years into the future, and to see his unfeeling master a miserable fugitive from London, and himself, hated of all men, disguised in the dress of a coal-heaver, hiding in an obscure tavern, and then, half dead with fear, hurried from the blows and curses of the rabble, and safe only as a prisoner in the Tower; he might have wished to be gentle to the aged divine placed unjustly at the bar. In that after time, in his own shame and suffering, he may have bitterly remembered, among his other atrocities, how he heaped insult and outrage upon him in his weakness and dishonour, when by brutal insolence and low invective he lost dignity and degraded the tribunal.

Baxter quickly acted upon the advice of his friends to appeal against the iniquity of the trial; and, as a clergyman of the English Church, he asked for the interposition on his behalf of the Bishop of London. "My Lord,—Being by episcopal ordination vowed to the sacred ministry, and bound not to desert it, when by painful diseases and debility I waited for my change, I durst not spend my last days in idleness, and knew not how better to serve the Church than by writing a 'Paraphrase on the New Testament,' purposely fitted to the use of the most ignorant, and the reconciling of doctrinal differences about texts variously expounded. Far was it from my design to reproach the Church or draw men from it, having therein pleaded for diocesans as successors of the apostles over many churches; though I confute the overthrowing opinion which setteth them over but one church, denying the parishes to be churches. But some persons, offended, it is like, at some other passages in the book, have thought fit to say that I scandalised the Church of England; and an information being exhibited in the King's Bench, at a trial before a common jury, on my owning the book, they forthwith found me guilty without hearing my defence, and I have cause to expect a severe judgment, the beginning of the next term. All this is on a charge that my unquestionable words were meant by me to scandalise the Church, which I utterly deny. If God will have me end a painful, weary life by such a suffering, I hope I shall finish my course with joy; but my conscience commandeth me to value the Church's strength and honour before my life, and I ought not to be silent under the scandal of suffering as an enemy to it. Nor would I have my sufferings increase men's prejudice against it. I have lived in its communion, and conformed to as much as the Act of Uniformity obliged me in my condition; I have drawn multitudes into the Church, and written to justify the Church and ministry against separation, when the 'Paraphrase' was in the press; and my displeasing writings (whose eagerness and faults I justify not) have been my earnest pleadings for the healing of a divided people, and the strengthening of the Church by love and concord on possible terms. I owe satisfaction to you that are my diocesan, and therefore presume to send you a copy of the information against me, and my answer to the particular accusations, humbly entreating you to spare so much time from your weighty business as to peruse them, or to refer them to be perused for your satisfaction. For expositions of Scripture to be thus tried by such juries, as often they are but called seditious, is not the old way of managing Church differences; and of what consequence you will easily judge.

If your lordship be satisfied that I am no enemy to the Church, and that my punishment will not be for its interest, I hope you will vouchsafe to present my petition to His Majesty, that my appeal to the Church may suspend the sentence till my diocesan, or whom His Majesty shall appoint, may hear me, and report their sense of the cause. By which your lordship will, I doubt not, many ways serve the welfare of the Church, as well as oblige your languishing humble servant."

It is uncertain whether the bishop was able to soften the heart of James, whose cold and cruel nature had neither misgiving nor clemency; but Jeffries may have counter-worked the intercession of the prelate, who no doubt did all which became his office to lessen the punishment to be inflicted upon the diseased and aged clergyman. There can be no question that the conduct of that ferocious judge contributed to the revulsion of public feeling against James, and to his ultimate downfall. The second edition of the "Paraphrase" contains a note, in which Baxter says: "Reader, it is like you heard how I was for this book, by the instigation of Sir Roger L'Estrange and some of the clergy, imprisoned nearly two years by Sir George Jeffries, Sir Francis Wilkins, and the rest of the judges of the King's Bench, after their preparatory restraints, and attendance under the most reproachful words, as if I had been the most odious person living, and not suffered at all to speak for myself. Had not the king taken off my fine, I had continued in prison till death. Because many desire to know what all this was for, I have here written the eight accusations which (after the great clergy search of my book) were brought in as seditious. I have never altered a word accused, that you may know the worst. What I said of the murderers of Christ, and the hypocrite Pharisees and their sins, the judge said I meant of the Church of England, though I have written for it, and still communicate with it."

On the 29th of June, Baxter was called up for judgment. Jeffries wished him to be publicly whipped through the city, a sentence which would have given pleasure to the king, and which would have satisfied the judge, after the sarcasms he had received in his court from the prisoner's counsellors; but the other judges would not consent that a man to whom a bishopric had been offered should be punished as a felon. Baxter was fined five hundred marks, to be imprisoned until it was paid, and to give security for his good conduct for seven years. Unable to pay the fine, he was taken to prison. There he remained for nearly two years, attended by his own servants; and he seems to have been spared forced labour and other indignities of a modern imprisonment. It is possible now to have only a few glimpses of those terrible days, but one is given in the Biography of Matthew Henry, the author of the well-known Commentary, and written by Sir Bickerton Williams, who wrote also the "Life of Philip Henry," one of the most valuable existing religious memorials of the period of the Tyranny. Matthew Henry writes from London to his father at Broad Oak: "I went into Southwark to Mr. Baxter. I was to wait upon him once before, and then he was busy. I found him in pretty comfortable circumstances, though a prisoner, in a private house near the prison, attended by his own man and maid. My good friend, Mr. S. Lawrence, went with me. He is in as good health as one can expect, and methinks looks better and speaks heartier than when I saw him last. The token you sent he would by no means be persuaded to accept, and was almost angry when I pressed it, from one outed as well as himself. He said he did not use to receive; and I understand since, his need is not great. We sat with him about an hour. I was very glad to find he so much approved of my present circumstances. He said he knew not why young men might not improve as by travelling abroad. He inquired for his Shropshire friends, and observed that of those gentlemen who were with him at Wem, he hears of none whose sons tread in their fathers' steps, but Colonel Hunt's. He inquired about Mr. Macworth's and Mr. Lloyd's (of Aston) children. He gave us some good counsel to prepare for trials; and said the best preparation for them was a life of faith, and a constant course of self-denial. He thought it harder constantly to deny temptations to sensual lusts and pleasures than to resist one single temptation to deny Christ for fear of suffering: the former requiring such constant watchfulness; however, after the former the latter will be easier. He said we who are young are apt to count upon great things, but we must not look for them, and much more to this purpose. He said he thought dying by sickness usually much more painful and dreadful than dying a violent death, especially considering the extraordinary supports which those have who suffer for righteousness' sake."

By paying the fine imposed by the court, Baxter knew he should not free himself from prosecutions in the future, and therefore he went to prison. Many of the Anglican clergy, who admired his character, and sympathised with him in his sufferings, visited him in his confinement, thus protesting against the injustice and cruelty of his trial; and if he had not freedom, he at least was preserved from the intrusion of spies, and had leisure to pursue his studies in peace, and to write some of his later books. Every kindness which his circumstances permitted was shown him by them who loved him, and the bitterness of imprisonment was lessened by the offices of friendship. While Baxter was undergoing the punishment to which Jeffries sentenced him, the king was harassing the Puritans with all imaginable severity: so that some of their ministers sought ordination, and returned to the English Church; and some of the clergy, protesting against the persecution of their religious fellow-citizens, joined the Nonconformists. In the villages around London, informers were especially active, assemblies of religionists were dispersed, and heavy fines exacted. Many of the Puritans removed their families to New England.

The unwise policy of Cromwell and of Charles II. was continued with increasing severity by James II.; but it was found impossible to heal religious differences by civil prosecution and the infliction of penalties. The more the Nonconformists were persecuted, the more resolute their dissent became: for compulsion is a bad argument. They used various methods of concealing the time and place of their assembling, and they agreed to meet in small numbers, late at night, or early in the morning; often changing their place of worship, and always keeping a careful watch against surprises. There are traditions, that where many Nonconformists lived in the same street, as often happened probably in Hackney, Stoke Newington, and in the northern parts of London, they opened communications from house to house; so that many families at once might hear the voice of the preacher, and that he might escape through one dwelling, if the constables entered another. The minister passed through the streets in various disguises; sometimes dressed as a mechanic, at others in the garb of a coachman. He had secret means of communicating with his congregation, and an active correspondence was maintained between them, which the Government was never able to discover. Sometimes clever informers detected the minister in his disguise, or found out the place of his preaching, which generally was a large room at a distance from the street, where no singing or music was used in the assembly; and frequent discoveries enriched the officers of the courts, and enabled the spies to live in the unenviable enjoyments of vice. It is probable that James adopted the same course of policy which Charles II. had pursued, in using excessive severity towards all classes of Nonconformists, that toleration might at length become necessary for the maintenance of the public peace, in the benefits of which the adherents of the Latin Church would have part. By the command of the king, who wished to familiarize the citizens of London to the sight of them, foreign ecclesiastics were seen in the streets; Franciscans, Carmelites, Benedictines, and members of other fraternities, dressed in the habits of their distinctive orders. Jesuit schools were opened in London, and in many parts of England. In some towns Roman Catholic chapels were built; even the bishops of that faith were consecrated in the palace; all men were forbidden to speak against them; and the king caused it to be announced, among the younger men at the Bar and in Parliament, that the surest way to quick preferment was to profess to be of his form of religion.

CHAPTER XXVI.

1686—1688.

THE trial and imprisonment of Baxter were soon followed by events which tested the strength of James's power to the utmost. The Earl of Argyll had landed in Scotland, and had raised an insurrection there, which was speedily quelled, and its leader taken and executed. In the west of England the Duke of Monmouth, one of the illegitimate sons of Charles II., disembarked with men and arms at Lyme, in Dorsetshire, rashly attempting the conquest of a powerful kingdom with small provision for success. He deserves the pity of posterity: the son of a profligate father, educated in a court to the last degree immoral, himself without virtue, ruined by indulgence, and deceived by flattery, he had neither the principle to resist temptation, nor the fortitude to meet danger. At first few persons of means or of rank joined him; but the country people flocked to him so largely, that in a few days he found himself at the head of several thousand men. He published a manifesto, which Bishop Burnet says, was "long and ill-penned, full of much black and dull malice." As he advanced he had at first some trifling successes, enough to inspirit the ploughmen and Mendip-miners who had joined him. With about six thousand men, large numbers of them armed only with the tools which they used in their daily labour, he ventured to attack the army James had ordered to oppose him, under the command of Lord Faversham. Early in July, Monmouth was entirely defeated on Sedgemoor, near Bridgewater. Hundreds of his followers were slain; and, fleeing across the country, in hope of reaching the coast of Hampshire, and of escaping by sea, he was captured in the dress of a shepherd, when he was resting himself in a ditch, wearied, unwashed, and nearly starved. He wrote a letter to the king, expressing his sorrow for his rebellion. James commanded him to be brought to Whitehall, questioned him on Monday, and ordered him to be executed on Wednesday. When he came to Tower Hill to be beheaded, he said, "I will make no speeches, I come to die." He saw the axe, felt its edge, said it was not sharp enough; and he told the executioner if he cut off his head cleverly, and "not so butcherly as he did Lord Russell's," his servant should give him his reward. His words terrified the man, who struck him three times, and then flung his axe down. The sheriff compelled him to take it up, and he struck four times more, before he severed the young duke's head from his body. Immediately after Monmouth's execution, James sent Jeffries into the western counties, directing him to spare none whom under any legal pretext he could kill. That cruel judge went with gladness to his revel of death. He condemned Lady Alice Lisle to be burned alive, for giving a meal and a night's rest to two men who had fled from Sedgemoor. They, who saw Jeffries in his feast of blood, said, that he was always either drunk or in a rage. To save time, as he alleged, he urged the prisoners to plead guilty, and he "ordered them," as men reported, "to be hanged at once, without allowing them a minute's time to say their prayers." He executed seventy-four persons in Dorsetshire, thirteen in Devonshire, and two hundred and thirty-three in Somersetshire. In all about six hundred men were hanged, drawn, and quartered by his sentence; which directed that the limbs of the dead, after being boiled in pitch, were to be placed on each church-tower and steeple in Somersetshire, that on every side farmers and their labourers might learn how terrible was the end of them who rebelled against the anointed of the Lord. It was known to all London that Jeffries sent the king every day an exact account of the trials and executions, and that James read it to the foreign ministers and to the other guests at his dinner-table and in his drawing-rooms, calling upon them with manifestations of joy to admire the speed and success of "Jeffries's campaign," as he called it. The grateful monarch immediately raised Jeffries to the peerage, and showed him other distinguishing proofs of his favour and satisfaction; for the destruction of his enemies was as sweetest music to dispel the gloom, and to gladden the heart of the king; and the pleasure was enhanced by the assurance, that the end he desired had been gained under every circumstance of cruelty, suffering, and indignity. No royal family ever more worthily deserved to be called, after the Hebrew designation, "a bloody house," than that of the Stuart kings. The blood of Sir Walter Raleigh stains the throne of James I. That of Charles I. is drenched by the slaughter produced by the civil war. That of Charles II. is foully soiled by the judicial murders of Lord William Russell, Algernon Sidney, and of others who resisted his perfidious tyranny. That of James II. is for ever steeped in the hideous massacre which, by his urgent direction, Jeffries perpetrated in the western counties, and for which that sanguinary agent pleaded as his justification, that he had not done half of that which the king commanded him to do.

It soon became clear, even to the dull apprehension of James, that he could not force his form of religion upon the people of England; and that his cruel repression of the rebellions, in this country and in Scotland, was beginning to raise dangerous questions among men of moderate opinions, which boded only evil to himself and to his government. A large number of the English clergy became convinced that the policy they had approved for the last twenty-five years had been unwise. They argued that, in face of threatening dangers, it were not prudent to increase the divisions unhappily existing among Protestants, nor to rely upon the word of the king. They wrote ably and zealously against the Latin Church, and endeavoured to arouse the

English people against either its violent aggression or its insidious encroachments. It occurred to many in the higher stations of the Church, that they might need the help of them to whose persecution they had consented. Their endeavour to gain the assistance of the Nonconformists fiercely angered the king, who was astonished and alarmed to find so many of them learned and skilled in controversy, and unwilling to be his instruments in further harassing Dissenters. Men began to interest themselves more and more in the chief points of difference and disagreement between the Latin and Anglican Churches. The terrible cruelties perpetrated, in violation of his word, by Louis XIV. against the Huguenots, his most loyal, industrious, and useful subjects, and who in their flight from France had brought to England the wealth of their skill in manufactures, led men to reflect upon the conduct of James, and added to their apprehension a distrust of his promise to maintain the English Church in its integrity. Controversy on the Protestant side was carried on with great ability and moderation by Stillingfleet, Tillotson, Tenison, Patrick, Sherlock, Whitby, Wake, and many others, against writers who defended their cause so badly, that all men not of their party declared that the Anglican divines had an easy victory. James found that he had raised a spirit of resistance to his designs, which could be quenched only by a violent exercise of his power.

King James was one of those men who, if they have more modes of action than one, invariably choose the most impracticable; and who always meet a difficulty with the distempered mind and the rough hand. His suspicion and distrust were largely increased by the statements, which were repeated from house to house in London, and in many parts of the country, that the sovereign had connived at the infamous conduct of Jeffries in selling pardons of the numerous prisoners taken after the repression of Monmouth's rebellion. It was said—and no one, who knew the man and the corruption of the times, doubted the fact—that Jeffries had greatly enriched himself by the nefarious sale. Some of the poorer prisoners gained their forgiveness and freedom at the rate of ten guineas apiece. From some of the richer prisoners as much as fourteen thousand guineas were demanded. The king ordered Jeffries to take a thousand prisoners from among the host of them, who were condemned to transportation as slaves to the merchants in the plantations, and to divide them among certain noblemen who were true to his interests. Enormous sums were received for their ransom. James commanded Sunderland to write to Jeffries, that "the queen has asked for a hundred more of the rebels." These, and the other prisoners who were unable to buy their own freedom, were sold as slaves to the proprietors of estates in Jamaica, and in other of the West Indian islands. Jeffries replied to the king's demand: "I beseech Your Majesty that I may inform you that each prisoner will be worth ten pounds, if not fifteen pounds, apiece; and, Sir, if Your Majesty orders them as you have designed, persons that have not suffered in the service will run away with the booty." Some young ladies at Taunton had embroidered a banner, and presented it to Monmouth. Seized and condemned by Jeffries, these imprisoned girls were given as spoils to the queen's maids of honour; and those virtuous attendants on the Court wrung more than two thousand pounds from the parents, before their children could obtain pardon. So completely had Charles II. and James II. demoralised their adherents, that the wives and daughters of dukes and of earls were not ashamed to purchase jewels, or to make investments among the goldsmiths in the city, with the price of blood. Jeffries, who returned with ensanguined hand to the presence of his sovereign to be caressed and honoured, with his share of the money obtained by the sale of pardons, was able to purchase estates, which cost him nearly thirty-five thousand pounds; and he boasted, when drinking brandy with the vulgar and dissolute men with whom he delighted to associate, that he had hanged more persons for rebellion than all the judges since the Norman conquest, six hundred years before.

No man was ever more clever than James II. in ruining his own interest; never learning from experience, and in the management of affairs seemingly unable to connect effects with their causes. With all his dull obstinacy of mind, he perceived he had gone too far; and he resolved to declare a universal toleration, and to employ the Nonconformists to resist and to punish the Church of England. He charged the Church with treating Nonconformists with cruel severities, and he resolved to humble the clergy whenever he had opportunity, and to favour the dissenters. Bishop Burnet, who vigilantly observed the events of the time, and who had long and well known James II., states: "Chief Justice Herbert went the western circuit after Jeffries's bloody one, and now all was grace and favour to them. Their former sufferings were much reflected on and pitied. Everything was offered that could alleviate their sufferings. Their teachers were now encouraged to set up their conventicles again, which had been discontinued, or held very secretly, for four or five years. Intimations were everywhere given that the king would not have them at their meetings to be disturbed. But wiser men saw through all this, and perceived now the design was to set on the Dissenters against the Church; and therefore, though they returned to their conventicles, yet they had a just jealousy of the ill designs that lay hid under all this sudden and unexpected show of grace and kindness." James attempted to imitate Louis XIV. He boasted that he would not yield, as his father had yielded, to his ruin: he showed no sincere regard for liberty: he not only approved of the despotism of the French king, and of his persecution of his Protestant subjects; but he ordered Claude's account of the oppression and massacre of the Huguenots, which had been translated into English, to be burned at the Royal Exchange by the hangman. The opening of a Roman Catholic chapel in the city of London caused a riot, which the train-bands were unwilling to quell; and to overawe malcontents, James formed a camp of thirteen thousand men at Hounslow. With the obstinate determination to proceed, without due regard to difficulties, and which always betokens the feeble or incorrect reasoner, by the fatal advice of his evil agent, Jeffries, he resolved to establish an ecclesiastical Commission-Court, something after the model of the tyrannical High Commission-Court of former days, and which was abolished in 1640. The new court was to have summary jurisdiction in all matters affecting the Church; and it was, in fact, the creation of a government which was practically absolute. While the king withheld the enforcement of the penal laws against the Nonconformists, his friends begged him to pause, before committing himself to open hostility with a power so great and coherent as the Anglican Church. The Quakers, who had been cruelly persecuted for twenty-five years, petitioned the king to relax the severities under which they were suffering. They represented to him, that fifteen hundred men and women of their sect were in prison, for refusing to take an oath which their consciences forbade, and that already three hundred and sixty of them had died in confinement. They represented that Newgate was crowded by their people, twenty thrust into one room, and that within a few days past several of them had died of the fever, from which at that time no gaol was quite free, and which sometimes swept away judge, jury, and prisoners, all contaminated from the same source. They added, that they were the continual prey of informers; and that some of them had nothing left to be seized, not even a bed to sleep on;—that in country places their corn, cattle, and tools had been confiscated, and that their misery was complete. James had judgment enough to make him understand that with both the Anglican Church and the Nonconformists opposed to him, he would be baffled; and he resolved to accomplish his purpose of granting toleration, by releasing every person who was imprisoned under the penal statutes which had been passed in his brother's reign. He was much disturbed by the information he received, that five thousand Nonconformists had died in prison since the passing of those penal Acts, and he resolved to hold no person any longer in confinement who had been condemned for an ecclesiastical offence.

Among the other sufferers the king remembered Baxter, who would not pay the fine imposed upon him, because he knew that it might be repeated and enforced on every occasion on which he attempted to preach, or whenever he wrote anything objected to by the Court; and he would not solicit release from an unjust imprisonment. It was generally believed in London, that Lord Powis had remonstrated with James upon the manifest hardship of detaining in gaol a man so loyal and so eminent as Baxter. There is little doubt but that in giving him freedom, the king hoped he would help the Crown in the conflict with the Church. On the 24th of November, upon giving sureties for his good conduct, Baxter was released from the King's Bench prison, in which he had been confined for nearly two years; and the tyrant, who had caused him to be prosecuted, gave him to understand that he might pass the rest of his days in London, without liability to penalty for infringing the Five Mile Act; and in February, 1687, Baxter took a house in Charterhouse Square. The king, notwithstanding his professed zeal for religion, followed the example of his brother, although in a manner which the public eye could not easily discern. In denial of his promise to abandon his personal vices, he continued his relations with Mrs. Sedley, whom he made Countess of Dorchester. While eager to make converts to his own professed form of religion, he abandoned none of his immoralities. The queen, who was cognisant of his habitual adultery, remonstrated with him, became seriously ill, and sought the intervention of her priests. The Court was disturbed, and the king, alarmed at the indignant protest, promised to give up the evil association, and to send Mrs. Sedley to Ireland; but when the commotion had subsided, following the instincts of his perfidious nature, Mrs. Sedley, who treated the priests with contempt and defiance, was soon permitted to return, and the royal dissoluteness continued as before.

James found his perplexities increasing; and in him, as in all men of the lesser mind, difficulties strengthened his obstinacy in his design to make the Latin Church supreme in the country. When opposition was offered to his proposals, he was accustomed to say, "I am a king, and I will be obeyed;" but he quickly discovered, that his demand for submission and surrender neither awed the Anglican clergy nor induced them to yield to his imperious commands. He summoned his council, and informed them that he had resolved upon publishing a Declaration, promising liberty of conscience to religionists of every class. In our own day, we have heard statesmen advocating with singular vehemence a course of policy which, a few months before, they had condemned as strongly; but the remarkable rapidity of the king's change of government, from forcible repression to complete license of differences in religion, caused men to suspect the honesty of his motives. He proclaimed in the Gazette, "That though a uniformity of worship had been endeavoured to be established within this kingdom in the successive reigns of four of his predecessors, yet it had proved altogether ineffectual. That the restraint upon the consciences of Dissenters had been very prejudicial to the nation, as was sadly experienced by the horrid rebellion in the time of His Majesty's father. That the many penal laws made against Dissenters had rather increased than lessened the number of them; and that nothing could more conduce to the peace and quiet of this kingdom, and the increase of the number as well as the trade of his subjects, than an entire liberty of conscience, it having always been his opinion, as most suitable to the principles of Christianity, that no man should be persecuted for conscience' sake; for he thought conscience could not be forced, and that it could never be the true interest of a king of England to endeavour to do it." Bishop Burnet says "This was strange conduct in a Roman Catholic monarch, at a time when his brother of France had just broke the Edict of Nantes, and was dragooning his Protestant subjects out of his kingdom." Many persons agreed with the opinion expressed by Burnet. They argued, that the bishops and clergy had been too severe with the Nonconformists, and that they who had suffered would do well, when the common Protestantism was in danger, to forgive and forget their mutual injuries, and to unite in opposing the sinister design of the court. The king, aware of the public feeling, made a progress throughout the country to ingratiate himself with the people, who bitterly remembered the cruelties perpetrated at the western assizes, and who suspected the king of a determination to overthrow the ancient Church in which their fathers had worshipped, whose advantages they had only lately recovered, after their violent withdrawment by the government of Cromwell, and for whose preservation many of them would hazard property and life. As he went from town to town, James lavished his favours on Nonconformists, made many of them magistrates, and on all sides requested them to be assured of his continual good will. But everywhere the king observed signs of resistance to him. The public instinct detected his perfidy, suspected his too eager protestations of gracious intentions, remembered that his race never forgave, and that they were the deadly enemies of liberty of opinion. They observed the king at the same time gradually increasing his army, and stealthily placing his creatures in command of the fortresses, and they were not prepared to accept his promises of giving and protecting universal liberty. His claim to possess dispensing power was resisted by Churchmen and Nonconformists alike. The former were determined at all hazards to maintain the integrity of their Church, the freest and the most comprehensive upon the earth, and to resist all attempts of the monarch to control their services, or to limit the liberty of their clergy. Their unanimity and firmness, and the strength in popular esteem which more moderate counsels had given them, made it impossible for James to use such severities against them as Cromwell had employed.

The Nonconformists on their part were resolved to resist the usurpation of the king. Baxter and John Howe refused to take any part against their brethren of the English Church; and when James sent for the latter, he told the king, "that it was his province to preach, and to endeavour to do good to the souls of men, but as for meddling with state affairs, he was neither inclined nor called to it, and must beg to be excused." James, who was often saying, that he was a king, and that he would be obeyed, was urged by his courtiers to take further steps, and to show his authority in composing differences of opinion in religion by the energetic exercise of his power; but the Church was neither to be awed nor to be won, and the Nonconformists were so firm in their opposition, that he said, "he saw the Dissenters were an ill-natured sort of people, that could not be gained;" and the courtiers, exasperated at the failure of their prince, spoke of them as "private, sullen, discontented, niggardly Nonconformists."

During the amazing follies, and the political agitations of the remaining years of James's short reign, Baxter lived in retirement, at rest from persecution, and harassed no more by the intrusion of insolent informers. He preached in his own house to a few persons who revered and loved him, and he assisted his friend Sylvester by giving such occasional exhortations as his increasing weakness permitted. The shadows were deepening and strengthening, but his sky was calm. He had endured the violence of persecution, but the tempest had ceased. He lived to see the revenges which time invariably brings. In those western English counties, where James's cruelties had been excessive, his strength and refuge failed him; where he had poured out blood like water, his power was broken, and his crown lost; for there his army went over to the standard of the invader, and the slaughter which called for retribution was avenged in the very place of the crime. The king, who had done such wrong, was forsaken by a nation—bishops, peers, country-gentlemen, merchants, lawyers, mechanics, every man who cared for his native land, opposing the tyrant, and leaving him without counsellor or friend; an exile from the Church he had dishonoured and sought to enslave, and from the State he had ruled in obstinacy, rigour, and superstition. Baxter also heard of the sudden ruin of the unjust judge, who had cruelly used him on the day of trial; fallen "like Lucifer, never to rise again"; and of his lurking among the sailors at Wapping, hoping to escape on shipboard from the scene of his fury, cruelty, and rapacity; and at last of his imprisonment in the Tower, where in the anguish of remorse, hated of all men, he sank and died. On that terrible night, when the citizens of London expected to be attacked by Irish soldiers, brought to England by James to overawe his Protestant army, from his house Baxter heard the shouts of the mob, and he saw the glare of the fire in which the Roman Catholic chapels which the monarch had built were destroyed. His visitors told him from hour to hour of the gradual defection of James's forces, of the rapid march of William of Orange, and of the entry of the Dutch army into London; and in a short time he heard with thankful heart the roar of the guns, which announced that the long night of the Stuart tyranny was at an end, and that a new day had dawned upon Britain, in which liberty would be assured to all men; that the Church in which he was ordained to holy service was saved; that persecution for religious opinion or practice was for ever at an end; and that truth, law, and freedom were preserved. In the peaceful evening of his days, Baxter was able in his twilight to recall the past: his successes at Kidderminster; his happy home, "and hauntings from the infirmity of love"; the persecution and the terror passed away; the labours of his pen in defence of the faith; and the infinite mazes of controversy. He still wrote large volumes, for his mind knew not the feebleness of age, and was never wearied. In 1689, and afterwards, he published his "Sense of the Subscribed Articles," "A Treatise of Knowledge and Love Compared," "The Scripture Doctrine Defended," "A Defence of Christ and Free Grace," "An End of Doctrinal Controversies,"

"The Glorious Kingdom of Christ Described and Vindicated," "Of National Churches," "Against Revolt to a Foreign Jurisdiction," "Richard Baxter's Penitent Confession," a remarkable small volume; "The Certainty of the World of Spirits, fully evinced by unquestionable Histories of Apparitions and Witchcrafts;" "The Protestant Religion truly Stated and Justified;" "A Paraphrase on the Psalms of David, with other Hymns;" "A Treatise of Universal Redemption;" "Monthly Preparations for the Holy Communion;" and "The Mother's Catechism."

The influence of his character, of his preaching, and especially of his writings, was very great in Britain and in America, in forming and strengthening religious life, and in producing in others that love for the souls of men which was the peculiar character of his heart. It is only just to attribute to him and to his example the revived zeal for missionary work, which is distinctive of our own age. He urged the importance of propagating Christianity in heathen lands, when missions were little understood among Protestants; and he maintained, that the Church for many centuries had disobeyed the last commands of its Lord, to teach all nations His condescension, mercy, and truth. Among his other laborious works, his mind was ever occupied by the thought that little had been gained of a world lost to goodness, and for whose recovery especially the Church was founded; to be not only the public and enduring witness of Christian truth, but the direct means of its promulgation. To him it was a grievous thought, that some of the fairest regions of the earth were inhabited by men ignorant of Him Who created and loved them, and that in such regions human life was woeful and wasted. For their recovery he offered his most fervent prayers, that the Saviour's kingdom might come where ignorance, superstition, and depravity reigned. His large charity wished that all should receive that religion, with its peace and gladness, which he himself possessed. It was his daily grief that, in scenes so enriched by the bounty of the

Creator, men should live neglected by the Church, alien to the faith, afflicting and afflicted. Such sentiments were worthy of the great divine, preacher, and writer, who was a conspicuous example of that self-denial, devotion, and benevolence, which he exhorted others to exhibit, and to possess themselves of those counsels and consolations which Christianity has provided for escaping present dangers and for securing future blessings. His own life was the exact exposition of the principles he held. His latest friend, who had long lived in Baxter's house, and had seen what practical effect true goodness has upon the conduct of him whom it governs, writes: "His personal abstinence, severity, and labours were exceeding great. He kept his body under, and always feared pampering his flesh too much. He diligently and with great pleasure minded his Master's work within doors and without, while he was able. His purse was ever open to the poor; where the case required it he never thought great sums too much. He suited what he gave to the necessities and character of those he gave to; and his charity was not confined to parties and opinions." Another, who loved him much, writes: "His patience was truly Christian; he was tried by many afflictions; many slanderous darts were thrown at him; he was charged with schism and sedition. He was entire to his conscience, and independent of the opinion of others; but his patience was more eminently tried by his continual pains and languishing. Martyrdom is a more easy way of dying, when the combat and the victory are finished at once, than to die by degrees every day. His complaints were frequent, but who ever heard an unsubmissive word drop from his lips? He was not put out of his patience, nor out of the possession of himself. In his sharp pains, he said: 'I have a rational patience, and a believing patience, though sense would recoil.' But my account is but an imperfect shadow of his resplendent virtues; indeed, if love could make me eloquent, I should use all the most lively and graceful colours of language to adorn his memory." Baxter became more and more conscious that his pursuit of truth must shortly end; and he carefully applied to himself those great principles of Christian conduct which for many years he had impressed upon others. He had been no timid apologist for Christianity, and to the end he sustained the conclusions he had carefully formed. He believed that which he had maintained—that there is no rest for man, either in his strength or in his decay, but in the will of God; and upon Him he could "in trembling hope repose." In the house in Charterhouse Square, to which he had retired, he was able to recall the various passages of his eventful life, and in view of the all-reconciling world for which he was preparing, he could apply to himself his "Dying Thoughts," which had consoled the brave and good whom the tyrant condemned to death, and which since have been as angels of mercy to many who were making ready to depart.

Baxter's doctrinal system differed from both Calvinism and Arminianism, and from the ancient opinions which these in some degree represent; holding a middle place between these schools of religious thought, and maintaining both the dogma of election and that of free grace. He held that some men were elected to the blessings contained in Redemption, but that all, to whom the gospel of the Saviour's mercy is made known, can secure their own salvation. His system has no place for the terrible tenet of reprobation. His great principle is, that all men may receive the conditional blessings of salvation, but that those blessings are assured to them who are elected: so that if the blessings were designed only for a few, they are really offered to all men. He founds this position upon the facts, that Christ took upon Himself the nature of man, and suffered for the sins of the whole human race; that pardon, which includes in it every other needful gift of mercy, is offered to all who will fulfil the condition of faith; and that the facts and benefits of redemption are to be proclaimed to all men. Whatever divergences of opinion there may be from either of the opposing schools, in Baxter's system of Christian doctrine, it is evident that exclusiveness forms no part of it. His large charity is conspicuous in all his theology. The great practical principles of it are, that if "common grace" be well applied, "saving grace" will be obtained; that the Redeemer commanded His Church to proclaim His Gospel, and thus to declare His mercy to all mankind; and that by His death conditional blessings are offered to all men. This creed, which Watts, Doddridge, and many of the Anglican clergy have held, seems now to be received by a large number of them who are termed orthodox religionists, excepting many of the Presbyterians in Scotland and in Holland; and it is probably that which has place more or less in the sermons of the English Church in our day. Whatever defects may be assumed to occur in it, Baxter's system of theology neither limits the Divine mercy, nor lessens the responsibility of man. It cannot justly be called latitudinarian; and in no narrow or obscure terms it expresses doctrinal truths, which demand from him who holds them a life of constant practical goodness.

CHAPTER XXVII.

1688—1691.

ONE of the most valuable works which Baxter left to his country is the Autobiography, to which there is frequent reference in this narrative, and from which considerable quotations are made in it: as they give his own character, drawn by the hand of a man thoroughly conscious of his infirmities, and who would never willingly deceive. The large folio volume which contains this memorial was happily published exactly as its writer left it, without the obliteration and alteration which would have removed the master-strokes of genius and power distinctive of the author. The latter part of the first book contains passages, which have often attracted the admiration, and received the praise of them who loved wisdom and reality in the life of a man, whose accurate self-knowledge, and whose great and varied experience, enabled him to mark his own growth in intellectual and religious strength; and which also reveals how truth ripened and passion abated, when, after a day of storm and conflict, its evening was that of calm reason, undoubting faith, childlike affection, and patient hope of bliss. No memorial of him, written by the most friendly hand, could represent his mental and spiritual life as he has drawn it; with all its unselfish labours, its constant prayers, successes, regrets, and sorrows; his tranquillity in scenes of agitation and suffering; the love of them for whose advantage he devoted years of unwearying toil and care, and the manifest proofs which he received of favour and acceptance from the gracious Saviour. The descendants of them, to whom he ministered at Kidderminster, have gratefully erected, in the centre of their town, a noble statue of him who taught and guided their ancestors in the ways of sacred Truth; but the really lasting memorial of the great English preacher and divine is the record of his life, written by his own hand, when he had gained that self-knowledge and that maturity of mind which are an inestimable treasure. The retrospect of his long and laborious course, given at the end of the first part of the "Reliquiæ Baxterianæ," should have the careful attention of them who have devoted themselves to the purest and noblest of all human work, the service of the Redeemer's Church: "I shall only give the reader so much satisfaction as to acquaint him truly what change God hath made upon my mind and heart since those unriper times, and wherein I now differ in judgment and disposition from himself. For any more particular account of heart-occurrences, and God's operations on me, I think it somewhat unsavoury to recite them, seeing God's dealings are much the same with all His servants in the main; nor have I anything extraordinary to glory in, which is not common to the rest of my brethren, who have the same Spirit, and are servants of the same Lord. The temper of my mind hath somewhat altered with the temper of my body. When I was young, I was more vigorous, affectionate, and fervent, in preaching, conference, and prayer, than ordinarily I can be now. My style was more extemporate and lax, but by the advantage of warmth, and a very familiar, moving voice and utterance, my preaching then did more affect the auditory, than it did many of the last years before I gave over preaching. But what I delivered then was much more raw, and had more passages that would not bear the trial of accurate judgments; and my discourses had both less substance and less judgment than of late. My understanding was then quicker, and could more easily manage anything that was presented to it of a sudden; but it is since better furnished, and acquainted with the ways of truth and error, and with a multitude of particular mistakes of the world, which then I was the more in danger of, because I had only the faculty of knowing them, but did not actually know them. I was then like a man of quick understanding that was to travel a way he never went before, or to cast up an account which he never laboured in before, or to play on an instrument of music which he never saw before. I am now like one of somewhat slower understanding, who is travelling a way which he hath often gone, and is casting up an account which he hath ready at hand, and that is playing on an instrument which he hath frequently used; so that I can very confidently say my judgment is much sounder and firmer now than it was then: for though I am now as competent a judge of the actings of my own understanding as then, I can judge better of the effects. When I peruse the writings which I wrote in my younger years, I can find the footsteps of my unfurnished mind, and of my emptiness and insufficiency: so that the man that followed my judgment then was likelier to have been misled by me than he that should follow it now. In my younger years, my trouble for sin was most about my actual failings; but now I am much more troubled for inward defects and omissions, for want of the vital duties or graces of the soul. My daily trouble is so much for my ignorance of God, weakness of belief, want of greater love to God, strangeness to Him and to the life to come, and for want of a greater willingness to die, and more longing to be with God in heaven, that I take not some immoralities, though very great, to be in themselves so great and odious sins, if they could be found separate from these. Had I all the riches of the world, how gladly should I give them for a fuller knowledge, belief, and love of God and everlasting glory! These wants are the greatest burden of my life, which oft maketh my life itself a burden. Heretofore I placed much of my religion in tenderness of heart, grieving for sin, and penitential tears; and less of it in the love of God, in studying His goodness, and engaging in His joyful praises, than now I do. I am less troubled for want of grief and tears (though I value humility, and refuse not needful humiliation), but my conscience now looketh at love and delight in God, and praising Him, as the top of all my religious duties; for which it is that I value and use the rest. My judgment is much more for frequent and serious meditation on the heavenly blessedness than it was in my younger days. I then thought that a sermon on the attributes of God and the joys of heaven was not the most excellent; and was wont to say, 'Everybody knoweth that God is great and good, and that heaven is a blessed place; I had rather hear how I may attain it.' Nothing pleased so well as the doctrine of regeneration and the marks of sincerity, because these things were suitable to me in that state; but I now had rather hear, read, meditate on God and heaven, than on any other subject. I perceive that it is the object which altereth and elevateth the mind, which will resemble that which it most frequently feedeth on. It is not only useful to our comfort to be much in heaven in believing thoughts; it must animate all our other duties, and fortify us against every temptation and sin. The love of the end is the poise or spring which setteth every wheel a-going, and must put us on to all the means; for a man is no more a Christian indeed than he is heavenly. Formerly, I knew much less than now, and yet was not half so much acquainted with my ignorance: I had a great delight in the daily new discoveries which I made, and of the light which shined in upon me, like a man that cometh into a country where he never was before; but I little knew either how imperfectly I understood those very points whose discovery so much delighted me, or how much might be said against them, or how many things I was yet a stranger to. I now find far greater darkness in all things, and perceive how very little we know in comparison of that of which we are ignorant. I have therefore far meaner thoughts of my own understanding, though I must needs know that it is better furnished than it was then. I now see more good and more evil than heretofore I did. I see that good men are not so good as I once thought they were, but have more imperfections; and that nearer approach and fuller trial do make the best appear more weak and faulty than their admirers at a distance think. I find that few are so bad as either malicious enemies or censorious separating professors do imagine. In some indeed I find that human nature is corrupted into a greater likeness to devils than I once thought any on earth had been; but even in the wicked usually there is more for grace to make advantage of, and more to testify for God and holiness than I once believed there had been.

"I less admire gifts of utterance and the bare profession of religion than I once did, and have much more charity for many who by the want of gifts do make an obscurer profession. I once thought that almost all who could pray movingly and fluently, and talk well of religion, had been saints. But experience hath opened to me what odious crimes may consist with high profession; while I have met with divers obscure persons, not noted for any extraordinary profession or forwardness in religion, but only to live a quiet, blameless life, whom I have after found to have long lived, as far as I could discern, a truly godly and sanctified life; only their prayers and duties were by accident kept secret from other men's observation. I am not so narrow in my special love as heretofore: being less censorious, and taking more than I did for saints, it must needs follow that I love more as saints than I did formerly. I think it not lawful to put that man off with bare Church-communion, and such common love which I must allow the wicked who professeth himself a true Christian, by such a profession as I cannot disprove. I am not so narrow in my principles of Church-communion as I once was. I more plainly see the difference between the Church as congregate or visible, and as regenerate or mystical. I can now distinguish between sincerity and profession; that a credible profession is proof sufficient of a man's title to Church admission; and that the profession is credible *in foro ecclesiæ*, which is not disproved. I am not for narrowing the Church more than Christ Himself alloweth us, nor for robbing Him of any of His flock. I am more sensible how much it is the will of Christ that every man be the chooser or refuser of his own felicity, and that it lieth most on his own hands whether he will have communion with the Church or not, and that if he be an hypocrite it is himself that will bear the loss. Yet I am more apprehensive than ever of the great use and need of ecclesiastical discipline; what a sin it is in the pastors of the Church to make no distinction, but by bare names and sacraments, and to force all the unmeet against their wills to Church-communion: though the ignorant and erroneous may sometimes be forced to hear instruction. What a great dishonour to Christ it is, when the Church is as vicious as Pagan and Mahometan assemblies, and differs from them only in ceremony and name! I am much more sensible how prone many young professors are to spiritual pride, and self-conceitedness, and unruliness, and division, and so to prove the grief of their teachers, and firebrands in the Church; and how much of a minister's work lies in preventing this, and humbling and confirming such young inexperienced professors, and keeping them in order in their progress in religion. Yet I am more sensible of the sin and mischief of using men cruelly in matters of religion, and of pretending men's good and the order of the Church for acts of inhumanity or uncharitableness. Such know not their own infirmity, nor yet the nature of pastoral government, which ought to be paternal and by love; nor do they know the way to win a soul, or to maintain the Church's peace.

"My soul is much more afflicted with the thoughts of this miserable world, and more drawn out in desire of its conversion than heretofore. I was wont to look but little further than England in my prayers, not considering the state of the rest of the world; or if I prayed for the conversion of the Jews, that was almost all. But now, as I better understand the case of the world, and the method of the Lord's Prayer, there is nothing in the world that lieth so heavy upon my heart as the thought of the miserable nations of the earth. It is the most astonishing part of all God's providence to me, that He so far forsaketh almost all the world, and confineth His special favour to so few; that so small a part of the world hath the profession of Christianity, in comparison of heathens, Mahometans, and other infidels; that among professed Christians there are so few that are saved from gross delusions, and have any competent knowledge; and that among those there are so few that are seriously religious, and who truly set their hearts on heaven. I cannot be affected so much with the calamities of my own relations or the land of my nativity, as with the case of the heathen, Mahometan, and ignorant nations of the earth. No parts of my prayers are so deeply serious as those for the conversion of the infidel and ungodly world, that God's name may be sanctified, and His kingdom come, and His will be done on earth as it is in heaven. Nor was I ever before so sensible what a plague the division of languages is, which hindereth our speaking to them for their conversion. Nor what a great sin tyranny is, which keepeth out the Gospel from most of the nations of the world. Could we but go among Tartars, Turks, and heathens, and speak their language, I should be but little troubled for the silencing of eighteen hundred ministers at once in England, nor for all the rest that were cast out here, and in Scotland and Ireland; there being no employment in the world so desirable in my eyes as to labour for the winning of such miserable souls; which maketh me greatly honour Mr. John Eliot, the apostle of the Indians in New England, and whoever else have laboured in such work. I am more deeply afflicted for the disagreements of Christians than I was when I was a younger Christian. Except the case of the infidel world, nothing is so bad and grievous to my thoughts as the case of divided churches: and therefore I am more deeply sensible of the sinfulness of those prelates and pastors of churches who are the principal cause of these divisions. Oh! how many millions of souls are kept by them in ignorance and ungodliness, and deluded by faction, as if it were true religion! How is the conversion of infidels hindered by them, and Christ and religion heinously dishonoured! The contentions between the Greek Church and the Roman, the Papists and the Protestants, the Lutherans and the Calvinists, have woefully hindered the kingdom of Christ. I am further than ever I was from expecting great matters of unity, splendour, or prosperity to the Church on earth, or that saints should dream of a kingdom of this world, or flatter themselves with the hope of a golden age, or of reigning over the ungodly, till there be a new heavens and a new earth, wherein dwelleth righteousness. On the contrary, I am more apprehensive that suffering must be the Church's ordinary lot; and true Christians must be self-denying cross-bearers, even where there are none but formal, nominal Christians to be the cross-makers: for though ordinarily God would have vicissitudes of summer and winter, day and night, that the Church may grow externally in the summer of prosperity, and intensively and radically in the winter of adversity; yet usually their night is longer than their day, and that day itself hath its storms and tempests.

"I do not lay so great a stress upon the external modes and forms of worship, as many young professors do. I have suspected myself, as perhaps the reader may do, that this is from a cooling and declining of my former zeal, though the truth is I never much complied with men of that mind: but I find that judgment and charity are the causes of it; as far as I am able to discover. I cannot be so narrow in my principles of Church-communion as many are, that are so much for a liturgy, or so much against it; so much for ceremonies, or so much against them, that they can hold communion with no church that is not of their mind and way. If I were among the Greeks, the Lutherans, the Independents, yea, the Baptists, owning no heresy, nor setting themselves against charity and peace, I would sometimes hold communion with them as Christians; if they would give me leave, without forcing me to any sinful subscription or action, though my most usual communion should be with that society which I thought most agreeable to the word of God if I were free to choose. I cannot be of their opinion that think God will not accept him that prayeth by the Common Prayer-Book, and that such forms are a self-invented worship, which God rejecteth; nor yet can I be of their mind that say the like of extempore prayers. I am much less regardful of the approbation of man, and set much lighter by contempt or applause than I did long ago. All worldly things appear most vain and unsatisfactory when we have tried them most. I am more and more pleased with a solitary life, and though, in a way of self-denial, I could submit to the most public life for the service of God, when He requireth it, and would not be unprofitable that I might be private, yet I must confess it is much more pleasing to myself to be retired from the world, and to have very little to do with men, and to converse with God and conscience and good books. Though I was never much tempted to the sin of covetousness, yet my fear of dying was wont to tell me that I was not sufficiently loosened from the world: but I find that it is comparatively very easy to me to be loose from this world, but hard to live by faith above. I am much more apprehensive than long ago of the odiousness and danger of the sin of pride. I am much more sensible than heretofore of the breadth, and length, and depth of the radical, universal, odious sin of selfishness, and therefore have written so much against it; and of the excellency and necessity of self-denial, and of a public mind, and of loving our neighbours as ourselves. I am more solicitous than I have been about my duty to God, and less solicitous about His dealings with me; being assured that He will do all things well; acknowledging the goodness of all the declarations of His holiness, even in the punishment of man, and knowing that there is no rest but in the will and goodness of God.

"Thus much of the alterations of my soul since my younger years, I thought best to give the reader; and having transcribed thus much of a life which God hath read, and conscience hath read, and must further read, I humbly lament it and beg pardon of it, as sinful, and too unequal and unprofitable. I warn the reader to amend that in his own, which he findeth to have been amiss in mine; confessing also that much hath been amiss which I have not here particularly mentioned, and that I have not lived according to the abundant mercies of the Lord. Having mentioned the changes which I think were for the better, I must add, that as I confessed many of my sins before, so I have been guilty of many since, which, because materially they seemed small, have had the less resistance, and yet on the review do trouble me more than if they had been greater, done in ignorance. It can be no small sin formally, which is committed against knowledge, and conscience, and deliberation, whatever excuse it have. To have sinned while I preached and wrote against sin, and had such abundant and great obligations from God, and made so many promises against it, doth lay me very low: not so much in fear of hell, as in great displeasure against myself, and such self-abhorrence as would cause revenge upon myself were it not forbidden. When God forgiveth me, I cannot forgive myself; especially for my rash words or deeds, by which I have seemed injurious, and less tender and kind than I should have been to my near and dear relations, whose love abundantly obliged me. When such are dead, though we never differed in point of interest, or any other matter, every sour or cross provoking word which I gave them, maketh me almost irreconcilable to myself, and tells me how repentance brought some of old to pray to the dead whom they had wronged, to forgive them, in the hurry of their passion. That which I named before by-the-bye, is grown one of my great diseases; I have lost much of that zeal which I had to propagate any truths to others, save the mere fundamentals. When I perceive people or ministers to know what indeed they do not, which is too common, and to dispute those things which they never thoroughly studied, or expect that I should debate the case with them, as if an hour's talk would serve, instead of an acute understanding and seven years' study, I have no zeal to make them of my opinion, but an impatience of continuing discourse with them on such subjects, and am apt to be silent, or to turn to something else;

which, though there be some reason for it, I feel cometh from a want of zeal for the truth, and from an impatient temper of mind. I am ready to think that people should quickly understand all in a few words; and if they cannot, to despair of them, and leave them to themselves. I know the more that this is sinful in me, because it is partly so in other things, even about the faults of my servants or other inferiors. If three or four times warning do no good to them, I am much tempted to despair of them, turn them away, and leave them to themselves. I mention all these distempers that my faults may be a warning to others to take heed, as they call on myself for repentance and watchfulness. O Lord, for the merits, and sacrifice, and intercession of Christ, be merciful to me a sinner, and forgive my known and unknown sins!"

They who well knew Baxter have represented him as tall in stature, attenuated by disease; in his later years much bent by suffering; with a countenance generally brightened by a smile, a keen and lustrous eye, and a very clear and rich voice, which he had trained with the utmost care. One of his ablest opponents declared of him, that "he could say what he would, and he could prove what he said." His industry in his parish and in the preparation of his treatises is almost incredible. In forty years he wrote one hundred and sixty-eight books, eighty-five of them quarto volumes; and, in addition, he took an active and prominent part in public affairs. There are few things more remarkable, in the literary history of our country, than the fact, that a man who suffered so frequently from disease and excruciating pains, and from afflicting nervous irritation, should have been able to produce so large a number of works, written clearly and forcibly, and with much close and effective reasoning upon the most difficult subjects of inquiry, especially on polemical, doctrinal, and practical theology; some of them now neglected or forgotten, but others still largely read, of great utility, and contributing much to maintain and strengthen religious life in all lands in which the English language is spoken. In his estimate of Baxter's books, Mr. Orme states, that if they were printed in a uniform edition, they could not be comprised in less than sixty octavo volumes, making nearly forty thousand closely printed pages. In his lifetime many of his publications were largely sold, passing through several editions, and they gained him the esteem of some of the ablest of his contemporaries. Bishop Wilkins, who knew Baxter well, said of him, that "he cultivated every subject he handled, and if he had lived in the primitive time, he had been one of the Fathers of the Church." His friend, Robert Boyle, the founder of the "Lecture" which bears his name, said Baxter was the fittest man of the age for a casuist, because he feared no man's displeasure, nor hoped for any man's preferment. Dr. Samuel Johnson classed Baxter with the most eminent theologians. When Boswell asked him what works of Baxter he should read, Johnson gave him the well-known answer, "Read any of them, for they are all good."

Baxter's last days were passed in Charterhouse Square, near the chapel of his friend Sylvester, to whose congregation he occasionally preached, so long as his strength remained; and he received persons eager to have his instructions, at his family-prayer every morning and evening. Dr. Calamy, who saw him in the last year of his life, says: "He talked in the pulpit with great freedom about another world, like one that had been there, and was come as a sort of express from thence, to make a report concerning it;" and his friend Dr. Bates states, that Baxter "continued to preach so long, notwithstanding his wasted, languishing body, that the last time he almost died in the pulpit." The very large calculus which had so long tortured him, and which, removed after his death, is said to be preserved in the British Museum, so reduced his strength that at length he was unable to leave his bed. Some of them, to whom he had for many years taught religious truth, visited him when he was waiting for his departure. To some of them he said: "You come hither to learn to die; I am not the only person who must go this way. I can assure you that your whole life, be it never so long, is little enough to prepare for death. Have a care of this vain, deceitful world, and the lusts of the flesh. Be sure you choose God for your portion and heaven for your home, God's glory for your end, His Word for your rule; and then you need never fear but that we shall meet with comfort." So they who were permitted to visit his chamber have recorded some of his last words, which the Church cannot willingly let die. They, who were near him in those days, heard him often praying—as afterwards the brilliant Von Haller accustomed himself to pray—"God, be merciful to me a sinner;" and Baxter would have agreed with the declaration of that man of remarkable genius, that he "was truly convinced that in the grace of God we have an almighty Helper, Who can free us from the bonds of sin, and lead us on to lofty and consecrated purposes." Some of his friends reminded him how many and what useful books he had written for the instruction of the Church. He replied, "I was but a pen in God's hand, and what praise is due to a pen?" When the sharpness of his frequent pains inclined him to pray that his suffering might mercifully come to an end, he would recover his fortitude and composure, and would utter those words which, since his day, many good men have spoken with humble penitence, in all time of their tribulation: "It is not fit for me to prescribe. When Thou wilt; what Thou wilt; and how Thou wilt." He said to them who saw him in anguish: "Do not think the worse of religion for what you see me suffer. I bless God I have a well-grounded assurance of my eternal happiness, and great peace and comfort within." The love for the Church in which he had been ordained returned with consoling effect upon him as his weakness increased. He said: "I find great comfort and sweetness in repeating the words of the Lord's Prayer, and I am sorry that some good people are prejudiced against the use of it; for there are all necessary petitions for soul and body contained in it." A few hours before his departure, to Mr. Mather of New England, who asked him how he was, Baxter replied: "Almost well." The terrible disease from which he suffered afflicted him each hour more and more, as though he, who was so revered by devout men, must enter by a rugged and thorny path upon the home which had been prepared for him by Eternal Goodness. They who prayed by his bed have recorded that the extremity of pain extorted strong cries from their dying friend; but at midnight the anguish suddenly ceased, and there came to him the tranquillity of one who waited in joyful hope for the welcome of his Lord. Turning his eye to Sylvester, who was at his side, Baxter spoke his last words on earth; and which testified that in the Christian life, in its weakest hour, charity never faileth—"The Lord teach you how to die!" In the early winter-morning, at four o'clock, on December 8th, 1691, in the seventy-sixth year of his age, the great preacher passed into the unsuffering Kingdom, and to the gracious Saviour he had served.

They who sorrowed that they should see his face no more buried Baxter in Christchurch, where he had placed his wife and her mother. A long train of carriages, and a great number of clergymen and Nonconformists, followed him to his grave.

Baxter directed the executors of his will to give his books to needy scholars; and he left his estate for the benefit of the poor.

He lived in an age when civil strife was sharpened by religious dissension, when difference of opinion often produced violent hostility, and when toleration was unknown. Men had not yet discovered, that it is for the health of the state that there should be diversity of sentiment. Divines did not then understand the distinction between what is essential and non-essential in doctrine and in ceremonial. Persecution in matters of conscience still produced grievous cruelties in many European countries. Unity was enforced, but morals were not improved. Among the chief exponents of sacred thought there was no desire to solve doubts, to calm troubled minds, and to preserve peace. Governments had not yet learned the folly of making religion a question of police, and of exactly prescribing the faith of a nation. Cromwell and the Stuart kings equally invaded the province of conscience; and the victorious religionists, both republican and royalist, cruelly persecuted their conquered opponents. They who clamoured for freedom, when they had gained it became tyrannical.

But consideration is due to the custom of the time, and to the long submission to a stern religious discipline to which the country had been habituated. It were unjust to estimate the principles and policy maintained in the seventeenth century by the ideas which prevail in our era. Few men have calm self-possession in times of discord and strife, nor can they reason temperately and act wisely when they are moved by indignant anger. The Anglican Church of to-day, with its vigorous life, its large sympathies, its diffusive charities, its wide comprehensiveness, is no more to be condemned for the persecuting spirit of its bishops, and for the intolerance of some of its clergy, who lived among the furious passions which obtained in the reigns of the Stuarts, than a man who has been restored to health is to be blamed for his words and actions in the delirium which attended his disease. Every wise Nonconformist must in his conscience censure the terrible and various severities with which Cromwell afflicted the unoffending clergymen of the English Church, especially in forbidding them the exercise of their religion. They, who now rejoice in the renewed strength and beneficent activities of that Church, must deplore that the prelates of a former age vindictively persecuted and punished the ejected Puritans, and especially that they sanctioned the cruel treatment of their fellow-servant, the great divine, whose history is here written.

Printed by Hazell, Watson, & Viney, Ld., London and Aylesbury.

www.ingramcontent.com/pod-product-compliance
Lightning Source LLC
Chambersburg PA
CBHW022024110726
47901CB00006B/1652

* 9 7 8 3 7 4 4 7 6 0 5 1 5 *